Nick. It was re

Sidney couldn't see his face, but she knew it was him.

She took off running. She crashed into the glass wall. Her palms splayed against it. "Nick."

He turned. His hands met hers against the glass.

Sweet Lord, was this possible? She stared, unblinking. If she closed her eyes, she was afraid he'd disappear.

He came around the wall through the door and reached toward her. She latched on to his hand, laced her fingers through his. He was thinner than the last time she'd seen him. His complexion was pale as though he'd been ill, but this was definitely her fiancé.

She lifted her hand toward his face and touched the V-shaped scar on his jaw.

"Oh, Nick, I missed you so much."

"It's okay. I'm here. I'm back."

But there was something different. When she peered into his eyes, she didn't see the man she had once loved with all her heart.

Nick Corelli looked back at her with the eyes of a stranger.

MOUNTAIN RETREAT

BY
CASSIE MILES

Published in Great Britain 2015
by Mills & Boon, an imprint of Harlequin (UK) Limited,
Eton House, 18-24 Paradise Road, Richmond, Surrey, TW9 1SR

© 2015 Kay Bergstrom

ISBN: 978-0-263-25293-4

46-0115

Harlequin (UK) Limited's policy is to use papers that are natural, renewable and recyclable products and made from wood grown in sustainable forests. The logging and manufacturing processes conform to the legal environmental regulations of the country of origin.

Printed and bound in Spain
by CPI, Barcelona

Cassie Miles, a *USA TODAY* bestselling author, lives in Colorado. After raising two daughters and cooking tons of macaroni and cheese for her family, Cassie is trying to be more adventurous in her culinary efforts. She's discovered that almost anything tastes better with wine. When she's not plotting Mills & Boon® Intrigue books, Cassie likes to hang out at the Denver Botanical Gardens near her high-rise home.

To my kids and friends and docs and therapists and everybody who made it possible for me to be sitting here at my computer. And, as always, to Rick.

Chapter One

Working as a barmaid at the Silver Star Saloon in Austin put Sidney Parker's eidetic memory to good use. She could easily remember the drink orders for this table of twelve. With thumbs hooked in the belt loops of her thigh-high jean skirt, she faced the group of well-dressed young people who were still wearing their security badges from the state capitol.

"What'll it be?" she asked.

They could have answered in one voice: beer. But the Silver Star was a designer brewery with products ranging from Amber Angel to Zoo Brew. Sidney mentally recorded the order and gave a nod.

"Wait a minute," said a woman with platinum blond curls. "Change mine from Chantilly Lace to Raspberry Rocket."

"Got it."

"Are you sure? You didn't write anything down."

Sidney inhaled a breath and repeated their order. "We're starting over here with two Pale Tigers, then a Blue Moon, a Lucky Ducky, Thor's Hammer Lite…" She continued around the table and ended with the redhead. "And you'll be having the Raspberry Rocket."

The gang applauded, and she swept a bow before heading to the huge central bar to fill her tray.

Keeping her brain occupied wasn't the greatest benefit of Sidney's part-time night job. The country-and-western sound track, the conversation and general clamor at the Silver Star provided her with a much-needed distraction during those lonely hours before dawn when tears swamped her pillow.

Behind the bar, Celia Marshall ducked down so the customers couldn't see her adjust the red gingham uniform shirt to better contain her cleavage. "I swear, I'm about to have a wardrobe malfunction."

"That's a problem I don't have." Sidney never needed to worry about her cup running over; her breasts were small and well behaved.

"I'd trade my chest in a minute for your mile-long legs."

"No deal." Sidney liked being tall. In her cowgirl boots, she was almost six feet. She gave her friend a closer look and noticed the puffiness around her eyes. "Something wrong?"

"Ray and I are fussing at each other again." Celia shook her head and frowned. "I always feel like a class-A whiner talking to you about man problems. Nobody has worse luck than you."

"It's not a contest." Sidney tucked a strand of her long, straight blond hair behind her ear. "And there's nothing I can do about my situation. You have options."

"Any word on Nick?"

"Not yet." She couldn't bear to think of Nick Corelli, her fiancé. The mere mention of his name conjured up a mental image of a tall, handsome marine with thick black hair and deep-set eyes the color of fine cognac. Her perfect memory filled in all the blanks as she recalled his wide grin, high cheekbones and strong jawline.

If she allowed herself to think about him, she'd be

sobbing in a minute. So she pushed his image aside and asked, "What's up with you and Ray?"

"It's all about his stupid hunting plans."

Sidney listened while she loaded her tray. It was going to take a couple of trips to serve her big table, and the domestic drama of Celia and Ray gave her something else to think about. They were both good people, understandable people with normal relationship issues. Not like her and Nick.

As she stood behind the bar, she spotted two men with impeccable posture and serious expressions enter the saloon. They weren't in uniform, but they might as well have been marching shoulder to shoulder, wearing their marine dress blues.

She set her tray on the bar. "Celia, you'll have to take over for me."

After a quick explanation to the shift manager, she fell into step between the two marines. She knew the drill. They were here to escort her to an interview with a CIA agent or someone high up in Marine Intelligence. She'd taken part in sixteen of these interrogations during the past six months after her fiancé went missing in a South American dictatorship. She always hoped that her marine escorts would be bringing good news.

They never did.

IN A DULL beige room at the local CIA field offices, Sidney paced back and forth behind the table. The heels of her boots clunked on the tile floor. In her barmaid uniform with the short denim skirt and gingham top, she felt a little ridiculous but not intimidated.

The first time she'd been sequestered in a room like this, her anxiety level was off the charts. The shock of possibly losing Nick had been staggering, and she'd been desperate for information. She'd begged, wept and pleaded.

The only facts she'd been able to pry from the case officer, CIA Special Agent Sean Phillips, were that her fiancé was MIA in the South American country of Tiquanna, his body hadn't been found and he was probably being held by the rebels. There had been no ransom demands.

That was in early May, six months and four days ago. Nothing much had changed in the details she'd been given, but her attitude had transformed. When she first came here, she was a nervous kitty cat. Now, a lioness.

She was half a tick away from going to Tiquanna herself, marching into the palace compound of dictator Tomas Hurtado and demanding an army to storm the rebel camps. She'd met Hurtado three years ago when he consulted with the oil company she worked for in the engineering department. Along with her boss at Texas Triton, she had actually traveled to the small country that was intent on developing its natural resources.

Sometimes, she wondered if that trip was the reason Nick had been selected for the assignment. When he told her that his platoon was being sent to Tiquanna, she'd given him all the inside information on Hurtado and his stunning wife, Elena.

The door opened and Special Agent Phillips entered. Sidney had heard that CIA agents liked to look anonymous so they could fade into crowds. If true, that meant Phillips was a CIA superstar. He was the most average-looking guy she'd ever met. With his thinning brown hair, brown eyes and average build, he was as plain as a prairie chicken.

"Why am I here?" she asked.

"Nice to see you, Sidney."

"Do you have news?"

A second person entered the room. Special Agent Victoria Hawthorne was higher in rank than Phillips, always dressed in black and as thin as a greyhound. Her dark hair was slicked back in a tight bun. She pulled out a chair on the opposite side of the table and sat. "Have a seat, Sidney."

"Am I being interrogated?" Still standing, she purposely kept her anger going. "This looks like an interrogation room with the closed door and the table and the big two-way mirror on the wall."

Special Agent Hawthorne scowled. Her thin lips pulled into an upside-down U. "You've been in this room before."

"And I've answered a million questions," she said. "I've been totally cooperative, and I think it's time I got an upgrade to a comfortable chair and, maybe, a room with windows."

Ignoring Sidney's demands, she asked, "Have you been in contact with anyone from Tiquanna?"

"Of course not. If somebody contacted me, I'd tell you immediately."

Hawthorne regarded Sidney through slitted eyes. "I have information if you're ready to hear it."

Hope flickered inside her like a pilot light that refused to be extinguished. "I'm ready. Tell me."

"On one condition. You must promise not to act on this information. Trust us to do our jobs without your interference. Is that clear?"

"Crystal."

"Hurtado and his wife will be in Austin next week along with several other South American leaders."

This was big news. Sidney might have a chance to

hear firsthand what was happening to Nick. "I want to see them."

"I can't promise," the thin-lipped agent said. "We'll do everything in our power to make that happen."

"Where will they be staying? How long will they be here?"

"You don't need to know." As she rose from her chair, Special Agent Hawthorne maintained steady eye contact. Her gaze was a warning. "If they agree to meet with you, we'll be in touch."

She turned on her heel and stalked from the room, leaving Sidney with a complicated tangle of anger, frustration and fear. She was afraid to expect too much, but she couldn't give up. It would be foolish to antagonize Hawthorne, but Sidney's anger demanded release.

Special Agent Phillips took Hawthorne's seat at the table, opened a folder and took out four photographs of men in camouflage fatigues. Three of them had beards. "Recognize anyone?"

"Do you think she'll let me talk to Hurtado?"

"I can't rightly say," he said in a Texan drawl.

Over the months, she and Phillips had developed a bit of rapport. He'd seen her at her worst when she broke down into hysterical tears, and she sensed that he was more sympathetic toward her than the other agents.

"I could negotiate with the rebels," she said. "I know it's against CIA policy, but I could—"

"C'mon now, Sidney girl." He poked at the photos. "Let's do this thing."

She didn't want to be a good girl. A lioness would tear these photos to scraps and throw them in his face. She was too docile. Nothing was getting done.

But what choice did she have? Could she single-handedly take on the whole intelligence community?

She huffed a frustrated sigh before picking up the photos. This was part of their routine. Because of her memory, the CIA used her to identify men whom she might have met when she visited the country. Thus far, there had been only four familiar faces.

These unposed pictures had been taken in a forested setting. "It's hard to tell with the beards. I don't think I know them. Who are they?"

"Rebels," he said.

"When I was in Tiquanna, I never left the palace grounds. Why would you think I'd know rebels?" She didn't expect him to answer. "Is it because the palace guards are defecting? Are they joining the rebels?"

"Let's just say that Señor Hurtado ain't exactly winning any popularity contests."

And the CIA wanted to keep Hurtado on their side. Though the dictator had a terrible record on civil rights for his impoverished people, he supported US programs and happily accepted our aid. More important, he was working with neighboring countries to form an oil and natural gas distribution system functioning with US companies.

When Phillips pulled out several aerial photographs of the palace grounds, she groaned. "Not again," she said. "I've told you everything I could about the palace."

"Focus on this area." He pointed to a far corner in the walled compound.

She stared. "It looks like the wall is broken. Was it an explosion?"

"Yep."

A wave of guilt washed over her. In a similar tactic, Nick had disappeared. Six months and four days ago, there had been an explosion targeting the front gates. Two marines had been injured. The last anyone had seen of Nick was when he was trying to rescue them.

Before he left on this deployment, she'd told him not to be a hero, which was impossible advice for a marine. The man lived to protect others. His courage was as much a part of him as his arms and legs. Oh, God, she missed him so much. Without him, her life was empty.

Her fingers gripped the back of the chair. Her knees were weak. Though she wanted to be fierce, the weight of her sadness dragged her down. She sank into the chair.

"Please," she said, "you've got to tell me something about Nick. Those pictures you showed me are snapshots. They were taken from surveillance at the rebel camp, weren't they? Your people have infiltrated the camp."

The corner of his mouth twitched. For Phillips, that slight change of expression was more than she'd seen from him in weeks. Sensing a possible crack in the stone wall that kept information from her, she asked, "Do you have photos of Nick?"

"You know how this works, Sidney. I'm here to get intel from you."

"I just want to know if he's all right."

"There's reason to believe that your fiancé is well."

The tiny flicker of hope burst into full flame. Something was different about Phillips. He knew something.

She asked, "Is Nick well enough to be rescued? What do you CIA people call it? Extracted. Can he be extracted?"

He pushed the aerial photo toward her. "We need to know about this part of the compound."

There was nothing to tell. She hadn't visited that part of the palace grounds, hadn't noticed anything about the far corner. For the first time, she wondered if it would serve her better to lie and build up the importance of that corner in the hope that she could get more information. But she wasn't about to play games with the CIA. They were on the same side. She needed to cooperate.

"I was never near that part of the grounds." She rose from her chair. "I've got nothing against you, Phillips. But I need more. Is there anybody else I should talk to? Anything else I can do?"

He leaned back in the chair and folded his arms across his chest. "If you left the room right now and went down the corridor to your left, I wouldn't stop you."

"Why? What does that mean?"

"You heard me."

She took the cue, not knowing what she'd find. Hoping for the best and fearing the worst, her fingers closed on the doorknob and she yanked the door open. Had it always been unlocked? She didn't know; she'd never tried it before.

After hours, there was no one else in the hallway. One side was all windows, and the other was closed doors. The route she'd always followed when escorted into the building was in the opposite direction. She'd never been this way before.

Moving fast before Phillips changed his mind, she rushed down the carpeted corridor. At the far end, a double doorway opened into a honeycomb of cubicles encircled by offices with glass walls. She heard voices to her left and turned.

In the farthest office, Special Agent Hawthorne stood behind a desk and spoke to four men. One stood apart from the others. His left hand was in the pocket of his gray suit jacket. He was tall with black hair and wide shoulders. Sidney couldn't see his face, but she knew him.

She took off running. Dodging around file cabinets and desks, she flew across the room. Her feet barely touched the floor. She crashed into the glass wall. Her palms splayed against it. "Nick."

He turned. His hands met hers against the glass.

Sweet lord, was this possible? She stared, unblinking. If she closed her eyes, she was afraid he'd disappear.

He came around the wall through the door and reached toward her. She latched on to his hand, laced her fingers through his. He was thinner than the last time she'd seen him. His complexion was pale, as though he'd been ill, but this was definitely her fiancé. She lifted her hand toward his face and touched the V-shaped scar on his jaw.

"Oh, Nick, I missed you so much."

"It's okay. I'm here. I'm back."

But there was something different. When she peered into his eyes, she didn't see the man she had once loved with all her heart. Nick Corelli looked back at her with the eyes of a stranger.

Chapter Two

Nick folded his arms around her and held her in a warm embrace. Tucking her head beneath his chin, Sidney gasped, trying to suck oxygen into lungs that felt paralyzed. She was frozen in time. Her world had stopped spinning.

"You're trembling," he said.

"I know."

She desperately wanted to kiss him, but she was afraid to look into his eyes again. What if he'd changed? What if he was no longer the Nick she'd built her life around? She needed reassurance, needed to know that this was *her* Nick, *her* fiancé, *her* lover.

"They told me it was better to wait," he whispered in her ear. "They said it would be easier for you."

"They were wrong."

And he should have known that. He should have realized how much she had needed to know that he was safe. Every moment he'd been missing, she had feared the worst.

"I'm sorry," he said.

"Don't say that." It wasn't right for him to apologize. He'd been through hell. "It's not your fault."

"You know I'd never do anything to hurt you."

"I know."

"Forgive me, Sidney."

A burst of anger shattered her fear. Her blood surged. Her muscles tensed. She pushed away from him, whirled and stalked into the office to face the CIA agents, who had been joined by Phillips. "I blame them."

Special Agent Hawthorne had lied to her only minutes ago. The woman was a monster. If Sidney truly had been a lioness, she would have pounced on the skinny agent, thrown her to the carpet and torn out her throat. Why had they kept Nick from her? What was their plan?

She didn't really care, didn't want to know. She'd happily leave spying to the professionals. All that mattered was Nick. He was alive. Everything else was water under the bridge.

"We're leaving now," she informed them. "Nick and I are leaving. Together."

"I'm afraid that's not possible," Hawthorne said. "Nick will be staying in a safe house until after the visit from Hurtado and his wife."

"Is he in danger?"

"I don't owe you an explanation." Hawthorne's tone was brisk. "Captain Corelli is a marine. He has his orders."

"Ma'am." A man with a thick neck and a body builder's shoulders stepped forward and shook Sidney's hand. "I'm Lieutenant Randall Butler. I want you to know that we appreciate what you've gone through."

"Is that so?" Anger pumped molten lava through her veins. "You knew he was safe. I should have been informed."

"Marine Intelligence has been working with the CIA on this mission. Special Agent Hawthorne is taking the lead."

In spite of her searing fury, she understood what he

was saying. "It was Hawthorne's decision to keep me uninformed. Why?"

Hawthorne unbuttoned the black jacket of her severe pantsuit and leaned against the edge of her desk. The plain office suited her dull, uncluttered personality. The bookshelves were arranged in order, a few diplomas—including one from Harvard—hung on the walls, and nothing seemed out of place.

Hawthorne's eyes narrowed to slits. "Part of my job is to assess your psychological profile. Though you're an intelligent woman who is capable of logic—"

"An engineer," Sidney said. "It doesn't get much more logical than that."

"Your behavior—especially when it pertains to your fiancé—is highly irrational. Therefore, I concluded that you would not be brought into the loop until after Captain Corelli's assignment is over."

Clenching her jaw to keep from screaming, Sidney replied, "I resent your assumptions."

"They aren't meant as criticism." Hawthorne arched an eyebrow. "It's clear that you care so much about Captain Corelli that you aren't capable of behaving in a dispassionate manner."

No one had ever accused Sidney of being too passionate. Her engineering work put her in contact with all-male crews who never showed emotion, and Nick was the only man she'd ever had a serious, long-term relationship with. In her twenty-eight years, there had been two other men she'd fallen for, but she had ultimately ended things with them.

Sidney wasn't going to waste time arguing with Hawthorne, who thought she was doing the right thing. Instead, she pointed out the obvious. "The situation has changed."

"Yes, it has." Hawthorne scowled.

"Keeping me in the dark is no longer an option. I'm here. What are you going to do about it?"

"You leave me no choice but to take you into protective custody."

"You're arresting me?"

"There's no need to be melodramatic. The only restriction is that you won't be allowed to talk to anyone. You'll be kept in comfortable accommodations, and it will only be for about a week."

Overwhelmed by rage, she saw red. "You can't do that."

"Actually, I can."

"What about my work?"

"We'll handle it," Hawthorne said. "This is inconvenient for all of us. It would have been easier if you'd just stayed in the interrogation room." She shot an accusing glance toward Phillips.

"Don't blame him," Sidney said. "After I saw the photos you took in the rebel camp, I took off running. I had a question for you."

"Go ahead and ask."

"I wanted to know if you'd seen my fiancé." She turned toward Nick, who had remained silent throughout this exchange. "The answer is obvious."

He came toward her and slipped his arm around her waist, a familiar gesture. Leaning against his chest, she was more comfortable than she'd been in half a year. Their bodies fit together so nicely.

His deep voice rumbled. "There's no reason for Sidney to be detained. She doesn't know anything about my assignment, except that I'm back in town. Hurtado and the rebels are aware of that fact."

"I don't want her talking to anyone."

"A simple instruction," Nick said. "She can handle it."

"Unacceptable," Hawthorne said. "I don't believe she can be trusted. She's a civilian."

"Which is why you can't take her into custody against her will," Nick said. "You're right about me. I'm obligated to follow orders. But Sidney wants to be home."

She appreciated the way he was taking care of her, putting her comfort ahead of his own. She tilted her head back so she could see him. "I haven't done much with the house."

Before he'd left, they'd purchased a bungalow together. She had intended to use the time while he was on deployment to do some decorating, but when he'd gone missing, she couldn't bear to make any new purchases. Cardboard boxes still packed with their belongings were stacked in every room of the house. In spite of a lovely walk-in closet, she was living out of a suitcase.

"I've been dreaming about our house," he whispered, "coming home and finding you waiting for me in the bedroom."

The tone of his voice hit precisely the right chords inside her. His words were music that touched her soul. She knew there was only one way she could be certain that everything was all right between them. She needed to kiss him.

"Try to understand," the lieutenant said. "The CIA is running this show. We need to do all we can to help them."

"Yes, sir," Nick said, "and I'm not refusing. But I want Sidney to be comfortable. She's been through enough."

"I agree," the lieutenant said. "It's important to be sensitive to the needs of the family."

"What if she's in danger?" Phillips asked. "The rebels could kidnap her and use her to influence you."

"If that's true," Nick said, "why wasn't she under protection before?"

She listened with half an ear to their discussion. The rest of her mind focused on one goal: *kiss him, kiss him, kiss him.* If she could feel his lips on hers and know their relationship was okay, she could handle anything.

Special Agent Hawthorne stomped around her desk and took a position behind it. The only overt signs of her anger were the flaring of her nostrils and a sharp gleam in her flinty eyes. Her voice was low, monotone. "I will agree to send Ms. Parker home while Captain Corelli stays in protective custody. There will be no communication between them unless it's cleared through me. Phillips will accompany her and keep an eye on her. Is that satisfactory?"

"It works for me," Nick said.

"And for me," she said.

She shifted her position within his embrace, turned toward him and tilted her head upward. Her eyelids closed, and her lips parted. The office wasn't an appropriate place for their first kiss, but she couldn't take the chance that Hawthorne would tear Nick away from her.

When his mouth joined with hers, a sweet rush of warmth spread through her body. His lips were firm. His taste always reminded her of honeysuckle. His scent was a pine forest after a rain. He held her with a perfect balance of strength and gentleness.

Even on a bummer day when he wasn't in the mood, Nick was the most irresistible kisser she'd ever known. Though his lips pressed against hers and invited her to respond, he seemed…detached. This kiss wasn't exactly right.

Silently, she cursed her eidetic memory that had recorded every nuance of their lovemaking in indelible detail. She missed the light scrape of his teeth against her lower lip, the quick stroke of his tongue and the fire.

Embarrassed, she pulled away. What had she been expecting? He certainly wasn't going to give her the kind of kiss she wanted while standing in an office surrounded by intelligence agents. This was no basis for judgment.

IN THE BACKSEAT of an unmarked SUV, Sidney sat beside Nick on their way to drop her off at their house. An agent she'd never met before was driving, and Phillips sat beside him in the passenger seat.

"Special Agent Phillips," she said, leaning forward to speak to him. "Thank you."

"It didn't feel right to keep you in the dark," he said. "I'm surprised y'all got Hawthorne to make a concession."

"She's a hard nut to crack."

"Just doing her job," Phillips drawled.

Though wearing her seat belt, her shoulder rubbed against Nick's and her naked thigh grazed the fabric of his trousers. She could feel him watching her.

"Interesting outfit," he said, "I never thought you went in for gingham."

"I have a new job at the Silver Star Saloon, night shift."

"Why?"

"It's kind of fun," she said, avoiding the sad truth. "The place is a microbrewery with ninety-nine different brands of beer, and I like to take big orders and show off by remembering every last one of them."

"You wanted to keep yourself busy," he said. "My God, Sidney, I'm so damn sorry."

There were so many things she wanted to know but was afraid to talk about. What had happened to him while he was held captive? Was he hurt? How was he rescued? Instead, she kept the topic light.

"I should warn you about the house." Quickly, she glanced up at him and then looked away. His nearness was also having a sensual effect on her. Did she dare to try another kiss? "I haven't done much with it, with the house."

"But you had such big plans for decorating."

"I wanted you to help me make up my mind. I haven't even painted the disgusting turquoise in the kitchen."

"What colors are you thinking about?"

Decisions that had seemed impossible yesterday became clear. "I like a soft beige with dark gold and brown granite countertops."

"And in the bedroom?"

"Blue," she said.

"Like the Colorado skies you grew up with."

He knew her so well. At this time of the year, in early November, they usually took a ski vacation in Colorado, where her parents had a vacation cabin. "I don't mind Austin, but I love my mountains."

"Tell me about this bar where you're working."

"Should I recite the ninety-nine varieties of beer?"

"Please don't."

Their conversation was cozy and natural and deliberately avoided dangerous topics. She felt as if she was walking through a minefield. They talked until they pulled up to the curb outside the one-story, redbrick bungalow with shrubs under the windows and a live oak in the front yard. The grass was a little raggedy in winter.

"It's even cuter than I remembered," Nick said as he unfastened his seat belt.

"Whoa," Phillips said. "My orders are for you to stay in the vehicle while I escort Sidney inside."

"You're going to have to hog-tie me to keep me from going into my own house." Nick clapped him on the shoulder. "I'll just be a minute."

Hand in hand, they walked up the sidewalk together. Being separated from him again would be hard, but she was willing to put up with a few days now that she knew he was safe. "You'll call me, won't you?"

"Every day."

"I wish you could stay here."

"Me, too."

She noticed that the porch lamp was dark. She thought she'd turned it on before she'd left for work. The bulb must have burned out. But there were two bulbs in the fixture. What were the odds of both burning out at the same time? "I must have forgotten to turn on the porch lamp."

As she reached toward the lock with her key, the front door yanked inward. A barrage of gunfire erupted.

Chapter Three

Before the bullets flew, Nick had suspected trouble. His beautiful, brilliant Sidney never forgot anything, especially not the locking-up procedures when she left the house. She knew to leave a light burning.

His right arm flung around her slender waist. He scooped her off her feet and pulled her against him as he flattened his back against the brick wall beside the front door. Bullets tore through the opened door and cut into the night.

Still holding Sidney, he stepped off the concrete stoop and ducked into the space between the shrubbery and the red brick wall. "Stay down," he said as he drew a Glock 9 from his ankle holster. He fired two shots toward the open door to let the intruders know he was armed.

It had taken a lot of negotiation to convince Hawthorne to allow him to carry a firearm, and his talk had been worth every minute. The gun felt good in his hand. When it came to survival, Nick trusted himself more than anyone else.

Special Agent Phillips and the other Fed who had been the driver were out of the vehicle and moving toward them.

"You good?" Phillips called out.

Nick gave him a silent okay signal and then motioned

him toward the live oak at the far left side of the front yard. He assumed the two agents would know enough to avoid the sight line from the front window. After he turned Sidney over to their protection, he'd go back to the house and catch the sons of bitches who set up this ambush. Shielding her with his body, he crept under the window ledge toward the corner of the house.

"Where are we going?" she whispered.

"I'm taking you to Phillips. He'll get you to safety."

She balked. "I'm not going anywhere without you."

He hadn't expected resistance. "It's better if you're out of the way."

"Not if I'm armed. I can help."

His attitude shifted from mild surprise to downright shock. Six months ago, Sidney hadn't known how to handle a weapon.

A fresh blast of gunfire exploded behind them. Shards of glass from the shattered front window rained over them. He looked down at the delicate, pale oval of her face. Her jaw was set. Her clear blue eyes showed no fear.

"You don't know how to shoot," he said.

"I learned," she said, cool as ice. "It's not a difficult skill, and I have excellent hand-eye coordination."

"Why?"

"I thought I might have to go to Tiquanna and rescue you. Learning to handle weaponry seemed prudent."

The idea of Sidney charging into the palace of a Third World dictator gave him pause, but he didn't dismiss the notion. She was a remarkable woman. "For now, let's do it my way."

"I'm tired of people telling me what to do," she said, "and that includes you, Nick. I'm part of this operation."

"I won't let you risk your life."

"Ditto."

"We can't stay where we are." He nudged her forward. "Stay low and run toward the live oak where Phillips and the other agent are waiting. I'll cover you."

"And you'll follow me," she said. "Promise that you'll be right behind me. If you aren't, I'll come back for you."

"Just go."

As she stepped out from the shrubbery, he dodged to the right and fired into the house through the shattered front window. From the corner of his eye, he saw her make it to the tree. Though he would have preferred heading to the rear of the house, he ran behind her.

Sheltered by the shade tree, Nick took command. "Phillips, you stay here and keep them pinned down. I'll go around to the back door and do the same. I want to take these guys alive."

"I assume that Special Agent Phillips has already called for backup," Sidney said, again surprising him with her savvy comprehension of a dangerous situation. "If we keep the gunmen contained in the house until the others arrive, we'll have the manpower to take them."

Phillips gaped at her, and then stared at Nick. "What the hell's going on with y'all?"

Nick didn't have time to explain. "Get her to safety."

"I can help," she said. "Give me a weapon."

In her short denim skirt and gingham shirt with her blond hair tucked behind her ears, she looked about as dangerous as Cowgirl Barbie. But he knew better than to doubt her abilities. "There's no reason for you to take any risks."

"I could say the same to you."

But this was his job. He'd been trained for combat. He knew how to handle himself. "I'll stay safe."

After another burst of gunfire from the house, Nick separated from the others and emptied the bullets from his Glock 9 into the front of the house. He loaded a fresh clip and ran, returning to the left side of the house, where he ducked down. Remembering the floor plan of their little bungalow, he knew that the windows above him opened onto a dining room that attached to the kitchen. The only exits from the house were the front entry and the kitchen door. He eased toward the rear of the house.

Stark, silvery moonlight glistened across the backyard patio and the waist-high chain link fence. Nick was painfully aware that he wasn't in a simple village in Tiquanna, where danger was a way of life. The complications of being in Austin were wide and varied. When lights went on in the house next door, he prayed that his neighbors had the good sense to stay inside. From down the street, he heard dogs barking. If this firefight continued, there were sure to be casualties.

Scanning the yard, he decided that the best vantage point for watching the kitchen door would be at the far side of the backyard, but that area offered little in the way of cover, and he wasn't carrying another ammunition clip. Every shot had to count. His best option was to stay where he was and fire at anyone who came through the door. He wanted to take these men alive, to find out why they were coming after him.

If this attack had been arranged by the underfunded Tiquanna rebels, he didn't expect sophisticated weaponry. They'd wear bulletproof vests but not body armor. How many of them were there in the house? He'd seen flashes from at least two weapons.

He heard more gunfire at the front of the house. The longer he waited for the gunmen to make their move, the greater the risk that somebody was going to get shot. Nick had to take the fight to the rebels.

Ignoring the chronic ache from a sprained ankle

that hadn't healed correctly, he vaulted the chain link fence and approached the kitchen door. The interior of the house was dark. There were shouts from inside and more gunfire.

From the street at the front of the house, he heard a police siren and winced. He could have handled the situation with two other marines. Now he'd be dealing with cops, Texas Rangers and backup from the CIA... and Sidney. He couldn't help being proud of her. She'd learned to shoot and had been planning to take on the whole country of Tiquanna to engineer his rescue. He regretted every minute he'd been away from her and every lie he'd ever told her.

Red and blue cop lights flashed like fireworks through the branches of the trees, lighting up the neighborhood. There were shouts and more chaotic gunfire. The situation was slipping out of control. If he hoped to take these guys alive, he needed to rein it in.

A young, fresh-faced Texas Ranger with a handgun appeared at the back gate.

"Don't shoot," Nick said. "I'm on your side."

"Put down your gun."

Nick couldn't blame the kid. If they'd traded places, he would have done the same. Another Ranger joined the first. Now there were two of them, yelling at him to disarm himself.

"Stand down." The order was barked with the authority of a marine. Lieutenant Butler had joined the Rangers. "He's on our side, boys."

There was an explosion at the front of the house. It sounded like a grenade, but Nick guessed it was a flash-bang device that made a lot of noise and fired off thick smoke to drive the gunmen from the house.

The kitchen door flung open and two men wearing

balaclavas rushed through. Nick was caught between the Rangers and the masked men. He pivoted and aimed at the rebels.

Bracing himself, he shouted, "Drop your guns." He repeated the command in Spanish. For a moment, it looked as if they might obey. Then three other armed cops came around from the front and opened fire. Nick dropped to the ground.

When the smoke cleared, the two masked men were sprawled facedown on the concrete patio. Two of the Rangers had also been shot. Their cries and moans struck a familiar chord in Nick's memory. The stink of blood and gunpowder dragged him back in time to other battles, other attacks. Adrenaline pumped up his senses. He staggered to his feet.

He didn't seem to be injured. By some miracle, he had been spared. Stumbling, he approached one of the downed rebels and yanked the mask from his face. He'd been shot in the head, but enough of his features remained for Nick to identify him. His name was Rico.

Agent Phillips dashed into view. "I don't want you to worry, Nick. She's going to be all right."

Sidney. If anything happened to her, he would never forgive himself.

SIDNEY WASN'T HAPPY about the blatantly obvious police presence in front of her house. Most of her neighbors were still strangers, and this wasn't how she wanted to be introduced. Still, making a bad first impression might be the least of her worries. Number one was, of course, that she and Nick had been targeted, which validated Special Agent Hawthorne's insistence on safe houses. Number two, Sidney had been injured. She sat on the rear step bumper of one of the two ambulances with a bandage wrapped around her upper left arm.

A bullet had grazed her. Though the EMT told her she needed stitches, he also assured her that the wound wasn't serious. She clenched her jaw, telling herself that it didn't hurt even though the straight slash across her biceps stung like hellfire. The EMT had given her something for the pain, but it hadn't kicked in yet. If only the bleeding would stop… Her bandage was already soaked through. Nick was going to be upset.

When she saw him plowing through the mob of law enforcement officers like a running back crashing toward the goalposts, she stood and adjusted the black POLICE windbreaker draped over her shoulders so he couldn't see the bandage.

His thick black hair—though neatly trimmed—stuck out in spikes. The lines in his face seemed to be etched more deeply, and he looked much older than his thirty years. This was a part of her fiancé that she didn't know. She'd never seen him in action. The battle-tested marine who had experienced the devastation of war and who risked his life on a daily basis was a good, brave, admirable man. She wanted to be closer to him, but he kept his warrior spirit hidden.

As he approached, she could tell that he intended to embrace her, which was really going to hurt her arm. She held up a hand, bringing him to a halt.

"This wasn't my fault," she said. "Phillips wouldn't give me a weapon, and I was trying to obey orders and go back to the vehicle, but others kept arriving and—"

"Were you wounded?"

"It's nothing serious." She turned away from him, hoping to hide the bandage. "A couple of stitches and I'll be good as new."

Gently, he removed the windbreaker. When he saw the bandage, he inhaled a sharp gasp. "You need medical attention."

"Several other people have been wounded. The EMTs have their hands full."

"You're pale, Sidney. Have you lost a lot of blood?"

"I don't think so." But she did feel a bit dizzy and unsure on her feet. "I took a pill."

"You could be going into shock." He wrapped the windbreaker around her again and held her against his chest in such a way that her left arm was untouched. "I'm sorry, baby. I'm so damn sorry."

"It's not your fault."

"I never should have left you alone."

Agent Victoria Hawthorne, wearing her own black windbreaker with CIA stenciled across the back, charged toward them. "Get in the back of the ambulance, both of you."

Glaring at her, Nick gestured toward the battlefield on their front lawn. "How the hell did this happen?"

"A misjudgment," she snapped. "Do what I say. I need to get you both out of here."

"Where are we going?"

Angrily, she gestured to the back of the ambulance. "Let's move. We'll talk on the way."

After Sidney refused to lie on the gurney, Hawthorne shoved it out of the way and they sat on plastic-cushioned seats with minimal seat belts. Wall space and drawers held an array of medical equipment, including oxygen tanks, defibrillators and stethoscopes. She reached for a blanket to cover her bare legs and settled back on the seat as they pulled away with the siren blaring.

Hawthorne barked into her cell phone, snapping out instructions to her staff. Sidney figured that if anyone should be offering an apology, it was the thin, angry senior agent. She was the one who gave the okay for Sidney to go home without having her house checked out first.

Her skeletal hand, holding the phone, dropped to her lap. She spoke loudly so they could hear her over the siren. "The only way this operation could be arranged so quickly was with prior knowledge. We have a leak, a mole."

"At the CIA," Nick said.

"I don't know. Several other agencies are involved in this operation, including Marine Intelligence." With a disgusted snort, she shook her head. "I never should have allowed you to come to the house with your fiancée."

"Thank God you made that misjudgment." His voice was cold, hard and angry. Sidney had never heard him speak so harshly. "If I hadn't been along, she would have walked into this ambush by herself, defenseless and vulnerable."

Hawthorne pinched her lips together. "Not necessarily."

"They would have taken Sidney hostage, used her to get what they wanted."

The ambulance careened around a corner, and she was thrown against his shoulder. Her wound still ached, but she appreciated the warmth of the blanket over her knees and the jacket around her shoulders. A comfortable heat spread through her, and she felt her eyelids begin to droop. Though she had plenty to say to Hawthorne, it was a struggle to merely stay alert.

"There's been a change in plans," Hawthorne said. "We'll swap vehicles shortly, and you will be taken to the safe house."

"I'm not going anywhere without Sidney," he said.

"Understood." She gave a terse nod. "For now, you'll be staying together."

Chapter Four

Propped up against several pillows, Sidney wakened slowly, cautiously. She peered through heavy-lidded eyes at a dimly lit bedroom with pine furniture. *Where am I?* Her legs stretched out straight in front of her on a king-size bed with a dark blue comforter. *Not my bed.*

Wiggling her butt to get comfortable, she winced at the sharp pain from her left arm. *I was wounded.*

Her memory began to kick in. She heard the echo of an ambulance siren. She remembered being moved into the backseat of a car, looking out the window. And there had been horses and open fields and moonlight. *And Nick, she'd been with Nick.*

"Not possible," she whispered. Her throat was dry and scratchy. Her tongue felt swollen. She couldn't have been with Nick because he was in Tiquanna.

Carefully, she turned on her side so her arm wouldn't rub against anything. Nick wasn't here, and she had to accept that fact. All the denial in the world wouldn't make a difference. She closed her eyes. If the only way she could see him was in her dreams, she wanted to sleep forever.

In her mind, she sorted through her memories as though picking from a jewelry box to choose the shiniest bauble. She selected the day they'd met at the mountain cabin that her friend and colleague, Marissa Hughes, and her new husband had purchased in the mountains outside Deckers in Colorado.

A year and a half ago, it was the summer solstice, June 21, when magic was in the air and young maidens performed candle rituals to see the faces of the men who would be their lovers. Though Sidney didn't believe in all that mystical stuff, her heart leaped when she was introduced to Nick Corelli, and she went all gooey inside when she gazed into his golden eyes. He shook her hand; the connection between them was palpable. They were meant to be together.

Eight other people had been staying at Marissa's cabin over the weekend. Sidney could recite all their names and could report on what they were wearing and what they had for lunch, but her attention focused on Nick. They paired up, and she found herself talking more to him than she did with others. She was positively chatty, which was very unlike her. She tended to be quiet and reserved and a little bit shy. An only child, she grew up mostly in the company of her parents, who were both scientists. Sidney had learned from an early age to amuse herself.

Nick invaded her quiet world with his gentle baritone, his laughter and his intelligence. Of course, she appreciated his physically imposing presence. No red-blooded female could ignore those muscular shoulders and tree-trunk thighs. His torso was lean and well-built and begging to be stroked. But she was also attracted to his mind.

Not only did he listen to her, but he actually seemed to care about what she was saying. Her engineering work was too technical to discuss with people who weren't in the field, and she'd expanded her interests into studies of the lands her firm chose for development, learning the history of the people who lived there and the geological development of these unique places.

During that first afternoon when she and Nick were getting to know each other, the group went tubing. In big rubber inner tubes, they bobbed along a stretch of the North Fork of the South Platte River. The summer sun baked her bare arms and legs while the sparkling, cool water refreshed her senses.

Such a shiny, perfect memory! This brilliant day was meant to be treasured forever.

Lying in the grass beside the river, she and Nick talked about the rock formations and glacial shifts and volcanic activity. Her memory replayed parts of their conversation. She could accurately recall every word, but his nearness distracted her. For long, blissful moments, her overactive brain shut down as she admired this tall man with his easygoing charm. His life experiences intrigued her. Being in the military, he'd seen much of the world.

That night, the group had built a campfire to celebrate the solstice—a night for lovers. At midnight, she and Nick had kissed for the first time.

That kiss, that perfect kiss.

She jolted awake and struggled to sit up on the unfamiliar bed. Her memory filled in the events of what had happened to her in the past few hours.

She'd been at the CIA office, and Nick was there. He was safe. But he was different. And when they kissed, it wasn't the same. A decent enough kiss, that was for sure, but it wasn't earth-shattering. She had to know why. She had to save the precious connection with the man she loved.

Throwing off the comforter, she swung her legs off the side of the bed. Sitting up, she was overcome by vertigo and had to lie back down.

They were at a safe house, a ranch outside Austin, being protected by the CIA. Shortly after they arrived, she had been seen by a doctor who stitched up the wound on her arm and gave her meds for the pain. No doubt, the sedatives were making her woozy.

But she couldn't relax, not while Nick was back and she was unable to comprehend what was happening. She had to regain control.

Struggling, she forced herself to sit up again and waited until the room stopped spinning. Though the curtains were drawn, enough moonlight spilled around the edges of the window that she could see a dresser with a mirror, an overstuffed chair and a bedside table. A digital clock showed the time: 2:37. On a typical Friday night, her shift at the saloon would have ended. She'd be off work and on her way home. Would those intruders have been waiting for her?

If Nick hadn't been there to shove her out of the way, she would have walked into a blast of gunfire. Or not. If she'd been alone, they wouldn't have needed guns to subdue her. She could have been taken hostage.

Leaning forward, she balanced on the soles of her bare feet. Her toes were cold. As soon as she shed the comforter, she shivered. All she was wearing was an oversize T-shirt that hung halfway to her knees. The white bandage on her upper arm gleamed in the moonlight.

She practiced taking one step forward and one step back, not wanting to be far away from the bed in case her knees buckled. As she straightened her shoulders, pain from her wound radiated across the upper half of her body. Fighting it, she clenched her jaw.

Her mouth was parched. She reached for a half-full water glass on the bedside table and wetted her lips. The liquid revived her. She drank it all, set down the glass and cleared her throat. Better, she felt better.

Calling out for help was one option, but she didn't

want to be seen as helpless. As an engineer, she worked mostly with men, and she knew they tended to see women as the weaker gender, easily pacified and disregarded. *Not this time.* Maybe she wasn't as fierce as a lioness, but she meant to be taken seriously.

At the lower edge of her bedroom door, she saw an outline of light. Outside this room, other people were awake and probably making plans. She would join them and become part of the team.

Easier said than done. Obviously, she had to change clothes. Stumbling into a cabal of intelligence agents in her oversize T-shirt and bare feet wouldn't gain her any respect. She shuffled to the closet and opened the door. The total darkness inside the closet dissipated when she flipped a light switch at the edge of the door frame. *Smart move, Sidney.* Turning on the bedroom lights should have been step number one.

With the overhead light on, she searched for something to wear. After fumbling around, she managed to get dressed in a flannel shirt, baggy sweatpants and moccasins that were a couple of sizes too big. Not exactly what she'd choose to confront the precisely groomed Agent Victoria Hawthorne, but this makeshift outfit would have to do.

She opened the bedroom door. To her left was a long hallway with rooms on one side and a carved, wooden balustrade on the other. Below her, on the first floor, was a vast, open room with a two-story moss rock fireplace. Standing at the banister, she looked down into a living room and a dining area where several people sat around a table.

Nick was there.

Her fingers tightened on the polished wood of the banister rail as she looked down at the back of his head.

He still wore the trousers from his gray suit but had shed the jacket. His white shirt was rolled up to his elbows, displaying powerful forearms and wrists.

The muscular lieutenant from Marine Intelligence sat beside Nick. Across the table was Agent Phillips. He sat with his elbows on the tabletop and his chin propped on his fist. The poor guy looked exhausted, barely able to keep his eyes open. Agent Hawthorne sat at the head of the table, of course.

From this angle, Sidney viewed Hawthorne in profile. Not a hair in her sleek brunette bun was out of place. On the table in front of her were folders and electronic equipment. Her tone was calm, and Sidney strained to hear what she was saying. It sounded like a recap of tonight's incidents.

At one point, Hawthorne reached over and patted Nick's arm. Her slender white fingers contrasted with his olive skin and the soft black hair on his forearm. The mere fact that another woman was touching him gave Sidney a pang of jealousy, and she was glad when he jerked away from her.

"In conclusion," Hawthorne said, "I assure you gentlemen that we will uncover the source of this information leak. I will need full cooperation from each of your services."

The marine officer shook his head. "Tell me what you want, and I'll take care of it."

"I prefer conducting my own interrogations."

"Not going to happen, ma'am. I have to protect the identities of my undercover operatives."

"We'll see," she said. "None of us like to think we have a traitor, but how else would information about Nick be made available?"

"What's done is done," Nick said. "I'm more concerned about what happens next."

"We proceed as planned," Hawthorne said. "Three days from now, on Monday, we transfer you into the hotel where Hurtado and the others are staying. You will have private talks and interviews with the oil companies, politicians and investors. At the banquet, you will praise the little dictator. Then, you're done."

"Seems like a lot of fuss for public relations," he said with some bitterness. "Tell me again why this is useful."

Sidney wanted to know the answer to that question, too. It might be better for her to stay out of sight and listen while they talked. She ducked behind the carved, polished wooden spokes holding up the banister rail.

"How many times do I have to say this?" Hawthorne abruptly rose from her chair and pressed her hand across her forehead as though physically holding back a migraine. "It's in the best interest of the US to keep Hurtado in power, and the Tiquanna rebels are garnering sympathy. It's your job to make Tomas Hurtado look like a hero."

"So the oil development firms will choose to do business with him," Nick concluded her speech.

"It's no big deal," she snapped. "All you have to do is put on your uniform, flash your charming smile and tell everyone about being rescued by Hurtado."

Those were stories Sidney wanted to hear. While Nick was gone, she'd imagined him suffering a horrible fate and then tried to convince herself that he was off at a picnic in the Tiquanna jungle. After he told her the real version, she might be able to let go of the tears she'd wept and the pain she'd imagined.

She sat cross-legged on the floor and peered down from the balcony. They wouldn't see her unless they were really looking, but she had a clear view of the table. Her simple surveillance was kind of ironic, considering they were spies.

"You're not telling me the whole story," Nick said.

"Of course, I am."

"If it's no big deal, why did the rebels come after me tonight with guns blazing? I deserve a real answer. My fiancée is lying in a bed upstairs with a gunshot wound."

When he gestured toward the balcony, their heads turned in her direction and she pulled back into the shadows.

Agent Hawthorne slapped her palms on the table and thrust her face toward him. In profile, her nose was as long and sharp as a ferret's. Her lips drew back from her teeth.

"I was going to ask you the same question," she said. "Is there something you haven't told us? Some bit of information you haven't seen fit to share?"

"My debriefings are complete. I gave you pages of intel on the rebel camps, on where they're getting their weapons and how their operation is run."

"How do you know it was the rebels who attacked tonight?"

Nick rose slowly from his chair and towered over her. "You tell me, Hawthorne. How did they know about Sidney?"

"A leak," she said.

"Could be something else," Phillips said. "They could have had Sidney under surveillance at the saloon."

Eager to get away from Nick's scrutiny, Hawthorne turned on him. "Why would they do that?"

"We haven't kept it a secret that Nick is here in town. He's part of the schedule for the Tiquanna meeting. The rebels might have figured that he'd contact his fiancée.

And when she left work in the company of two official-looking guys, they'd draw the obvious conclusion."

Sidney nodded. Though she hated to think of being watched by rebel thugs, Phillips's explanation made logical sense. She wished that he was in charge of this operation instead of Hawthorne.

The thin female agent returned to her seat at the head of the table. "I knew it was a mistake to pick her up tonight."

"She would have found out that I was at the meetings with Hurtado," Nick said, "and there would have been hell to pay."

Phillips drawled, "Y'all wouldn't want to make Miss Sidney angry."

"Oh? Why not?" Hawthorne said.

Nick chuckled. Sidney couldn't see his face, but she knew he was grinning as he said, "My fiancée was planning a coup on the government of Tiquanna. You'd be wise not to underestimate my woman."

"Let's talk about another woman, shall we? I'd like to hear more about your relationship with Elena Hurtado."

Sidney vividly remembered Elena. An exotic, raven-haired beauty, she played the role of South American bombshell to perfection. Elena was a woman who deservedly inspired envy. If Nick had a relationship with her, Sidney wanted to know.

Not wanting to miss a word, she leaned forward. Her forehead bumped against the spokes holding up the railing. Just a quiet, little thump. But it was enough to draw the attention of the military guy and Phillips.

She was discovered. There was nothing she could do but stand up. Trying to ignore the pain in her arm, she pasted a smile on her face and shuffled along the balcony toward the staircase in her oversize moccasins.

Chapter Five

Nick rushed to the staircase, where Sidney carefully descended, clinging to the banister and taking one step at a time. Less than half an hour ago, he'd been sitting on the edge of her bed watching her sleep soundly. Unable to keep his hands off her, he'd stroked her fevered forehead, brushing aside a gleaming hank of smooth blond hair. He'd longed to kiss her, to make love to her. Hell, he would have been happy just to hold her close.

But she needed her sleep. Her breathing had been steady and regular. The doc had given her enough painkillers to hold her until morning.

He climbed the staircase and slung an arm around her waist for support. "You shouldn't be up."

"I was hungry," she said.

"Let me bring something to the bedroom."

"I'd rather join the team."

When she raised her arm to wave to the others, he felt her sag against him. She barely had the strength to stand. Her complexion was pallid. Her beautiful blue eyes were bloodshot. But her determination was intact; she wasn't going back to bed unless he picked her up and carried her.

He made one more attempt to reason with her. "I'll come to bed with you."

She hobbled down another stair. "I'll be fine."

"I guess it's true what they say. You can't keep a good woman down."

"Please don't refer to me as your woman," she said. "We aren't Neanderthals."

Her body was weak, but there was nothing wrong with her razor wit. He returned, "Whatever you say, baby-cakes."

"Honey lamb," she muttered.

"Pookie pie."

At the foot of the staircase, Hawthorne confronted them with a cold, I-mean-business glare. "How are you feeling, Sidney?"

Nick felt a surge of strength go through her as she straightened her spine. No way would Sidney let Hawthorne know how much she was hurting.

"Don't worry about me," Sidney said. "Please continue with your debriefing. I believe you were talking about Elena Hurtado."

From Nick's point of view, Sidney's interruption had come at a good time. He wanted to avoid discussion of Elena until he had more information. He continued down the staircase. "We're going to the kitchen, Hawthorne. Sidney's hungry."

They made their way across the spacious front room and dining room into the attached kitchen, where two armed agents dressed in cowboy gear were drinking mugs of coffee. This safe house outside Austin had once been a working cattle ranch with a barn, bunkhouse and outbuildings in addition to the two-story main house. The kitchen was big enough to cook for twenty or thirty hungry ranch hands.

After he got her seated at a round wood table, he grabbed a bottle of water from the fridge, placed it on the table beside her and sat. He noticed a tremble in her fingers as she screwed off the lid on the water bottle.

According to the doc, her injury and the resulting loss of blood weren't particularly serious, but Nick couldn't help worrying about her. "Are you in pain?"

"My arm hurts a little." She chugged the water. "Mostly, I'm dizzy. You know how I hate to take pills."

She didn't like being intoxicated and losing control. He'd never seen her drunk. "Do you remember getting stitched up?"

"Not very well. I had twelve stitches, right?"

"It's going to leave a scar."

She gave him a goofy grin. "Cool."

Most women would be upset, but not her. "Really? You think it's cool?"

"I like the drama. If somebody asks about my scar, I can tell them I was injured in a firefight with terrorists. Is that right? Were they terrorists or rebels?"

Nick thought of the man he'd recognized when he pulled off the mask. Rico Suarez was a cool, handsome businessman who worked with Hurtado and had connections with the oil companies. "It's hard to say who they were or what they were after."

"Don't you know?"

"There's a lot I don't know." And more that he couldn't talk about. He'd spent six months involved in a political dance where the partners seemed to change every day. "What do you want to eat?"

"Something easily digested. I haven't been nauseated, but I don't want to push my luck. Maybe crackers or a cookie?"

He asked the other two agents where to find food, and they pointed him in the direction of an earthenware cookie jar. He brought her a couple of homemade sugar cookies on a napkin.

She nodded. "Coffee?"

"That's a negative," he said. "You need your sleep."

She pushed back the sleeves of her plaid flannel shirt. "Do you like my outfit?"

"Very cute."

"I call it hobo chic." She picked up a cookie and took a ladylike nibble. A crumb fell onto her chin. He wanted to brush it off but didn't trust himself to touch her. One simple caress would lead too quickly to another, and before he knew what was happening he'd be kissing her, scooping her into his arms and carrying her up the staircase to the bedroom.

For the past six months, he dreamed about making love to her. Being so close and not being able to taste her mouth or run his hands through her straight blond hair was driving him crazy. He was desperate to feel her sweet, slender body pressed against his.

He had to be careful, had to hold back. Sidney was smart and perceptive. He wasn't ready for her to know the whole truth, not just yet.

Hawthorne came into the kitchen. Scowling, she announced, "It's almost three in the morning. We'll call it a night and start again tomorrow."

"Agreed," Nick said. He had considered talking to Lieutenant Butler about Rico. Butler was the closest he had to a confidant. But after tonight's attack, Nick wasn't sure he trusted the lieutenant. Butler had arrived at the scene quickly; he'd been in the backyard at the right time to shoot Rico.

Hawthorne pivoted and marched into the other room. The two other agents shouldered their weapons and went out the back door. Nick was alone with Sidney in the kitchen. Not that they were truly alone. This was a CIA safe house; he'd be wise to assume that every conversation was bugged.

Unable to resist her, he moved a little closer. "I missed you. I kept thinking about you and what you were doing every minute of the day. Rubbing lotion on your long legs. Combing your hair. Brushing your teeth while you hummed the *Jeopardy* theme song."

"That tune lasts a minute," she said. "It's important to spend at least a minute, twice a day, on oral care."

He closed his eyes and inhaled deeply, catching a hint of her special scent through all the other odors in the house.

"That routine pretty much covers what I was doing," she said. "My days were the same as always, except for when I fell into the panic-and-depression thing, which I don't intend to talk about. Oh, and I went to a psychic."

He was surprised. "You don't usually go for nonscientific explanations."

"When logic fails, I'll try other methods." She finished one cookie and started on the other. "This was a Navajo woman who mostly deals with herbal remedies. She told me we'd be together again."

Her lips pressed together, and he could tell she was holding something back. "What else?"

"She said something would come between us, but she wasn't specific or logical."

Turning her head, she stared at him with wide, curious eyes. Quickly, she averted her gaze. He had the sense that she didn't like what she'd seen.

Nick had secrets he'd kept from everyone. He'd passed through a battery of interviews from several intelligence agencies, talking to people who were trained to spot deception. As far as he knew, none of them suspected him. But Sidney knew him better than anyone else.

Her voice was soft and subtly persuasive. "Tell me what happened to you in Tiquanna."

"It's a long story. We should go upstairs to bed."

CLIMBING THE STAIRCASE to the second floor took effort, but Sidney managed. In the bedroom, she kicked off the moccasins and slipped out of the sweatpants, her back to Nick. Too tired to remove the flannel shirt, she crawled into bed and lay on her side with her injured arm facing the ceiling. She allowed herself a little smile. Her scar would be a badge of honor, totally impressive to all the tech guys at work.

Under the comforter, warmth wrapped around her like a gentle cocoon. Sleep beckoned. If she relaxed a tiny bit more, she'd be unconscious. But she wasn't ready to let go.

Her mind hopscotched from one point to another and back again. Nick was her fiancé, the man she wanted to spend the rest of her life with. She should be able to embrace him without reservation. The less analytical part of her brain told her to open her arms and accept him. *Forget the doubts. Take the kisses.* It would all work itself out. Or would it?

She'd never been a woman who would settle for less. Before Nick left for Tiquanna, their happiness had been as close to perfection as she could imagine. They'd bought a house. They were getting married. And now… he was different.

She hadn't gone through six months of hell, not knowing if he was dead or alive, to end up with a troubled relationship. Until she could look into his eyes and see the truth, she'd keep him at arm's length. No matter how much she wanted to succumb, she'd resist. No kissing. No touching. Definitely, no lovemaking.

Nick turned off the bedside lamp and unbuttoned his shirt. Her strong resolve crumbled when she saw the outline of his bare chest. Her heart beat faster. She had memorized those swirling patterns of hair and the ridges of hard muscle. Her fingers itched to touch him.

"No," she said aloud.

In the dim moonlight shining around the edge of the window, she saw him pause. "Did you say something?"

Though she wanted him with all the pent-up yearning of six long months, she said, "Don't you have your own bedroom? I figured Hawthorne would enforce a no-fraternization policy."

"There's another room. But the view isn't anywhere near as pretty."

"Maybe you should go there, anyway."

The mattress bounced as he sat on the bed beside her. Gently, he stroked the hair off her forehead. "Are you throwing me out?"

"I don't feel good." She squeezed her eyes shut, unable to bear looking at him. "Just for tonight, it's better if I sleep alone."

"I'll stay with you until you're asleep." His hand caressed her cheek. "It's been a hell of a day."

"It has." She couldn't help turning her head and lightly kissing his palm.

"I'm sorry about what happened at the house."

"I can't imagine what our neighbors think." Her memory pulled up a grim recollection of police vehicles and ambulances, flashing lights and gunfire. After that circus, she was pretty sure that nobody on their block would ask her to babysit. "We'll have to make it up to them. Maybe have a barbecue."

"Yeah, nothing says 'I'm sorry' like pulled pork."

His voice went still. A heavy silence invaded the bedroom. The distance between them spread like a fading echo.

Was she doing the right thing? The temptation was great to put aside her concerns and make love to him, but she had to make things right. She wanted their relationship to be the way it was before.

"As long as you're here," she said, "I want to know what happened in Tiquanna."

He leaned down and kissed her forehead. Then he stood and walked away. She opened her eyes and watched as he went to the window and pulled the curtain aside to look outside. Moonlight traced his profile. "It's a long story, and you're tired. Maybe tomorrow."

He was avoiding the topic. He didn't want to tell her, but she had to know. "We've got time."

"Okay," he said. "Remember what the country was like when you visited a couple of years ago? Tropical climate, lush and humid. Rain forests. Villages with thatched roof huts. Tourists in the capital city on the Atlantic coast. Abundant natural resources."

Her most vivid memories were the heat like a steam bath, the brilliant green of indigenous foliage and odd creatures like lizards and frogs and insects. Less charming was a filthy hospital, beggar children on the streets and a long line of women waiting by a supply truck for freshwater. "I remember."

"Your company didn't invest in oil exploration there," he said.

"Lack of infrastructure."

He nodded. "Like roads and plumbing."

Thinking of the children, she said, "More than that. It was a beautiful place but sad."

"It's gotten worse," he said. "Hurtado and his hand-picked ministers siphon off all the aid money. Anybody who objects gets tossed in jail. The rebels claim to be representing the people, but they're nearly as corrupt as the dictator. The level of violence is brutal."

"Why were you sent there?" she said.

"The ambassador requested a squad of marines to protect the embassy, but we didn't stay there for long. Hurtado was hosting a bunch of companies that wanted to invest in Tiquanna. These top executives stayed with Hurtado. Pretty soon, that's where we were stationed. Our job was to add a layer of protection for American VIPs."

"What happened when you were taken?"

"An explosive device tore a hole in the wall surrounding the presidential compound."

"Presidential," she said. "Hurtado became president?"

"A couple of years ago. Sham elections."

Though she knew better than to get worked up about political fakery, she was disgusted. "Let me guess. He's president for life."

"The rebels are making noises about calling for a new election. Each time an opposing candidate steps forward, he's charged with a crime and ends up in prison."

She suppressed a shudder. "Let's get back to you. After they blew a hole in the wall, what happened?"

"A couple of my guys were injured. I went to help them. It was night. Smoke from the explosion streaked the air and stung my eyes. I put on my infrared goggles. In the street beyond the wall, I saw flashes of gunfire. I wanted to shoot back, but the rebels weren't alone."

"Who was there?"

"Civilians. I saw women and kids running from house to house, trying to get away. There was no way I could open fire."

Her heart ached for him. She'd always known his pro-
fession, had always been aware of the risks in the military
and the hard decisions he had to make. And she had to
believe that his sacrifices fulfilled an important purpose.

"After that," he said, "I don't know what happened. My
mind went blank. When I woke up, I was in a thatched
hut."

"Were you injured?"

"I've got a couple of scars I can show you." He stepped
away from the window and went to the overstuffed chair,
where he sat, leaning back with his long legs stretched
out in front of him. "I was moved from place to place,
sometimes in a house and other times in the forests."

"Was it the rebels?"

"I don't know." He hesitated for a long moment. "Who
else would bomb Hurtado's palace?"

"You don't sound sure."

"Like I said, I don't remember. I was a hostage for six
or seven weeks before I started making sense of things.
There was an old man with a grizzled beard who gave
me food and played chess with me. His name was Estaban. He told me that I got beat up pretty badly and almost died."

Her heart clenched. "Oh, Nick…"

"Stop," he said. "It's over. It's done, and I survived.
Probably the worst thing that happened was a stomach
infection, probably from drinking the water."

Peering across the unlit room, she tried to see his eyes.
She wanted to hold him and comfort him, but she knew
he'd reject anything that smacked of pity. "I noticed you
have a small limp."

"I tried to escape, took off running through the forest.
Do you remember those forests?"

"Incredible." Her mind traveled back to a hike through

Tiquanna where she saw intensely green foliage at the edge of the rain forest. The reds and blues were so brilliant that they seemed to vibrate. The birds and animals were remarkable. "Did you see any of the poison dart frogs?"

"Some."

Those tiny jewel-toned creatures actually were toxic enough to kill. She had heard their venom was used in torture. "What happened in your escape attempt?"

"Long story short, I tripped over a tree root and got a sprained ankle. It's still not completely healed."

She heard detachment in his voice, as though he was reciting a story about some other hostage. It was going to take time for him to open up. "Nick, I want you to know—"

"It's okay." He sank back in the chair. "You need your sleep. We'll talk tomorrow."

Pulling away, he was pulling away from her. The space between them loomed as wide as the Grand Canyon. "Good night, Nick."

Chapter Six

The next morning, Sidney awoke with the certainty that Nick was keeping something from her. She didn't know what, didn't know why, didn't know how he'd gotten the notion that he could be less than honest with her. But today, she meant to find out.

Ignoring the stab of pain when she moved her arm, she threw off the comforter and hauled herself out of bed. Her movements were clumsy, her muscles felt kind of stiff and she had a nagging little headache. Though she'd never experienced anything like yesterday, she was reminded of the day after a car accident when she'd separated her shoulder. Her fault, she'd been driving too fast and had gone into a skid on an icy mountain road and ended up in a ditch. She remembered the hangover from painkillers. God, she hated taking pills.

On the floor beside the window, she found the big black suitcase that was usually stashed in the back of her closet. With a sense of dread and trepidation, she unzipped the back panel on the bag that looked exactly like thousands of other practical suitcases. But this piece of luggage was different. On the inside was a long, flat metal box with a keypad lock that she used as a safe. The men who had broken into their house weren't thieves, but she was still worried about these precious belongings and had requested that this specific suitcase be brought to her.

Inside the back panel, she keyed in the number to unlock the safe. The lid clicked open. She sorted through velvet bags containing a pair of diamond studs, a couple of antique brooches, a string of pearls and—most important—her engagement ring. Holding the diamond in her hand, she breathed a relieved prayer that it hadn't been taken. Last night, she'd left her ring in the safe, not wanting to wear it while she worked at the saloon.

She was a little surprised that Nick hadn't mentioned the ring. A ray of sunlight crept around the window curtain and lit up the glittering facets of the marquise cut stone. A beautiful piece of jewelry, it was meant for special occasions. She placed the ring back into the blue velvet box and returned it to the safe.

After zipping the back panel, she pawed through the rest of the clothing and shoes. The person who had packed for her seemed to have planned for several possible occasions. In addition to jeans, shirts and sweatshirts, the individual had included a nice black dress and a couple of skirts.

Eager to get a start on the day, she gathered up a handful of clothes. Two doors down from her bedroom was a huge bathroom. She locked the door. A shower would have been quicker, but she opted for a bath in the quaint claw-footed tub so she wouldn't get the dressing on her wound wet. The injury was problematic when she washed her hair. Raising her left arm above her head hurt, but she managed.

There was a knock on the door.

"Nick?"

"It's Agent Hawthorne. I trust you found the clothes we picked up from your house."

"I appreciate having my own things," Sidney said.

"Take your time getting ready. Other than a debriefing on the events of last night, we shouldn't have to bother you."

"I want to help."

"There's nothing you can do. Just relax and recuperate."

But Sidney wanted to be part of the investigation. "I might be able to share some insights on the resources in Tiquanna. My data is a couple of years old, but I doubt much has changed. Is Rafael still the minister of energy?" Her voice echoed hollowly in the tiled bathroom. "Hello? Agent Hawthorne?"

There was no answer. Apparently, Hawthorne had walked away and left her hanging. She'd been dismissed. Sidney glided the flat of her right hand across the surface of the hot water in the tub. She hadn't counted on being treated well by Agent Victoria Hawthorne, but the disrespect was still irritating.

It didn't matter what the CIA and the other intelligence people thought. Nick was her focus, and she was confident that she could make sense of him. Her training and her memory were geared toward problem solving. Starting with the assumption that he was keeping something from her, she worked deductively. Why wouldn't he tell her? He might be trying to protect her. If so, whom was he protecting her from?

Last night, the rebels had broken into her home. They might have taken her hostage and forced her to cough up information. Nick hadn't anticipated the attack at the house. He'd been acting as if she was in very little danger. Therefore, she reasoned, he wasn't withholding information to protect her.

More likely, he was keeping secrets as a part of his

assignment— one of those "tell no one" things. And why would that secrecy extend to her? She wasn't part of the political scene. Her company had no interest in Tiquanna.

Was Nick protecting someone else? *Elena Hurtado.* A gorgeous woman like her would have dozens of men— possibly even Nick—leaping forward to take care of her. Not that she needed them. The dictator's wife was one of the strongest women Sidney had even met.

Once out of the tub, she got dressed, choosing jeans and a sleeveless shirt that would allow easy access to the bandage on her arm and pulling a light blue cardigan over it. After toweling her hair dry, she dragged a comb through it. The thoughtful suitcase packer hadn't tossed in a supply of cosmetics, so she used the lipstick in her purse and wished for mascara to darken her blond lashes.

If she asked Nick directly about what he was holding back, she wondered what kind of response she'd get. He knew her well enough not to play the "I'm doing this for your own good" card. Nick had never been dismissive with her, never.

The more she thought about it, the more she knew that all she needed to do was get him alone and have a direct conversation. *He'll tell me.* When he told her the truth, she'd see the doubt clear from his eyes. Then she could open her heart to him.

As she descended the staircase into the large front area, she had a new appreciation for the rugged charm of this former ranch house. Morning sunlight poured through pine-framed windows and splashed against sandy-colored walls. Rough-hewn wood furniture was arranged in a conversation area near the two-story fireplace. Earthy blues, greens and browns from woven rugs added warmth to the slate floors. It was a little too tidy and classy for a working ranch. This was more like a dude ranch where urban cowboys would kick up their boots and relax.

Agent Phillips, looking very comfortable and Texan in his jeans and boots, came into the dining room from the kitchen and gave her a weary wave. "Are you feeling like breakfast?"

"I could eat."

"Help yourself to chow in the kitchen. After that, I think the doc wants to take another look at your arm."

None of the other agents were in sight, and she had the feeling that Phillips had been left to "handle" her. Since he'd established a foundation of trust with her over the past several months, he was the logical choice. But she didn't want to be shuffled out of the way.

"Where's Nick?" she asked.

He set down his coffee mug beside a plate of scrambled eggs and bacon. "In a meeting with Agent Hawthorne and some others. This smells like heaven."

She glanced down at his plate. "With all that bacon, I'd have to say it was hog heaven."

He grumbled, "A man deserves a little bacon now and again."

She sat beside him. "Does anyone ever call Agent Hawthorne Vicky?"

"Not if they value their ass."

"I'm guessing that she doesn't want me interrupting whatever big-deal meeting she has going on with Nick and the other agents. I think she considers me a loose cannon."

Phillips picked up a strip of bacon. "The loosest."

"I'm not going to let her railroad me." For six months, Sidney had followed the rules, and her cooperation had gotten her nowhere. "My house was shot to pieces. Men were killed on my patio. I've got a stake in this game."

Phillips finished his bacon and picked up his coffee mug. "What are you fixing to do?"

"I'm not sure. I need more information." The combined aromas of coffee and bacon were having an effect on her. Though it probably wouldn't hurt to grab a bite before she took on the CIA, she needed to keep her priorities straight. "Where are they meeting?"

He shrugged. "If you poke around in that back hallway, you'll find them. This isn't that big a house."

"What are they talking about?"

"Stop your worrying, Sidney. There's nothing clandestine going on."

She had no reason to mistrust Phillips. He'd been more straightforward with her than anyone. If he hadn't pointed her in the right direction at the CIA office, she might not have found Nick. Leaning close, she gave him a hug with her good arm. "What did your twins wear for Halloween?"

He reared back in his chair. "How do you know about my kids?"

"One of the times I was in the office, you mentioned that it was their fourth birthday. Two boys. Ron and Eric." She tapped the side on her head, reminding him of her eidetic memory. "So? Were they Tweedledee and Tweedledum?"

"Ninja turtles," he said. "Thanks for asking."

In the kitchen, she met Delia, the cook and housekeeper, and a couple of guys who worked here at the ranch, taking care of the horses and such. Sidney wrapped a blueberry empanada in a napkin, filled a coffee mug and set out in search of the meeting.

The third door she opened was an office space with a long sofa, a couple of chairs and a big carved-oak desk.

Nick rose to greet her and directed her to a chair near the coffee table.

Predictably, Hawthorne objected. "Sidney, there's no reason for you to be here."

"I'll be quiet," she said.

Hawthorne had shed her black suit in favor of jeans, a white turtleneck and a puffy vest that added a little bit of bulk to her skinny frame. "I have to be frank," she said. "You're in the way."

"She's staying," Nick said. "We can use Sidney's expertise when I'm talking to Gregory about the oil development."

He introduced her to another CIA agent—Jim Gregory—who had a stack of maps, grids and documents piled up on the floor beside him. He worked mostly with Underwood Oil Exploration, but he also knew a couple of men who worked for her firm, Texas Triton.

She shook his hand firmly. "We've met."

"I don't think so." He blinked behind his glasses.

"I didn't know your name," she said, "but I saw you at my house when the bullets were flying."

"That's correct. I was with the first response team."

Curiously, she eyed his research-and-development paperwork. "I'm surprised you brought so much material with you."

"We do our research," he said proudly.

She actually hadn't been wondering about the amount of information he had compiled. She questioned why he brought hard copies. Her team kept most of its data on computer and flash drives. Giving Gregory the benefit of the doubt, she decided he'd brought paper so he could have information at his fingertips and more easily explain to the other agents. "Are you an engineer?"

"I used to be an accountant."

He looked the part with his tortoiseshell glasses and khaki trousers. Gregory was probably the only person in the room, other than her, who wasn't armed. She gave him an encouraging grin. "I'd be happy to help with any information."

She wondered what had changed to make Tiquanna a more appealing site for oil investment. Three years ago, when she visited the country, she had concluded that there were significant oil reserves, similar to Venezuela, but they would need to invest far too much initial capital in pipelines, roads, refineries and housing.

"All right, Nick." Hawthorne snapped his name, compelling his attention. "We've covered the basics of what you need to say to the executives from Underwood Oil. Emphasize the brutality of the rebels, especially when talking about how they injured your leg. Don't forget to practice with that cane I got for you."

She waited for Nick to correct Hawthorne. Last night, he'd told her that his injured ankle was the result of an escape attempt, not due to mistreatment by the rebels. He didn't say anything. Instead, he nodded.

Had Sidney misunderstood last night? She didn't think so. He'd been specific about tripping on a tree branch. And he'd talked about poison dart frogs. Or was that something she'd been thinking? Last night, her brain had been fuzzy. And what difference did it make how he'd hurt his leg?

She sipped her coffee and studied his profile. Blaming his sprained ankle on the rebels made them seem more dangerous. When he talked about the old man who cooked for him, he hadn't been hostile or afraid.

A possibility occurred to her. He might be lying to Hawthorne. But that didn't make any sense. Why would he want to mislead the CIA?

To keep herself from blurting out something that would get her tossed from the meeting, she took a gooey bite of blueberry empanada. Nick sat on the sofa next to the muscle-bound Lieutenant Butler. Another CIA agent was at the desk with a laptop open in front of him. Hawthorne approached him. "As long as Sidney is here, I might as well show her the photos of the men who were killed last night."

The agent behind the desk scrambled to find an electronic tablet, which he passed to Hawthorne. She held the screen toward Sidney. "Take your time."

After brushing the sugar off her fingers, Sidney took the tablet. A glaring light illuminated the face of a dead man with red blood streaking through his thick black hair and down his forehead. His eyes were open. His jaw hung slack. A tattoo of a spider web crawled up his throat.

Sidney had never been squeamish. When she was a little girl, she helped her anthropologist mother sort and catalog human and animal bones from various dig sites. Still, it was disturbing to look into the flat, empty eyes of this man, who couldn't have been much older than twenty.

Carefully, she studied his features, trying to imagine what he looked like three years ago when she was in Tiquanna. "He's not familiar."

Hawthorne changed the picture on the screen. "How about this one?"

He'd been shot in the head. The left frontal bone of his cranium was shattered. He hadn't yet been cleaned and prepped for autopsy, and blood matted with his hair. In places, she saw the white of his skull and the ooze of brain matter. His left eye was gone.

She concentrated on his well-shaped lips and the side of his face that was still intact.

"Rico Suarez," she said.

Hawthorne glared at her. "You know him?"

She looked away from the grotesque photo. "He was a dashing, handsome man who dressed well and wore a lot of gold jewelry. I met him at the palace. He took the representatives from my company out for a night of mojitos and salsa dancing."

"You must be mistaken," Hawthorne said.

Agent Gregory took the screen from her. "She's right. It's Rico. How could I have missed this?"

In a voice that was too innocent to be believed, Nick said, "Sidney said she met him at the palace. Was he a friend of Hurtado?"

"He must be working with the rebels now," Hawthorne said as she dodged behind the desk. "This requires a change in strategy. Would you all please leave? We'll continue this meeting later."

Still clinging to her coffee mug, Sidney hustled out into the hallway, where Nick slipped an arm around her shoulders. "Nice job," he said. "We could have been stuck in there for hours."

"Can we go somewhere alone, just you and me?"

"Thought you'd never ask."

Chapter Seven

Without stopping or consulting with any of his handlers, Nick escorted Sidney through the kitchen and out the door, heading toward the barn behind. For reasons he couldn't explain to her right now, he needed to get away from the safe house and the multitude of surveillance that surrounded them.

"Nice day." He squinted up at the sun and inhaled a gulp of fresh air. The quiet rustle of wind through autumn leaves, the sounds of horses and occasional bird squawks replaced the dark hum of tension inside the house. "Warm enough that we won't need jackets to go for a ride."

"A horseback ride? I'd like that."

The bright note in her voice made him wish that they could simply be together and relax. Not yet. "We need to hurry."

"I'm right behind you."

Inside the wide-open double doors of the barn, he left her sitting on a hay bale to finish her coffee. He went to the corral behind the horse stalls and recruited one of the ranch hands to help him saddle up two horses, a pinto and a bay.

He brought the horses to where she was sitting. "How's your arm?" he asked. "Riding won't bother you, will it?"

"Not a bit."

"Would you tell me if it did?"

She downed the last of her coffee. "I don't mind a little 'owie' if it gets me closer to what I want. We need to talk."

"And we will." *But not yet. Not here.*

They needed to be alone, truly alone and away from the house. There was no one he could trust, not even this crusty old cowboy who didn't appear to have any connection with the CIA. Everyone was watching and listening. Nick was just as much a captive here in Texas as he had been in South America. Maybe even more so; the CIA surveillance was more subtle. He couldn't see all the hidden bugs and cameras that were keeping tabs on his every movement.

Last night, he'd made a big mistake when he started to talk to Sidney about Estaban and his time with the rebels. He was certain their conversation had been bugged when Special Agent Hawthorne presented him with a cane this morning and reminded him that his sprained ankle hadn't been due to a stumble. The CIA wanted his injury to look like torture.

Before they mounted up, Lieutenant Butler marched into the barn. "I wondered where you two went running off to."

Not a clean getaway. But Nick wasn't going to let Butler stop him. He took the coffee mug from Sidney's hand and set it down on the hay bale. "I wanted to grab some alone time with my fiancée."

"It's not safe. I should come with you."

The last thing Nick wanted was a chaperone. "Lieutenant, I'm armed. I paid attention to the briefing last night, and I know where the safe boundaries for this property lie."

"None of that protects you from a sniper." His short,

military-style haircut was hidden under a cowboy hat. He tugged on the brim. "There's a leak. Someone could be watching."

"Sidney and I need some time, sir. She went six months without knowing whether I was dead or alive." He fixed the other marine with a steady gaze. "You know what it means to leave loved ones behind."

They were both military men. Both had faced the loneliness of battle and the struggle of coming home again. If anyone could understand the need for a moment of privacy, it had to be the lieutenant.

"Be back at eleven hundred hours," Butler said, "and don't go beyond the safe area."

"Okay."

Nick helped Sidney mount the pinto. As soon as she was in the saddle, Butler reached up and patted her on the knee. "You've got a good man there."

"I know," she said.

"Nice work in identifying Rico from the photo. Hawthorne looked like she'd been kicked in the gut by a mule. I guess she doesn't know everything, after all," Butler said.

"Guess not," she said.

Before the lieutenant could change his mind, Nick flicked his reins and rode out of the barn with Sidney following close behind. A swift breeze swept through his hair, and the morning sun warmed his face. The high prairie grass and sage had faded to a dull khaki, and the live oak and cedar forests in the distance mingled the gold and orange leaves of late autumn.

After they were beyond the bunkhouse, he slowed, and she trotted her pinto up beside him. The sunlight picked out strands of gold in her straight, maize-colored hair. Graceful and athletic, she sat comfortably in the saddle.

For a moment, he was mesmerized by the sight of her. She was even more beautiful than he remembered.

"This is nice," he said, "just you and me."

"Nick, I have some questions."

He knew she was suspicious, and he wanted to put off the explanations for as long as possible. There wasn't much he was free to say. "There's something I've been thinking about," he said. "Something you and I do that no other couple does."

Her blond eyebrows shot up. "What are you talking about?"

"You know." If they'd had more time, he would have teased until she exploded. But she was already close to eruption, and he knew better than to poke the bear. "I want you to tell me one of your stories."

"Oh, Nick. Not now."

He liked playing this storytelling game using her eidetic memory. After he gave her a date, she'd tell him exactly what had happened. "March 14, 2013."

"Pi Day." She gave him an indulgent smile. "You didn't even know it was a special occasion until I explained that pi was three-point-fourteen, which makes me the biggest nerd girl on the planet."

"You're my nerd girl," he said.

"You flew into Lackland Air Force Base, borrowed a Hummer and got to my apartment at 10:48 in the morning. We hadn't seen each other for six days." A dreamy expression softened her features. "And we made up for lost time."

"Details," he said. "I want details."

"I made you an omelet with mango salsa and cheese."

"And what did we do before we ate?"

"I remember a kiss," she said, "a really long and passionate kiss. I knew you'd caught a late-night flight and it had taken a while for you to drive to my place from San Antonio because your stubble was growing out and your cheeks were already scratchy. I liked the way it felt when you kissed me here." She arched her neck and pointed to the hollow of her throat. "And here." She cupped her breast.

As she continued, her voice got husky, low and sexy. He wondered if she was reliving the sensations of their lovemaking as she described unbuttoning his camo uniform shirt and slipping out of her pink cotton nightgown. He was definitely feeling it, hanging on every word.

"And after we made love—"

"Hey," he interrupted. "You're leaving out the best part."

"I think not," she said archly. "The best was right before sunset at 7:39."

"There was a lot of time between ten and seven." And they had kept busy. He actually didn't need a lot of description of their lovemaking. The feel of her silky skin, her scent and her taste were indelible parts of his memory.

"7:39," she said firmly. "We were dressed to go out for dinner. You were wearing a black suit with a gray shirt and a burgundy necktie. And you went down on one knee."

"Even better, you said yes."

"And you gave me a pi diamond, 3.14 carats." She held up her bare left hand. "The ring is too beautiful to wear, really. I took it off before work last night and left it in the safe in my suitcase."

But she hadn't put it on. *Interesting.* She must really be mad at him, and he had the feeling that it was going to get worse when he revealed the real reason for bringing her out here.

"Whoa." She reined her horse to a sudden halt. "You've gotten me completely distracted. I have questions."

"You're wondering about that cane, right?"

"Well, yes. I've noticed you walking with a slight limp, but you definitely don't need a cane."

"A bit of theatrics to please Hawthorne," he said. "This is her show, and she has her own ideas of how it should play out."

"It's not just the cane," she said. "It's the story that goes with it."

Sitting tall in the saddle, he scanned the area and spotted surveillance equipment on a fence post. He needed to get outside camera range before he used his burner phone. The forested land would provide shelter from the watchers, but it was too far away to ride there and get back in time to meet Butler's deadline. The best way to send his secret text message was to use the horses and Sidney for cover. "Do you mind if we walk a bit?"

"Here's what I mind," she said. "You keep changing the subject. You're hiding something from me."

She was too smart and knew him too well. No way could he hope to deceive her, but he couldn't explain the intrigues that spun around him in a web of lies. Half of what he knew was guesswork. The other half was based on intuition. He didn't want to drag her deeper. She'd already been injured. Every time he thought of that scar on her arm, he cringed. It could have been worse. It never should have happened.

He directed his horse to a rutted dirt road, nothing more than a couple of tire tracks through the high grasses. He dismounted. The grasses were as high as his thigh.

When he went to help her down from her horse, she waved him off, kicked the stirrup out of the way and slid to the ground. Her cheeks flushed pink from the exertion of riding…and probably because she was getting angry. "Nick, you've got to tell me what's going on."

He stood with his back to the surveillance camera and spoke softly. "I need to send a text, and I couldn't do it from the house."

"Why not? Nobody can overhear a text message."

"Some other time I'll give you a lesson in spy technology and cell phones. For now, I need to get this message out. I can't tell you who I'm calling or why."

She looked down at the toe to her sneaker. When she lifted her chin, her blue eyes stabbed him like lasers. "Just do it."

He started to maneuver to hide his actions, and she grabbed the collar of his shirt and pulled him toward her. They stood together between the horses, hidden from observation. "Like this," she said, "it'll look like we're kissing and you won't be seen by the camera on the fence post."

"You noticed the surveillance."

"I'm not blind, Nick. Send your message."

He took a burner phone from his pocket, plugged in a battery and hit three call numbers. He typed in a name, a date and a time, sent it and went off grid again. "This isn't the way I wanted it to be when I saw you again."

"My fault. I showed up too early."

"Don't blame yourself." As soon as he arrived in Austin, he had considered the probability that she would become accidentally involved. "I brought you to me. I wanted you to know I was alive, safe. And I thought I could take care of you."

"What are you saying?"

"You're in the oil business. And you're one of the few people in this city who is familiar with Tiquanna. I was afraid that you'd get wind of the meetings with Hurtado."

"When they brought me to the CIA office," she said, "you told Phillips to point me in your direction."

He nodded. "I didn't want you to show up at a bad time."

"A bad time?" She gave a quick, ironic laugh. "Something worse than having our house shot to pieces?"

"You tell me," he said. "You're the one who learned to shoot so you could launch a one-woman attack in Tiquanna to find me."

"How did they know, Nick? How did the rebels know about our house? Why set up the ambush?"

"If the rebels were behind that action…"

"Rico Suarez," she said. "Not a rebel, he was one of Hurtado's men."

It seemed unlikely that Rico was playing both sides against each other. His focus was profit, and the rebels had precious little in the way of monetary resources. If Rico hadn't been killed, what would he have said? Whom would he have implicated?

The death of Rico Suarez had been convenient. And it hadn't escaped Nick's attention that the kill shot could have come from Butler, Phillips or Hawthorne. They were all at the house. And so was Agent Gregory, the accountant. Sidney had seen him there.

Part of Nick wanted to confide in her. She was smart and perceptive. She could help him make sense of these intrigues. Spending time with her made him smarter, too. It was one of the things he liked best about their relationship. When he was with Sidney, he was better in so many ways. His IQ jumped ten points. He saw the world more clearly.

"I won't put you in danger." He was speaking as much to himself as to her. "There's nothing more I can say."

Her hands dropped to her sides, and she turned away

from him. "You never kept secrets before. Or maybe you did, and I just didn't know. I really don't know what you do when you take off on your assignments."

He wanted to tell her. But where would he start? He couldn't reveal one detail without telling another and another. He'd been trained by the best in the world, the navy SEALs, and they would advise him to maintain his silence.

He checked his wristwatch. "We need to get back if we're going to make Butler's deadline."

She spun around to face him. "I'm suspicious of Special Agent Gregory. I'd like to take a look at his information on the oil resources and infrastructure in Tiquanna."

"Sidney, you've got to stop. You're not an investigator."

"Well, maybe I should be. I could probably do as well as Hawthorne."

"Mount up. We need to get back."

She placed her right hand on his shoulder. "Nick, I saw part of the text message you typed."

"What?"

"I'm not blind," she said for the second time.

"I shielded the screen."

"And I read the letters as you typed them. I didn't get the numbers, but you typed the word *Elena*."

Too damned smart for her own good.

Chapter Eight

Sidney watched as he mounted the bay. Nick's jaw clenched so tightly that he could have cracked walnuts. His brow furrowed. It didn't take a genius to see that he was angry.

And so was she. The dictator's wife was remarkably beautiful. More than the long, thick, black cascading hair and the glowing, unblemished skin, she radiated charisma. When Elena Hurtado walked into a room, all eyes went to her. And Nick had spent six months in her company.

He hadn't actually been with her the whole time, but he'd been close. And the text message he'd sent to covert ops showed there was still a connection between them.

In normal circumstances, Sidney didn't consider herself to be a jealous person. And she didn't want to believe that there was anything romantic going on between her fiancé and Elena, but Nick was only human. If he'd fallen in love with another woman, it would explain why his eyes didn't quite meet hers when they looked at each other. He was different. His kiss was different.

Infidelity was an ugly word. Nothing like this had ever happened to her before. Plenty of her girlfriends had confided in her about their cheating men, and she'd always told them to be sure of their facts. The same applied to her. Sidney had opened this Pandora's box, and she had to face whatever evil spilled out.

She mounted the pinto and rode up beside him. Their horses proceeded at a steady walk. "Tell me about Elena."

"I'm to meet her at the hotel in Austin. Then I take her to a specified location and turn her over to handlers. The text I just sent was to verify the time and date."

"Why couldn't she go to the embassy in Tiquanna?"

"Hurtado suspects something. He has her on a short leash, constantly surrounded by guards. If he finds out that she's going to betray him, he'll kill her."

She took a moment to digest this information. With Nick being held hostage, she'd kept up with news from Tiquanna. The Hurtado regime was more infamous for being greedy than brutal, but the country's prisons were full. "Where do you come in?"

"Hurtado's men know me. If I escort Elena away from the meetings, they won't stop us."

"Because you and Elena are…friends?"

He reined his horse to a stop. "There isn't time for a full explanation, but know this. Elena helped me escape. I owe her."

Every layer of this story got worse. Not only was Elena gorgeous, but she was brave and had saved Nick. How could he help falling in love with her? "Why does she want to be in the US?"

"She wants to end her marriage."

Sidney's breath caught in her throat. "Is she in love with someone else?"

"Yes," he said quickly, too quickly.

In a small voice, she asked, "Who?"

"The worst possible match you could think of."

No, no, no, not him, not Nick. "Say the name."

"Miguel Avilar, the leader of the rebels."

She exhaled in a whoosh. An international conspiracy that might topple a government and cost millions in oil investments felt insignificant compared with having Nick fall in love with the magnificent Elena.

Gazing up at him, she couldn't help admiring his broad shoulders and lean torso. He was such a handsome, masculine man. The collar of his shirt was open a few buttons, and she could see a curl of chest hair. "Is there anything else you need to tell me about Elena?"

"She's smarter than you'd think. She's tough, bordering on ruthless. And she's ambitious. I wouldn't be surprised if she tossed the men aside and took over the running of Tiquanna herself."

"And she's beautiful," Sidney said.

"Remember how Eva Perón became the most powerful person in Argentina? Elena Hurtado thinks of herself in that pattern."

Again, he was talking politics. The answers she wanted were personal. "How do you feel about her?"

"She's high maintenance, a little scary."

Sidney had never been subtle. She couldn't keep dancing around the issue. "Are you in love with her?"

"Hell, no."

He stared directly into her face. His light brown eyes shone with the warm, strong light she remembered. He was telling the truth.

Ignoring the pain from her injured left arm, she reached toward him. He caught her hand and pressed his lips into her palm. "There's room in my heart for only one woman. That's you."

Her Nick—the man she wanted to spend the rest of her life with—was back. "I've missed you so much."

"Being away from you was the hardest thing I've ever done. For a while, I was sick and I welcomed the fever because it helped me forget that we were apart..." His voice faded. "You shouldn't be here. It's not safe."

"There's only one place I want to be, and that's with you."

He gave her hand a final squeeze, and then sat up straight on his horse. His smile was so sweet and so tender that her heart fluttered. "I have a couple of rules."

"Okay."

"Try to stay out of the line of fire. Don't play Nancy Drew and start investigating. And here's the big one—trust no one."

She nodded. "I can do that."

"The safe house is one big spider's nest of surveillance. Assume that anything you say will be overheard. Anything you do will be watched."

"Even in the bathroom?"

"Spies have no shame."

He tapped his heels against the flank of his bay and took off at a gallop. She did the same.

BACK AT THE HOUSE, she and Nick were alone in the upstairs bathroom. Sidney perched on the edge of the claw-footed bathtub as he carefully removed the dressing on her battle wound. The slash across her upper arm still hurt, but not enough to take mind-numbing painkillers. She wanted to stay as alert as she could.

"How's my scar?" she asked. "Do I look like a biker chick?"

"Oh, yeah. A regular kick-ass." His fingers glided down her arm, and his thumb lightly caressed the sensitive skin inside her wrist. "You're unbelievable. An MIT-trained engineer who works part-time at a saloon and is healing from a gunshot wound."

"I try to keep it fresh."

Recalling what he'd told her about surveillance, she glanced around the bathroom. Was anyone watching? Even if they were, it wouldn't hurt for her and Nick to kiss. They were engaged, after all.

"There's no infection," he said, "but I'd still like to have a real doctor check out your wound when we get into town."

"And when will that be?"

"The meetings are scheduled for Tuesday. We'll probably move to the hotel in Austin on Monday night."

Today was Saturday. "So a couple of days. Since I'm going to miss work on Monday, I should call my office."

"Let Hawthorne take care of the phone calls," he said. "That way she won't worry that you've said the wrong thing to the wrong person."

"You mean like tipping off my bosses about the oil development in Tiquanna? I can assure Hawthorne that my company isn't interested. We checked it out three years ago."

"The situation might have changed."

She wondered if those changes would make a difference to Texas Triton. As far as she knew, the company hadn't been invited to the meetings with Hurtado, which seemed strange since it'd shown an interest in Tiquanna earlier. These politics might be of interest to her and the people she worked with.

She couldn't ask Nick if there were other financial incentives being offered or other perks. Those topics would surely be off-limits if their conversation was being bugged.

With a gentle touch, he applied an antiseptic to the stitches and put on a smaller bandage. "All done."

She stood and faced him. Cameras be damned, she

needed a kiss, needed it now. Her right hand glided up the front of his shirt and slipped behind his neck.

For a long moment, she simply stared into the facets of his deep-set brown eyes flecked with pure gold. His lashes were thick and as black as his hair, once again proving that Mother Nature was unfair. Men always got the great eyelashes. The depth of his gaze recalled their past. These were the eyes she'd known before. This was the man she'd fallen in love with.

When she joined her lips with his, an electric buzz went through her. It was a wake-up call to her senses. The inside of his mouth was hot and, for some unexplainable reason, tasted sweet as honey. The surface of her skin prickled with awareness. Her pulse jumped. She could almost feel the blood surging through her veins.

His arm wrapped around her waist and yanked her closer. He took charge of their kiss. His tongue plunged deep. He held her so tightly that she could barely draw breath. Who needed oxygen when she could breathe him?

Their earlier kiss was nothing compared with this. She'd spent six months waiting for Nick, and he was worth every second. How could she have doubted him? Gasping, she broke the kiss and looked up at him. "Nick, I trust you. I'm so—"

"Hush."

He laid a finger across her mouth to silence her. Others could be listening. She had to be careful. "There's so much I want to say."

"Show me," he murmured.

She leaned into his embrace, needing to be closer, to mold her body to his. Her legs twined with his, and she felt his erection pushing against the fabric of his jeans. When her hand slipped between them and she rubbed his hard sex, he stiffened.

His response sent a thrill straight to her core, and she trembled. It had been way too long since she'd been with him. Memories of their lovemaking exploded behind her eyelids like fireworks.

And he pulled back. "We have to stop."

"No," she moaned. "No stopping."

"Somebody's at the door."

When she heard Hawthorne calling his name, Sidney imagined the skinny agent watching them on surveillance and choosing the worst moment to interrupt.

"Nick," Hawthorne repeated. "We're having a meeting downstairs."

"Be there in a minute," he responded.

"You need to hurry. It's important."

Sidney collapsed against his chest and murmured, "Can I kill her?"

"Probably not a good idea."

"I know how to handle a gun, and I'm pretty accurate."

His arms still enclosed her. He brushed his lips across her forehead. "But then you'd get arrested and I'd have to break you out of jail and we'd have to go on the run together."

"Like Bonnie and Clyde." As she accurately recalled, they'd died in a hail of 163 bullets. "Or you could just go to Hawthorne's very important meeting."

He ended the embrace. "Come with me."

"If you don't mind, I'd rather not listen to Hawthorne drone on."

A look of concern crossed his face. "What are you planning to do?"

"I promise not to get into any trouble. I'll stay in my room. Or maybe go down to the kitchen and see what's for lunch."

She understood the rules he'd laid down. And she had absolutely no intention of breaking them.

NICK DIDN'T TRUST her promise to avoid trouble. Not that Sidney would purposely set out to aggravate him. But she was inquisitive by nature, and he had opened the door to questions she'd want answered. When they parted at the top of the staircase in the safe house, he saw a preoccupied look in her bright blue eyes. She was already thinking, already figuring things out.

He wouldn't want her to be different. Her curiosity was one of the things he loved about her. As she explained, her need to know came from being raised by her scientist parents. As a kid, she'd ask why the sky was blue, and her mom or dad would hand her a reference book and make her question into a teachable moment. Someday, when they had kids, he hoped to follow the same pattern.

In the office, he joined the others, taking a seat on the sofa and making a big production of checking his wristwatch. "I hope this isn't going to run long. It's time for lunch."

Phillips, Gregory and Lieutenant Butler echoed his sentiment. Everybody was hungry, but nobody was going anywhere until Hawthorne had her say.

"Gentlemen," she started, "we have a problem. There have been a number of defections among Hurtado's loyal followers. Rico Suarez was the tip of the iceberg."

"And now poor Rico is on ice," Phillips joked.

"Not funny, Special Agent Phillips."

"Yes, ma'am."

"We can't allow a threat to the president of another country while he is in the US."

As she ran through various modifications in their basic plan, Nick listened with half an ear. His only concern was to find Elena and deliver her to his handlers in the covert operations branch of Marine Intelligence.

Facilitating Elena's defection wouldn't be easy. For weeks, he'd been passing information about her finances and possessions to the people in charge. Every divorce was difficult. But divorcing a dictator came with its own set of complex problems, the greatest of which would be avoiding a bloodbath when Hurtado realized he'd been betrayed.

He tuned in to Hawthorne's monologue. "What did you say?"

"Pay attention, Nick. Just because your girlfriend is here doesn't mean you aren't playing a part."

"My fiancée," he corrected.

"The best way around this threat," she said, "is to shake up the prior plan of organization. I've spoken to the regional director, and he agrees."

His patience was running thin. When Hawthorne was unsure of herself, she tended to overspeak, using ten sentences where a couple of words would do.

"You're talking about a change in plans," he said. "Fine. What do we do different?"

"I want Hurtado under our protection. Therefore, I'm changing the timetable. He and his entourage will arrive on Sunday instead of Monday."

"Tomorrow? They'll be here tomorrow?"

"And they'll come here to the safe house, where we can keep an eye on them."

His disabled cell phone was burning a hole in his pocket. He needed to send a text message about the change in schedule, immediately if not sooner.

Chapter Nine

Upstairs in her bedroom, Sidney stood at the window, watching a tall man in a cowboy hat and grungy down vest saunter across the dry, dusty grass toward a live oak with rust-colored autumn leaves. She didn't recognize the man. Everybody, agents and cowboys alike, was wearing jeans and casual clothes. A couple of trucks and an open-top Jeep were parked by the white corral fence beside the barn. The shiny CIA vehicles were not in plain sight, probably hidden inside a closed garage so they wouldn't attract attention.

From her vantage point, she couldn't see the two-lane asphalt road or the long driveway leading to the front door. To the casual observer, this place would look like a nicely tended ranch, nothing special, certainly not a safe house. Things weren't always the way they seemed. Layers of deception clouded her vision. Nick had warned her to trust no one.

She ran her thumb across her lower lip, still tasting his lips against hers. It felt so right to be in his arms. A residual shiver of excitement slid down her spine. Her pulse rate still hadn't returned to normal. All she could think about was him, being closer to him, making love for the first time in six months. Right now, they should have been twined together on her bed like any other normal engaged couple.

To be certain, there were dozens of other things to worry about, but nothing else compared in importance. Her gaze flitted around the room, trying to spot the surveillance he'd told her to expect. Even now, at this very moment, some CIA-trained computer geek might be watching her. She hated the idea. And she intended to do something about it.

Though she'd promised Nick that she wouldn't play detective, she didn't think he'd mind if she figured out a way for them to grab some privacy. Her plans would have absolutely nothing to do with international intrigues or Elena or the oil reserves in Tiquanna. She just wanted to be with her man. He wouldn't object. And if he did, she'd change his mind. They weren't one of those couples who fought and bickered all the time. They seldom disagreed about anything.

The closest they'd come to a real argument was, ironically, March 14. When he gave her the pi diamond, she was happy, of course, to be engaged. But the ring dismayed her. That big beautiful diamond wasn't practical and was too expensive, and she'd rather have something less spectacular that she could wear all the time.

When she'd voiced those concerns, he was hurt. The light in his golden eyes dimmed, and his voice dropped to a deep, serious tone. He'd told her that he'd never expected to settle down. Marriage didn't fit with his work in the military. Too often, he had to be gone for extended periods of time. And there was the constant threat of danger.

She crossed the bedroom to the closet, pulled out her suitcase and opened the keypad lock. The blue velvet box felt warm in her hand. The 3.14-carat diamond sparkled with an ethereal light.

When Nick had talked about absence and danger, she hadn't really understood what he meant. Basking in the glow of being newly engaged, she'd been unable to imagine those negatives. That had been before Tiquanna. These past months had tested their relationship. She'd been furious and sad and terrified. Yes, she'd thought she might have made a mistake by getting engaged to him. But not once, not even for a moment, had she quit loving him.

On Pi Day, he'd said that being with her made him hope for the impossible. He wanted her to have a diamond so big it could be seen from outer space. That was how much he valued her, how much he valued their relationship. How could she argue with that kind of wild, romantic logic?

Newly resolved to make this work, she placed the ring on her finger. Her next move was to find a way they could be alone in the safe house.

The logical first step was to find out where the camera feeds were being observed. She imagined a dark room with floor-to-ceiling screens as she'd seen at the movies. And there would be a massive control panel with blinking lights, and the whole operation would be touch screen. It would take some expertise to set up this operation or a more modest version of it, which meant there had to be an expert.

At the meeting earlier this morning, an agent had been stationed behind the desk with a laptop and a couple of electronic screens. His name, she recalled, was Curtis. He had carrot-red hair and the kind of bloodshot eyes that came from playing video games until late into the night. He might very well be the tech guy who kept the surveillance equipment humming.

Leaving the bedroom, she went down the hall to the

banister overlooking the front room and dining area. At the top of the staircase, she got her bearings. The two-story room with the fireplace seemed to be the hub of the safe house, with other rooms and corridors radiating from it. The dining area led to the huge, professional kitchen, which opened onto a covered outdoor patio and barbecue. The office where they'd met this morning was down a long corridor to the left of the front entrance. A short hallway stretched to the right and opened into a television room.

Either she could ask for directions or she could wander until she stumbled into the surveillance headquarters. The first alternative seemed the least suspicious. She followed her nose into the kitchen, where a vat of spicy, fragrant chili was simmering on the stove top. After politely offering to help and being turned down by the housekeeper, Sidney asked, "Do you know where I can find Curtis? I had a question about my cell phone."

"You're probably wondering where it is," Delia said as she pulled a tray of golden-brown corn bread from the oven. "Nobody gets to keep their phone while they're in the house. Not even me."

"Why is that?"

"Something about the GPS signals. This is supposed to be a safe house, you know."

"Are you an agent?"

"Me? No way." She set down the corn bread and straightened to her full height, which had to be nearly six feet. Delia was a robust woman with short, sandy brown hair and a ruddy complexion. "Somebody told me you're not an agent, either."

"Nope, I'm an engineer. I work for an oil company." She'd never make a good agent. Lying made her skin crawl. Even this tiny fib to Delia was uncomfortable. "I'm looking for my phone so I can call my office."

"Good luck with getting Curtis to share. He's protective of his gadgets. The only thing he lets us use is the television, and that's because if we didn't get our weekly dose of football, there'd be a mutiny."

Sidney noticed her maroon jersey. "You're for Texas A&M."

"Gig 'em, Aggies. The game starts at one. That's why I've got lunch ready to go. Who's your team?"

"I went to MIT, but I've lived in Austin for the past five years." She knew better than to mention the University of Texas Longhorns to a robust woman in a maroon jersey. "I'm an Aggie fan."

"Good answer." Delia leaned close and glanced to the left and the right. "You didn't hear this from me, but you can usually find Curtis and all his equipment in a room at the end of the back hallway behind the TV room."

"Thanks, Delia. The chili smells great."

"Be sure to sit down for lunch early. I've got a full house, and these guys can eat."

Sidney rushed past the dining table and down the short hall to the TV room, where half a dozen men in jeans were already watching a college game. She recognized the black-and-gold uniforms. "University of Colorado Buffs."

"That's right," one of the men drawled. "And the Oregon Ducks are kicking the Buffaloes' butts."

She couldn't have asked for a better distraction. For the duration of the football games, none of these agents or cowboys would pay the least bit of attention to her. If Special Agent Curtis happened to be a fan, the surveillance would be lax this afternoon.

The last door at the end of the hallway was closed, and she tapped on it before opening. "Special Agent Curtis?"

He sat behind a long desk console before a double row of six screens mounted on the wall. It wasn't the high-tech marvel she'd imagined, but it was fairly impressive all the same.

She'd caught him playing a video game. He turned the screen to blank and bolted to his feet. "You shouldn't be here."

"Nice setup." She closed the door behind her and moved toward the screens. Some of the images changed every thirty seconds. Others remained the same. "Are these feeds from rotating cameras?"

"Seriously," he said, "this area is restricted access."

"No need to worry about me. I'm just a civilian."

"You have to leave."

For a moment, she considered playing the part of a dumb blonde, the kind of babe he'd find in one of his online games. Then she decided that she wasn't a good enough actress to pull it off. It was better to find common ground and encourage him to open up to her.

"The only reason I'm at the safe house is to be with my fiancé." She pointed to the engagement ring as proof. "I'm not a threat, but I am an engineer and I've done a lot of geological mapping and triangulation. I'm interested in how you constructed your surveillance patterns."

"You didn't come looking for a lesson in remote cameras." Though Curtis was a grown man, there was enough of the insecure teenaged nerd in him to be confused by attention from a woman. He eyed her suspiciously. "What do you really want?"

"To use my cell phone to call my office," she said. "I've got a project due on Monday, and I should talk to my assistant."

"Hawthorne hasn't authorized the use of your phone." He rubbed at the corners of his eyes. "If she gives the okay, no problem. Otherwise, forget it."

She had edged close enough to the desk console to be impressed with his neatness and attention to detail. The screens were numbered. The masses of wires and cables were neatly organized. She pointed to a screen built into the console that showed the CIA logo of an eagle's head above a compass rose. "Is that where you access information from official databases?"

"Yes, and it requires a password to open."

She truly was fascinated by the equipment. "If you sent a photo to this computer, would you get an ID and other information?"

"Correct."

"Can you do me? Get a picture of my face and run it?"

"It's not a toy." He squinted and blinked.

"You look like a man with eye strain," she said. "I get the same thing when I spend the whole day at the computer. Why don't you sit down and let me give you a temple massage?"

"A what?"

She directed him into the swivel chair and took a position behind him. "Sit back and relax. First, I'm going to work out some of these knots on your neck. Then I'll massage your temples and forehead."

The touch of her fingertips on the nape of his neck relaxed him immediately. After years of working with people who hunched over precision equipment and computers with fierce concentration, she had learned how to alleviate the pressure on those knotted muscles and tendons.

"You should get a goldfish for your desk," she said in a soothing voice.

"Why?"

"For one thing, a fish is more fun than plants. For another, watching the random swimming movement is good therapy to relax eye strain. Once an hour, take a one-minute pause and check out the fish."

A lazy smile spread across his face. "Maybe I'll do that. What are other stress-relief techniques?"

"Sex." As soon as the word jumped out of her mouth, she bit her tongue. "Sorry, I didn't mean to be a jerk."

"It's okay. I happen to agree with you."

"Good." She continued her massage across his scalp. "You could also do yoga."

"Don't have the patience for it."

She completely understood. Though she tried to meditate, she found it nearly impossible to empty her mind of all thoughts. She looked up at the rows of screens ranged across the wall: six on top and six on the bottom. "I'm guessing you have your surveillance set up in six quadrants outdoors and six indoors. How many cameras are in each quadrant?"

"It depends on obstacles and sight lines," he said. "I took care not to be redundant so I don't have more than one view of any particular area. The outdoor cameras are infrared so I can see in the dark."

"But not the indoor ones?"

"The ambient light is sufficient. Plus there are audio feeds. If an area looks suspicious, I can turn up the bug and hear what's going on."

"Nick told me that you had cameras in the bathrooms."

He turned in the chair to look at her. "I swear that I'm not spying on people doing their business. As soon as someone goes into the bathroom, I blank the screen."

"I appreciate that."

"I'm not a Peeping Tom."

But he didn't mind telling her about a breech in his

surveillance security. She should have felt as if she was taking advantage of Curtis. She was using him. But her end goal was positive. Finding a way to be alone with Nick was worth a twinge of guilt.

Chapter Ten

Nick stabbed his spoon into a meaty bowl of chili and glared across the dining table at Special Agent Hawthorne. No wonder the woman was so scrawny; she'd loaded her plate with a wimpy green salad and taken only a spoonful of the great-smelling Texas chili. He hoped she'd choke on a crouton.

Her change in plans for the Hurtado meeting created massive complications for him. He was supposed to meet Elena *at the hotel*. He should have been able to stroll with her to a location where she'd easily be transferred into protective custody.

Not anymore.

The dictator and his wife and their entourage of three would arrive at the safe house ranch tomorrow afternoon and would stay until Monday afternoon. During that time, the only way Nick could separate Elena from her husband and his men would be to make a run for it—a dangerous alternative. And he'd need help from somebody inside, somebody who was already here at the ranch.

He shoveled the spoonful of chili into his mouth. The spicy heat came from the perfect combination of cayenne and chili peppers. His taste buds lit up. He groaned with pleasure and reached for a glass of sweetened iced tea to wash it down. "Damn, that's good."

The others murmured in agreement. Could he trust any of these three to work with him? Butler, Phillips and Gregory all had agendas of their own. If they refused to play along with his plans or told Hawthorne what he was planning, Nick's assignment completely fell apart. He would have wasted a lot of time setting this in motion. Worse, he'd be putting Elena in danger.

"Y'all got to admit," Phillips said, "ain't nothing as good as real Texas chili."

"Amen to that," said the lieutenant.

Butler was the most logical person for Nick to approach. They were both marines, brothers. They shared much of the same training, knew many of the same people. But Butler was a spit-and-polish officer who looked like a recruiting poster with his close-cropped hair and his muscular build. He wasn't somebody who bent the rules, much less broke them. More than once, he'd made comments about how Nick just couldn't stay out of hot water.

And Nick hadn't forgotten how quickly Butler had responded to the attack at the house. He had explained his presence by saying he'd followed their car because he wanted to talk to Nick in private about having Sidney stay with him. Butler had been in the right place to shoot Rico Suarez. A coincidence?

The easygoing Texan, Special Agent Phillips, was somebody Nick intuitively connected with. He had trusted Phillips to give a message to Sidney so she'd come looking for him at the CIA office. But Phillips was CIA. If he helped Nick, he'd be hurting his own career. That was too much to ask. Phillips might be okay with looking the other way if he caught Nick breaking the rules. But he couldn't participate in an unauthorized action with Elena.

Nick didn't waste much time considering Special Agent Jim Gregory. He was more of a numbers man, hiding behind his glasses and his stacks of information. Besides, Sidney was suspicious of Gregory.

The sound of her laughter preceded her into the room. She was walking beside Curtis the computer guy, who usually faded into the woodwork in spite of his flaming red hair. With Sidney at his side, Curtis stood a little taller, grinned a little broader and had a swagger in his step.

He stopped beside Nick's chair and patted him on the back. "A pi diamond," he said. "That's very cool, man."

Sidney flashed her engagement ring for them all to see.

"Thanks," Nick said to Curtis without taking his eyes off his lovely fiancée. She'd make a good accomplice on the inside. She was smart, quick-thinking and— according to her—knew how to handle a weapon. But he didn't dare put her at risk.

AFTER LUNCH, ALMOST everybody gathered in the TV room to watch the Aggies play football. Sidney snuggled next to Nick on a sofa against the back wall. Not the best vantage point, but she was far more interested in being close to him than in watching the game. She kicked off her sneakers, tucked her legs under her and rested her head against his shoulder.

The time she'd spent with Curtis hadn't been wasted. Not only did she find she had a lot in common with the computer guy, but she also had an idea of how to circumvent his surveillance. Figuring out the way through the cameras would take some serious math skills, but she was confident.

When she laced her fingers with Nick's, she felt the tension in his grasp. She leaned close to his ear and whispered, "What's wrong?"

"I need to send another text."

There was a quick solution to his problem, but she hesitated to tell him. Curtis had trusted her, and she didn't want to betray him. On the other hand, the whole idea of being under the constant scrutiny of hidden cameras didn't seem right or fair.

Curtis had explained that the surveillance was there for their protection so they'd have advance warning of anyone trying to sneak up on the safe house. But it felt more as if they were the prisoners—rats in their cages, being watched so they didn't pull any kind of stunt or try to escape. Nope, she didn't like those cameras. Plus, she believed in Nick's cause. He was trying to save Elena, to rescue her from a dangerous marriage.

The Aggies made a touchdown, and the room erupted in cheers. They were all on their feet.

Using that noise as a cover, she whispered to Nick, "Go into the bathroom. Within a few minutes, Curtis will turn off the camera. Run the water for the shower to cover the sound."

Skeptical, he raised an eyebrow. "Why would he kill the camera feed?"

"He's not a Peeping Tom."

He slung an arm around her shoulder and gave her a squeeze before they sat again. After ten minutes, he left the TV room.

She perched on the arm of the sofa so she'd have a better view of the huge screen mounted on the wall. Football wasn't her favorite sport. She preferred the symmetry and logic of baseball, but she kept her unwavering gaze pinned to the television so she wouldn't be sneaking peeks to see where Nick was. Based on her conversation with Curtis, her advice ought to work, but nothing was foolproof.

To her surprise, Special Agent Hawthorne sat on the sofa and patted the space beside her. "Sit with me, Sidney."

This felt like a trap. Sidney eased her butt onto the sofa and gave the agent a nervous smile. "How's it going?"

"As well as can be expected." She sipped from a coffee mug. Though the agents were technically on duty, most of them were drinking beer. Not Hawthorne. She was by the book.

"As you know," she said, "the defection and death of Rico Suarez caused some problems, but I've come up with a solution. Has Nick told you?"

Her gaze was cold, piercing and a little bit predatory. Every conversation with this woman felt as hostile as an interrogation. *No problem.* Sidney had nothing to hide. "Nick hasn't told me anything."

"This might interest you because you've been to Tiquanna and have met the president and his wife."

"He wasn't a president when I met him," Sidney said. "Just another dictator."

"Times have changed. He's now our ally, and it's our responsibility to protect our allies. Hurtado and his wife will be arriving tomorrow with their bodyguards, and they're coming here to the safe house."

"That's big." She understood why Nick had to send another text message. His plans had been totally disrupted.

"But very efficient. We will have complete control of his security."

Her narrow lips twisted in a self-satisfied smirk. If her

hands hadn't been occupied holding the coffee mug, she would have been patting herself on the back.

"You like being in control," Sidney said.

"As a woman in an occupation that's dominated by men, I find it necessary to assert myself. Don't you?"

"I don't think about it much."

On the big screen, the Aggies fumbled. The guys let out a chorus of groans.

Hawthorne stared pointedly at her diamond. "I suppose your career isn't as important as your other concerns. When's the wedding?"

Sidney didn't like the implication that getting married meant she'd be quitting her job, but she wasn't going to rise to the bait. She didn't have anything to prove to Special Agent Hawthorne. "Why would you think I'd be interested in your plans for the Hurtados? I've met them, but we're certainly not friends. Our meetings were strictly business."

"But you've visited Tiquanna," she said. "It's such a beautiful country with the sultry air and the verdant foliage. When I was there, I fell in love with it."

Really? Was ice-cold Special Agent Hawthorne waxing poetic about Tiquanna? "Did you visit the rain forests?"

"The forests, the beaches, the little shops. Charming."

She sounded almost human, and Sidney wondered if she'd misjudged her. It might just be possible that Special Agent Victoria Hawthorne wasn't a completely soulless harpy who had purposely kept her apart from Nick.

Sidney looked toward the door and saw Nick. He motioned for her to join him. To Hawthorne, she said, "Excuse me. Enjoy the game."

She picked her way through the Aggie fans on her way toward her tall, dark and handsome fiancé. He would never ask her to give up her job for him, and she wasn't sure if she would. Her work wasn't as important to her as her dreams. There was a lot of world she wanted to explore. She'd given some thought to building her own one hundred percent green house. There were classes she wanted to take, studies she wanted to pursue. Nick had always encouraged her. He never set limits. With him, anything was possible.

As she moved closer to him, her heart beat faster and her stomach tightened in a knot. In his faded jeans and his plaid shirt, he could have been an advertisement for any number of rugged and manly products. She'd buy whatever he was selling. His black hair was spiky and wet. He must have actually used the shower in the bathroom.

He enveloped her in a hug. "It worked."

She'd almost forgotten the real reason he'd left the room. "I guess that's good."

They walked together in silence into the large front room with the moss rock fireplace. She heard someone messing around in the kitchen. Otherwise, no one was in sight. There was so much she wanted to say to him, but the audio surveillance was operational and it made her uncomfortable to know that Curtis was listening and recording their words.

Nick guided her toward the staircase. "I thought we might take a little nap."

"In bed? Together?" That was either the most wonderful idea she'd ever heard or the most insane. With the way she was feeling, she didn't think she could lie beside him and not make love. "I don't know if I have that much willpower."

But she didn't hesitate to climb the stairs. Her arm suctioned around him like a barnacle on a rock. She didn't let go until they were in her bedroom.

He closed the door and scooped her off her feet. They fell together onto the bed, already entangled. His thigh separated her legs. One of her arms circled his shoulder while the other hand slipped around to his muscular back.

Their kiss was hungry and deep. His tongue plunged into her, and she savored the taste of him. So good, he was so good for her, with her. She wanted him inside her even though she knew they could only go so far, since they were being watched. Frenzied, she clawed at him. They pressed tightly against each other, separated only by their clothes, but she wanted him closer, wanted him to be an indivisible part of herself. Those desires didn't make sense, and she didn't care. No thought or logic intruded on her pure, physical need.

Rough and impatient, he tore her shirt free from the waistband of her jeans and ran his hand over her ribcage to her breast. His touch was familiar and exotic at the same time. Straddling his hips, she arched above him, baring her throat to a trail of fevered kisses that started at her jaw and ended at her breast. He pushed the silky fabric of her bra aside and teased her nipple into a tight peak, sending her to a higher level of excitement.

She was already trembling at the edge of an orgasm. It had been six months. There was a lot to make up for.

Waves of sensation crashed over her, and just when she thought she might drown from too much excitement, he flipped her onto her back. There was a sudden intense calm. She locked gazes with him. This was the moment when they should have been naked and making love. Their clothes should have melted away.

It wasn't going to happen. Not now, not while they were being recorded. "I guess I'm not cut out to be a porn star."

"Don't stop."

She knew there were people who got turned on when they thought they might get caught in the act. She wasn't one of them. "What about the cameras?"

He pulled up the blanket from the foot of the bed and covered them. Reaching inside, he unbuttoned the waist of her jeans. His hand slid down her belly.

Her frantic desire centered on his stroking touch. She bucked and gasped, unable to control the shuddering, trembling sensations that ratcheted higher and higher until she exploded. Spasms of tension rocked her body. She was flying and falling at the same time, totally out of control.

With a fierce moan, she collapsed against him, breathing as hard as if she'd run a marathon. Would she quit her job for him? Oh, yeah. She'd follow him into a burning building. She'd do anything for him…almost anything.

Chapter Eleven

For the rest of the afternoon, Sidney focused on a project that reminded her of when she was a little girl. Her scientist parents had a love/hate relationship with computers. They appreciated the way the internet opened a wider scope of communication and research, but they didn't want her to solve every problem with the jiggle of a mouse. She needed to have a solid understanding of the basics. The end result was that Sidney spent a lot of time working out equations and logic problems the old-fashioned way, by hand.

Since Hawthorne had confiscated all the phones and wouldn't allow the use of computers without supervision, she sprawled on her stomach across her bed with a yellow legal pad and a pencil. Her notes were designed to calculate the range, rotation and visual scope of Curtis's cameras. Once she'd found the gaps in his system, she could plot a pathway to walk through the surveillance undetected.

In his explanation of the schematics, Curtis had inadvertently shown her a couple of areas that didn't have cameras. The loft in the front section of the barn would be their destination tonight. If she and Nick could get there unseen by cameras, they would have privacy.

And she could hardly wait. Their intimate moments

together in the bedroom had been even better than she expected. But she hated that a camera had recorded them and couldn't help imagining Special Agent Hawthorne spying.

Being watched constantly was ridiculous. There should have been a way she and Nick could pull the curtain. Their private life was nobody's business but their own.

He joined her in the bedroom and stretched out beside her. The bed was too short for his long legs, so he turned on his side. He reached out and patted her bottom as he looked down at her legal pad.

"What's all this?" he asked.

"How much do you remember of your basic geometry and algebra?"

"There was something about the square of the hippopotamus."

"Hypotenuse," she corrected. "So…nothing?"

He shrugged. "I spent most of my time in math class counting the minutes until recess."

"These equations are kind of a game," she said, being mindful that someone was probably listening. "Something I learned as a kid."

On the legal pad, she wrote in tiny letters: *Making a map to show us how to get past the surveillance cameras.*

After he read the words, she scribbled over them with the tip of her pencil. When she was done, it might be wise to burn these pages. "What have you been doing?" she asked.

"Waiting for recess."

"As in school?"

"As in dead-boring meetings."

His hand slipped under her sweater and caressed the bare skin of her back. His touch was gentle and meant to be casual, but she still felt a little shiver of excitement down the length of her spine.

Being close to him was driving her absolutely crazy. They'd always been good in bed, but this kind of intimacy was different. She had nothing in her memory banks to compare with the heart-pounding lust she was feeling.

When she was separated from him and feared the worst, she'd kept busy and held her emotions in check. Now she was brimming with crazy desire. She looked down at the legal pad where she'd drawn a little heart. *Really?* Was this the way a twenty-eight-year-old engineer behaved?

As Nick spoke, she watched his lips, mesmerized.

"Super-Special Agent Victoria Hawthorne," he said, "is figuring out security to protect Hurtado and his party while they're here. Her primary game plan is to bring in more men. When we move to the hotel in Austin, we'll have an entire floor to ourselves."

He continued to lightly massage her back, apparently unaware of the thrilling effect on her. She forced herself to pay attention, noting the disgust in his voice. "Wait a minute. Why is Hawthorne talking about security? Isn't protection more up your alley than hers?"

"That's right," he growled. "If you want something kept safe, you send in the marines. If I was running this show, there wouldn't be cameras and bugs and fancy little devices. I wouldn't need a battalion of armed guards. All I'd need would be six trained men."

Six was the same number used by Curtis to divide the area into quadrants. "Why six?"

He explained exterior sight lines, directionality and triangulation. Much of the language he used echoed what Curtis had told her about covering the entire area. "You're a lot better at math than you think."

"But I'm not in charge, and Butler is content to sit back and listen to Hawthorne." He shrugged. "What do you think of Butler?"

She had plenty to say but wasn't sure she ought to speak up. On her legal pad she wrote: *Bugs?*

Nick took the pencil from her and scribbled: *Can I trust him?*

She framed her thoughts carefully before she spoke. "Lieutenant Butler is obviously disciplined. One look at his body tells you that he follows a daily routine with his exercising. He impresses me as being one hundred percent marine, which is a very good thing."

"Agreed."

"When he's given an order, he follows through. If he was under your command, he'd be totally trustworthy."

But someone else was giving Butler his orders. Next to Nick's question on the legal pad, she wrote: *No.*

He leaned close to her. When he whispered, his breath was hot on her neck. "Have you figured out how we can be alone tonight?"

"You bet I have."

If it required reformatting the pattern of stars in the night sky, she'd find a way.

He nipped her earlobe. "I can't wait."

FOLLOWING SIDNEY'S INSTRUCTIONS, Nick climbed out a downstairs bathroom window at twenty-three hundred hours that night. He had no worries about alarms because Sidney had already disabled the motion detector. His beautiful fiancée was a woman of many talents. Outsmarting any sort of electrical system was one of them.

He crouched below the window and waited for her. The November moon was on the wane. Last night, the night sky had been brighter. Tonight, hazy clouds obscured the moon and stars, and the shadows spread in a murky gloom across the yard between the house and the barn.

His position was hidden by a couple of prickly shrubs, and he was motionless, watching for the newly arrived security team that Hawthorne had enlisted to keep them safe. Part of the reason Nick wanted to follow Sidney's map was to check out the current precautions.

He spotted two armed men in dark windbreakers wearing baseball caps. By the odor he could tell one of them was smoking. If Hawthorne caught him, she'd have his butt on a platter. They meandered across the open front of the barn, walked the line of the corral fence and continued toward the multicar garage until they were almost out of sight. Then they returned on roughly the same route. He knew there was another guard posted on the wraparound front porch. And a sniper on the roof.

To his left, he heard the snap of a twig and the crackle of footsteps through dried leaves. Sidney stood at the corner of the house and motioned for him to join her. She'd tucked her straight blond hair up inside a baseball cap. With the brim pulled down, she looked like a tomboy, but her black turtleneck outlined curves that were one hundred percent female.

She'd already told him to follow her moves exactly. His job was timing, making sure they avoided being seen by the guards. He gave her the go-ahead.

At the ninety-degree corner of the house, she set out in a transverse angle, walking in a straight line to the live oak in the backyard. Her path was so direct and so bold; he couldn't believe she wasn't being picked up by a surveillance camera, even though she'd explained how the range of the different cameras left gaps. He followed her.

At the tree, she zigzagged to a fence post where she paused and waited for him. When he joined her, she whispered, "Here's the only part that will show up on tape. Stay low and keep to the shadows."

He had spent enough time in stakeouts watching flat screens to know how boring surveillance could be. The system Curtis used alternated views from several cameras on each screen, so the odds against having him spot them were good. Still, Nick felt the prickle of unseen eyes on the back of his neck as he moved to a point farther down the fence.

After checking to see that the bodyguards were down by the garage, he motioned her forward. They crossed the open yard to the east side of the barn. Beside a closed door, she leaned against the weathered wood and gave him a huge smile.

"We made it," she said quietly.

Nick wasn't so sure. The smell of cigarette smoke hung in the air, but the guard who'd been smoking was a hundred yards away. Even if Hawthorne's guards did their job and found them, Nick and Sidney weren't in any real danger. They could make an excuse about trying to get privacy and would get off with nothing more than a slap on the wrist.

But he sensed a change in the atmosphere. They were under observation. Hostile eyes tracked their movements.

He drew his Glock from the holster on his hip and opened his senses to the night. He scanned the flat side of the barn. Ten feet from them was a waist-high storage bin. A stack of metal fencing for a movable corral leaned against the wall. According to Sidney, this side of the barn was not within range of any camera. Had someone else discovered the anomaly?

Nick gestured for her to get down while he made sure they weren't walking into a situation. A tall man with a cowboy hat hiding his features stepped out of the shadows from the storage container. "Hello, Nick."

The deep voice, lightly accented, needed no other introduction. "Miguel Avilar."

The leader of the Tiquanna rebel movement stood before him with his hands raised in the air. Nick didn't lower his gun. He was ambivalent about Avilar, didn't know if he was friend or foe, even though Elena had vouched for him and his cause.

Nick believed he'd been taken hostage by Avilar's men. Though he couldn't recall details, he hadn't forgotten the pain. He'd been stripped, beaten and starved. He knew Americans were involved. He'd heard their accented Spanish. But he had thought Avilar was in charge. And he couldn't forgive the way the rebels had captured him. Two other marines had been seriously injured.

In a voice pitched as low as a whisper, Nick asked, "Did your boys shoot up my house in Austin?"

"You know better. I would never work with Rico Suarez."

Sidney peeked around his arm. "How did you get past the security cameras?"

Avilar swept the cowboy hat off his head, took a step closer and gazed into her eyes. "You must be Sidney Parker. I have heard much about you."

The rebel leader was a good-looking man and charismatic enough to have captured the heart of Elena Hurtado. But Sidney seemed unimpressed. "Yeah, I've heard about you, too. And I didn't think you were clever enough to get past the safe house surveillance."

"You were wrong."

"Did you hack into the computer system? Dummy up the camera feeds for this quadrant?"

"Let it go," he said.

"I don't like you, Avilar. Because of you, Nick was held hostage. I thought he was dead. Because of you, my heart nearly shattered." Her accusations were more dramatic because she spoke in a quiet, matter-of-fact tone. "Give me one good reason why I shouldn't scream for the guards and have you taken into custody."

Disbelief flickered behind his eyes. He hadn't expected to encounter an angry woman with a grudge. His right hand moved toward the back of his belt, reaching for a weapon.

Nick raised his gun. "Don't even think about it."

Avilar donned his hat and straightened the brim. "Here's your reason, Sidney. We're on the same side. We want the same thing. To keep Elena safe."

Nick wasn't sure how much Sidney cared about Elena, but he tentatively decided to accept Avilar as an ally. "Why are you here?"

"Elena will be brought to this safe house tomorrow. I will rescue her and take her away with me."

Not according to Nick's orders. "That's not the plan."

He heard the clumsy approach of the two guards who were patrolling this area. If he was found with Avilar, he'd never be able to complete his assignment. All this planning would have been for nothing.

He nodded toward the storage bin where Avilar had been hiding. As they ducked into the shadows, he knew it wasn't sufficient cover for all three of them. If the guards came closer to investigate, there would be no escape.

To Sidney, he whispered, "Take us to the loft."

Stealthy as a cat, she glided to the end of the east wall. At the corner, a corral fence with four wood slats attached to the barn. She climbed quickly and dropped into the hay on the opposite side. He followed. Avilar came after him.

They waited in silence, measuring each breath.

The guards rounded the opposite corner of the barn where they had been standing a moment ago. They exchanged quiet comments. Nick heard them coming closer.

The stalls were just inside. Moving past the horses was risky, but there didn't seem to be an alternative.

Sidney darted across the corral enclosure and slipped through the open door. As far as he knew, the only time she'd been in the barn was this morning, and she might have observed the layout on the camera surveillance. Still, she moved with the confidence of someone who had been in and out of the barn dozens of times before.

He knew that she was visualizing the interior of the barn in her remarkable memory. Without a single misstep, she led them to a wood ladder built into the wall and climbed.

When they were all three in the loft, they lay flat on the wood floor. Below them, the guards made their search. They rattled the door on one of the stalls, and the horse inside whinnied and stamped his feet.

"Now look what you've done," one of the guards said. "You got the animals all riled up."

"I'm telling you that I heard something. And I smelled cigarettes."

"That was me, you idiot. I smoke. Deal with it."

The guards left the barn, and Sidney sat up. She pulled off her baseball cap and shook her head. Her straight blond hair fell to her shoulders. She gave him a baleful glance. "So much for our privacy."

"Just for tonight," he said.

Avilar sat up to face them. His swagger had toned down a few notches. "I'm glad I ran into you tonight."

"Sheer luck," Nick said. Their meeting couldn't have been planned because he hadn't even been sure when they'd leave the house. "Now I'm going to give you advice that will save your life. There's no way you and your men can take Elena by force. Not without getting her killed in the process."

"I got through the surveillance cameras easily," he said. "Using our computer signals, we can jam all transmissions."

"Listen to me," Nick said. "You don't want this to turn into a shootout. Hurtado would rather see Elena dead than to have her go with you."

"I have no choice." Though Avilar was whispering, Nick heard real emotion in his voice. "If I don't get her away from him, he'll kill her tomorrow night. All along, this has been his plan. He had to get Elena away from our native country, where she is much beloved. If she was killed in Tiquanna, there would be riots in the streets."

Nick doubted the reaction would rise to the level of rioting, but he was aware of Elena's many supporters. "Go on."

"He will assassinate her here, and blame her death on the rebels. That was why you were attacked at your house, to establish the supposed presence of the Tiquanna rebels in your country."

His narrative made sense, except for one piece. "Who informed you that I would be returning home with Sidney? How did you know where I live?"

"I didn't know," Avilar said. "Hurtado's men arranged the attack. They had the information."

Their CIA team was in contact with Hurtado and his energy minister and the head of his security. Hawthorne probably communicated with Tiquanna once or twice a day. This was more than a leak. It was a sieve.

Chapter Twelve

Sidney strained to hear as Nick and Miguel Avilar spoke in hushed tones. The rebel leader confused her. She'd taken an immediate dislike to his arrogance, an attitude so typical of men in power. But he seemed sincere in his love of Elena and his concern for her safety. If his forces had the technical skills to hack into the CIA's surveillance equipment, she had seriously underestimated them. What else were they capable of?

Was Avilar an enemy or a friend?

"Not here," Nick said. "Don't try to take her from the safe house. Wait until we're at the hotel."

"You can't guarantee Elena's safety," Avilar said. "What's to stop Hurtado from shooting her and blaming her death on my rebels?"

"I won't let that happen."

"I trust your intention, my friend. But there are forces beyond your control."

Avilar's light accent reminded her of Tiquanna. She appreciated the tropical beauty of the country and understood how the oppressed population needed better leadership. But did the rebels have the right answers? Hurtado had been in charge for years. He'd made the transition from dictatorship to elections, even though he would undoubtedly be president for life. And he was bringing new money and business from developing the oil resources. At the very least, Hurtado represented stability for his people.

As Avilar prepared to leave them, he turned to her and said, "Remember me, Sidney."

"I couldn't forget you if I tried."

Avilar disappeared through the hatchway and down the wooden stairs into the barn.

As soon as he was gone, she inched across the slatted wood floor to be closer to Nick. Her movements kicked up a layer of dust sprinkled with dry hay stalks. She lay on her side next to him. Her plan for tonight had been to find a private place, but her need to make love was eclipsed by her hunger for information. If she didn't grab this chance to talk, she might never get answers.

"I need to know," she said. "Who are the good guys and who are the bad guys?"

"It's not that simple."

"The CIA is backing Hurtado. Hawthorne and her pals are doing everything they can to help him set up a business relationship with Underwood Oil."

He took her hand, brushed a light kiss across her knuckles. "I don't work for the CIA."

"Your orders come from somewhere else. Where? Who are you sending your text messages to?"

"It's complicated."

Though ready to scream with frustration, she kept her voice low. "I understand that there are other forces at work. I need to know who and why."

Even in the dim light, she saw his gaze turn secretive. He was holding something back from her. She wanted to trust him, needed to believe in him.

The deep, quiet tone of his voice soothed her. "My assignment is to keep Elena Hurtado safe."

How could that be bad? Saving the life of an abused wife ranked high on Sidney's list of noble actions. But the CIA wasn't on Nick's side. And he was friendly with Avilar, the leader of the rebels. She hated the dark thoughts that bubbled up from the back of her mind.

Sidney had never been much interested in politics. Her work dealt in numbers, facts and absolutes. She liked things to be black-and-white. "I have to ask this question, Nick."

"Go ahead. Clear the air."

She inhaled a deep breath. "Are you on the right side?"

"I'm not a traitor, Sidney."

"Of course not, I'm just—"

"I've spent my life in service to the US Marines. I'd die before I'd betray my country."

How could she doubt him, even for a moment? He was a good man, a good person. And yet… "Help me understand. I believe you're loyal. But what does that make Hawthorne and the CIA?"

"Misguided."

"Why can't you explain to them?"

"If I could, I would. But I'm not a philosopher or a statesman. I don't make speeches. I deal with actions, not words. And I have to do what I believe is right."

"Didn't you tell me that Avilar was responsible for your kidnapping?"

"I told you the palace was attacked, and it made sense that the rebels would be responsible."

"But you don't blame Avilar."

"I never saw him." He shook his head and looked away from her. "We already talked about this stuff, Sidney. Do we have to go over it again?"

"Someone grabbed you and took you away from me

for six months. I need to know who it was, full disclosure. I deserve an answer."

"What if I don't have one?"

"We'll figure it out together," she said. "Tell me what happened when you were taken hostage. Don't leave anything out."

"They hit me with a stun gun. I was hooded. Everything went black. When I woke up, I was on the ground. My ankles and knees were tied with heavy rope. My wrists were tied in front of me. I tore off the hood."

"Did you see your captors?"

"My vision was hazy. For a while, I thought I was going blind. Then my eyes accustomed to the night. I was in a hut with a thatched roof. Two men were watching me, both armed.

"I wanted to escape, to get up and run. But I could barely move. My muscles wouldn't respond. It took all the strength I had to sit up."

His voice faded to silence, and she waited for him to continue. Talking about his ordeal was hard for him. Hard for her, too. She hated to think of what he had suffered, but it was better to know, always better to talk about the pain than to keep it bottled up inside.

Earlier when he'd told her about his time in captivity, he made it sound like a bad camping trip. This was different. This time, she heard the pain and the rage in his voice.

"They'd taken my clothes and my boots," he said. "I was stripped down to my skivvies and my dog tags.

"The inside of my mouth was dry. My tongue was swollen. I couldn't summon up enough spit to lick my lips. I tried to ask for water, but the only sound I could make was a croak. One of the men took pity. He kicked a plastic water bottle toward me. I used my teeth to get the top off, and I drank. I've never tasted anything so damn good. That was the last bit of kindness they showed me for a long time."

Hot, angry tears gathered behind her eyelids, and she dashed them away. He'd been tortured. "How can you stand to look at Avilar?"

"I never knew if it was him. I didn't know if I'd been taken by the rebels or by someone else, someone working for Hurtado. They wanted information from me. They beat me up pretty good. The doctors tell me my shoulder was separated, twice. I was sore all over, filthy and hungry. Then they let up, and things got better."

"You were with the old man, Estaban," she said.

"I was in a camp, wearing the same rags they wore, eating the same food. There were other hostages with me, people from the town. They kept us together. That's when I met Avilar."

"Is he the leader of all the rebels?"

"There are several factions. His group is the largest, the best equipped and the most powerful. Miguel Avilar is college educated and comes from a wealthy family, all of whom have left Tiquanna. When he met me, he apologized for the way I'd been treated. And he said he wasn't responsible."

"And you believed him."

"Not at first," Nick said. "I thought this was just another tactic to get information from me."

"What changed your mind?"

"Elena was with him. She pretty much took charge and arranged for me to be returned to the presidential compound. As far as I know, she's never lied to me."

Sidney regretted every nasty thought she'd ever had about Elena. "She saved your life."

"Not because she's Saint Elena. The supposed rescue

of an American citizen made Hurtado look like a hero. And Elena gained leverage. As long as I was there as a witness, her husband had to treat her right."

"If Elena and Avilar are allies," she said, "Hurtado is their enemy."

"He's greedy and he's cruel. A dictator. But he's not going forward with this multimillion-dollar development by himself. Somebody else is pulling the strings."

"Oh, my God, Nick. You don't think the CIA was behind your kidnapping, do you? What would they have to gain?"

"I don't know."

"I hope you aren't suggesting it's an evil oil development company," she said. "Those are the people I work for. Texas Triton tries really hard to be ecologically and socially responsible."

"Can you say the same about your competitors?"

"Them? Oh, well, they're the scum of the earth." She grinned. "Not really."

"And that takes us right back to the beginning," he said. "It's complicated."

Though they hadn't resolved a thing, she felt better. At least he was talking to her. "Go ahead, Nick, say it."

"Say what?"

"I told you so."

His large hand grasped the small of her waist and yanked her toward him until her body aligned with his. His natural heat permeated her clothes and warmed her skin. Unable to resist, she snuggled against him. With her ear to his chest, she listened to the strong, steady thump of his heartbeat. Her pulse synchronized with his.

There were no cameras here. If there had been surveillance, the guards would have known Avilar was here. They would have been found out. Though she was satisfied that they weren't under observation, she hesitated. "This doesn't feel private."

He squeezed her closer. "Not real sexy."

"It's like that creepy feeling on the back of your neck when someone's watching."

He lightly kissed her lips, and then pulled her up so they were both sitting. "No more sneaking around. When we make love again, it'll be perfect."

She patted the wood floor. "At least, we should have a bed."

"Silk sheets and champagne," he said. "When this is over, we'll take a trip to a mountain cabin in Colorado. Just you and me, we'll be completely alone. At night, we'll build a fire. And we'll make love until dawn."

For a long moment, she stared at him through the darkness. There was no equation for how to deal with his absence or his return to her. Somehow, she had to trust that they'd find their way back to normalcy.

THE NEXT DAY, Special Agent Hawthorne was in a frenzy of organization. She reshuffled several of the rooms to make sure Hurtado and his wife had the master suite with the attached bathroom. The dictator would be accompanied by two bodyguards who would share a room on one side of his suite. Hawthorne posted CIA guards directly outside the room and had beefed up security in general, which Sidney found a little sad since Avilar had so easily slipped inside last night.

Not that she was an expert on how to keep a safe house safe. Sidney didn't have much to add to any of the bustling around, which suited her just fine. The only directive she received from Hawthorne was to address the dictator as "President Hurtado."

In the morning, she took one of the horses out for a

run. A light rain was falling, but her ride was refreshing. With the ongoing drought conditions in Texas, nobody complained about the moisture.

After lunch, she milled around, wishing she had access to a computer so she could hook into work and get something done. She offered to help out in the kitchen, but Delia had the roast beef and scalloped potatoes under control. Sidney tried to nap but wasn't tired. Finally, late in the afternoon, she grabbed a few minutes with Nick. They sat on the porch swing, looking for rainbows behind the barn.

"You've had lots of meetings," she said.

He slung an arm around her shoulder. "Your buddy Curtis is keeping busy. Hawthorne treats him like her personal assistant, making her phone calls and setting up reminders."

It was a shame to waste the tech skills of somebody like Curtis. He was smart and funny and insightful, but he lacked the ambition and aggression to shove his career into high gear. People like Hawthorne would always try to use him.

"What about you?" she asked. "How does Hawthorne treat you?"

"She's wary, doesn't know what to expect. She's afraid I might do something that will cause her trouble."

And she was correct in that assumption. When Nick got Elena away from Hurtado, the dictator was going to go ballistic. Or maybe not. Maybe he'd be glad to get rid of a troublesome woman. "How long before the big arrival?"

"Any minute now." He checked his wristwatch. "Hawthorne expects them to arrive around four o'clock, which gives them a chance to see their room and get changed before dinner. I guess we'll be having cocktails before we eat."

"Am I supposed to get dressed up?" She remembered the little black dress that had thoughtfully been packed in her suitcase.

He shrugged. "You look beautiful just the way you are."

She didn't expect him to understand. Being in the same room with the gorgeous Elena Hurtado was enough to make any normal woman feel insecure. Sidney decided it wouldn't hurt to spend a few extra minutes on her grooming.

He pulled her close and whispered in her ear, "Tell me a story. Fourth of July, last year."

"That's a totally indelible memory." When she thought of that day, she couldn't help smiling. "We were in Aspen. There were fireworks in the sky and in the hotel bedroom."

"Give me the details."

It was the first time they'd made love, and she remembered shedding their clothes, seeing him naked for the first time, tasting his honey mouth. The memory made her feel warm and gooey inside. "Not appropriate. I have to act like a proper person, and I'll get all excited if I give you a blow-by-blow description."

"Blow-by-blow," he said with a grin. "That's what I want."

"Not going to happen."

A black SUV pulled up in front of the porch, and Special Agent Gregory got out. As usual, he was carrying a satchel full of written information and looking self-important. Maybe she could talk to him later, assess his trustworthiness. If he really was an expert on oil exploration, they might have something in common to discuss. Or he might have something to hide.

She heard the thwhump-thwhump of the chopper blades before she saw the running lights. The black helicopter dipped through gray clouds and prepared to land in the open area between the house and the road.

She couldn't help but whisper under her breath, "Showtime."

Chapter Thirteen

With all of Special Agent Hawthorne's fussing about preparations, Sidney felt as if the helicopter should have arrived with more fanfare, maybe a brass band or a heavenly choir.

"Nice transportation," she said.

"Butler set it up. They were flown into Lackland Air Force Base."

"That doesn't look like a military chopper."

"I'm guessing it's a little something from the CIA."

Hawthorne appeared on the porch wearing one of her trademark black suits, but her blouse was teal silk and her dark brown hair hung in loose curls to her shoulders. Her cheeks flushed pink, and her lips were glossed to a high sheen. She looked like a robot trying to transform into a Kewpie doll.

She motioned to Curtis, who popped open an umbrella and followed her to the chopper.

Hurtado, make that President Hurtado, emerged first. He wore the same kind of uniform as when Sidney met him three years ago: a khaki-colored jacket with a matching belt and a blue ascot. There appeared to be even more medals on his chest.

A tall man in his late forties, he wasn't bad-looking with his high forehead and narrow, patrician nose. He had a great tan, and his fingernails were manicured and buffed. This was a guy who knew how to take care of himself.

All the buffing and fluffing in the world couldn't draw the attention to him when Elena stepped out of the helicopter. Her long black hair cascaded past her shoulders. Dramatic eyes stared out from a flawless complexion. Her royal blue designer dress hugged her curves, and a patterned shawl added an aura of feminine mystery.

Sidney heaved a sigh. "She's as beautiful as I remember."

"Not my type," Nick said.

"Oh, pul-eeze, she's every man's type."

"Not for me," he repeated. "I like straight blond hair, long legs and attitude."

"And here I am. What a coincidence!"

The two bodyguards wore beige uniforms and blue berets. They carried automatic repeating rifles.

As she watched them approach, she was hit with a memory. Still mindful of the bugs, she whispered to Nick, "Three years ago. I was in Tiquanna. We were out on Hurtado's yacht. Rico Suarez was with us. He was trying to get my boss to invest a half million dollars in a resort hotel that could turn the beachfront into a tourist's dream location. He mentioned Underwood Oil."

"What did he say?"

"Underwood Oil was making investments in their country, providing for their needs. I asked if he was referring to building schools or providing medical aid, but that wasn't it. Then I lost my train of thought." She chuckled. "Hurtado was wearing a Speedo."

"And you got distracted."

"But not in a good way."

"That's actually a helpful memory. I can check records and see what they were investing in."

Nick had pasted a smile on his face as they waited for the group from Tiquanna to approach. When Sidney looked up at him, she saw an example of perfect diplomacy. But she felt tension in his arm. Anger glimmered in his golden eyes. It was obvious to her that Nick viewed Hurtado as the enemy.

Had the dictator arranged for Nick's abduction? It didn't make sense for him to blow a hole in his own palace compound. And what could he hope to gain? She realized that the whole episode had worked out well for Hurtado. By pretending to rescue Nick, he became something of a hero. But he couldn't have expected that outcome.

He approached her with arms outstretched for a hug. "Miss Sidney Parker, you're the girl who remembers everything."

When his arms enclosed her, she was overwhelmed by the heavy leather scent of his cologne. "Nice to see you again, Mr. President."

"When Vicky told me you were here, I couldn't believe it."

Vicky? As in Victoria Hawthorne? Finally, Sidney had her answer. If you were the head of a nation, you got to call Special Agent Hawthorne by a nickname.

Elena had gone directly to Nick, who politely kissed her hand and said, "I hope you'll enjoy your stay in our country."

She scanned the rain-soaked horizon. "I'm not as much interested in ranches and cowboys as I am in shopping. Perhaps Sidney can show me around."

Hawthorne stepped up. "We'll arrange a day for you at Neiman Marcus."

"Lovely." She faced Sidney and took her hand. Her violet eyes were serious. "I thought of you so many times. It must have been terrible to have your fiancé missing."

Sidney hadn't expected empathy. Elena was either a thoughtful and trusted ally as Nick believed or she was cleverly perceptive in knowing what to say. "Thank you."

Hawthorne herded them toward the front door. "We'll get you settled inside, and then we can talk about dinner."

Upstairs in her bedroom, Sidney quickly changed into her little black dress. Since it was sleeveless, she covered up with a dark rose cashmere cardigan. Her shoes were comfortable black flats. If she'd been at home, she would have added jewelry, but the person who packed her suitcase had skimped on accessories. Her spectacular engagement ring would have to be enough.

In the hallway, she met Nick, who was wearing his dress blue uniform with gold buttons down the front and real medals on his chest. He was so handsome that he took her breath away. What was it about a man in uniform? When she placed her hand on his arm, she was trembling.

"You look great," he said.

"Not me. You."

In his formal attire, he was ready to escort her to somewhere wonderful. She was already rethinking the sleeping arrangements for tonight, trying to figure out a way she could get him into her bed without camera surveillance or bugs. Being this close and not making love was driving her crazy.

Downstairs, the rest of the crew had gathered. In addition to Phillips, Gregory and Curtis, there were three other CIA types in suits and the chopper pilot.

Nick went directly to the pilot. "Are you headed back to Lackland tonight?"

"No, sir. I'll be transporting a group to the hotel to-morrow morning."

Lieutenant Butler, in his own resplendent uniform, joined them. "Looks like Hawthorne has everything under control."

Sidney wasn't sure what that meant. As far as she knew, the major change in plan was the date. "Are you expecting trouble?"

"Nothing to worry about." He looked down into a crystal tumbler of amber liquid. "We've picked up some chatter on the internet. According to our sources, the rebels are in Austin. Avilar might be with them."

Beside her, Nick stiffened. "Why wasn't I informed about the chatter?"

"Not your purview. You're here for the show. You'll meet with the people from Underwood Oil, tell them what a swell guy Hurtado is, and then you're free to get out of here."

She could tell that Nick wanted more. He'd invested his time, his energy and his blood in the struggle be-tween the rebels and Hurtado. He had more experience with their politics than anyone else. As far as she was concerned, he should be in charge.

Butler leaned close enough that she could smell the whiskey on his breath. "I don't mind saying that I wish I could leave with you."

"Why is that?" Nick asked.

"I've got no problem with taking orders from a fe-male. My CO is a woman. But Hawthorne won't listen to a damn word I say. She acts like it's a sign of weak-ness to seek other opinions."

"Like the way she set up guard duty," Nick said.

"Hell, yes." Butler grumbled into his drink. "I could

have handled that responsibility with half the men and twice the effectiveness."

As the two military men fell into a discussion of surveillance strategy, Sidney's gaze shifted toward Special Agent Phillips, who was doing a great job of fading into the woodwork in his brown suit. He gave her a wink. When it came right down to it, she trusted Phillips more than anybody else. He was a kindhearted man. He had a family. She didn't want to think that he was working for the bad guys.

Gregory was another story. There were lots of secrets behind his horn-rimmed glasses. If she ever got a chance to be alone with him, she'd make a point of talking to him about their common interests to see what he might reveal.

A hush dropped over the room as the dictator/president and his wife descended the staircase in a practiced manner. These two were accustomed to making an entrance. He was dignified, and Elena was stunning. Her designer dress in coral and cream managed to look formal without being too fancy.

Though Sidney could imagine Elena running off with Avilar, she didn't think this pampered princess would be happy living in a rebel camp. She probably looked great in camouflage fatigues, but Sidney didn't think the lady had ever shopped at an army surplus store.

Agent Hawthorne—Vicky—trailed behind them, looking very much like a disgruntled lady-in-waiting. She'd taken off the black jacket to her suit to show off the attractive draping of her silk blouse, but she was still a long way from glamorous.

A burst of gunfire shattered the genteel mood. From outside, Sidney heard guards yelling. More shots were fired.

Hurtado's guards leaped in front of him and Elena

with their weapons held at the ready. The agents in suits dropped their drinks, pulled their guns and sought cover.

In those first seconds, she was too shocked to be scared. Was this really happening? Why were they being shot at?

Nick shoved her down behind the dining room table away from the windows. He hadn't been wearing a sword with his dress uniform, but he had a Glock in his hand.

"Stay down," he said.

"Do you have another gun in an ankle holster?" She really had practiced shooting, not so much because she intended to take on the world but because it seemed smart to be able to protect herself. The extra bonus was that she liked it—the noise and the feeling of power when she squeezed the trigger.

He gave her a worried look but didn't argue. As he placed his second Glock in her hand, he said, "Don't get shot again."

"One scar is cool. Two are excessive."

The weight of the gun in her grasp brought her back to reality. They were in a serious, dangerous situation. Adrenaline rushed through her, and her pulse jumped into high gear as the battle outside grew louder. The booming rattle from repeating rifles mingled with single shots. And there were a lot of indecipherable shouts. One of the large windows that opened onto the patio shattered, spewing glass across the floor.

Butler appeared next to Nick. "Sounds like chaos out there."

Nick looked over his shoulder, and she followed his gaze. The Tiquanna guards were hustling Hurtado and Elena from the room. She wondered why Hawthorne wasn't with them. Having the leader of a foreign nation attacked on American soil had to be the special agent's worst nightmare.

Nick asked Butler, "Where are they going?"

"Didn't you pay attention in the meetings? The safe room is the wine cellar under the kitchen."

"I'll accompany them."

He gave her a quick kiss and took off. Sidney understood his reasoning. If Avilar was correct, Hurtado wanted to have Elena assassinated and blame the rebels. This was a perfect opportunity for that scenario.

She looked to Butler. "What can I do to help?"

"You stay here. I'm going to organize this crew."

She ducked down and pushed aside the white linen tablecloth so she could watch Butler take charge. His military training served him well. Nobody—not even Hawthorne—objected when he ordered the various agents into teams and sent them to various locations with specific assignments.

Sidney's job was to stay out of harm's way. As the front room emptied, she moved into the kitchen, where Delia had armed herself with a hunting rifle. Down on one knee, she braced the rifle on the window ledge and peered out toward the barn.

"What do you see?" Sidney asked.

"It's a dark night. Rainy." She adjusted the night scope and squinted into it. "I can't tell what's going on. There's a bunch of guys running around. Looks like they're headed toward the barn. That's bad."

"Why?"

"They're going to scare the horses."

Thinking of Nick, she asked, "How do I get to the wine cellar?"

"There are stairs to the basement behind the mudroom. Once you're down there, you'll see a heavy wooden door. It locks on the inside and the outside. If you get in there, you're safe. Unless the house falls down on your head."

The wine cellar sounded like a clandestine place. Anything might happen there. She decided to join Nick, to be another witness in case Hurtado tried to hurt Elena. First, she asked Delia, "Is there any way I can help you?"

"I don't think so. Nobody is headed our way."

A gigantic explosion rocked the house. A fierce orange light burst through the windows toward the front. Sidney's heart thumped hard against her ribcage, and she inhaled a deep breath to fight her rising panic. It felt as if the whole world had exploded, leaving her disoriented with the inside of her head ringing.

With Delia, she darted along the hallway toward the front of the house. Both women held their guns at the ready.

Another huge boom erupted. The noise was so loud, it hurt her ears.

Peeking around the corner of the hall into the front room, she saw the metal skeleton of the helicopter going up in flames.

Chapter Fourteen

Nick stayed close to Elena in the wine cellar. Hurtado might not have qualms about shooting his wife and blaming the rebels, but he couldn't get away with killing both Elena and Nick, a decorated marine with friends in high places, without many questions being asked. Still, Nick didn't make the mistake of counting too much on his citizenship or his reputation. Those factors hadn't saved him from being abducted and beaten in Tiquanna.

This time, he was armed. As soon as they entered the wine cellar, he imagined several possible actions where he took out the guards and Hurtado. Riding his current wave of anger and frustration, he figured he could handle three men with no sweat. He almost hoped for a confrontation.

The dull light from a few bare bulbs did nothing to lift the chill of the climate-controlled temperature and humidity. Rows of bottles were stored on their sides on specially made racks. This underground room was solid. Down here, the sound of gunfire from outside sounded as harmless as popcorn in the microwave.

Nick set up a table and chairs behind the racks, giving them cover if attackers came through the heavy wooden door, which was locked on the inside. He had only one complaint about this "safe room." There was only one way in and out. They were trapped.

Then they heard the explosion.

"What the hell was that?" Hurtado demanded.

"The chopper," Nick said. He was honestly surprised. "How would the rebels get their hands on that kind of firepower?"

"Simple," Hurtado said. "A stick of dynamite."

"But they'd have to come close to throw it."

Avilar wasn't a fool. He wouldn't risk his men by trying to penetrate so deeply past the heavily armed perimeter surrounding the safe house. And that brought up the obvious question: Why had he staged this attack?

Nick guessed that the purpose was to force Hurtado to move to the hotel. Blowing up the chopper would send that message. Going to Austin suited Nick just fine. The sooner he could turn Elena over to his handlers, the sooner she'd be safe. And he could go home.

Hurtado straightened his shoulders and puffed out his chest, preparing to make an announcement. "I warn you, Captain Corelli, these rebels cannot be underestimated. They have made secret alliances."

"Are you sure this is the action of the rebels?"

"Who else?"

"I have to point this out, sir. You have other enemies."

"That's true," Elena said quietly. "Your own cousin is putting together an army."

"He's organizing a few men for his own protection," Hurtado said. "My cousin, the fool, is a frightened little toad. He finally understands that he must use force against Avilar."

While he was recovering, Nick spent nearly a month in the presidential compound, where he could observe Hurtado in action. His regime was rife with deceptions and intrigues. It was nearly impossible to locate a single grain of truth amid all the lies.

Nick wasn't a card-carrying member of the Miguel Avilar fan club, but he much preferred the rebel to the dictator. And he wasn't above getting in his digs at Hurtado. "The rebels must be growing stronger. Financing this attack in the US had to cost a lot of money."

Hurtado scowled. "Not so much as you might think. I could have financed such an attack."

"I suppose you could." And possibly did. He wouldn't put it past Hurtado to arrange his own attack so the rebels would look bad. Avilar had suggested that the shootout at Nick's house was the work of Hurtado's men, and the proof was Rico Suarez.

"They must be stopped," Hurtado said. "Your government must help me stop them."

Nick cringed. Words of war. He hated them and hated the men like Hurtado who saw force as the only option. "You might want to think about this," he said. "How did Avilar locate the safe house? Does he have a contact on the inside?"

"A traitor to my cause?"

Hurtado's gaze went to Elena, which wasn't the direction Nick wanted him to pursue. His job was to keep her safe. There were plenty of other people to throw under the bus. "Special Agent Hawthorne thinks there's a leak in the CIA."

"Does she?"

"That's why she wanted to bring you here," Nick said. "A spectacular failure."

In her flimsy dress, Elena shivered. Nick unbuttoned his uniform jacket and draped it over her slender shoulders. She was a lovely woman, but he hadn't lied when he said Elena wasn't his type. She was super high maintenance. The man who hooked up with this beauty would be dedicating his entire life to her whims.

Sidney was a partner who gave as good as she got. Living with her would never be boring.

He heard a voice from outside the wine cellar. "It's Hawthorne. Unlock the door."

One of the guards unfastened the latch while the other held his weapon at the ready. Hawthorne rushed inside and yanked the door closed. "It's over," she said. "Are you all right?"

Hurtado answered for all of them. "No injuries to report. Vicky, how could this happen?"

"I'll have a full report later, sir."

"This was the action of the Tiquanna rebels," he said. "Captain Corelli agrees with me."

Nick didn't recall any such agreement. "I'm not so sure."

"Who else could it be?" Hurtado made a fist and punched it into his other hand. "We must hunt them down like dogs. They can't get away with this. Not on American soil."

Nick wasn't in the mood for the dictator's pontificating. There was nothing Hurtado could say that would impress him. He approached Hawthorne. "Casualties?"

"Nothing serious." A puzzled frown creased her forehead. "It sounded like a battlefield with bullets flying, but we had only a few minor hits. Either these guys are really bad marksmen or they were shooting into the air."

"Drawing everyone toward the barn," Nick said.

She nodded. "Then the chopper blew."

The helicopter had been the mark from the first. All that other firepower was meant as a distraction. Nick appreciated the strategy. "If this was Avilar, he was making a statement. Nobody has to get killed."

"No," Hurtado said emphatically. "These dogs can't be permitted to live."

Hawthorne placed a consoling hand on his arm. "Please accept my deepest apologies, sir."

He shook her hand off. "I will never align the interests of my country with cowards."

Head held high, he stalked toward the door, threw it open and marched out. His guards rushed to follow, and Hawthorne brought up the rear.

Nick was left alone with Elena. He shrugged. "That went well."

"You have no idea."

Her smile was cool and secretive. He suspected that she knew all about this attack, had maybe even planned it with Avilar, but he didn't bother asking. She'd tell him when she was ready and not a moment before.

SIDNEY SUMMED UP the helicopter explosion as good news versus bad news. The bad part was, of course, the destruction of an expensive piece of machinery. The good news was the rain. If the fields had been dry, flames from the explosion would have spread across acres and acres of prairie grass. The safe house—which she'd come to think of as the "unsafe" house—might have burned.

She and Delia helped where they could, hauling buckets of drinking water for the ranch hands and guards who were fighting the fire. She ran back and forth to the barn, fetching various tools and implements. Her little black dress was ruined after the second trip, carrying hoes and shovels in a wheelbarrow, but she didn't care. At least she was useful.

Thick, metallic, black smoke billowed straight into the air in an angry plume against the dark night sky. The sparks below sizzled and hissed. People from neighboring ranches showed up and got busy. When the local fire brigade arrived, every hope for CIA secrecy was gone.

Sidney had wondered how the former ranch was explained to the people in the area without telling anybody it was a government safe house. Lodge or dude ranch were the most common explanations.

As Hawthorne mobilized their group to evacuate, Sidney had to fight for her place in one of the SUVs that would form a convoy to the hotel in Austin. Sidney wasn't considered to be a number one important person at these meetings. But Nick was. And he insisted on having her with him. After she wiped the smudges of smoke off her face, she changed into jeans and a sweatshirt, packed her suitcase and lugged it downstairs, where she found her place in the second vehicle with Nick, Gregory, Phillips and Lieutenant Butler.

They drove away immediately, following the vehicle carrying the Hurtados and Special Agent Hawthorne. Another SUV fell into line behind them.

She and Nick sat in the farthest backseat. They weren't alone, but it felt private. She snuggled against him.

"Don't take this personally," he said, "but you stink."

"That smoke was awful."

"I might be the smelly one," Phillips said. "Have y'all ever seen anything like that explosion? I wish I'd recorded it on my phone to show the kids. They don't think their daddy has an exciting job."

"What do you tell your twins about your job?" she asked.

"I just tell them that I'm an analyst for the government. They don't care. They're only four." He glanced over his shoulder and made eye contact with her. "When my boys are older, I could have a problem not telling the whole truth. But I can't very well say that I'm a secret agent. If I did, it wouldn't be a secret."

"What about your wife?"

"Y'all ask a lot of questions, Sidney."

"I can't help being curious."

"That's true," Nick said. "She wants to know everything."

"Me and my wife don't talk about my job." He frowned. "If something comes up, like this fire, I change the subject. Here's what I'd say. That fire could have been a real disaster, but those ranch hands really know what they're doing."

"All true," she said. But he avoided any detail that would have been a breech in secrecy. It must be exhausting to live like that, hiding your real work.

"I'll tell you this," Butler grumbled from the front seat. "Those cowboys were a hell of a lot more efficient than the CIA. The bodyguards were running around like chickens with their heads cut off. No leadership whatsoever."

"Could have been worse," Phillips said. "Nobody got shot."

Butler turned in his seat to glare at all of them. "The enemy achieved their objective, which was, obviously, to torch the chopper. They distracted the security force with gunfire at the rear of the house while they did whatever they wanted at the front."

"Do you have any idea what caused the explosion?" Nick asked. "Any chance it was long-range weaponry?"

"I doubt they needed anything that sophisticated," Butler said. "If we've learned anything from Iraq and Afghanistan, it's that it doesn't take a lot of expertise to put together a bomb."

"What happens when we get to the hotel?" Gregory asked. "I don't think we have reservations for tonight."

"Hawthorne has it under control," Phillips said. "I think we have an entire floor booked for a week, including some fancy suite for the president and his wife."

"I'm aware of that," Gregory snapped. "I'm handling the meeting preparations for Underwood Oil, so I've been talking to the hotel. I just want to know about tonight."

She nudged Nick in the ribs. "Maybe they won't have a room for us, and we'll have to fend for ourselves."

"All by ourselves. That wouldn't be so bad."

"Not for you," Gregory muttered. "I've been working on this for years. Finally, it looks like everybody is on board. Finally, I can get some solid agreement."

"About what?" she asked. The negotiation of drilling rights shouldn't be so complicated. When her company checked out Tiquanna, their main concern had been lack of infrastructure. "How much is Underwood Oil willing to finance in building roads, providing housing and clean water? Are they going to deal with the lack of schools? What about medical conditions?"

"Humanitarian aid is *not* my problem." He pushed his glasses up on his nose. "And it's none of your business."

She was about to protest. The mistreatment of these people should be everybody's problem. Clearly, the rebels saw a problem in the way their country was being developed. She remembered the squalid conditions in the slums of the capital city.

Before Underwood Oil turned on the tap and sent a gush of money flowing into Tiquanna, there needed to be considerations for the people who lived there.

If the only purpose for these meetings was to ensure Hurtado's wealth and fortune, she wanted to make it her business. But it wouldn't do much good to poke at Gregory. He had his strategy mapped and wasn't going to change his mind.

No matter who got hurt.

Chapter Fifteen

Sidney waltzed through the door to their hotel room on the fifth floor. It was a typical room with a queen-size bed, a dresser, a television, a desk and a bathroom. The walls were painted a soft gold. A floor-to-ceiling window was covered with a nubby curtain. The carpet was beige. Nothing spectacular, but she thought it was the most fantastic room she'd ever seen. This space—this wonderful space—belonged to her and Nick alone.

There hadn't been a room available for them on the floor that the CIA had rented, so they got their own random vacant room at the hotel. No surveillance cameras. No bugs. Finally, they had privacy. And that was a thing of beauty.

While Nick tipped the bellman, she flopped across the bed and stared up at the ceiling. "I love this place."

"You're easy to please."

"Seriously, Nick. If I want to talk in a normal voice about why Hurtado is an evil dictator, it's not a problem. Nobody is listening to us. Nobody is watching."

He sat on the bed beside her. "We can get into all kinds of trouble."

It felt as if they should do something outrageous to celebrate. Her arm slithered toward him, free to touch wherever she wanted. "Do you want to talk dirty?"

"Do you?"

"Well, it's never really been my thing. But if I wanted to sleaze it up, I could."

"Knock yourself out."

"Oh, baby, I want you. I want your…" She grabbed his leather jacket and yanked him toward her. "You know what I want."

He gathered her in his arms and kissed her without holding anything back. Though she wanted to record every second, she couldn't keep track as his hands coasted over her body, exploring and teasing. His rough caresses demanded a response, and her instincts took over. She hadn't been aware of how restricted she'd been when she thought they were being watched. Now she was free and loving every touch, every twitch, every gasp.

What she didn't love was the stink. She drew back. Her nose wrinkled. "I smell like smoke."

"We need a shower."

"Yes, please."

The simple, white-tiled hotel bathroom seemed like a garden of earthly delights when she turned on the hot water and steam rolled out from behind the curtain. For the past few days, she'd been dying to get her hands on his body. Though a sexy striptease would have been a treat, she was too eager to waste time with game playing. They tore off their clothes in a matter of seconds. She stared. His broad-shouldered body was even better than she remembered, too good to be true.

The yearning that had tortured her for months transformed into pure desire. Nothing in the world existed beyond him, her fiancé, her lover, her man. Naked, they stepped under the hot shower.

He leaned down and kissed her upper arm. "Your battle wound looks good."

"I almost forgot about it."

"It's going to be a sexy scar."

She tilted her head back and let the water sluice through her hair, rinsing out the stench from the fire.

"Look at you," he murmured as he peeled the wrapper off a bar of soap. "You're the prettiest thing I've ever seen. You're perfect."

"Now who's easy to please?"

He worked up the lather in his hands. "Come here, dirty girl."

He rubbed the soapsuds over her breasts and waist. Then he turned her around and washed her shoulders. His fingers traced her spine and cupped her bottom as she stood facing the spray of hot water. She knew his strength; he was a big, muscular man. But his touch was infinitely gentle.

He opened the shampoo and washed her hair. The sandalwood fragrance of the soap gradually erased the ugly stench of smoke. Though she could have stood there for hours, enjoying the purely sensual massage, her needs were more demanding. She'd been dreaming about him for six months. It was time.

They traded places. He was so tall that he had to duck to get the shower spray on his head. The water slicked his shining black hair and coursed in rivulets down his body. She treated herself to a slow study of his long, lean torso.

There were new scars. She touched a poorly stitched line on his upper chest. "Whoever did this to you deserves to die."

"Let's not talk about it now. This time is for us."

With an effort, she pushed back her anger. She wanted justice for him. She wanted retribution. But he was right. They had earned their moments of privacy.

She soaped every part of him, and when she was done,

she leaned her cheek against his broad chest. The cascading sound of the shower played a natural harmony that synchronized with the throbbing of her pulse. Their bodies suctioned together and pulled apart.

They'd made love in the shower before. The first time was on November 15th, almost a year ago. She had that memory preserved in her mind. But this felt like the first time. She marveled at his taut muscles, and she laughed when she stroked his side and he flinched in a tickle response. His kisses were deeper. His touch was more demanding. She spread her legs and rubbed against him.

"I'm still taking my birth control pills," she said.

"Good."

When he'd been gone three months, and she didn't know if he was alive or dead, she had considered dumping the pills. That had been a low point for her, when she'd almost given up hope that she'd ever see him again. If she lost Nick, she never wanted to make love with another man. No one could ever come close to taking his place in her heart.

Staying on the pill became an important part of her schedule, a daily affirmation. She needed to be prepared for the moment when he returned to her.

She looked up at his face. Her gaze locked on his golden eyes, and a rush of adrenaline coursed through her veins. "I knew you'd come back to me."

He traced her lips with a fingertip. "I'll never leave, never again."

Still standing, he lifted her thigh, adjusted his position and entered her. The shock of finally joining together thrilled her. Her moans of pleasure echoed in the shower as her greedy hands pulled him closer.

He filled her completely. His thrusts were slow at first, driving her wild. Her back arched. In a desperate frenzy, she writhed against him, wanting more and more, deeper and deeper. He plunged harder, drove her to the edge. She couldn't stop if she'd wanted to. A bolt of excitement shattered her. She came completely undone.

Trembling, gasping and falling, she clung to him, unable to stand on her own two legs. He had taken her beyond her imagination and her memories. He was her everything.

NICK TOWELED HER DRY, carried her to the bed and tucked her under the covers. Making love to her was more than sex. Not that the sex was anything to be disregarded. But this was pure love, blooming all around him, sweeter than the fragrance of gardenias and softer than the touch of morning sun. He knew what had to be done for him to live with Sidney, and he was ready to finish this assignment and get on with their future.

There would be changes for him. Less excitement and more desk work. But she was worth it. "Tell me about your plans for the house."

"Everything gets painted, like I said before. No more dark turquoise. Definitely, no more orange. Whenever I walk into that room behind the kitchen, I feel like I'm inside a juicer about to get pulped."

"What do you want to do with that room?"

"It'd make a nice guest bedroom, but it's kind of far from the bathroom. I'm thinking of a home office. It's big enough that we both could use it."

"Do you think we could share an office?"

Her full lips twisted in an adorable scowl. "I suppose we could. I've been working at a bar, and I kind of like that cheesy country music you always play."

"And my guitar."

She groaned. "Why would you play your guitar in the office?"

She was cute when she got irked with him. It made him want to tease her more. "The twelve-string helps me think."

"Or maybe we don't share an office," she said. "It could be an exercise room. Or a plant room in case I get into gardening."

"Or a nursery."

Her blue eyes widened. They hadn't talked much about having kids. Of course, they both wanted children. And their little brick house with the big backyard would be a good place to start a family.

"Someday," she said.

There were a lot of other things that had to happen first. "Can we get a border collie?"

"Only if we get it from the pound," she said.

If he slipped under the covers beside her and felt the silky texture of her skin, he wouldn't be able to resist making love again. Not a problem. He was already half-way aroused again and ready for a full night of passion.

A glance at the digital clock on the bedside table showed it was after ten o'clock. He wondered how late room service was available. "Hungry?"

"You bet I am. All afternoon I could smell the pot roast Delia was making for dinner."

He put on a terry cloth bathrobe provided by the hotel, grabbed the phone and placed their order: a hamburger for him, roast beef for her and a bottle of the house red wine. Going out to dinner would have been great, but he'd promised Hawthorne that he wouldn't leave the hotel.

With all the other distractions, he wasn't worried about using his secret cell phone to send a message. The response to his text was immediate. Tomorrow at one-thirty, he should bring Elena to the roof of the building.

Why the roof? As he removed the battery from the phone so it couldn't be traced, he decided that before that meeting, he would check out the roof. He needed to be aware of escape options if something went wrong.

Sidney had opened her suitcase and found her own pastel blue robe decorated with snowflakes. She perched on the edge of the bed and dragged a comb through her straight blond hair. "I want to take you to the Silver Star Saloon, where I was working. They have incredible beers."

"This could be over tomorrow," he said. "And we're going on a real retreat, someplace in the mountains where nobody knows us and nobody wants anything from us."

"How do you think this is going to turn out? What happens after Elena disappears?"

"It's not my problem, but I'd say that's the beginning of the end for Hurtado."

"Good. I've decided that he's the bad guy."

"Even though it's likely that Avilar blew up the chopper?"

"I've been thinking about that," she said. "I don't think it was accidental that no one was seriously injured. Avilar wanted to make a statement. He wanted to get Elena away from the safe house early, and he accomplished that without casualties. Kind of impressive."

He agreed. A dead helicopter bothered him less than the loss of human life. "If Avilar is behind this, he's put together a significant force inside the US. How is he being financed?"

"You mentioned that his family has money."

Nick was well aware of the resources available to the rebels. In some ways, they looked like a ragtag army, poorly funded and struggling. But their weaponry and access to computer technology were first-class.

Finding their financial backer was one of the reasons he'd been stationed in Tiquanna. At first, he thought they were being armed by Underwood Oil. Earlier today when Sidney mentioned an investment from the oil company, he was reminded of the many times he had tried to follow the money trail. Somehow, Underwood Oil money always led back to Hurtado and his friends.

When room service came, he scarfed down half his hamburger without taking a breath. He sipped the wine, savoring the tang. "It's good."

"Delicious," she said, finishing her roast beef. "I'll bet Delia's beef is better. She's a really good cook. Is she part of the CIA? How does the safe house work with the locals?"

"Delia and a couple of the ranch hands are live-ins. I expect they have some kind of security clearance, but they aren't officially CIA or FBI. They know the ranch is owned by the government and if they want to keep their jobs, they don't talk about the people staying there."

"With all the cameras and such, that seems a bit lax."

"It's the other way around," he said. "If they were overheard talking about anything suspicious, they'd be in trouble."

"I'd hate to live like that. I've never been good at keeping secrets."

He heard a tap on the door and went to answer. Holding his gun, he peeked through the fish-eye and saw Special Agent Curtis standing in the hallway, shifting his weight from one foot to the other.

Hoping that Curtis wasn't bringing news of a new disaster, Nick opened the door. "What is it?"

"Is Sidney here?"

As soon as she heard Curtis's voice, she left her chair and bounced up to greet him. "What can I do for you?"

He gave her a shy smile. His cheeks were almost as red as his hair. "Actually, I have something for you. Your cell phone."

She took it from him. "Is it okay for me to call my office?"

"Hawthorne asked that you not give your location or make plans to meet with anybody until the Tiquanna meetings are over. But information about Hurtado and Elena being at the hotel is common knowledge. Tomorrow, they'll be talking to the press."

"I appreciate this," she said.

"Have a nice night."

Nick closed the door and watched as Curtis went back down the hall to the elevator. "How did he know which room we were in? I didn't tell anybody."

"He's CIA," she said. "They know everything."

"You like him, don't you?"

She shrugged. "He's sweet. Within a few minutes of meeting him, he let me give him a neck massage."

Nick wasn't surprised. "You can be very persuasive."

"Stop being a guy for a minute," she said. "It wasn't a sexy massage."

"Uh-huh." As if he believed that.

"Curtis and I bonded on a nerd level." She sipped her wine. "He understands me."

"How do you figure?"

"I was asking him tons of questions about degrees of angles and camera rotations. He probably knew that I'd try to circumvent his surveillance. But he also knew that I'm not a dangerous person."

He took the cell phone from her. "Do you have the information on your cell backed up?"

"Yes, it links up with my computer."

"Good."

In the bathroom, he removed the battery. Using the heel of his boot, he smashed the phone and tossed the pieces in a water glass.

"You killed it," she said.

"We don't need any more cameras or bugs." He was pretty sure that picking up surveillance on them had motivated the supposedly nice gesture of returning her phone. "Your pal Curtis might be a nice guy. But he still works for Hawthorne."

Nick still needed to be cautious. The game wasn't over. Not by a long shot.

Chapter Sixteen

After a night of passion that took up rows and rows of space in her memory banks, Sidney might have been content to roll over and sleep until noon. With any luck, she'd miss any more fireworks, Nick could fulfill his orders with Elena, and they could leave this chaos behind them in the rearview mirror.

Whatever happened in Tiquanna wasn't her problem. She was just one little person who had gotten swept up in an international intrigue. Not. Her. Problem.

Unfortunately, whether she liked it or not, Nick played a role in this battle. He'd been kidnapped and tortured, rescued and recruited to help Elena. He had a stake in the outcome. Tiquanna was important to him. Therefore, she was involved.

At eight o'clock in the morning, she was dressed and ready to go. Her little black dress was destroyed after last night, but she had a light wool plaid skirt that she wore with a blazer. She chose flats instead of heels in case she needed to move fast.

Nick came out of the bathroom wearing the heather-gray sweater she'd bought for him on his last birthday, March 22. He looked preppy and cool as he slipped on a sports jacket to cover the gun at the small of his back.

He glanced at her outfit. "You don't have to come with me."

"I want to."

"There's nothing to worry about," he said. "Nothing dangerous about today."

"You've been wrong about that before," she pointed out. "Bad guys shot up our house. We bumped into a rebel leader in the barn. And there was that exploding chopper..."

"Okay, I get it."

She took a sip of the instant coffee she'd made using the machine in the bathroom. The taste was gross, but caffeine was caffeine. "What's our plan?"

"We go to the ninth floor, where Hawthorne has the whole operation set up. We hang around there until it's time for me to take Elena to the drop-off point."

"And what time is that going to happen?"

"I'd rather not tell you when."

Too bad for him. She refused to be left in the dark. "I'm not insisting on coming along, but I want to know."

"Last night, you admitted that you aren't good at keeping secrets."

"Yes, I did say that. And yes, it's true." If he told her the time, she'd be checking her wristwatch and doing mental countdowns. "Can you tell me where?"

He thought for a moment, and she imagined his mental process. The location where he would hand over Elena seemed to be bothering him. He'd like to have her input. But he wanted to keep her at a distance.

His common sense won out. "Okay, I'll tell you."

"Where?"

"According to my instructions, I'm supposed to take Elena to the roof. I want to go up there this morning and check for obstacles."

"Makes sense to go to the roof," Sidney said. "They'll pick her up with a chopper."

It was his turn to look surprised. "You figured that out pretty fast."

She shrugged. "Their problem is to get Elena out of the building without being harmed. If the exits are watched by armed men, she's an easy target for a sniper. Or she could be followed on the street."

"True."

She continued, "It's already been established that the rebels are willing to use force. They'd be blamed if Elena was attacked. Hurtado could pretend to be a grieving widower, and he'd be excused for using force on his enemies."

"You have a knack for this," he said.

"Thank you."

In the hallway outside their fifth-floor room, she was fairly sure they'd be picked up on hotel surveillance and probably CIA, as well. With all these cameras, she ought to feel like a movie star. Instead, she was annoyed.

She glanced at the green exit sign above the door to a stairwell. "I'm guessing all the doors to the stairwell open on this side and lock when they're closed."

"Good guess," he said. "But I know a way around the locks."

"You've done this kind of thing before."

He had a lot of interesting skills that she knew nothing about. His abilities went far beyond basic training for a captain in the marines. She followed him into the stairwell.

Whitewashed concrete walls closed around them. Their steps on the staircase echoed as they climbed past the ninth floor to the roof on the fifteenth.

Sidney was in pretty good shape, but hiking up ten

flights left her huffing and puffing. She leaned her back against the wall and caught her breath while Nick took a metallic tool from his pocket and fiddled with the lock on the door labeled Roof. There was a soft popping noise and the smell of gunpowder. He pushed open the door.

Outside, the rain had faded to a gray drizzle that obscured what would have been a beautiful view on a clear day. She looked down at the wide Colorado River as it cut through town. The capitol building wasn't in her sightline. Nor was the Silver Star Saloon. For a moment she wondered what had happened to her car, which she'd left parked behind the saloon.

Nick walked across the gravel-topped roof to the center of a concrete circle. "Heliport."

"We were right," she said.

"Not much cover up here." He turned three hundred and sixty degrees, and then he hiked to the edge of the roof, where a beige brick parapet rose two feet high.

She joined him and looked down a wall made of alternating brick and glass. A sense of vertigo caused her vision to telescope, and she took a step back.

"Careful." He reached out and braced her.

"That's steep."

"I wanted to see if there was some alternate way down from here. There's supposed to be a restaurant or something."

As in climbing down fifteen stories? Was he crazy?

"Nothing here. You're out of luck."

He led her to the corner of the building and pointed down to a terraced area, lavishly decorated with potted plants. The glass-top dining tables surrounded a circular pool. "Here's the escape."

"That's a thirty-foot drop onto concrete, otherwise known as a suicide mission."

"It's not so bad. There's an overhang above the door. That's only about fifteen feet. And it's possible to jump all the way to the pool."

There was no way she'd allow him to come up here with Elena by himself. Whether or not he wanted her company, he needed backup.

ON THE NINTH FLOOR, Sidney and Nick were met at the elevator by an agent she didn't recognize who provided them with prepared name tags to hang around their necks. This was usually a concierge level with an open reception area. At both ends, there were high ceilings and lots of windows that gave an open feeling to conversational groupings of sofas and chairs. Behind a Plexiglas wall, there was a meeting in progress. As Sidney watched the various agents seated around a long table, she was reminded of a fishbowl.

Though there were armed guards posted at intervals, Special Agent Hawthorne had done her best to create an upbeat, relaxed atmosphere for the meetings involving Hurtado, various politicians and Underwood Oil. When Lieutenant Butler swooped down on them and pulled Nick aside, she made a beeline for the silver coffee urn.

Not knowing when she'd get another chance to eat, she grabbed two muffins and packets of cream cheese before she sat at the end of a sofa. Two women in business suits sipped coffee at the other end of the sofa. Their ID badges showed they were with the governor's office, and Sidney wondered if she'd ever served them at the Silver Star Saloon.

"Excuse me," one of the women said. "Have you met her?"

"Her?"

"Elena Hurtado." Her voice quavered with excitement. "I've been told that her photographs don't do her justice."

"She's very beautiful," Sidney said with sincerity. "Always wears designer clothes."

"I've had private correspondence with her about early schooling and vaccination programs in Tiquanna. In spite of her husband's policies, she might really be able to help the poor people of her country."

Don't get your hopes up. Sidney nodded.

From a room with double doors at the far end of the hallway, she watched as President Hurtado emerged in his impressive uniform. Special Agent Hawthorne marched beside him, and his two bodyguards fell into place behind him.

Halfway down the hall, their procession halted.

"May I have your attention?" Hawthorne said. "Ladies and gentlemen, thank you for attending this impromptu breakfast. The president will be available for the next half hour to take questions."

"What about Elena?" someone called out.

"His wife isn't feeling well," Hawthorne said. "I'm sure she'll be here for lunch."

Sidney glanced over at Nick. A simple way to foil Elena's defection would be to keep her locked up. After excusing herself to the ladies from the governor's office, Sidney joined her fiancé. "What do you think?"

"I'd like to see Elena join the group."

"I can handle this." Being a woman would come in handy. "I'll have her mingling in no time."

Sidney quickly made her way to the end of the hallway, where she informed the uniformed guard that she was a friend of Elena's and needed to be with her.

"Sorry, ma'am. My orders state that no one but her husband is allowed to see her."

Sidney tried another tactic. "Vicky Hawthorne said I could go inside." The guard didn't budge.

She tried one more direction. "My fiancé would want me to check on Elena and make sure she was all right. My fiancé, Captain Nick Corelli."

"Yes, ma'am." He snapped to attention and opened the door.

The interior of the opulent suite glowed, even though the rain-filled light through the tall windows was gray and flat. Elena rushed toward her in a swirl of ostrich feathers and coral chiffon from her peignoir. She was a vision of energy, vivacious and very much alive. She grasped both of Sidney's hands. Her violet eyes were electric. "I have to get out of here."

Sidney was a little overwhelmed by the direct attention. "Your husband said you're sick."

"Sick of him," she muttered as she turned away and stalked across the room, trailing bits of feather.

Some of her big personality was purely for dramatic effect. This was a woman who liked constantly being on camera, and Sidney was one hundred percent certain that they were currently under surveillance. She had to wonder what was underneath the flourishes and pirouettes. Did Elena truly believe that her husband wanted her dead?

Sidney cleared her throat. "I spoke to a woman outside who came here specifically to see you. She wants to talk about schools for the children of Tiquanna. It'd be a shame for you to stay in this room."

"Vicky Hawthorne says I must not risk going out. She looks at Tomas as though he's a god. I would be happy for her to take my husband far away from me."

Sidney went to the silver coffee service on a glass-topped table in the center of the suite and poured a cup.

She'd had tastes of the instant and the stuff in the outer lobby, but her need for more caffeine was still present. Her thoughts weren't clear. She couldn't tell if Elena was afraid of the rebel threat or of her husband. "Do you mind if I ask a personal question?"

She arched a beautifully shaped eyebrow. "Of course not."

"Why don't you just divorce him?"

Elena threw her head back and laughed. Again, this was big drama, the kind of gesture you'd expect to see onstage. Somehow, she pulled off the diva routine without looking crazy.

"Divorce is not possible for the machismo man, such as Tomas," she said. "The woman doesn't make such decisions. We are married, and that's final, *finito.*"

"An Italian word," Sidney said.

"I was born in Milan."

Sidney hadn't known that. She was hazy on Elena's biography. "I thought you grew up in Tiquanna."

"With my parents, I traveled Europe until I was fourteen. My father was killed in an accident. We lost our fortune, and my mother was forced to bring me to Tiquanna to live with her family." Her full lips parted in a toothy smile. "I fell in love with Tomas. I was ready to marry him, but he insisted that I get an education in America."

"Because you were only fourteen at the time." Even in Tiquanna, the dictator couldn't justify marrying such a young girl.

"With my mother as chaperone, I went to school in California. I studied international business and politics. I speak six languages, four of them fluently. When I returned to Tiquanna, I was prepared to marry Tomas and become first lady of my country."

Her story was unbelievable and fascinating. Sidney

imagined the dramatic rooftop escape in a helicopter to be just another chapter in Elena's operatic life. It was time to move forward with that plan.

She took Elena's hand and made direct eye contact. "My fiancé appreciates everything you've done for him."

"Nick is a good man. He loves you very much."

It did Sidney a world of good to hear those words from Elena. "I'm certain that he would want you to leave your suite and meet with the people who have gathered here."

"My husband wishes for me to stay."

Sidney noticed a glimmer of fear behind the big personality. She suspected that Tomas hadn't been gentle in teaching life's lessons to Elena. If there hadn't been surveillance, she could have told the woman that the time for her escape was near. It would be only a few more hours.

"You can't disappoint the people who have come to see you," Sidney said. "Get dressed, Elena."

She darted into the bedroom.

Within two minutes, the door to the suite swung open and slammed hard. Special Agent Hawthorne stood there with her fists braced on her skinny hips.

"What the hell are you doing, Sidney?"

Chapter Seventeen

Sidney felt absolutely no need to justify her actions to Special Agent Hawthorne. Her grudge against this woman was long-standing. During the months Nick had been held hostage, he'd told her Hawthorne had gathered detailed information about his condition that she hadn't seen fit to pass along. She could have arranged phone calls or online visits between Sidney and Nick. Instead, she'd kept them separate.

Hawthorne had called it "keeping control" of the situation. Sidney called it "payback time." This situation was about to get very, very messy.

"It's a miracle," Sidney said. "Elena is feeling better. She's going to get dressed, and we'll join the others."

"This isn't about her health. I want her in this room. It's the only way I can be sure she's safe from the rebels."

"You can't seriously believe the rebels would attempt an attack at the hotel. Not with all the law enforcement present."

"I'm doing my best to avoid a confrontation." Hawthorne pursed her narrow lips. "I don't have to explain to you."

"If there's a real danger," Sidney said, "why is Hurtado parading around in the hallway? Wouldn't the greater threat be directed toward him?"

She couldn't argue with that logic, and Sidney pressed her advantage. "The real reason you want Elena to stay in her room is because her husband wants it that way. For some reason, Tomas is keeping Elena locked away. And you're helping him."

"It's my job to make sure he stays happy with us. We need for him to be on our side."

"What about Elena?" Sidney took an educated guess. "There are people in government who trust her opinion more than his."

Apparently, she'd struck a chord. A muscle at the corner of Hawthorne's eye twitched. "I forbid you to get involved."

"You forbid me?" Who did she think she was? The Wicked Witch of the West? "I'm delighted to be the one to inform you that you're not calling the shots anymore."

"And who is?"

The door to the bedroom flung wide, and Sidney gestured. "She is. The first lady of Tiquanna."

Elena sailed through in full diva mode. Her green-and-white-patterned dress clung to her slender waist like a designer's caress. The deep V of the neckline showed off a platinum and emerald necklace. Her black hair billowed around her shoulders.

"Come," she said to Sidney, "I have people to meet."

Hawthorne blocked the doorway like a pugnacious bulldog. "I'm sorry, Mrs. Hurtado. I must insist that you stay in your room today."

"I am not a coward," Elena said with her head held high. "It is my duty to represent my country and my people. This is my responsibility."

Sidney pushed past Hawthorne and opened the door. "Right this way, Elena."

"Thank you."

As soon as Elena the Diva entered the hallway, the atmosphere changed from political discussion to party, party, party. The women were fascinated by her sense of style. And the men were drawn to her beauty.

When Sidney stepped aside to let Elena shine at full voltage, Nick joined her. "Good job getting her out here."

"All I had to do was remind her that she's a superstar."

"She's impressive."

Sidney hadn't realized how truly impressive Elena was. She had prepared herself to take a position of power, and her husband was right to be worried about her sphere of influence. If Elena and the handsome rebel leader hooked up, they might take over the world.

IF SIDNEY HADN'T been with him, Nick would have been knee-deep in a swamp of negativity. How the hell did he expect this to work? A helicopter escape off a hotel building? It wasn't exactly subtle. Even though the plan started as a secret, the truth would be out in a matter of minutes. The media would be alerted. Talent agents would be casting the miniseries.

Just because Elena's defection could turn into a publicity circus, it didn't negate the danger, especially for him. Elena would be flying away, but how was Nick going to get out of the building without being arrested by Hawthorne and her gang? He'd be lucky not to end up in a CIA prison.

As he chatted with people in the meeting area, it didn't help that most of his conversations tracked back to his time as a hostage and how heroic he was to have endured. Playing the role of a war hero made him uncomfortable. He was a soldier, a marine, and he didn't do his job for medals or pats on the back. It was his job to serve his country. His satisfaction came when a mission was accomplished.

As he watched Sidney interact with many of the women present, he decided that her engagement ring had paid off in clarifying their relationship. When other women checked out the pi diamond, they oohed and aahed and crossed him off the list of eligible men. The only one who wasn't impressed by its size was Sidney, who wanted something smaller and more efficient.

She sidled up beside him and went up on tiptoe to whisper in his ear, "Now?"

"Not yet."

It had been a smart move on his part to keep the departure time a secret from Sidney. She was anxious enough without knowing the details.

At twelve-thirty, with less than an hour to go before the meet, everyone had settled at five-person tables for a casual lunch of beet salad and some kind of chicken breast with a sauce. He noticed that Sidney had rescued Elena from her expected position at her husband's side and seated her with a group of women. They were talking about food.

"A typical dinner in Tiquanna," Sidney said, "might include a fish stew, lentils, plantains and fried corn bread. The seasonings tend to be a combination of Caribbean and Mexican."

"And the drinks are rum," Elena added. "My country has a lighthearted side. And we love music, as you do in Austin. If there were more development in our country, tourists would flock to Tiquanna."

"Not enough development. That's your real problem," said a woman in a red suit with an ID badge from the governor's office. "Lack of infrastructure. When you get the oil business up and running, there will be plenty of people willing to invest in hotels and such."

"Before the hotels," said a nervous little blonde, "you need schools and hospitals. Otherwise, they'll never get built."

Nick motioned to Sidney, and she excused herself from the discussion that was rapidly evolving into a cultural exchange program with Austin and Tiquanna. She bounced over to him, smiling broadly.

"And that," she said, "is how the world's problems get solved. Five or six women sitting around a table will come up with a plan to make everything right."

"I believe it," he said, "as long as Hawthorne isn't at the table."

"Yeah, she's a pill."

His deadline was approaching. The time had ticked down to twenty-eight minutes before he needed to be on the roof with Elena, which meant he had to make his move in twenty minutes, give or take. "I'm going to need help separating Elena from her adoring fans."

"Right now?"

Excitement brightened her eyes, and he was reminded of his early days when he was less cynical and war-weary. There had been a time, long ago, when he didn't look at the downside. "In a few minutes."

She whispered, "Does Elena know what's going on?"

"Yes."

She didn't have the details, but she was aware of the arrangements being made for her defection. And she knew that Nick was the only person she could trust. If only he'd had a backup, he would have felt more confident.

Sidney gave him a wink. "I've got an idea."

"Oh, good."

"We've been talking about weddings. There's something I wanted to ask Elena."

He wasn't sure where she was going with this, but he played along. "Okay, sure."

Agents Gregory and Curtis stepped up to join them, and Sidney turned to them. "I'm going to ask Elena to be the matron of honor at our wedding. What do you think?"

The two men exchanged a glance and a shrug. Curtis asked, "What if she's in Tiquanna?"

"Well, I have to work out the schedule." She looked up at Nick and batted her eyelashes. "Will you ask her with me? It would mean so much."

He understood what she was doing. Sidney's ruse provided him with an excuse to get Elena away from these people. He had to admit that she was clever. What could be more innocent than a wedding? "Just give me a wave when you're ready."

"Maybe we can slip into one of the meeting rooms." She beamed a smile at the other two men and dashed back to the table. "Hope you guys are having fun."

Curtis looked at Nick. "She's something else."

"I'm a lucky man."

"You'd better get your woman in line," Gregory said. "She's got the engineers from Underwood Oil all worried about their survey figures."

"As if I could control her," Nick said.

In twelve minutes, he'd escort Elena from this room into an elevator. Then, he'd take the elevator to the top floor. He'd already prepped the door to the roof. They'd step outside. The chopper would be waiting. And she'd lift off.

As quickly as possible, he'd come back for Sidney.

Then, they were out of there. They'd take a cab directly to the airport.

"Does she really remember everything?" Gregory asked.

"Oh, yeah."

"After you're married, it'll be hard to put anything over on her."

"Why would I want to?"

His life with Sidney would be completely free and open, based on trust. There would be no secrets. No surveillance. Their whole life would be like last night, when they were free with each other.

Six minutes to go.

Curtis was looking at him as if he'd asked a question and wanted a response.

"Sorry," Nick said, "I didn't hear you."

"How long will you be stationed in Austin?"

"For a while. That's why we bought a house here."

"Does that mean you won't be traveling as much?" Curtis asked.

Why did he care? Nick wondered if Curtis was trying to strike up a friendship. "Are you stationed in this area?"

"I live in Dallas," he said.

The time for conversation was over. Nick had to put his plan into effect. He looked across the room to where Sidney sat beside Elena, waiting for his signal. He gave her a nod.

"I'll see you guys later," he said. "I need to go talk about weddings."

Though he strolled casually through the tables, he felt people watching him. Hawthorne's gaze had been disapproving from the moment she saw him without the cane she had provided for him. Hurtado glared with distaste. Nick glanced to the left and, for an instant, made eye contact with Lieutenant Butler, who quickly looked away. There was only one relatively friendly face, and that was Special Agent Sean Phillips, who didn't seem to be in the room.

Nick paused beside Sidney and Elena. "Ladies."

Sidney did the talking. "Elena, we have something to ask you. In private."

"Very well." She patted her lips with her napkin and rose. "I'll be back in a moment."

He escorted Sidney and Elena toward the elevators. A single uniformed marine, one of Butler's men, stood guard. The most direct escape would have been to hop on the elevator and ride to the top, but he knew better than to attempt a bypass on a marine with clear orders.

He brought the ladies down the hall, where they turned into a kitchen. This route—that Nick had found earlier— would add four minutes to their timing. "We need to hurry."

Sidney looked down at Elena's high-heeled platform shoes. "Can you move fast in those?"

"I've been running in heels since I was fourteen."

From the kitchen, they took an elevator all the way to the basement of the hotel, then down a concrete corridor past a laundry, then back to the central elevators. They rode all the way to the fourteenth floor, one down from the roof.

In the hallway outside the elevator, Nick shepherded Elena into the stairwell. He turned to Sidney. "Stay here."

She nodded. "Be careful."

The doors to the second elevator swooshed open. Special Agent Curtis jumped out. He braced a Glock 17 in both hands. Before he could shoot, Nick pulled Sidney into the stairwell.

"What is it?" Elena demanded.

"We've been found out," Nick said.

"How?"

"Curtis must have planted a trace on one of us."

"Now what?"

"Up to the roof," he said as he drew his weapon from the holster at the small of his back. He pulled his second gun from his ankle and gave it to Sidney. "The door's open."

While the women climbed, he prepared to return fire. Curtis had the advantage. He had a door to hide behind. All Nick had going for him was a fierce will to live and pinpoint accuracy as a marksman. He liked his chances.

Chapter Eighteen

Sidney pushed open the door leading to the roof of the hotel. A burst of damp air slapped her in the face. The rain had stopped, but the gravelly surface beneath their feet glistened with moisture and the clouds hung low.

There was no helicopter.

This can't be right. Frantic, she scanned the skies and the roof. *No chopper.* They were trapped up here with no place to go and Curtis closing in.

Sweet, carrot-top Curtis was the traitor. It made sense. He had access to all communication and could easily alert anyone to where they were and what plans had been made. Had he intercepted the texts from Nick's cell phone? Had he led them to this place?

"Sidney, where do we go?"

She didn't know what to tell Elena. Sidney wasn't supposed to be here. She wasn't part of the plan.

From the stairwell, she heard the ricochet of gunfire.

She stared at the Glock in her hand.

In her shooting lessons, she learned that she didn't have to release the safety on this model. All it took was a squeeze of the trigger. Though her hands were trembling, she was careful to hold the weapon so it wouldn't accidentally discharge.

Should she return to the staircase? Could she help

Nick? *Too many questions.* There wasn't time for her to examine the situation from every angle and come up with a rational conclusion. She needed to go with her instincts.

But she had no instinct when it came to battle. She imagined what Nick would tell her to do. He'd want her to fulfill the mission. Sidney shook off her panic. "This way, Elena."

Sure-footed in her high heels, Elena dashed onto the rooftop. "Where?"

"Over here." She pointed toward a metal vent that opened onto the roof. It was closer to the concrete circle for the heliport. "We'll hide behind this."

"Do you have another weapon?"

"No." Sidney was carrying her purse but was armed with nothing more lethal than a fingernail file. She didn't even have another ammunition clip for the gun. That meant she had only fourteen or fifteen rounds. Every bullet needed to count.

The door to the roof opened, and Nick dived through. He went to the left, found a ledge to hide behind and prepared to return fire. Sidney did the same, bracing her wrist and staring down the barrel. Her vision blurred. She shook her head and squinted hard. She wasn't much good at this, but Nick was a sharpshooter. All marines had high rankings in marksmanship, but he was better than most. He had an award for accuracy.

She hoped that would make a difference. Not that gunning down Curtis would get them home free. He had to be working with somebody else. There would be others with guns. They might be gathering right now, behind that door, waiting to swarm onto the rooftop.

A cold wind blew against her cheeks, causing her eyes to water. Sidney was trying her best to hold steady, but her fears multiplied by the second. Then she heard the most beautiful sound, the *thwhump-thwhump* of the helicopter blades.

"It's coming," Elena cried out. "The chopper."

The door from the hotel opened, and Curtis charged through. Two other armed men followed him. They were all bundled up in Kevlar vests while she and Elena wore flimsy skirts and dresses. Almost without aiming, Sidney fired a shot to let them know she meant business.

Nick fired twice. One of the men with Curtis went down, clutching his leg. The other two spread out. Curtis was closest to her.

He'd probably chosen his position strategically, knowing that she was inexperienced with weapons. She hated that he knew her well enough to make that judgment. During the time when they'd been talking in the surveillance room, she'd thought they were bonding and had so much in common. If she'd known his true character, she would have strangled him instead of giving him a neck massage.

The chopper was coming closer.

To Elena, she said, "As soon as the door opens, make a run for it."

"I don't want to leave you," she said. "Come with me."

"I will."

Jumping into the chopper seemed like the best way to get off the roof. Sidney didn't like the odds of surviving in a shootout, and she wasn't going to risk leaping off the roof onto the terrace swimming pool they'd seen two stories below.

The helicopter touched down with blades still circling. The side door swung open. Gunfire erupted from inside. A heavily armed man leaped out and rushed toward them.

Nick dodged across the roof, shooting as he came closer.

The man from the chopper grabbed Elena. Shielding her with his body, he carried her to safety. She was inside the helicopter.

Sidney tried to aim her weapon for one last shot before she ran to join Elena. But she couldn't see Curtis. She leaned out from behind the vent.

The gun was slapped from her hand. An arm circled her waist, pinning her arm to her side. She felt the bite of cold steel against the side of her neck. Curtis had her. She'd been caught.

"Don't move," he growled.

"No." She wouldn't go quietly. This was Curtis. He wasn't a big man. She could fight him.

Her free arm lashed out, and she hit his vest. She twisted in his grasp, struggling to free herself.

A blinding pain exploded on the right side of her face. Her head jerked back. For an instant, the world turned black. But she didn't pass out. Being unconscious would have been preferable to the throbbing hurt. My God, had he broken her jaw? She reached up and touched her face. Her fingers came back wet with blood. He'd hit her with his gun, hit her with force.

He yanked her upright. "Do what I say, and I won't kill you."

She wished she could have made a brave or clever response, but it was all she could do to stand without having her knees buckle. She'd never been hit by another person. There were injuries. Bumps and bruises from car accidents. Sports injuries. But never an assault. This was a new experience for her memory. She hoped it wasn't the last thing her brain recorded.

She looked across the roof at Nick. He stood facing them with his gun aimed at Curtis.

"Don't make me shoot her," Curtis yelled over the

noise of the helicopter. For emphasis, he poked his gun into her neck.

"Let her go."

"If you get Elena back down here, I'll let Sidney go."

"Not going to happen." Shoulder hunched, Nick kept moving. "Put down your gun, and I won't kill you."

"You won't take a chance," Curtis said. "You might hit Sidney."

"That was your last warning," Nick growled.

Curtis dragged her behind the vent. He exhaled a wheezing noise, almost as though he was crying. "Sorry, Sidney. This isn't personal."

"It feels real damn personal." The chopper lifted a few feet off the roof. She saw her chance for escape floating away. "Why are you doing this?"

"Money. I'm getting paid a lot."

"Who's paying you?"

"Unbelievable." He tapped the gun against her skull and scoffed. "You're trying to interrogate me. Don't you get it, Sidney? Game over. You lose."

"Whatever you're getting paid isn't worth it," she said. "Put down the gun."

"And spend the rest of my life in prison? That's not for me."

"You could get a deal." Was she actually trying to reason with a man who held a gun to her throat? "Please, Curtis. This isn't like one of your video games. When you die, you won't get a new set of bullets and a fresh start."

She looked down and saw red spatters of her blood smearing his sleeve. Each thud of her pulse drove home the pain. She wasn't crying, but her eyes watered.

Curtis leaned close. His breath was hot on her ear. "Do you really think Nick will kill me?"

"He's a marksman. You know that."

"I've heard. He's the kind of guy who can shoot the wings off a fly at fifty yards."

"Something like that," she said. "He trained with the SEALs."

Just then a shot whizzed by Curtis's head. A warning shot from Nick. The next one wouldn't miss.

"I'm sorry." Curtis, obviously realizing he had no choice, placed his gun on the rooftop. He raised his hands above his head and stood.

As soon as she was free, Sidney ran toward Nick. The pain was so intense that she felt nothing else. All she knew was that her legs were moving.

A spray of bullets exploded. She looked over her shoulder.

Curtis had been shot, not by Nick but by his own man. She heard herself cry out. She wanted to help him, to save him. But it was too late.

Nick grasped her arm and propelled her toward the chopper that had been circling. *Thwhump-thwhump*, the noise was overwhelming. She could see Elena through the door, beckoning her forward. The men in the chopper reached for them. Nick pushed her forward and someone caught her arm. They were pulled inside.

As the helicopter ascended, she looked down at the rooftop, where Curtis lay sprawled on his back. Dark blood circled his head. He shouldn't have had to die.

A DAY LATER, Sidney was still disoriented, maybe even more so. She and Nick had left the drab, rainy weather in Texas. They were on their way to their mountain retreat, the pot of gold at the end of the rainbow.

Bundled up in a brand-new parka and jeans, she leaned back in the passenger seat of an incredibly comfortable SUV and stared through the windshield at a clear, blue

Colorado sky above glistening, snowcapped peaks. Her jaw wasn't broken but the entire right side of her face was swollen and bruised, which meant that—once again—she was taking painkillers that didn't help with her mental clarity.

She glanced over at Nick, who seemed to know exactly where he was going and what he was doing. Smiling for no reason, he hummed along with a twangy tune from his never-ending country-and-western playlist. She surprised him by singing along on the chorus.

"Whoa," he said. "How did you learn that?"

"I worked as a barmaid at a saloon. I probably know more of these songs than you do."

"But do you love them?" he asked.

She was more drawn to the almost mathematical precision of classical music, but she had to admit that she loved the outright emotional sentiment of country-and-western songs.

Changing the subject, she said, "How'd you hear about this cabin?"

"I told you before."

"Yeah, well, my brain isn't really working at tip-top condition."

"No prob. All you have to do is sit there and look pretty."

She touched her bruise. "Like the bride of Frankenstein."

"The cabin belongs to a friend of a friend. It's a little two-bedroom on the edge of a national forest with good trails for cross-country skiing or snowmobiling. I brought enough food and wine to last us for a week."

"I don't care about food," she muttered. No way would she attempt chewing with her sore face. This time, the stitches were below her jawline. "Not unless it's ice cream or soup."

"You're lucky they didn't wire your mouth shut."

"Real lucky."

Though tired, she kept her eyes open. Whenever she dozed, her memory replayed on an endless loop. She saw Curtis dying on the rooftop over and over and over again. Nothing she could do to stop it. No way she could change fate.

"You're thinking about him," Nick said.

"He said he'd gotten a lot of money. I wish I knew who was paying him off."

"It's not our problem. I fulfilled my orders, which were to deliver Elena to the people who will protect her."

She cast a suspicious eye in his direction. "And who are those people?"

"The good guys," he said, purposely evasive.

"What's going to happen to her?"

"Again, it's not my problem. Elena needed to get out from under her husband's control, and we provided an escape. What happens now is up to her."

"But wouldn't you like to have all the details tied up in a neat little package with a bow on top?"

He shrugged. "Life isn't so tidy. We made a small step forward for the people of Tiquanna by rescuing their first lady. Though I'm not so sure they'll see it that way. But it's enough for me."

Something about his involvement in this whole situation bothered her, but she couldn't exactly figure out why. Maybe later. Or maybe not. They had a week for themselves, plenty of time to get their lives as an engaged couple back on track.

Nick followed GPS directions, turning off the highway into an old-growth forest where the road narrowed to a two-lane that climbed in hairpin turns. They crested the summit above the timberline for a panoramic view.

The pinkish tinge of sunset colored the cumulus clouds above the mountaintops.

She sighed at the sheer beauty of the landscape. Colorado was the place they would come to heal. What else could possibly go wrong?

Chapter Nineteen

After Nick got her settled on a plaid, overstuffed sofa and built a cheery fire, he unloaded their luggage and food. Their escape off the rooftop in the chopper meant they had to leave all their belongings behind. Sooner or later, those things might be returned to them after the CIA had the chance to study each garment and toothbrush. He didn't really care. Except for the engagement ring, which she'd been wearing, the rest of it was just stuff.

He wasn't sure what part all the different people had played in Elena's rescue but was informed that his future liaison would be Special Agent Sean Phillips, who was acceptable to both the CIA and the elite Marine Corps Undercover Intelligence Agency, MCUIA, that had initially sent Nick to South America. His highly classified group trained with the SEALs and was deployed on special missions with wide-ranging responsibilities. They had no office, no meetings and no real chain of command.

When Nick first started working for MCUIA, he thought of himself as a spy among spies. His missions were clandestine, and he reported to no one. If he was found out, he was on his own without backup, and he liked the loner aspect.

Not anymore.

As he tiptoed across the front room of the cabin to

the kitchen, he looked down at Sidney. Her eyes were closed, but he doubted she was sleeping. The brutal death of Curtis affected her deeply. She wasn't the kind of person who bounced back and returned to battle in the blink of an eye.

He regretted her involvement. Her poor face was badly bruised, and she'd been shot. If he could have taken the pain for her, he would have. Her injuries were his fault. The danger of his life had boiled over, and she'd gotten burned. This wasn't the way he wanted to live.

Not anymore.

She deserved better, and so did he. They ought to be able to build a satisfying life, to have kids and a garden and a collie dog named Rex. He was done with spying, being surrounded by people he couldn't trust, holding on to secrets that didn't matter to him.

As soon as Sidney was feeling better, he'd tell her about his real job. She wasn't going to like the fact that he'd kept things from her. She was all about truth and trust.

After he put away their clothing, he turned up the propane heater in the bedroom and made the bed with extra blankets to ward off the night chill. His cell phone buzzed.

He answered, "I didn't think I'd get reception here."

"Sorry about that," said Special Agent Phillips in his Texan drawl. "How are you and Sidney doing?"

Phillips was a friendly guy, but he hadn't called to check on the state of their health, and Nick didn't have the patience to chat. "What do you need?"

"Elena and Avilar want to meet with y'all."

Nick glared at the phone. He truly cared for Elena Hurtado and believed that her intervention had probably saved his life when he was a hostage. But this had to end. "When?"

"Tomorrow at noon. They'll come to you."

"Not here," Nick said. "I want our cabin to be private."

"And were you thinking that your little hideaway is secret and untraceable?"

In a world filled with GPS satellites, surveillance cameras, drones and liars on every corner, Nick had no illusions about disappearing. If someone wanted to find him, they could. "Hell, you're right. Send them here."

"And there's one more thing you should know." Phillips cleared his throat. "Hawthorne's gone off the grid."

"Not working for the CIA anymore?"

"She hightailed it out of Austin when Curtis was shot. We don't have all the pieces put together, but I'm going to go ahead and assume that the two of them were working together."

"Who was paying them?"

"That part, I don't know."

"What a shame that she's gone, flown off on her broom." Nick grinned. "Are you going to miss her?"

"Like a bad case of the flu."

"What about Hurtado?"

"The president is still in Austin, still chatting up the executives from Underwood Oil. The politicians are putting distance between themselves and the current government of Tiquanna, but the money people have already made some commitments."

Diplomacy and deal making were two parts of the job that Nick could do very well without. "Good luck with all the crazy people."

"I'm going to need it."

In the front room of the cabin, Nick considered what Phillips had said about the lack of privacy. A certain amount of danger came in the aftermath of his assignments. He needed to make sure that he and Sidney would be safe. Tomorrow morning, he'd set up some basic protections.

Firelight shone on Sidney's face as she opened her eyes and looked up at him. "Who were you talking to?"

"Phillips." He sat on the coffee table next to the sofa and took her slender hands in his. "How are you feeling?"

"My stomach is growling, but I don't think I can chew anything without busting into tears."

He smoothed her straight blond hair and kissed her forehead. "I'll heat up soup. Chowder or tomato?"

"Tomato with crackers broken up in it."

Taking care of her made him feel warm inside. It was a different kind of heat from the sensual fire when they kissed or when his hands slid over her sweet, soft skin. This gentle glow felt innocent, almost pure. This was the kind of warmth that lasted.

She tried to smile. Instead, she winced and put her hand to her cheek. "What did Phillips have to say?"

"We're going to have visitors tomorrow. Elena and Miguel Avilar."

"How does this work with the CIA? How can they be friendly with both Hurtado and Avilar when they're on opposite sides?"

She was still trying to figure out who were the good guys and who were the bad. In politics and in spycraft, those answers changed without logic or reason. Truth was ephemeral. Loyalty was nearly nonexistent. "Don't try to figure it out in your condition. It'll just make your head hurt."

"Elena and Miguel seem like a, um, nice couple."

"Sure they are," he said, "if you ignore the fact that he

sometimes blows up helicopters and she has ambitions
to rule the world."

She exhaled a sigh. "I'm glad we're not them. We
don't have secrets."

He was going to have to tell her. All he could do was
hope that she'd forgive him.

THE NEXT MORNING, Sidney took her time waking up. She'd
cut back on her pain meds enough that she could distinguish three separate centers of hurt. The one on her jaw
where Curtis hit her with the butt of his gun was the
worst, and the bruising looked like hell. No amount of
makeup would cover the purple fading to a sickly yel-
lowish color. The stitches also hurt. And there was the
continual light drumming of a headache.

At least her hunger pangs had faded. She'd lost some
weight, not that she could tell from the fit of her new
clothes. All she'd worn since they left Austin were shape-
less sweatpants and turtlenecks. And today she'd be seeing the perfect Elena. That should be enough to slash
her self-confidence to ribbons. Sidney decided that her
big project for the day would be to get out of bed and
get dressed.

Step one: out of bed. She flung her legs over the edge,
took a moment to stabilize when she was standing and
went to the window. Last night, it had snowed, and the
surrounding hillsides were crusted with glistening white.
Such a beautiful setting. Being here was exactly what
she needed.

Nick came into the bedroom with a tray of oatmeal.
"Morning, sunshine."

She pointed to her mouth. "Imagine that I'm giving
you a great big smile."

"There are a couple of other things I'd like to imagine your mouth doing."

"Don't make me laugh."

"Where do you want your oatmeal?"

"The kitchen?"

"There's a little something I want to try in the bedroom first." He set down the tray on top of the dresser and guided her toward the bed. "I can't keep my hands off you."

"No kissing," she said.

"None for you," he murmured. "There's nothing wrong with my jaw."

Not with his jaw or his lips or his tongue. He lowered her onto her back on the bed and kissed the hollow below her chin. While she was distracted by the ripples of sensation that spread from each kiss, he unbuttoned the top of her pajamas to bare her breasts.

As gentle as rain, he kissed her tender flesh. His caresses were pure tenderness. Her response was all out of proportion. Her heart pumped too fast. She gasped. Her face throbbed.

"I don't want you to stop." She moaned. "But you have to stop. I could have a heart attack."

He rose quickly from the bed, and she missed him.

"As soon as you're ready," he said.

"I am," she said miserably. "But I'm not."

"Oatmeal first."

She followed him down the hallway and past the front room, where a fire flickered on the hearth. He placed the tray on the kitchen table and sat. "Is it better for you to move around or stay in bed?"

"I'm not sure." She was one of those people who never got sick. It had been only a couple of days, but she felt as if she'd been wiped out forever. She settled herself at the kitchen table and scowled. "I hate being an invalid."

"I like taking care of you, watching you while you're sleeping. It feels peaceful."

She dug her spoon into the oatmeal, took a bite and turned her gaze on him. "I'm just beginning to figure out that you haven't had much peace in your life. Right after college, you enlisted. Since then, you've been a soldier."

"That wasn't long after nine-eleven," he said. "Being a marine seemed like the right thing to do. No regrets."

There were few things in her life that she'd felt so certain about. She envied his decisive nature. "Today, I'm going to get dressed. Maybe even take a walk."

"No rush. I talked to your office before we left Austin, and your boss said you should take all the time you need."

"You talked to my boss?" She dipped her spoon into the oatmeal. "What did you tell him?"

"Just a quick recap. You'd been shot by terrorists, stayed in a CIA safe house and escaped off the roof of a hotel in a chopper."

She imagined the head of engineering at Texas Triton going into shock. "Did he believe you?"

"I actually told him you'd been injured and needed a little time to recuperate. I thought you should entertain the gang at the office with the tales of Sidney Parker."

"That'll be fun. Anything I can't say, you know, because of national security?"

"Don't use real names," he advised.

"But how can I talk about Hurtado and Elena without saying who they are?"

"It gets complicated, doesn't it?"

She finished her breakfast, took a leisurely bath and got dressed in a pair of black jeans, hiking boots and a sweater. By the time she and Nick took a short walk along the road outside the cabin, it was approaching the time when Elena and Miguel would arrive.

Sidney was content to sit at the kitchen table and watch while Nick put together a plate of sliced cheese and sausage and crackers. She reached for a cracker. "What else have you got for me?"

"Yogurt with blueberries."

"Yum."

With his sweater pushed up to his elbows, she could see the interplay of muscles in his forearms and the efficient movements of his large masculine hands. She remembered the skill and creativity in those hands when he made love to her. Oh yeah, she was definitely on the road to recovery. Maybe tonight…

The former first lady of Tiquanna and her companion arrived with zero fanfare in a black SUV. With her luxurious black hair pulled up in a simple ponytail, Elena looked almost like a regular person, except that her knee-high black leather boots were high-heeled, and her parka was lined with faux fur that was as thick and shiny as mink.

Avilar trailed behind her. He carried a briefcase and a laptop, which he placed on the kitchen table in front of Sidney. Apparently, they weren't going to waste any time on niceties. Elena was a woman with a purpose. When she sat at the table, Sidney felt energy and ambition radiating from her.

"This isn't a social visit," Sidney said.

"So much has happened so quickly." Elena glanced up at Nick. "There was a question you asked dozens of times, a question that didn't seem to have an answer."

He gave a curt nod. "Where did the rebels get their money and their weapons?"

She looked to Avilar. "Tell him."

"My family," he said. "When my father left Tiquanna, he had amassed a fortune. The same was true for my uncles and my cousins."

"Money that you failed to report," Nick said.

"Yes." His jaw tightened. "With offshore accounts and other investments, my family's wealth is nearly untraceable. We needed it all, every peso, to finance the rebellion and take our country back from Hurtado."

"Why keep it secret?" Sidney asked.

"Two reasons," Nick explained. "The first has to do with taxes and international monetary policies that are far too complex for me to comprehend or explain. The second, and more important reason, is perception. The rebels of Tiquanna wouldn't want to be recruited into another rich man's army. Avilar wanted to appear as one of them."

"They believed in me," he said. "And I didn't fail them. With Elena at my side, we can still take back our country."

Sidney could tell that Nick was angry. He had expected more transparency from Avilar.

"There is another source of money," Elena said. "I believe Sidney can tell us where it comes from."

They turned expectantly toward her, but she wasn't sure she wanted to play this game. If she helped them, where would it lead? When would it end?

Chapter Twenty

Nick saw Sidney's hesitation. He wanted to get out of the espionage business, not to be drawn deeper in. "Stop right there, Elena."

"Why?" She spread her hands wide in appeal. "Surely you want to help us."

"I expect you'll be a better leader than Hurtado," Nick said. After the time he'd spent with Elena in Tiquanna, he knew she wanted schools and roads, clean water and medical facilities for her people. Her heart was in the right place, but she wasn't a saint. She also wanted wealth and power. "I don't want to be part of setting off a civil war. Your country is a powder keg about to explode. People will be hurt."

"People already have been hurt," Sidney said. "Curtis is dead. He was prepared to surrender, and he was shot."

"All I ask," Elena said, "is for Sidney to use her expertise."

One little favor. That was how it started. Nick knew better than to get Sidney involved. "Find another way."

"Wait a minute." Sidney gestured to the documents and the laptop that Avilar had set on the table. "If all I have to do is interpret some statistics, I can handle that."

"So can dozens of other people," Nick said. "Elena needs to start building her own connections in the field of oil exploration. If she needs to use you, she should go through your company."

"There isn't time. Please," Elena pleaded. "My husband is already in bed with Underwood Oil. The meetings in Austin are continuing. By the time he returns to Tiquanna, there may be final agreements."

"How can you stop them?" Nick asked.

"By showing the prior surveys and projections are invalid," Sidney said. "From the very start, I wondered about Underwood's enthusiasm. When Texas Triton checked out Tiquanna, we decided it wouldn't be profitable without significant investment from Hurtado on the infrastructure."

"Please, Sidney. You're the only one who can help," Elena said. "Do you remember those original figures?"

"I remember everything."

Sidney sat up straighter in her chair. Her injuries had weakened her, but she was still ready to respond to a challenge. Nick hoped she wasn't opening a can of worms.

She took a folder from the briefcase. "Give me some time and space to go through this stuff."

Nick shepherded Elena and Miguel outside onto the porch of the cabin. The skies were clear and the temperature rising. It was one of those brilliant Colorado days that hid the potential for danger. Snowfall had been heavy for this early in the winter season, and there was a solid base under eighteen to twenty-four inches of new snow at the top.

Earlier, he'd surveyed the area, determining how best to protect their cabin. Though sheltered by forest, the little one-story house faced a steep, open slope. A blast of gunfire into the air might trigger an avalanche. He hoped he wouldn't need to resort to that tactic.

On the porch, Elena confronted him. "Why do you oppose me?"

"You're my friend. I want the best for you." He glanced at Avilar. "I'm not so sure of you, but if she trusts you, I'm willing to forget our differences in the past."

She braced her fists on her hips and tossed her head. The woman just couldn't help posturing. Sidney referred to Elena as a diva, and that description was accurate.

Elena snapped, "You tried to get Sidney to say no."

"I'm getting out of the political game," he said. "I don't want anything more to do with it. I'm neutral. Call me Switzerland."

She lowered her voice. "You will no longer be a spy."

"No more." He owed Sidney that much.

"We suspect Special Agent Gregory of being involved with Underwood Oil. He has disappeared. I wouldn't be surprised if he's already in Tiquanna."

That made two on the run: Gregory and Hawthorne. Gregory didn't worry Nick much. The guy was a pencil pusher, looking for a safe place to hide. But Hawthorne was unpredictable. She'd lost status, control and position. At this point, she had to be desperate.

"Will you two return to Tiquanna?" he asked.

"Not until it's safe," she said. "Miguel's family has offered to protect me, and I have many contacts in the US."

She would build her power base here, a smart move. He had no doubt that Elena would land on her feet. In a few years, she might be running the show in Tiquanna.

"And you?" she asked. "What are your plans?"

"First thing," he said, "a border collie named Rex."

SIDNEY PICKED OUT enough data from the surveys and charts they'd brought to indicate areas where further study might be needed. Some of the issues were highly technical and would require the type of thorough research done in development. Others were obvious mistakes.

"Mileage," she said as she pointed to a map. "The distance between the drilling field and the processing facility is twice what's indicated, which means that the cost will be double the estimate. It wouldn't hurt to check all the roads. And estimate the need for freshwater."

"Infrastructure," Elena said.

"Exactly." Sidney refolded documents. "Tiquanna is a beautiful country rich in resources, but it is largely undeveloped. Not to mention there are many restrictions about maintaining the natural rain forest."

"Hurtado has done a poor job," Avilar said.

"And you have a chance to do it right." Sidney met his dark-eyed gaze. "I'd advise you to seek the opinions of experts in the US and around the world. When I was in Tiquanna, I noticed that the main requirement for being appointed to a political position was being loyal to the dictator."

"It's true," Elena said. "We need educated advisers. Instead of rushing into expensive mistakes, we need to be wise."

"You're already a step ahead," Nick said. "You know people who can be trusted."

The diva pulled an exaggerated frown. "I wish the two of you would join us."

"Only as tourists," he said.

After Elena and Miguel drove away in their SUV, Sidney sat on the porch with a mug of steaming coffee in her hands. The afternoon sun reflected off the snowy slope and warmed her injured face. In her puffy green parka, she felt comfy and cozy. But not contented.

Too many issues had arisen during the past few days. Just as Elena and Miguel needed answers, Sidney had persistent questions. And Nick was the only one who could answer them.

He joined her on the porch. On the wood table between their two rocking chairs, he set down the plate of cheese and crackers. She picked up a flavorful sesame cracker and let it dissolve in her mouth.

"By tomorrow," she said, "I should graduate to soft food."

"Mashed peas and pudding?"

"Disgusting," she grumbled.

"Warm enough?"

"I'm fine. I like being out here." She didn't want to be angry at Nick, but she couldn't keep ignoring these questions, these voices in her head. "I think I did the right thing by giving that information to Elena. All I really did was point out the truth."

"But now it's over," he said. "I don't want her or Avilar to get the idea that you're working for them."

She nodded. "You're right. They need their own experts and advisers. Not me. And not you, either."

"Nope."

"When you told Elena she already knew people she could trust, were you talking about your handlers?"

"Yes." He was terse.

Technically, she'd met his superiors. When she was scooped off the rooftop in the chopper, Sidney had entered Nick's world. There were men dressed like SWAT officers, people shouting orders into headsets and a medical person. She wished she'd been more alert. Everything was a frantic blur of action, pain and the constant *thwhump-thwhump* of the blades. The painkillers had pretty much knocked her unconscious. "Who were they?"

"Is this one of those good-guy-or-bad-guy questions?"

"No, I'm sure they were good guys. They helped us.

And they didn't fire the bullet that killed Curtis." That was important to her. She hated that he'd been gunned down before he had a chance to change his mind. "There were a lot of them."

"Mostly marines," he said.

"Would it help me understand if I knew their names or job titles?"

"Probably not."

He was dancing around the issue, trying to keep from telling her anything, but this time she wouldn't be easily assuaged. This time, she would pin him down.

She paused for a moment, organizing her thoughts.

"Here's the thing, Nick. I really don't understand what you do. I know you're an ace marksman. And I know that you're given orders that must be followed. But I don't know who you're working for."

"I could say the same about you and your work."

"What?" She turned her head so quickly that her jaw hurt. "There's nothing mysterious about my job."

"You seldom talk about it."

"My projects are detail-oriented and, if you aren't familiar with the technology, you'd be bored to death with an explanation. Nobody wants to hear the various processes that make the engine in their car work. They just want to turn the key and have the ignition start."

"I could say the same."

"And I wouldn't believe you." She stared down into her coffee. "There's a reason you aren't telling me. You're keeping secrets. I saw it in your eyes when we met at CIA headquarters. You don't trust me."

"Oh, hell, no. That's not even close."

"Why else would you lie to me?"

She could feel their relationship coming apart. Huge

chunks broke off and floated away. Had he lied when they first met? Were any of his assignments the truth?

"Not lies," he said.

"Were you in Afghanistan when you told me you were?"

"Most of the time."

But not always. "Were you assigned to an embassy in Paris?"

"No."

"What about Cuba?" she demanded. "Did you go to Cuba?"

"Yes."

"I don't want to sort through our life, picking out what's true and what's not." She surged to her feet. "Tell me your job, Nick. What the hell do you do?"

He stood to face her. "I'm a field officer in the Marine Corps Undercover Intelligence, trained with the navy SEALs. My assignments are highly classified, covert and undercover. I have only one handler. Other than that person, I work alone."

"So…a spy."

"I think of my work as research, gathering intel."

"Why were you really in Tiquanna?"

"I knew I'd be taken hostage, but I didn't expect to be gone for more than a month."

Rage flared inside her. "You knew and you didn't tell me? You put me through hell."

"I wouldn't do that to you." His voice was sincere but his intentions meant nothing. "There have been other times when I didn't contact you for as much as a week."

"So what?"

"You weren't supposed to hear about the hostage situation. I was supposed to get in and get out. I needed to infiltrate the rebels and find out where they were getting their weapons. Something went wrong. Instead of hanging around with Avilar's crew, Hurtado's men took over. The hostage situation and the beatings turned real. I had no escape."

The level of danger in his work was extreme. If she'd known, she would have worried about him night and day. "So, everybody lied."

He reached toward her. "I didn't want you to be upset."

She slapped his hand away. "Why would you take such a risk?"

"I'm careful. I know how to interrogate and negotiate. I have all the skills."

"And you love the work," she said.

In a horrible way, she understood why a man like Nick would thrive on this kind of challenge. If they were walking down the street and he saw a house on fire, he'd run *toward* the flames and try to rescue the people inside. He was smart and strong and brave. He'd been trained to penetrate behind enemy lines.

She turned her back on him. Suddenly cold, she returned to the house and stood in front of the dying embers of the fire. Nick was the sort of man she admired. He was everything a woman could dream about...a real-life hero.

And she couldn't marry him. She couldn't live with that kind of fear, knowing that he was putting his life on the line. Was it really so different from being a soldier? Yes, it was. In Nick's line of work, he had no backup, no one else he could turn to. And the threat was constant. If he was found out, he'd be killed as quickly as Curtis was shot down on the rooftop.

She couldn't endure the ever-present danger.

She knew what she must do.

"I shouldn't have told you," he said from behind her.

"By all means, keep lying to me." She huffed. "You know how I love that."

"It's over, Sidney." He stepped up close behind her. "Tiquanna was my last field assignment. I won't be going undercover anymore. My focus will be research."

She whipped around to face him. "Desk work?"

He gave a quick, curt nod. "I'm ready to settle down."

"Are you making this change because of me? Because we're getting married?" She took a few angry steps away from him and then back again. "I won't have it. I won't have you blaming me for quitting the work you love."

"It's my decision," he said. "I can't do this anymore."

Nor could she. Sidney was done with his elaborate deceptions. She knew he could never change. And she wouldn't force him to. But there would be no desk job in his future and she couldn't live like that. She tore the pi diamond off her finger and slapped it into his hand.

"Goodbye, Nick."

Chapter Twenty-One

Sidney adjusted the seat in the SUV, fastened her seat belt and drove away from the cabin. She hadn't packed her suitcase and didn't have any idea of her destination. She knew only that she had to put miles between herself and Captain Nick Corelli or else she would shatter into a million pieces that could never be put together again.

She didn't want to hear his rumbling baritone voice, speaking excuses that she would never believe. It was all lies, every word he spoke. She could never trust him again.

She couldn't bear to see his thick black hair or to look into his golden eyes or to bask in the heat of his smile. Touching him was out of the question.

Her fingers drew into a fist, and she hammered on the dashboard. "You can't change who you are." He would always be a hero. And she would always miss him.

It was over, well and truly over. The past six months had taught her what it was to live without him. She'd survive. She'd be miserable and lonely and painfully depressed. She'd want to curl up and die, but it wouldn't happen.

She drove along the twisting two-lane road into the forest and cut the engine. She was about two miles from the cabin, far enough that he couldn't see her. *Where am*

I going? What am I doing? She was still taking painkill-ers, shouldn't be operating a vehicle. As if that was a big risk? Nick routinely lived with more danger before break-fast than she experienced in a year.

She threw back her head and screamed as loudly as she could. The local wildlife would cover their ears and run away. Birds would drop from the trees. She screamed again.

Her throat vibrated. Her gut clenched.

Before leaving, she hadn't made any kind of plan with Nick, hadn't said she was going for a little drive and would be right back. Maybe she wouldn't return. She had her purse, her credit cards and her brand-new cell phone. Maybe she should point the SUV due west and keep driving until she hit the Pacific Ocean. Hawaii would be pleasant at this time of year.

She started the SUV and drove again, swooping above the timberline and then descending on the hairpin turns. It was darker on the shadowed side of the mountain, but there were a couple of hours to go before dusk.

At the edge of the forest, she hit the brake. Another SUV had pulled off on the side of the road. Elena and Miguel's car? Their front wheel was in a ditch. Had there been an accident?

Parked behind them, she climbed out of her car and gingerly approached. "Elena? Are you all right?"

The back window was shattered. Bullet holes pierced the rear fender. Both back tires were flat. The air bags had deployed in the front seats.

Sidney darted back to her car and dived behind the wheel. This was no accident. Elena and Miguel had been attacked. She yanked her cell phone from her purse. Call 9-1-1. That was the sane, sensible thing to do. Alert the police and get a search under way.

Her fingers hesitated above the phone. They had a better chance of survival if she called Nick. She hated what he did, but she'd be a fool to deny it.

His cell number was the only one on speed dial, and she tapped the number. Nick would know how to locate Elena and Miguel. He'd make sure they were all right.

She felt the impact of the first bullet hitting the back of the SUV at the same time she heard gunfire. She didn't think twice before throwing her SUV into gear, whipping a U-turn and heading back toward the cabin. Her only option was to run.

"Sidney?" His voice came over the phone. "Sidney, what's going on?"

She barked at the phone. "Elena and Miguel's SUV is in a ditch and all shot up. Somebody's chasing me."

"Where are you?"

"Not far. About six miles from the cabin at the twisty part of the road."

The back window exploded inward. She let out a scream.

"Sidney." His voice was harsh. "Sidney, concentrate."

She dropped the phone on the passenger-side seat. "I didn't fasten my seat belt."

"Don't worry about that now. Drive as fast as you can. Don't stop for anything."

Her foot tromped the accelerator. The SUV fishtailed around a curve but stayed on the road. Another bullet clanged against the side of the car.

Her hands gripped the steering wheel. Every muscle in her body was tense. "I'm scared, Nick."

"Keep driving. Don't stop for anything."

Finally, she hit an open stretch of road where she might be able to put distance between her SUV and the pursuers. She glanced in her rearview mirror. It was a blue truck behind her. Someone leaned out of the passenger-side window brandishing a rifle.

More bullets smacked against the back of her vehicle. If she got to the summit of this hill, there was only a stretch of forest and then she'd be in the open field beside the cabin. She wasn't far, really. She might make it.

Her back tire was hit. The SUV wobbled, nearly out of control. She fought to keep it on the road. "Nick, they're shooting the tires."

"Keep going. You can make it."

In the thickly forested part of the route, she struggled to stay on the road. Her other tire was gone. She yanked the steering wheel.

The air bag deployed with a loud pop. The ignition died. These damn safety devices were killing her.

She fought her way free from the white powdery explosion, crawled across to the passenger side and shoved open the door. She grabbed the phone. "Nick, I'm on foot. In the forest."

She shoved the phone into the pocket of her parka. If he needed to track her later, he could use the GPS signal. *Why do I know that? Why do I have that knowledge at my fingertip?* Because I'm engaged to a spy. Not anymore, she corrected herself. That relationship was over. Or not…it might be best to postpone the breakup until after she'd escaped from whatever international criminals were trying to kill her.

She dashed into the forest. Her boots left clear tracks in the snow. It wouldn't be hard to find her or hunt her down like an animal.

"Give up, Sidney. You must be exhausted."

Hawthorne! She should have known that she wasn't through with that woman.

"Let's not waste time chasing each other. Especially

since I know Nick isn't with you. You really don't have a chance."

Why wasn't she in pursuit? Probably because she didn't know if Sidney had a gun. It wouldn't hurt to bluff. She yelled back, "Don't come any closer. I'll shoot."

"You've never actually shot another human being, have you?"

"You'd be my first, Hawthorne."

Sidney charged deeper into the forest but kept the road in sight. If she somehow managed to escape, she didn't want to be lost in the vast lands of the national forest.

When she looked over her shoulder, she saw the shadowy silhouette of a tall man coming after her. "Stop," she yelled at him. "I'll shoot."

He kept coming. She had nothing to protect herself, and there seemed to be no point in resisting. In a matter of minutes, he had yanked her hands behind her back and fastened her wrists with a zip tie.

She looked into his face. "You're one of Hurtado's guards. How could you leave him unprotected?"

"The president is safe," he said.

Hawthorne stepped forward. "And I needed the assistance of his guard."

Her hair was tucked up inside a black knit cap. She wore a black parka and matching pants with no discernible style. She gave the guard a friendly smile. Apparently, her style of leadership was different with the men of Tiquanna. Sidney didn't think she'd ever seen Special Agent Victoria Hawthorne grin at her CIA cohorts.

This was Vicky. Not Victoria. "You're different."

"How clever of you to notice! This is where I was meant to be, living my passion. I was always stifled in the CIA, dealing with all those petty bureaucrats. In Tiquanna, I'll flourish."

If she believed that, she was seriously delusional. Sidney figured there were lots of agencies waiting to press charges against Hawthorne for all kinds of treason and espionage. "You always looked happier when you talked about Tiquanna."

"Of course, I did." She beamed. "Tomas Hurtado is my lover."

Sidney wasn't sure what that meant for her, and especially for Elena. But she assumed Hawthorne's new relationship with the dictator wasn't good news.

THAT MORNING, NICK had taken the time to explore the cabin and prepare for danger in case he needed to protect Sidney. Though he planned to quit his undercover work, old habits die hard. And his preparations were turning out to be necessary.

On the snowmobile he'd found in the shed behind the cabin, he sped across the open field toward the forest. Hoping against the odds, he desperately wished that he'd see Sidney and the SUV emerge onto the main road. No such luck.

He couldn't take the snowmobile much farther. It made too much noise. He'd alert whoever had grabbed her and attacked Miguel and Elena. His first guess was that Hawthorne was behind this attack. He didn't know why, but he figured she was playing out some twisted agenda to get herself back into power.

At the forest's edge, he abandoned the snowmobile and grabbed a set of snowshoes. Using these, he could quickly and silently move through the trees. In addition to the long-range rifle slung over his shoulder, he carried two handguns.

As soon as he heard voices, he dumped the snowshoes. His primary objective now was to move silently. He came into sight of Hawthorne, a bodyguard and Sidney with her wrists fastened behind her back.

Hidden in the trees, he was in control of this situation. With two quick gunshots, he could take out Hawthorne and her man. But if he shot them down in cold blood, Sidney would never forgive him. And it wasn't the way he wanted to operate.

Nick wasn't a killer. There were other undercover guys who were assassins, pure and simple. That had never been his thing. He was more of an analyst. His goal in this situation would be to protect Sidney and take the other two into custody.

Hawthorne was talking in a strangely animated voice. "At first, when I'm in the presidential compound, my presence will be clandestine and secret. Tomas and I will share the sultry tropical nights and the brilliant sunlight."

"Has this affair been going on for a long time?" Sidney asked.

"Over a year." Hawthorne chuckled. "Right under Elena's nose. Her husband preferred me to her with all her fancy designer clothes and costly jewelry. He wanted a real woman."

"You've got it all figured out," Sidney said.

"It might take a while to get right with the CIA, but I'll get all my pardons in order. And the oil will be flowing from Tiquanna. And Tomas will be the leader of one of the richest and more powerful nations in South America."

Nick had heard enough. Clearly, Hawthorne was whacked-out. No way would Hurtado protect her. Once he'd gotten the oil contracts he needed, Hawthorne would be tossed aside like last week's old news.

Anticipating her moves, Nick got into position. Somehow, he needed to make sure Sidney was out of the line of fire, deal with the hulking bodyguard and disarm the crazy lady. And if that failed, he could always shoot Hawthorne.

He dodged through the trees until he was standing closest to the driver's-side door. The bodyguard reached for the door handle. Nick waited. Timing was everything.

Then he stepped back into the forest. Someone else was approaching. He heard the vehicle. A beat-up sedan parked behind the truck. The three men who got out were dressed in camouflage and looked like hunters. They reported to Hawthorne.

Nick should have known that Special Agent Hawthorne would need an army at her command. She wasn't the kind of person to handle a single-person operation. Her backup would have backup.

A young blond man said, "No luck. We still can't find the woman."

"She didn't disappear into thin air," Hawthorne snapped. "Didn't you see those high-heeled boots she was wearing? How could she get away from you?"

"Her boyfriend was laying down some pretty serious gunfire. We couldn't get too close."

"Elena is the one I really want," Hawthorne said. "The rest of them are collateral damage."

Nick wished he'd taken the shot at her when he had the chance. Now he had to deal with more armed men and a widespread operation.

Chapter Twenty-Two

Sidney jostled along in the backseat of the sedan with one
guard keeping a casual watch over her. With her wrists
zip-tied behind her back, she felt vulnerable, but it was
clear that she wasn't important as a hostage, nothing but
collateral damage, as Hawthorne had said, in her crazy
vendetta against Elena.

Vicky Hawthorne hadn't ever been a warm, thoughtful,
kind person. The only glimmer of humanity came when
she spoke of Tomas Hurtado, her dictator lover. Now she
was completely ruled by her desire for vengeance.

Elena had caused her trouble. It wasn't difficult to be
jealous of that gorgeous woman, but Elena's affront to
Hawthorne was personal. Hurtado had loved Elena and
married her. She would always have a place in his heart,
no matter how hard Hawthorne tried to erase her.

Sidney wondered if her memory would haunt Nick's
life. Would the women who came after her be curious?
Sidney had wanted to know about his other women. In
the interest of full disclosure, they'd talked about former
lovers. Had he been telling her the truth?

She wanted to ask him. Their relationship couldn't really be over. There were too many loose ends. All she'd
done was storm off in a huff. She wanted another chance.

The three men in the car with her were talking about

dinner and how much they were getting paid for this job. It sounded as if they'd been recruited from the local population. This was a quick way to make extra bucks.

Their job was to return to the crash site for Elena's SUV and start searching again.

The young man beside her nudged her shoulder. "What happened to your face?"

"It ran into the butt of somebody's gun."

He gave an appreciative snort. In spite of his beard, he looked young. "Are you a spy like Vicky?"

"I'm an engineer. I work for an oil company."

Apparently, her job wasn't exciting enough for him to pay attention because he turned away. Fine with her. She wished she could make herself small enough and insignificant enough that they'd forget she was here.

When they parked behind the SUV with exploded air bags, she thought that was exactly what would happen. All the guys got out of the car and started talking about which way they should go to search. She ducked down in the seat and prayed that they'd forget she was here.

The bearded guy who had been sitting beside her poked his head into the backseat. "We didn't forget about you."

He picked her up, carried her around the car and dumped her in the trunk. There was nothing pleasant about riding in a trunk, especially since this one stank of oily rags and junk that had been tossed and forgotten. Like her. Tossed and forgotten.

She wriggled around, trying to find something she could use to cut the zip tie. There was a crowbar. No sharp edges on that tool. A Phillips screwdriver might work.

From outside the trunk, she heard Hawthorne giving orders on how to search in quadrants. The door to her truck slammed. Sidney heard it drive away. The voices of the young men faded as they set out on their search.

The stale air in the trunk settled around her. It was quiet. And cold, her hands were cold. The swollen bruise on her face hurt.

Then she heard someone fiddling with the lock on the trunk. Had the young men come back? Had they already found Elena? Her muscles tensed.

"Sidney, it's me. Don't say anything."

"Nick?" This was a miracle. "How did you…"

"Quiet," he said.

The trunk lid popped open. He reached inside, lifted her out and sat her on the snowy road behind the car. He closed the trunk and ducked down beside her. "Stay down so they won't see us."

"Get this zip tie off me."

He pulled a fierce-looking knife, scrrated on one side, from a sheath and cut the tie. Her arms wrapped around him. She never wanted to let go. "How did you find me?"

"I hitched a ride in the back of Hawthorne's truck." He held her close. His lips nuzzled behind her ear. "We need to get out of here."

"How?"

"We've got a perfectly good car right here."

"Do you know how to hot-wire a car?"

"Yeah, I do. But it's hard with newer models, almost impossible. And not necessary." He dangled the keys in front of her. "Our boys aren't any too bright. They left the keys in the ignition. That's how I got you out of the trunk."

She dashed around to the passenger side and climbed in. As they drove away, she saw one of the young men in camo running after the car. "What do we do now?"

"This isn't the kind of single-person op I usually handle. There's nothing wrong with calling in backup." He passed her his cell phone. "Special Agent Phillips is number two on speed dial. Call him and bring him up to speed."

"And where are we going?"

"We could keep driving all the way to Denver and wait for this to blow over. Or we could get a room in Vail. Or we can do a little reconnaissance and see if we can find Hawthorne's hideout."

"I want to look for Hawthorne."

"You're sure?"

She couldn't bear the thought of Hawthorne hurting Elena and Miguel if she could help. "Don't get me wrong. I'm not a secret agent, but I'm loyal to my friends. If I can help Elena, I want to try."

"That's how you get hooked in," he said. "You make one attempt to help. Then another. Then you're stationed in Tiquanna pretending to be a hostage."

Helping Elena was pretty much the opposite of the stance Sidney had taken when she broke the engagement and ran away. Didn't she accuse him of being a liar in a nest of liars? Didn't she say she couldn't live with that sort of constant deception?

She exhaled a sigh. There would be time enough for apologies later.

Nick headed in the direction he'd seen the blue truck going. Tracking through unmarked roads in the national forest was like following a maze. Some routes led to developments. Others circled around and were dead ends.

After Sidney got off the phone with Phillips, he said, "Look for roads with recent tracks through the snow. And see if you can spot the truck."

She glanced out the window. "We don't have a lot of daylight left. What makes you think she's got a hideout?"

"She left Miguel somewhere. He wasn't with the guys in this car and wasn't in the truck."

"So she must have more men and a place where she's holding him."

"Don't underestimate her. The woman is an evil genius."

He'd spent enough time with Hawthorne over the past several days to know that she planned each detail, and then planned it again. She'd make sure she had plenty of men, guns and vehicles.

"She might have already dumped the truck."

"What did Phillips say?" he asked.

"I really like him, you know. He's a good person and he actually has a sense of humor. If it turns out that he's double-crossing us, would you please not tell me?"

"You want to preserve the myth that there's at least one decent man on earth."

"It's not a myth."

When he looked at her, his cynical heart swelled and he wished that he could take a ride on her rainbow. He wanted to believe that they were going to get married and everything would be all right. He wanted it. But that didn't make it true.

"Anyway," she said, "Phillips is coordinating with local law enforcement, and he'll get back to us with names. He was going to try to get a search chopper in the air before nightfall. And he said that the next time we take a vacation, we might try for someplace less dangerous, like an active war zone."

Nick guided the sedan along a narrow road where heavy ruts were forming in the melting snow. The cabin at the end of the road was dark with no tracks leading to it. They could circle around here for a long time without finding Hawthorne.

And he didn't think the car would hold out that long. They were down to a quarter of a tank of gas, and the engine light showed it was running hot.

"New plan," he said. "Let's go back to the cabin and pack up our stuff. When Phillips calls, we'll get ahold of the people in charge and offer to help."

"Very sensible."

He drove away from the snarled back routes toward the main road. The drive to the cabin would take a solid twenty to thirty minutes, and he didn't think they could maintain silence that long.

They had touched on her rage. And she'd been the one to suggest going after Elena. But there was still the matter of the engagement ring that was burning a hole in his pocket.

"Sidney, is there something you want to say?"

"It's about the lies."

"I know."

"I won't have you lying to me. Never again. Even if you think I'm going to be mad, you've got to tell me the whole truth."

"Works both ways," he said.

"Truth, this had better be the truth." She leaned forward so she could make direct eye contact. "Will you miss being an undercover intelligence agent?"

Without a moment's hesitation, he nodded. "Hell, yes."

"I thought so."

"Most of the time, I'm just standing at attention in my uniform trying not to look bored. But there are moments…" His voice faded, unable to express the feeling. "…moments of sheer excitement. And there are exotic locations. And I'm using a specialized skill set."

"Why would you quit?"

"That's a whole different question." He paused, wanting to express himself clearly. "I know I'm jaded. I've seen too much on the dark side. But I also know that I'm a lucky man, been lucky all my life. I had a good family and good friends. I'm pretty good at most things. And I found you—the woman I love with all my heart."

"It's not just luck," she said.

"But luck plays a part. I've gotten out of more than my fair share of dangerous scrapes, and I figure that I've just about used up my share of luck. Someday, I'll leap off a burning building and my parachute won't open."

"Mathematically," she said, "the odds don't work that way."

"There's a reason I don't want to push my luck," he said. "Until now, until I had a future with you, I didn't care. Win, lose or draw, I could handle anything. But I can't stand the thought of losing you. No job is worth taking that risk."

She unfastened her seat belt so she could climb over the center console and kiss him. Her lips pressed against his cheek, and immediately she reacted. "Ouch."

"Your jaw isn't healed enough for kissing."

"Let me try again." Another tiny kiss. "Ouch. Ouch."

"Stop it, Sidney. There's a lot we can do besides kiss."

"But I can't wait to use my mouth again. For talking and laughing and eating, especially for eating." She hugged him. "I love you, Nick."

"And I love you, too."

A sense of peace wrapped around him in a warm embrace as he drove across the wide field. The long shadows of dusk slid down from the peaks and reached toward them. The bright blue of the sky faded to a softer, gentler color.

When he pulled up to the porch, Nick was tempted to settle in for the night and pretend that he and Sidney were living in a soft little world of their own. But he thought of safety first. He scoped out the area as well as he could.

"Let's get packed," he said. "Ten-minute drill."

"Aye, aye, Captain Corelli." She pulled open the front door and sauntered inside.

What was wrong with this picture? He was certain that he'd locked the front door before he left. He drew his gun from the holster at the small of his back as he entered.

Hawthorne leaned against the counter that separated the kitchen from the front room. In her right hand, she held a small device.

"This," she said, "is a dead man's switch. In this case, a dead woman's switch. If I release this lever, the package of C-4 explosive sitting on the kitchen table will detonate."

Chapter Twenty-Three

Nick had to seize control of the moment. This wasn't about luck. It was training. He had to find the trigger, to figure out what made Hawthorne tick and what would make her back down.

The fading light through the windows emphasized the hollows on her face. She was so thin, skeletal. When she bared her teeth in a smile, the effect was gruesome. "I'm sure you're familiar with the concept of the dead man's switch, Nick."

"Every soldier in Afghanistan knows about the dead man's switch and IEDs."

"If you shoot me or startle me or cause me to let go of the lever, the immediate explosion will kill us all."

Keeping his distance from her so she wouldn't feel threatened, he sank into a chair near the door. He had been trained for situations exactly like this one. He knew what to do. "What do you want from us?"

"We're going to wait right here until Elena comes back."

Nick started with logic. "What makes you think she's coming back here?"

"She doesn't have anywhere else to go. The cars are destroyed. My men are patrolling, and it's getting cold.

She won't spend the night outside. This cabin is her only sanctuary."

She'd given too much explanation, a sign that she was nervous about her decision, trying to justify it to herself. He needed to decide which buttons to push with Hawthorne.

"I should warn you," he said, "I've already put in a call to the special agent who replaced you on the task force. He'll be arranging the search."

"Who's replacing me?"

She sounded affronted, as though she was doing a good job and the CIA should be giving her a bonus. Nick figured that she was vulnerable to an attack of her professional pride. "Special Agent Sean Phillips got the job. Everybody thinks he'll do great."

"That dumb Texan? He can't handle this type of widespread operation. They'll be sorry that they didn't treat me better."

"You failed, Hawthorne. You got yourself kicked out of the CIA. If you die pulling off this stunt…and it's likely you will…you won't earn a star on the Memorial Wall. Special Agent Victoria Hawthorne will be referred to as a cautionary tale about a woman who traded her career for love."

Her cheeks flushed a feverish red. Her eyes narrowed to angry slits. Nick had been going for an emotional response, and that was what he'd gotten. She whined, "Why would you say that to me? Do you have a death wish?"

"You're not going to let go of that lever," he said. He'd found her trigger. "Not until you get your revenge on Elena. She's the one who screwed up your plans."

"Damn right, she did. When Tomas and I met, it was love at first sight."

Nick played along with her. "Seeing Elena suffer is

the only thing that matters. You don't want to die until you know she's dead, too."

"Don't push me, Nick."

"I get you. We're a lot alike." They were nothing alike, not in the least, but he needed for her to identify with him. He was her last, best friend. "You deserve your revenge."

"I do," she said.

Nick turned to Sidney. "I want you to turn around and walk out the door. Get some distance between yourself and the cabin."

Sidney's gaze flickered. He could tell that she didn't want to leave him.

"Don't you dare move another step," Hawthorne said.

"If you release the lever," Nick said, "you'll kill yourself and Elena will get off scot-free. Maybe she'll even go back to her husband."

"He'll never take her back." Spittle gathered in the corners of Hawthorne's mouth. "Go ahead, Sidney, get out of here. I never wanted to hurt you."

Sidney walked backward to the door. Her movements were slow and deliberate, nonthreatening. She was outside. She was safe.

Now it was Nick's turn.

He met Hawthorne's gaze. "You're going to let me go, too."

"Without you, I don't have a hostage. I have no leverage."

"The search helicopter is going to be here soon. They'll find Elena before you will. All she has to do is signal them."

A sob caught in Hawthorne's throat. "It's not right."

"It wasn't right when you tricked Curtis into helping you and then had him shot."

"I didn't have a choice," she said.

"What about Special Agent Gregory? He falsified documents. His career is destroyed."

"He did that on his own, thought he was being clever."

"You could have stopped him," Nick said. "Over the past few days, there's been way too much talk about what's right or wrong, good or bad."

"Elena is bad. She might have you fooled right now, but she will destroy you all."

She took a step toward him, and he uncoiled from the chair, ready to make a dash through the open front door. "Leave the bomb here. Let's go. Both of us. Nobody has to die."

From outside, he heard a shout. He went through the door to the porch. Hawthorne was right beside him.

Elena was hiking through the snow, coming up the hill toward the cabin. Sidney ran to meet her, to stop her from taking another step.

"I figured it right," Hawthorne said. "I knew she'd come back here. And now, I'll watch her die."

What the hell was she talking about? Elena was out of range for an explosion from the cabin. Nick stepped off the porch. He felt the snow move under his feet. The earth trembled.

He looked up at the ridge of snow that perched on the mountains above the steep field. It was moving. He started running toward Sidney.

Hawthorne dashed into the trees. She threw the dead man's switch. The cabin burst into a ball of flame. The massive noise from the explosion rumbled through the hills and canyons. The snow erupted. Avalanche.

Sidney and Elena were in the path of the churning white wall of snow and ice as it roared down the steep slope. Like a tidal wave, it uprooted trees, lifted boulders. It changed the very shape of the landscape.

Nick wouldn't lose her like this. His thighs burned as he charged through the snow that was getting deeper with every passing second. He fought with both arms, struggling to stay atop the sliding snow. He reached the two women as the snow crested over them in a heavy, concrete curtain. He couldn't breathe. Everything went black.

SIDNEY HAD NEVER been so cold. Buried in snow, every part of her body was frozen. She forced her eyelids to open, and she could see the light of the afternoon sun. She knew which way to dig.

One arm was pressed against her chest, and she wiggled her bare hand higher until she reached her mouth. She hollowed out a little place where she could inhale tiny gasps of air. Then, she punched upward with her arm. At first, she barely made a dent in the snow. The next hit was harder. Again and again.

Her other arm was pinned helplessly behind her back. But she could wiggle her feet. She kicked and she slipped to a new depth.

Her toe poked a step in the ice, then another. And she kept punching like a boxer on his last legs. Her fist broke through. She saw the sky, a dismal gray haze.

She heard Elena's voice.

Where was Nick? She'd seen him running toward her. He'd touched her hand, and then the snow crashed over them. She had to find Nick. It didn't take long to suffocate in an avalanche.

With Elena helping, Sidney dragged herself out of the snow. Gasping, she lay on the rugged sheets of ice. "Nick, where are you?"

"We'll find him," Elena promised. "He was close to us. We'll keep digging. We'll keep looking."

She heard a loud, guttural yell and looked toward the

cabin, which was a ball of orange flame. She saw Hawthorne pacing at the edge of the snowy scree. "Why won't you die?"

Elena ducked down. "Hurtado is yours. My pig of a husband doesn't want me."

"You hurt him."

There was no point in trying to reason with Hawthorne. In her world, Elena was a she-devil who had to die even if it meant blowing up a cabin or triggering an avalanche.

Hawthorne pulled her Glock from a shoulder holster. She braced it in both hands as she took aim at Elena. Before she squeezed the trigger, another shot rang out. She went down.

Sidney turned and saw Nick behind her, holding his weapon. "I tried not to kill her." He spat out a mouthful of snow. "But I don't really care if she's dead."

She stumbled across the snow, flopped down beside him and kissed him on the lips. "Ouch."

THREE DAYS LATER, Sidney and Nick were staying in a luxury suite in a Vail hotel, paid for by Avilar's wealthy family, who were grateful for his rescue and release from the men hired by Hawthorne. She had survived, and Sidney was glad she wouldn't have to waste one instant feeling guilty about Vicky/Victoria's demise.

Draped in a silky white robe for dinner, she paused beside the hot tub. She and Nick really needed to install one of these at their house in Austin. Finding a place to put it wasn't a problem. Privacy was. They lived in a family-oriented neighborhood. And what good was a steamy, sexy hot tub if you couldn't bob around naked?

In the outer room of their fabulous suite, she joined him. Her jaw was recovered enough for light kissing and, more important, for eating medium-chewy foods like hamburger. They sat at a room service dinner for two with microbrew beer, burgers and fries. Sidney savored the first juicy bite.

"That's almost as good as sex."

"Should I be insulted?"

"I said *almost*."

The gold flecks in his eyes seemed to sparkle in the soft light of their suite overlooking the village. These past three days had been all about recuperation and making love. They'd both been hurt and were on their way toward healing.

"I have something for you." He placed a small velvet box on the tabletop. "It's not a replacement."

She opened the ring box and took out a white-gold band with a simple, reasonably sized diamond. "This is perfect. I love my pi diamond, I really do, but…"

"It's not practical," he said.

She slipped the ring onto her finger. "If not a replacement, what is it?"

"Backup," he said. "Everybody needs backup."

"No more single-person ops?"

"Never again." He raised his hand as though swearing an oath. "I will never again undertake a mission that I can't tell you about."

She bounced from her chair, rounded the table and sat on his lap. She placed a light kiss on his delectable mouth.

"Aren't you going to read the inscription?" he asked.

She took off the ring, held the band and read inside: True Love.

For them, that said it all.

* * * * *

"You're serious?" Pete challenged. "Someone's trying to kill you and you want me to leave you here, defenseless?"

"And I appreciate you saving me. Twice. But I can't tell you anything else, so isn't it more important to catch that creep and find clues at the accident?"

"The scene and *Suit Man* aren't my priority. You are."

His blue eyes searched hers. If she'd known what he needed to hear, she would have said it. But she was a little frightened or worried or maybe just confused from the blow to her ear.

What was she thinking? These men had rammed her car off the road with the intention to kill her. And in all probability they had killed the man she'd been trying to help.

"I'll concede that you don't know me, but I'm not defenseless." The soreness in her jaw screamed otherwise. "I can take care of myself."

"Not tonight." He stepped back, one hand pushing through a thick head of short, light brown hair. "I'm escorting you home until someone decides what to do with you."

THE SHERIFF

BY
ANGI MORGAN

MILLS & BOON

Published in Great Britain 2015
by Mills & Boon, an imprint of Harlequin (UK) Limited,
Eton House, 18-24 Paradise Road, Richmond, Surrey, TW9 1SR

© 2015 Angela Platt

ISBN: 978-0-263-25293-4

46-0115

Angi Morgan writes Mills & Boon® Intrigue novels "where honor and danger collide with love." She combines actual Texas settings with characters who are in realistic and dangerous situations. Angi and her husband live in north Texas, with only the four-legged "kids" left in the house to interrupt her writing. They recently began volunteering for a local Labrador retriever foster program. Visit her website, www.angimorgan.com, or hang out with her on Facebook.

Thanks so much, Jan, you've been a rock star this year.
Jill and Allison, your understanding and
support is unsurpassed.

Chapter One

"This is not happening. Aliens are landing and I can't find the camera."

Lights moved in an erratic pattern low in the sky. Not aliens, but it was fun to think so. Someone on the ground? No. The lights were moving too swiftly. It had to be a chopper. It could not be a phenomenon. And especially not a UFO.

Andrea Allen was very familiar with everything that flew. She had to be when she was the only child of an astronaut and a pretty good pilot herself. It was definitely not a plane. It didn't look like a chopper, but it had to be. The lights weren't in the correct place. It hovered and disappeared.

Pulling the cords from her ears, she heard the faint drumbeat of "Bohemian Rhapsody" rocking in the background, but no mechanical sounds echoing in the distance. She rubbed her eyes and found the hovering object with the telescope. Whatever it was, it just wasn't producing enough light to distinguish an outline above the desert with a mountain ridge in the background.

Normally, she was bored out of her mind with the study on the Marfa Lights. Even though several tourists had posted seeing activity recently, no one with credentials had verified anything. Tourists posted all the time. Didn't they know it was just an occurrence similar to the aurora borealis? Everyone had heard of the northern lights, right?

The UT students studying the local phenomenon from the McDonald Observatory got excited, clamoring for a turn to watch the uneventful sky. Three nights later with no activity, everyone assumed the sighting had been taillights from the highway and then they all wanted the weekend off for a party.

Bored. Tonight had been no exception.

Nothing happened in this West Texas desert except lots of star time. Which she loved. She loved it a lot. Much more than she missed friends and family. Staring at a clear night sky was something even her astronaut dad didn't understand.

Since it hadn't been her night to stare through a telescope at the far distant universe, her coworker Sharon had begged Andrea to take her place on the university study. Sharon wanted the night off because she had a hot date with her boyfriend, Logan. Granted, the young student had been here three nights in a row, since it was part of her class assignment. Andrea didn't mind. She needed to switch sleeping to days anyway.

Another sparkle of red twinkled. Just a bit closer than the last spot.

With her spare hand she dug around in the disorganized bag her coworker had dropped in her front seat before leaving the observatory. "Where's that silly camera?"

She lost sight of the floating light through the scope and bounced her gaze to the horizon. Nothing. Had it disappeared?

If the darn thing came back, she needed the camera to record it. Dumping the satchel upside down, she searched through the assortment of items that resembled a loose picnic basket. Snacks, bottles of water, gum wrappers, a notepad, a small tripod, a spoon to go along with the empty yogurt containers, three different bags of candy—the butterscotch made her pause and unwrap a piece to stick in her mouth. No video camera.

She scooped everything back into Sharon's UFO-watching sack.

Where's the camera? It was just here. She closed her eyes to visualize getting in the car. Sharon had run outside with the bag in her hand as the car backed out of the parking space. The window had been down. "Passenger side. It must have fallen under the seat."

"My gosh." The adrenaline rush grew each time she saw the light a bit closer. A burst of red. A burst of blue. A plane would have red or green running lights on its wings and a white strobe light would be a consistent flash. A chopper, same thing. There were ways to identify what was in the air. Flight patterns.

Amazed, she just stared.

"Camera!" She ran to the car, pausing when she caught sight of the red flash again. She still couldn't distinguish an outline of what was flying haphazardly and low to the ground. It couldn't be a UFO. There were no such things.

Did she really believe that? No life in the universe other than on Earth? No time to debate, she needed pictures. Lots of pictures and evidence.

No one was around for miles to break into Sharon's tiny compact car, so it wasn't locked. The keys were still even in the ignition. Andrea yanked open the door, immediately feeling under the seat. "Gotcha!"

The strap was caught on something. The sky behind her was empty as she switched to the backseat, dropping to her knees again to get low enough to search.

If she could obtain evidence of the Marfa Lights, she could publish in addition to her PhD, make a name for herself as an astronomer. Finally be worthy of her Allen heritage. It all hinged on concrete evidence. Could it happen?

She recognized the sudden nausea and shakiness as fear. Fear of jumping to conclusions and being discredited. She'd verify the facts.

"What am I thinking? I have my own study to finish. I'm not chasing another subject. This is university work. I. Can't. Switch. Again." Her teeth ground against each other in frustration—not only with the silly camera strap, but also with the lack of focus her parents had accused her of. "What is this stuck on?"

The flashlight was back on the viewing platform with the UFO bag, and the dome light had been out for months. She couldn't really see anything under the seat, even bent at another awkward angle. But she finally came up with the handheld video camera, pressing Record and immediately scanning the sky for her mystery lights.

Andrea maneuvered from the tiny car, resting the camera on the door frame. "I don't know if it's appropriate to talk while recording, but I think it's better to describe what I'm seeing. Mainly because I don't know what I'm seeing. Five minutes ago there were flashing lights. Nothing about it suggests standard aircraft. And yet nothing suggests the Marfa phenomenon."

The corner of her eye caught a blur, something running from the darkness in her direction. She swung the camera toward it.

"I can't tell what that is. For the record, I'm Andrea Allen and alone out here. There's nothing close at hand to defend myself from wild animals or— Good grief, what is that?"

She kept recording, squinted. Still couldn't make it out. "The lights have disappeared. I don't know what's weaving toward me, but I think I'm going to get back in the car and roll up the windows."

Proud of herself for continuing the recording, she felt with one hand until finding the window handle. It was the first time she was grateful she'd paid extra for electric windows. But she wasn't in her car, she was in Sharon's old sedan. Backseat ready, she pushed the lock and shut it, then moved to the front door.

During the transfer, she lost where the movement was, spotting it again when she found the handle. Closer. More in focus. A man. Staggering.

She dropped the camera on the seat, using both hands to tug at the window stuck on the old car. "Not now. Uh. Give me a break."

"Help."

"Help? Not likely." She ran to the driver's side. If she couldn't get locked inside her car, she didn't have to stay there.

Marfa was nine miles away. This was a police matter.

"Please. Help. Night of aliens."

She heard him loud and clear as he tripped and stumbled into her. Shirtless, his skin horribly dirty. His lips parched and cracked. With his short-cropped military cut, she could see the gaping wound on the side of his head. There were cuts and bruises all over his arms. Some fresh, some old.

Where was the nearest hospital? Alpine. She couldn't leave him.

He fell into her arms, knocking her into the car frame. She kept him moving, guiding his fall onto the backseat. She pushed at his legs, tried folding them so the door would close.

"Come on, man. Help me...out...here." He was unresponsive and most likely unconscious. She ran to the other door, forgetting it was locked, wasting precious time reaching through the window. She yanked and pulled until he budged enough to bend his knees on top of his body and shut both doors. It had to be uncomfortable, but the man wasn't complaining.

"Hospital!"

She left everything on the viewing platform, including

her cell phone, only having a moment of disappointment about not documenting evidence. This guy was clearly not from a UFO. It looked as if he'd been in the desert for days.

There was no question the man's life was much more important than any research. She pointed the car east toward Alpine. Marfa was closer and had a doctor but no hospital. The dashboard lights showed smudges of the man's blood on her hands and forearms. She felt the stickiness of a heavy damp saturation just above her hip.

"Are you bleeding to death?" she screamed at the unconscious stranger and threw on the brakes. "Were you attacked by coyotes or something?"

Twisting to look at him closer, she searched the middle compartment for anything, even napkins. There was nothing here to stem the loss of blood. She pulled her long-sleeve shirt over her head and shifted to reach his body, searching with her hands until she found a wound. Her fingers found a distinct puncture. She'd never seen one in real life, but there was no mistaking the bullet hole.

Dear Lord. "What happened to you?"

She pressed the shirt into his side, moving his arm into a position to hold it in place. He moaned.

"Thank God you're alive, but who knows how long that will last."

The lights were closer, then gone again.

Using all the training her father had taught her about control, she forced her thoughts to slow and hold herself together. She readjusted in the seat and buckled the seat belt in place before putting the car in Drive.

One at a time, she swiped her hands across her jeans to remove the man's damp blood before pulling out of the parking lot. She dipped her head to her shoulder, trying to push a loose piece of hair, stuck across her cheek, off her sweaty face.

What in the world was she getting involved in? A secret

chopper? Maybe a new stealth plane? "Are you military or something? I sure hope you're not a fugitive or a drug runner. But whoever you are, you're dying and I have to get you to a hospital."

Nothing was around for miles. No homes, no businesses, no help. *Help?* She should call for help. Where was her stupid phone?

Oh, no. It was in the chair where she'd dumped Sharon's bag. She needed to call, tell someone she had an injured man and get directions to the hospital in Alpine. She turned in the small lot, prepared to jump from the car and dial on the way back. A one- or two-minute delay was better than getting lost. Maybe they could send an ambulance to meet her.

Bright spotlights blinded her in all her mirrors. She couldn't see and tilted the rearview up. *Forget the phone.* She punched the gas and could smell the smoking rubber of the slightly balding tires.

"It's following us!" Whatever *it* was, it was practically on top of the trunk.

The road was straight so she couldn't stop or it would crash into her. There was no way to outrun it in an old four-cylinder economy.

"Now what?"

Colored lights flashed. The inside of the car looked like a blinking neon sign. She could barely see the two-lane highway, and then whatever followed rammed the little car. Andrea's neck jerked back. Her body smashed against the seat belt. Her wrists slammed into the steering wheel. Her father would be proud she didn't scream—as much as she wanted to let out a string of obscenities at whoever was flying that thing.

Another hit. The thing had to be a chopper. The man in her backseat had to be in serious trouble and now so was she.

The car skidded sideways onto the shoulder and beyond. She maintained her grip, steering through the grass on the side of the highway. The chopper blocked her path back to the road. They bounced a few seconds before she aimed at the wire between fence posts and gunned the little engine again.

She had no idea what was out here. She could be headed straight to a small boulder or a ravine. The unknown was definitely frightening, but not as much as the chopper on her tail.

As suddenly as the thing appeared behind her, it was gone. No lights. No sounds. She wanted to slow down, but it wasn't safe. Too late she wished she had when a slab of broken foundation forced the car sideways.

It rolled.

She screamed.

Chapter Two

Driving this empty length of pavement could put him to sleep if he wasn't careful. Pete Morrison stretched his neck from side to side, turned the squad car's radio up a bit louder and rolled down the window for fresh air. A quick trip out to the Lights Viewing Area and back to the office for some shut-eye.

Probably just a plane and a waste of taxpayer gas.

"I saw some strange stuff out there," a trucker had told Dispatch. "I don't believe in UFOs or nothing like that, but if it is, I want the credit for seeing it first. Okay?"

"Sure thing" had been the standard reply to every driver who thought he'd seen a UFO. And each report had to be checked out. It was Marfa, after all.

Griggs would get an earful in the morning about honesty and the law. This was the third time in two weeks Pete had covered the son of a gun's night shift at the last minute because of *illness*. Everyone knew the deputy had gone to Alpine to party. If he wanted to change shifts, he just needed to ask. There were twelve other deputies on the payroll, and yet Pete was covering. Again.

Partying hadn't been something he'd personally wanted to do for the past couple of months. But since Griggs had transferred from Jefferson Davis County, he'd been covering his shifts a lot. Covering wasn't the problem. He got extra pay and could normally sleep on the back cot. Nothing ever happened in Marfa beyond speeding citations and public intoxication.

Tonight was one of the exceptions. He'd make a quick pass by the official Marfa Lights Viewing Area, drive back and get some shut-eye.

"Dispatch, I've got an all clear. Not seeing anything unusual. But I might as well make a run to the county line."

"Okey dokey, Pete. This is Peach. See you in a while."

He laughed at Peach's official acknowledgment. No sense trying to get her to change. Everyone called her Peach. She insisted on it. Her sister, Honey, got the day shift since she was older. He supposed nicknames were better than Winafretta and Wilhilmina. They'd been in Dispatch for as long as his dad had been a deputy or sheriff of Presidio County. Or longer. His dad swore no one could remember hiring either of them. They'd just shown up one day.

When his dad officially retired, the new sheriff could request replacements for them, but he'd like to see anyone tell Peach she was too old to handle things at night around the office. A shot of regret lodged like a clump of desert dirt in his throat. He'd have to withdraw his name from the election so someone else would step forward. Galen Rooney had only been on the force for a couple of years and just didn't have the experience needed to run things.

No matter who the county elected, they'd most likely keep him on as a deputy. If not… Unfortunately, he hadn't thought past quitting the race. The idea of withdrawing gnawed at his gut like a bad case of food poisoning. He'd never quit anything. His dad—he couldn't ever think of the man who'd raised him as anything else—wouldn't be happy.

"Crap. What the hell was that?"

He successfully dodged a long object in the middle of the road. He swiftly U-turned the squad car, flipped his lights on and drove a couple of seconds. Parking across the road, he turned the floodlight until it shone on a black bumper resting on the yellow line.

Joe Morrison had raised him riding shotgun in a squad car. The mental checklist of what he did exiting his vehicle was as natural as walking. Even if Peach wasn't a stickler for the rules, he still needed to let her know exactly what he was doing.

"Dispatch, I swung back west to pick up some road debris. Guess a bumper dropped from a car and the driver didn't stop to take care of it. Almost sent me off the road."

"Wow, Sheriff Pete. It's a good thing we got that call to take you out that way tonight, then," Peach replied through the speaker. "What if an eighteen-wheeler had hit that thing? Oh, gosh, and what if it had been transporting fuel or hazardous waste? It might have spilled and leached into the water supply. We could have had deformed livestock or mutant wolves running around for years without anyone knowing."

"You reading another end-of-the-world novel, Peach?"

"How did you know?" she asked.

"Lucky guess." He laughed into the microphone. Peach and Honey's theories of espionage and Armageddon changed daily with each book they read.

"Well, I'm at a good spot in the story, so I'll let you clear the garbage. Shout out when you're heading back," she said.

"You got it. And, Peach, will you stop with the sheriff title? You know I'm the acting sheriff until the election."

"I feel the same way about my dispatch title."

"Point taken."

Picking up the plastic bumper from a small car, he noticed some skid marks on the asphalt. He flipped his flashlight on and followed their path to the gravel and farther into the flattened knee-high grass. A vehicle had obviously gone off the road. He tossed the bumper to the side and started walking.

About twenty yards away, the fence wasn't only down, but a section had been demolished and disappeared. There was nothing in range of the flashlight beam, so he shut off the light and let his eyes adjust to the well-lit night.

He finally spotted the car, the underbelly reflecting the starlight about four hundred yards into the field. He ran the short distance to the vehicle. The driver might need a hospital. A serious injury, he'd need to transport himself.

"Dispatch." Back in his car, he pointed the spotlight directly in front of the hood and followed the path through the fence. "Peach?" He raised his voice to get her attention.

"I'm here, just finishing the chapter. You heading back?"

"Looks like a vehicle went off the road about half a mile east of the Viewing Area. I spotted it. Driving there now. Check if there are any cattle around that could get loose, and notify the owner."

"Time to wake the sheriff."

"Don't wake Dad. He's officially retired."

"You know that's not going to stop him. Neither could a heart attack."

"Give me five minutes to check out the vehicle, Peach." And do something on his own without his dad shouting instructions in his ear. "I need to find the driver and see if we need assistance."

"He's gonna be mad," she sang into the radio. "You know how he hates to be the last told."

"My call."

"But you know how he is," she whined.

"Remember that he's retired. Five minutes."

"Yes, sirree-dee, Acting Sheriff Morrison."

Yeah, but for how long? He watched the land closest to him, searching for ditches or large rocks. Closer to the vehicle, it was apparent it had hit the foundation of an old building. Whoever had been driving the car had been traveling at a high speed, hit the broken concrete and flipped the vehicle.

He approached with caution, flashlight in hand, gun at his fingertips. "County Sheriff. Anyone need help?"

No answer. Nothing but the cool wind.

He switched the flashlight, looked inside the car. One body. Nonresponsive.

"Sir?" He felt the man's neck for a pulse. "Damn."

Dead.

The body was mangled pretty badly. "You should have buckled up, stranger. How'd you end up in the backseat?" He'd seen weirder things happen in car accidents than the driver being thrown around.

Back at his car, he pulled his radio through the open window. "Peach, send for an ambulance. We have a fatality."

"Poor soul."

"Yeah." He tossed the microphone onto the seat.

"Unit says they're about an hour out, Pete," he heard through the speaker. "There was an accident in Alpine and since it's only a pickup they aren't in a hurry."

"Not a problem."

No shut-eye anytime soon. He was stuck waiting here an hour unless Peach called him for a Marfa emergency. Fat chance. He'd get the pics they'd need for their records and maybe catch a nap after. He grabbed the camera from the Tahoe.

Careful not to disturb the body, he started snapping away, including the outside of the car and the tags. When he reached the driver's-side door, he noticed blood on the outside and then the tracks, patterns in the dirt as if someone had crawled from the car.

"Anyone out here?" he yelled, tilting the beam as far as it would project and following distinct shoe impressions. "I'm with the Marfa Sheriff's Department and here to help."

He shoved the camera in his pocket and picked up his pace. Two or three minutes passed, the footprints grew more erratic and then the bottom of a shoe came into view.

"Hello?" He ran to a woman lying facedown in the sand. She was visibly breathing, but unresponsive to shaking her shoulder. He verified no broken bones and no wounds, then rolled her over.

There was a lot of blood on her white tank, but no signs of any bleeding. He dusted the sand from her young face. Smooth skin. *That won't go in the report.* Caucasian. Short brown hair. Blue eyes, responsive to light.

"Ma'am? Can you hear me?"

The accident couldn't have happened that long ago. The hood of the car had been warm. Should he move her? There could be multiple things wrong with her. He ran his hands over her body checking for broken bones. She wasn't responding to stimulation. She needed immediate care and the ambulance was an hour out. That sealed it. He scooped her into his arms and rushed her back to his car.

Once he had her buckled, he picked up the microphone. "Peach!"

He returned along the same tire tracks, picking up his speed since he knew the path was clear.

"Bored already?" Peach asked.

"I'm transporting a survivor to Alpine General. Found her fifty yards or so from the car."

"Lord have mercy. I'll let them know you're on your way."

The car hit a bump and he heard a moan and mumbling from next to him. Good sign. "Hang in there, ma'am."

Slowing as he hit the road's pavement, he could swear the woman begged him not to let the aliens get her.

The Marfa Lights sure did attract a lot of kooks.

Chapter Three

"I've told you several times now, I'm not sure what rammed me off the road. It had to be a chopper, but the lights blinded me and I never got a good look at what model."

Everyone seemed to know the man who had brought Andrea to the hospital. He leaned his broad shoulders against the wall closest to the door. He'd scribbled notes and asked questions while the doctors looked her over. And almost every other sentence had been spent correcting someone congratulating him for his new position as sheriff.

Pardon, *acting* sheriff.

A sprained wrist, a minor concussion and dirty clothes, that was the extent of her accident injuries. Her favorite jeans were ruined. Not to mention Sharon's car.

The nurse said she could get her a hospital gown, but the good-looking deputy hadn't offered to leave the room while she changed. Ruined and filthy clothes would just have to do. She'd feel too open and exposed in front of *Acting* Sheriff Pete Morrison.

It was hardly fair to have such an attractive lawman interrogating her. It made her mind wander to forbidden topics, so it was much safer to remain completely covered.

"How tall are you?" he asked, flipping another page in his notebook.

"Five-nine. How could that be important?" As tall as

she was, she'd have to tiptoe to kiss him. What was wrong with her thinking? Had she hit her head a little too hard? Of course she had. Hello. Concussion!

"Just being thorough."

She watched him sort of hide a grin, draw his brows together in concentration and drop his gaze to her chest. So he'd noticed the pink bra? No worries. Why? *Because he's extremely cute, that's why.*

"You're certain you didn't hear anything? The man who 'came from the desert,' as you put it, he didn't say anything?" he asked.

"I don't think so. By the way, how is that guy doing? Is he still in surgery? I keep asking, but no one seems to know anything about him. This is the only hospital, right?"

The nurse looked confused when Andrea had asked earlier. This time she turned to the sheriff, who shook his head, then shrugged. Everyone coming into the room had looked to the young sheriff for permission to speak and been denied.

"Can you tell us who your friend is?" he asked, flashing bright blue eyes her direction.

"Check your notes, Sheriff Morrison. I'm certain I told you he wasn't my friend. That was sometime between having my temperature taken and my wrist x-rayed."

"Yes, ma'am, you did say that." The sheriff looked at his notes and flipped to the previous page. "No need to call me Sheriff. Pete will do."

"Guess there's nothing wrong with her memory, Pete," the nurse said as she continued to wrap Andrea's left hand, pausing several times to smile at the hunky man.

Andrea had regained consciousness in the emergency room with a horrible smell wafting under her nose. It wasn't her first time for smelling salts. She'd gotten rammed a couple of times as a shortstop on the softball field in college. She could just imagine what her mother would say when she told her parents about this sprain. Peggy Allen would be glad her daughter was uninjured and it was simply a miracle how her middle daughter had managed to avoid a car accident until the ripe old age of twenty-six.

Not a miracle to her father, who had taught her how to drive like a naval aviator late for a launch at NASA. That was a phone call she dreaded. At least it could wait until morning. No sense worrying her parents tonight.

"How's that, Miss Allen?" the nurse asked, securing the last bit of elastic bandage around her wrist. Miraculously—to use her mother's word—the slight ache was the only pain she experienced. Other than a headache from the concussion.

"Great. Thanks. Can I go now?"

"I just need to get the doctor's signature and I can get your discharge papers." The nurse put her supplies away, smiled prettily again at the annoying officer. "See you, Pete."

"What's your hurry?" the good-looking man asked as she left.

At first she thought he was flirting with the nurse. He dipped his dimpled chin, raised his eyebrows, expectantly waiting...

"Oh, you mean me? I'm not overly fond of hospitals." Oh, Lordy, he really had a dimpled chin. She was a sucker for that little cleft under rugged, nice lips. *Whoa.*

How could his straight brows rise even higher? It was as if getting asked a question made him feel guilty for not answering, or he assumed she'd seen a lot of hospitals. Either way, she immediately regretted giving the officer any insight into her character. "The answer to your question, Sheriff, is no. I haven't escaped from a loony bin. I told you, I'm a PhD candidate working at the McDonald Observatory."

"I didn't say a word."

"Your face says enough without your lips moving." She covered her mouth with her good hand to make herself shut up. The annoying man just laughed and grinned even bigger. "What are you waiting on, anyway? I told you I can phone and get a ride home. The student I was covering for is already in Alpine. Somewhere."

He pulled a cell from his pocket. "Use mine."

She held her hand out, wincing at the soreness already setting into her muscles. It didn't matter, she had no idea what Sharon's number was without recovering her cell from the Viewing Area.

"I don't know her number."

She hated to think what a cab ride to the north side of Fort Davis would cost. If they even had cabs in Alpine, Texas, that traveled the fifty miles or so outside the city. She'd probably have to bribe the driver by paying him double.

"We tried to locate the owner of the car, but the listing is in Austin."

"I did mention she's a student."

He stood straighter, slipping the cell back in his chest pocket. "To answer your question, I'm still here because I need your official statement and I thought you might need a ride back to wherever you're staying in Fort Davis."

"Oh. Thanks. That's very considerate of you. I'm at the observatory, actually. I guess you do things differently here."

"Spent a lot of time with the law back home?"

She just stared at him. The man was actually being extremely nice. And seemed to be charming. Part of his expressive nature, she surmised.

"We'd never get along." She clamped her hand over her mouth again.

"I don't know about that. I like a woman who speaks her mind. Kinda refreshing."

"They gave me a pain pill. It must have gone straight to my mouth."

He nodded and covered a grin by rubbing long fingers over his lips. "I was here before the pain pill. You weren't exactly holding back then, either."

For some reason she wanted to push her hands through his slightly mussed hair and see the sandy waviness up close. *Wow.* What had the doctors given her to make her think like this? She had to remain professional.

"Do you think I did something wrong, Sheriff?"

"Miss Allen—"

"Please, my name's Andrea." She checked out her torn black jeans and ragged undershirt still stained with blood, not feeling like a Miss anything.

"Andrea. We've done some checking."

"Don't tell me, there weren't any planes or helicopters flying in that area. So I actually saw a UFO." She was trying to be cutesy or sarcastic or just funny. A giggle even escaped, but the expression on the officer's face didn't indicate that he was laughing with her. In fact, he looked dead serious. "I'm joking, you know."

"You did mention that aliens were chasing you."

"I was referring to illegal immigrants. Or maybe I was just delirious from being knocked out cold. I never once seriously thought I was being chased by an extraterrestrial, something foreign to this modern age of flying machines. I study the stars. I don't live in them." Exhausted, she wanted to lie back on the examining table and sleep. "I'm here working on my last dissertation."

The room tilted. Or maybe she did. It was hard to tell. She was conscious of falling, knew it was about to happen before it did. The heaviness of her arms prevented her from stopping herself. She didn't hit the floor.

Instead, a firm grip kept her in place, then lowered her to the pillow.

He had the best hands. Strong, short practical nails. Firm. And she shouldn't forget how quick. He'd taken a step and caught her as she swayed.

"Maybe we should talk later?"

"I'm sorry, Sheriff." She rubbed her head and winced at the little bump. "I'm...sort...of...woozy."

"Not a problem. I'm not going anywhere. And it's Pete."

"I'm Andrea." She could really get into liking that mouth of his. "You have a super-cute smile. Did I—" A yawn escaped and she almost couldn't remember what she was saying. "Oh, yeah. Did I tell you I like your smile?"

"I think you did, Miss Allen. I think you need to get some shut-eye."

She turned into his hand, still holding her shoulder. She caught a clean, musky scent before letting her heavy eyelids close and stay that way. "Can't think of a better place to do it."

THE SHERIFF WHO'D taken Andrea's statement stood outside the door, which was open just a crack. The person he spoke to was in scrubs. Maybe the nurse who'd checked her out earlier, maybe someone new. Shoot, it could be the doctor there to discharge her. She didn't know. She grabbed the side of the bed and began pushing herself upright, jerking to a stop as a hiss of pain whistled between her teeth.

"Wow, that really hurts." Her wrist was bandaged. Funny, she could remember everything except that her wrist was sprained.

"I'm headed back to the scene," Pete said. "I'm waiting on the local PD who are going to stay with Miss Allen until we have a few more facts."

"What if we need the room?"

"Mrs. Yardly, it might be a Friday night in downtown Alpine, but when was the last time the ER filled up?"

The casual stance and charm disappeared quickly as a

balding man approached, flipping open a flat wallct. The kind she'd seen many times before.

The Suit Man seemed to have no personality. He wasn't attempting to make friends. His straight, thin lips never curved into an approachable welcome. "Steven Manny, Department of Homeland Security. I'm here for Andrea Allen."

"I was told local police would be here to escort her to the observatory," the sheriff answered, shifting his right hand near the top of his gun.

"I have a few questions and will make certain she gets returned to her residence. You're relieved." A light knuckle tap on the door and Suit Man walked inside. "Miss Allen, are you ready?"

She nodded but locked eyes with Pete, silently imploring the sheriff not to leave her alone. Before she verbalized the words, he stepped into the room behind the new guy and closed the door.

"She passed out a few minutes ago and they're not ready to discharge her."

"We understand your concern, but we're moving. Now. Miss Allen." He gestured for her to head to the door.

As anxious as she was to escape the hospital before landing in Pete's arms, she was scared to leave without him. The guy demanding she put on her shoes wasn't the average government-issued suit.

"Where are we going?" she asked.

"That's classified."

"I won't tell anyone." Pete seemed taller, firmer. He waved his hand for her to stay put. "Think you can give me another look at your badge?"

When Pete took another step, ready to do battle, the Suit shoved his forearm across the sheriff's windpipe. Andrea jumped to her feet to help but received a backhand with the Suit's free arm, knocking her across the small emergency room bed.

Pete was no slouch. He was younger, three or four inches taller and in really good shape. His strength kicked in and he shoved Suit Man straight into the path of her hospital-socked feet. Without shoes she couldn't do much damage, but she did put a heel in Suit Man's gut, hurtling him into the supply cabinet.

Pete was there, swung his left fist and connected with Suit Man's jaw, sending him flying backward into the door. Her rescuer swung again, connected a second time. She recognized the panic in Suit Man's eyes. He knew he'd failed.

Suit Man had something in one hand and the other hand on the door handle.

"Watch out!" she yelled.

Pete ducked, but she couldn't get out of the path. The metal hit her square in the ear, and she tumbled to the linoleum.

There was some yelling, really close to her ear, but the world was spinning sufficiently enough that it didn't register. She saw the blur of black dress shoes running from the room. It was all she could do to focus on not passing out. Then the strong arms she admired lifted her to the table.

"Everything okay in here, Pete?" the voice she'd heard earlier from the hall asked through the intercom.

"Yardly, I need a doctor, and where's security?"

"It's just a bump. My ears are ringing. That's all." She'd seen double for a few seconds, but that had already passed. "What are you waiting for?"

A nurse and then a doctor entered. Pete slipped out, but she could hear his raised voice in the hall. She saw his phone to his ear. Watched him pace in front of the rectangle of a window and then speak with the doctor before coming back in the room.

"Why aren't you chasing Suit Man?" she asked between the blood pressure cuff and insisting she was fine.

"You're stuck with me while I ensure your safety. That's your best option." He didn't seem at all satisfied being saddled with the position of her protector.

"I can wait for the police. There are plenty of people here. So go."

"You're serious?" He followed the nurse to the door, looked down the hall and slammed it shut. "Someone's trying to kill you and you want me to leave you here, defenseless?"

"And I appreciate your saving me. Twice. But I can't tell you anything else, so isn't it more important to catch that creep and find clues at the accident?"

"The scene and *Suit Man* aren't my priority. *You* are."

She watched his Adam's apple bob nicely as he swallowed hard. His blue eyes searched hers. If she'd known what he needed to hear, she would have said it. But she was a little frightened or worried or maybe just confused from the blow to her ear.

What was she thinking? These men had rammed her car off the road trying to kill her. Okay, technically, it was Sharon's car. And in all probability, they had killed the man she'd been trying to help. She'd been knocked silly-unconscious by a complete stranger with really good counterfeit DHS credentials who also wasn't afraid to show his face and try to kill her with security cameras everywhere.

"I'll concede that you don't know me, but I'm not *defenseless*." The soreness in her jaw screamed otherwise. "He caught me off guard. That's all. I can take care of myself."

"Not tonight." He stepped back, one hand going to his hip and the other pushing through a thick head of short, light brown hair. "I'm escorting you home until someone decides what to do with you. The local authorities will find Suit Man."

"Are you sure about that?"

She'd lost her chance. He'd made his decision. And it was probably best. The only personal possessions she still had were her earphones. They'd hooked around her neck and somehow not fallen off. If she'd been alone when the *Suit* attacked, she would have been dead before she could press the nurse call button.

Or maybe worse. She might have actually been woozy enough to leave with him. Then what?

The sheriff opened the door. "Yardly!" The nurse he'd been speaking to came running. "We're not waiting to give an incident report. We're leaving. Do what you have to do to get us out of here. *Now.*"

"Well then…it isn't just another boring Friday night, after all."

Chapter Four

Pete kept Andrea Allen in sight through the sliver of an opening in the door. There weren't any windows in the exam room, and he needed to keep an eye on her. Victim or perpetrator. He didn't know if that was an unsuccessful rescue attempt or an averted abduction.

Whichever, something didn't sit right and he wanted to know what she was doing. She was the prime suspect or witness in a man's death.

"I've got things under control, Dad. I don't need backup at the hospital. I'll be gone before anyone can get here. We're just waiting on a prescription. There's nothing you can do. I know you're already at the office. Just stay there and handle that end of things. When exactly did Peach call you?"

"Now, son, it's no reflection on your abilities that she called. We've been working together for a couple of decades."

When were any of his instructions going to be followed?

He'd been at the hospital almost three hours waiting on Andrea to be treated and discharged before Suit Man—it was as good a description as any—had shown up. And to get the okay for her to leave was taking a lot longer than he'd anticipated. The murderers seemed to be a lot more organized than the hospital staff, who couldn't get them out the door.

"Who am I kidding? Peach called the *real sheriff* as soon as I reported the dead body. Right?" A guy who went missing by the time the ambulance showed up twenty minutes later.

"You are the sheriff now and never mind how long I've been here," his father said, sounding wide-awake and probably on his third cup of coffee. He'd dodged answering like he usually did. "The picture you sent popped a red flag. I'm waiting on a call from the DEA and DHS."

"You think this guy was working undercover?" His charge was lying on an ER bed, ice bag on her ear.

"Could be, Pete. They're waking up some top-dog bureaucrat to get instructions. I don't want the call to drop on my way out to the Viewing Area. But I want to take a look at that car before it disappears, too."

"So you believe our Sleeping Beauty's story about the flashing lights?" His dad would take over the crime scene while Pete babysat the witness. This night just kept getting better and better.

"Well, something's not right. Dead bodies don't just walk away. The paramedics are sure there was no sign of animal involvement?" his dad asked.

"They actually accused me of yanking their chain when they returned to the hospital." A quick look into the room confirmed Andrea was still asleep, secure and safe.

"Then whoever was in the chopper chasing our witness didn't want the body found."

"Did Peach get anyone at the observatory to verify her ID?"

"Yeah, the director confirmed everything. She's lucky you got there as soon as you did or she'd be dead twice over now. Don't let her out of your sight until we get this thing figured out."

"I hadn't planned to. I know my job, Dad." He wasn't normally a pacer, but he couldn't lean against the wall much longer. He looked at the nurses' station, where there was still no sign of activity.

"You'll make a fine replacement. I'm looking forward to sleeping in," his dad said.

"That'll never happen. You'll just be at the café for breakfast earlier." He left the replacement statement hanging. He couldn't get into a conversation they'd been avoiding for almost six weeks while in the middle of what was becoming a major mess. "Listen, you know you're supposed to take it easy. I'll stop by the crash site on my way back."

"I'm not an invalid."

"You should be after a quadruple bypass."

Andrea yanked the door open.

"He's dead?" She was obviously panicked, more upset than she'd been earlier after the Suit had backhanded her jaw. "The man who stumbled out of the desert is dead? Did he die in the crash? Did I kill him?"

"Gotta run, Dad. Get a deputy there to pick you up. You shouldn't be driving." He slid the cell into his pocket and faced her. "I'm sorry you had to hear like that. How he died wasn't clear when I viewed the body, so I don't have the answer to your question."

"I need another shirt. Now."

He witnessed her realization she still wore the man's blood. Her chest began rising and falling more rapidly, and she was about to completely lose it. Good or bad? He didn't know. They didn't get too many cases like this bizarre situation in Jeff Davis County.

One second he was sticking his head out the door calling for clean scrubs and the next he saw Andrea tug the back of her shirt over her head.

"What are you doing?"

She threw the shirt across the room. "I think that's

self-explanatory. What? You've never seen a woman in a bra before?"

"Here." He shifted the pillow from the bed to block the view of her breasts.

"I'm not claiming harassment, if you're worried—"

"This is a small town and people will talk no matter what you claim."

"Someone's trying to kill me. I have no idea why. And you're worried about seeing me in my bra." She stared at him, hugging the pillow to her stomach.

She wanted a logical explanation. There wasn't one. "They're covering their bases."

"But I don't know anything," she whispered.

"They don't know that."

The door swung open, and Ginny held a pair of pink scrubs. She handed them to him without a word and turned to leave.

"Wait." He stopped the nurse after the disapproving look she shot his way. "I'll leave and you help Miss Allen get cleaned up and changed. Bag all her clothes, will ya?"

"Sure, Pete." Ginny smiled, raising an eyebrow to match the questions in her voice.

He stepped outside and pulled the door shut behind him, leaning against the wall and refusing to beat his head against the drywall. He was attracted to Andrea Allen in a major way and needed to set it aside until this mess was cleared up.

It didn't matter that her belly had been faintly stained with blood. He'd barely been able to think like a sheriff while admiring her other...assets. His red-hot American boy shouted at him to take notice.

The woman he'd been watching closely was completely in shape, sleek muscles in spite of being a scholar. That is, they still needed to verify her identity. They hadn't found any ID at the scene. Nothing on the viewing platform the way she claimed. And if he hadn't seen the dead man himself, they'd be questioning her story about that, too.

Maybe that's what she'd intended? Get him distracted so she could slip out of the hospital. Andrea Allen might just be a legitimate name she acquired so she could pretend to be someone from the university.

She was either the most carefree, speak-her-mind woman he'd ever met or the best con artist he'd ever witnessed. Being a looker helped. Spirited. Easily embarrassed on one hand and then contradicting it by stripping her shirt off without blinking an eye. Dark brown hair, skin that hadn't seen sun in a while and at least five necklaces, varying in length, drawing his stare to a pair of perfectly shaped breasts.

Ginny closed the door behind her. "She sure is upset that mystery guy is dead. You better watch her, Pete. No tellin' what you've stumbled across now. Guess that's the breaks when you're the sheriff." She dragged a finger across his nameplate. "Give me a call the next time you're in Alpine."

That ship had sailed a long time ago. "Thanks. Got an estimate on that prescription?"

"I'll go check for you."

He knocked on the door. Andrea sat on the bed, tapping the nails of her right hand on those of her left.

"So they think I'm crazy or lying. What do you think?" She had a pretty pout.

He shrugged and leaned on the wall again. "Maybe the man isn't dead after all. Maybe he came to and wandered into the desert. Search party will find him or evidence. They're usually good at that."

He cleared his throat, shifted his stance and forced his thoughts back to this case. A real case. A case that would prove he could be sheriff on his own merit. Not just because his dad had to step down after his heart attack. A case that would cinch an election.

He could hear questions being asked in the hall and no answers given to Ginny. But as much as the nurse kept her mouth shut here, he knew from firsthand experience she'd be sharing that he hadn't left the room. It would be all over the county as soon as she got on her social media devices.

So be it. Her gossiping was one of the reasons they'd stopped dating. Among other things.

If the woman he'd found had been caught in the wrong place, she needed protection. She could be a witness to a mysterious crime. Or part of it. He didn't know, but he would be discovering the truth soon.

Whatever was going on, until he figured it out, Andrea Allen was stuck with him.

BEING LOOPY IN the same room with a handsome man in uniform was humiliating enough. Then Andrea had taken her shirt off. *Oh, my gosh.* And he *was* handsome. She melted a bit when he put his hat on while leaving the hospital. *A cowboy? Really?* She was a rock 'n' roll girl all the way. Classic rock and definitely not country. This guy wore boots. Real boots. Still, she wanted to find out what kissing him was like.

She absolutely adored cleft chins. Especially this one. Then there were his eyes—kind and serious, or embarrassed and sweet.

"In case you're curious, we're heading down Highway 90 to Marfa instead of directly back 118 to Fort Davis. Just in case Suit Man is waiting with friends. There are plenty of cops on 90 tonight."

"Thanks."

She refused to further embarrass herself by making small talk. Her mouth had a habit of saying exactly what she was thinking, and the more time she thought about a subject, the more she'd end up blurting out trivia about herself.

"You warm enough?" he asked.

An innocent question. Small talk. She nodded, refusing to verbalize anything. It would open a floodgate of words that would inspire an entire conversation. And what if she ended up really liking him? How could he think of her as anything but a lunatic after what had happened?

"Sorry, is that an affirmative?"

"Yes." *Keep your cool. Maybe pretend to fall asleep and he won't ask anything.* She closed her eyes and leaned her head against the cool glass of the window, trying to see the stars and constellations.

"It's okay to talk, you know. Why don't you tell me about why you're in West Texas."

Was he just making conversation? Being polite? Or pumping her for information? Did it really matter? "I don't think I should say anything. You're treating me like a suspect."

"Do you feel like a suspect? I thought I was treating you like someone who needed a lift home. I do that. It's part of my job."

"I don't know why I'm being so paranoid."

"Maybe it has something to do with a dying man falling into your arms in the middle of nowhere or being chased by unknown assailants?" He scratched between his eyebrows for a brief second. He'd done that several times as he'd dipped his chin. "Or maybe it was the guy posing as Homeland Security who attacked you."

"Yeah." She laughed for a second, surprising herself. "That might have something to do with it."

"Pretty good badge, too. Had me fooled, even down to his shoes. Most of 'em forget the shoes."

She covered her eyes, sliding her hand over her mouth. *Small talk, remember the small talk consequences.* She did not want to reveal who her father was or who he worked for. His job title was a red flag, warning off guys too frightened to stand near him. Or others would fall into hero worship when the former astronaut showed up. Either of her father's personas would make her feel like the background, and she'd lose interest in a potential relationship.

"You can rest if you want. Use the blanket I took from the trunk for a pillow. I promise it's clean."

Rolling the dark cotton into a cylinder, her brain jumpstarted as the road veered directly west again. They were getting close to the Viewing Area. She could see warning lights down the road, still miles away, but bright for a clear night on a flat piece of earth. Not anything like what she'd experienced earlier.

"I probably should just keep my mouth shut, but I don't want to forget this." She pointed at the hills to the south. "The lights I saw first appeared back that direction. There was something strange about them."

"People see lights out here all the time."

"Don't dismiss me like a tourist."

"Pardon me, ma'am. I forgot for a minute you were an astrologer."

"Astro*n*omer, but you already knew that. Trying to insult me?" From him, it didn't come across as an insult. "Can we stop to get my things, Pete? I think I'm clearheaded enough to have a discussion with your colleagues about what happened. And I'll never get to sleep if I don't have my music."

He tugged at the front of his shirt, shifting behind the wheel. "I don't think that's a good idea."

So when Pete didn't want her to know something or he was holding back, he kept a straight face and couldn't smile. Interesting. He was definitely holding back. She'd seen a lot of guys in uniform in her lifetime and they all stood a little straighter, forcing the confidence to come through as the truth.

"I don't really want to see Sharon's car or have that memory with me forever. But isn't it better than wondering about it for the rest of my life? Which is worse?"

"I can't answer that, Miss Allen." He pulled to the shoulder of the road and put the car in Park. "What I can tell you is that nothing was there except the car."

"You aren't taking me back to the observatory. Are you?"

"No, ma'am."

"So you think I murdered that man and wrecked my friend's car and made up a story about weird chopper lights to cover everything up? He was shot. Did you find a gun? And really, I came into the desert without anything? No cell, no purse, no shovel, no identification whatsoever to get rid of a dead man?" She'd started talking and couldn't stop. "Granted, if I were getting rid of a dead man, I probably wouldn't carry my ID. But alone? Get real. And if you knew me at all, no snacks and no water? Well, that just isn't going to happen."

"Wow." He draped his arm over the steering wheel, turning more of his body toward her and smiling once again. "That's impressive."

"I have a vivid imagination and think really fast. My dad rubbed off on me. I don't understand how you can assume that I'm guilty without any proof. There isn't any proof. Right? I mean, I'm not being framed, am I? Lots of people knew where I'd be tonight."

"Just hold on a minute." He straightened the arm closer to her, reaching out to pat her shoulder. "If you can take a breath and slow down to my speed, I can explain what's going on. To a certain degree."

She faced forward and shoved her fingers under her legs. Watching his sincerity was clouding her ability to analyze the situation correctly. She'd allowed him to distract her far too long and should have called her parents immediately. She knew *that* number by heart. "Okay, I'm breathing."

"You've been in protective custody since I got a phone

call from the paramedics that there wasn't a body in the vehicle. No one's arresting you."

"But you saw him? I'm not…" She'd been about to say *crazy.*

He nodded. "I have pictures of a man at the scene matching the description you gave me earlier. Neither of us imagined it."

"Thank goodness." The sigh of relief was more than just verbal, it was liberating, and she physically felt lighter. For a moment, she'd doubted if she was experiencing an actual memory. Part of her imagination could have been distorted from the concussion.

Was that a possibility? She had definitely passed out after the accident. Could she have warped what really happened? Should she throw that scenario into the mix? No. She wasn't paranoid, just overthinking as usual. It was better to wait on the investigation and not doubt herself.

"Look, Miss Allen. Until we know what's going on, everyone believes it's better for me to stick close."

"I can't do my work just anywhere. Even under protective custody at the observatory would be difficult. Don't I have to consent or something? And who's everyone?"

For once, the man with all the answers seemed at a loss for words. It couldn't be plainer he was choosing his words carefully.

"I'm not trying to scare you, but being new around here you may not know that we've had a lot of drugs and guns crossing the border recently. Strange activity involving a helicopter and a disappearing body seems more than a little suspicious. It's better to be safe."

"And better to keep me close while you verify that I don't have anything to do with it."

"Hmm, there is that."

He grinned again, and she realized that there wasn't anything calculating about it. He seemed to be a good-looking, concerned officer who took his job very seriously to help her feel safe and at ease. Correction, he was absolutely terrific-looking and naturally charming. And off-limits?

Pete Morrison should be off-limits. She was completing her study and then getting a job halfway around the world. No reason to get involved. It wasn't logical. She didn't have time for a relationship.

Satisfied he was there to help and she needed to curb her attraction, she slapped her thighs, ready to cooperate. "I have a passport to verify who I am. It's at the observatory housing where I'm staying until I get my telescope time. I'm only here for three weeks."

He put the truck in motion. "So it was just coincidence that you were at the Viewing Area looking for the lights? Tourist or PhD work?"

"Filling in for a student. It's an ongoing study by UT. That's why I was driving her car. I hope her insurance covers accident by strange helicopter. She's going to kill me."

"No comment. I don't let people borrow my truck." He put the patrol car in Drive. "Not even my dad."

The circular building where tourists stopped to watch for the Marfa Lights phenomenon passed by amid several parked vehicles, including another squad car identical to the one she was inside. The radio squawked, and Pete lifted the hand microphone to his lips. It certainly was easy to think of the man by his first name.

"Yeah, Dad?"

"And what if it hadn't been me?" answered a gruff voice through the static.

"It's always you." Pete laughed after he'd released the talk button and couldn't be heard. "Remember that I have a ride-along."

"I ain't that old, buster Pete. Not much new here, but DHS wants you to meet them at the station with the witness."

"Headed there now. Out."

He stowed the microphone, and she waited for an explanation, but waiting wasn't really her thing. She was more of a straight-to-the-point, fixer type of person and yet she really didn't want to explain right now.

"Real DHS?" she asked, gulping at the potential conversation she'd be forced to have soon.

"The Department of Homeland Security. Looks like our missing body rang some official bells."

"Dang it." *Are they here for a missing body or because of my involvement?* It didn't take much to come to the conclusion it was about her. "Did they mention why they want to talk to me?"

"They probably need your statement. This is a good thing. They'll move the investigation forward a lot faster. You should be glad. We'll be out of your hair that much sooner."

Her instinct and her luck shouted differently.

"Not likely. Why is this happening now? Oh, I know you mentioned the guns and drugs and border thing. But I'm so close to finishing this dissertation. Shoot."

They entered Marfa and turned north toward the county jail. Pete let his department dispatch know they were on their way in.

"Did they say who would be coming here?" she asked.

"You know someone at Homeland Security?"

Hopefully, she wouldn't have to explain herself. She'd give her interview, they'd say everything was a huge mistake, no one's actually trying to kill you and she could return to finish her short time in the Davis Mountains. "I'd rather not get into it."

"Andrea, you're the one who brought it up."

"And I'm the one who's not going to talk about it." *Not unless I really, really have to.*

Chapter Five

Close to nine in the morning, an official government vehicle pulled in front of the Presidio County Sheriff's Department. One uniformed man got out. Navy, lots of rank. He openly assessed the street, then spent several minutes checking his phone.

Pete watched everything, but his main focus was Andrea. Her posture changed. She looked defeated. After she'd said she didn't want to discuss the DHS, she didn't discuss anything. Gone was the chatty, confident woman who spoke her mind. Now she was withdrawn, closed off, silent, and stood with her hands wrapped around her waist.

The officer acknowledged Pete, but his eyes had connected with Andrea and he wasn't looking anywhere else.

"Commander," Andrea said on a long, exasperated sigh and led the way to his dad's office. She clearly didn't want the DHS representative to be the man who'd walked into the sheriff's office.

"Andrea," the DHS expert acknowledged with a similar annoyed exhale. He shut the door behind him, leaving only silhouettes against the opaque window—letting Pete know they were on opposite sides of the small room.

Interesting. His witness recognized military rank and the DHS officer seemed to know her. She'd been tight-lipped since they arrived at the station. Either pretending to be asleep on his cot in the back or flat out refusing to answer any questions.

"Do you want something to eat, Pete?" Honey asked.

The shift change had occurred at eight o'clock sharp, just like every normal day. Peach and Honey insisted on working seven days a week, knowing his dad would let them off anytime they wanted. They liked staying busy, but they liked staying out of each other's hair more. They'd each confided in him—and probably everyone else in town—that it was the only reason they continued to live in the same house.

"No, thanks, Honey. I thought I'd take Miss Allen to the café when she's done."

"Are you sure she's not going to be whisked away by aliens or a secret government agency?" The older woman laughed, making fun of several theories Peach had shared before leaving. "The sheriff is hung up at the scene for at least another hour, Pete. He wanted me to let you know."

He could guess why his father hadn't spoken to him directly. Most likely to keep his cool at the lack of cooperation. "He still fighting for information?"

"I can only assume so," Honey said, picking up her pen. "You know those government types. They never let us in on the fun."

"You adding this to your novel?" he asked, and was ignored since she was already engrossed in writing her sentence.

Peach came up with the stories and Honey was the aspiring writer who wrote them down. They'd kept the local women busy debating the realism of their tales for several years. It was obvious even to strangers that they were best friends who happened to be sisters.

A yawn escaped him. It was the first double shift he'd completed without a wink of shut-eye in a long while. But he couldn't head back to the ranch until DHS instructed them on what was to happen with Andrea. His dad would be at the scene awhile. That left him with nothing to do but catch up on paperwork and wait for their guests to finish. He'd be lucky if he could go home afterward.

"Since things are covered at the moment, I'm going to grab a quick shower in the back and wake up. Alert me if they," he said, hooking his thumb toward his dad's closed office door, "finish up."

"I have a feeling they're going to be there awhile," Honey said. "Don't you think it's a bit strange that he's here to interview a witness and didn't even introduce himself?"

"I suppose you have a point. I'm not certain what protocol is for something like this. We normally don't share murder jurisdiction with anyone."

"You certain there's not going to be another murder soon?"

Voices were definitely rising on the other side of the window, but the old building had walls thick enough that he couldn't distinguish the words. Should he step inside and allow them to cool off? If he was closer, maybe he could understand what the argument was about.

"Do you think you should join them and referee?" Honey asked.

Pete took definite steps toward the arguing and stopped. It only took those three steps to realize he'd been waiting on encouragement from Honey so he could barge in and rescue Andrea again.

Son of a gun.

He was more interested in this fascinating woman than the murder and the disappearing body. He pivoted and headed into the back.

"Ten minutes. That's all I need for a shower."

"*I* could eavesdrop?"

"Get back to your writing, Honey."

"Yes, sir."

The door slamming had nothing to do with his actions. They'd been meaning to fix the mechanism that slowed the heavy door from crashing shut. He hadn't thought about it until the loud crash echoed in the concrete hallway. He threw his stuff into the locker and jumped under an icy spray, not giving the water time to warm.

Holding cells and the jail were on a different floor. He needed to put some effort into this case. His thoughts were centered more on Andrea's relationship with Homeland Security than getting his notes together for the investigation or why someone would steal the body of a dead man.

He'd offered to try to identify the missing man but had been specifically instructed not to even print pictures from the camera. Normally, he hated being shut out and treated like a wet-behind-the-ears rookie. Today, it had hardly crossed his mind. But it had, and soon after, he'd copied the pictures to a memory stick and stuck it in his pocket.

On the flip side, he couldn't *stop* thinking about Andrea Allen. He had no reason to book her and no criminal record he could find. DHS had just asked her to be held until they arrived.

Who was she? Where was she going after the observatory? What was her life like? Where had she been? How had she gotten that jagged old scar under her chin and the small one just above her collarbone?

Three weeks wasn't a long time to get the answers. Might be even less time. She'd mentioned three weeks total but had never mentioned how long she'd been here.

Pete toweled off and stuck his legs in his pants as quickly as a surprised rattler about to strike. He wasn't about to miss the opportunity to speak with the officer when he left. He considered shaving, but it would take too much time.

Looking in the mirror one last time, he shoved his

hair straight back and caught movement behind him. His weapon was still secure in his locker, so he spun, ready for—

"Andrea? How'd you get back here? I didn't hear the door."

"Some of us know how to close one without slamming it. They probably heard you come through it on Proxima Centauri."

"Prox what?" He leaned against the sink, crossing his arms and just enjoying how she could look so dang sexy even in teddy bear scrubs. The meek, insecure side of the woman he'd been admiring was gone. Spunky, speak-your-mind PhD candidate was approaching him one sure step at a time.

"It's the nearest star to earth, with the exception of our sun, of course. But it's not my favorite."

"The sun? I'm sort of fond of it."

"As I can see by your tan. No, Proxima Centauri. It's such a stuffy name."

She halted within arm's distance. A dangerous distance. Close enough to see his attraction reflected in her soft blue eyes. The desire to put a hand on each of her hips and draw her to him was tremendous. He had to clear his throat to think of something other than the pink lacy bra he'd seen earlier.

"I should go speak with the DHS officer." He took a step to move past her and ended with a slender hand on his chest.

"The Commander's gone to the scene. He said to stay put until he returned. Looks like you're stuck with me, Sheriff Morrison."

"*Acting* sheriff. Why don't you call me Pete." Was he insulted? Or too dang excited he didn't need to dart off to talk shop? *Excited.*

"I need to show you something."

"I don't think that's appropriate."

She threw back her head, laughing. He barely heard it as he admired the bend of her neck. "Silly. Do you have any gel?"

"Huh?" *Silly* wasn't the word filtering through his mind.

"Styling gel."

"I used it already."

"Not enough to do anything." She reached around him, brushing his arm as she squeezed goo into her hands.

Stunned into silence? Choking on his words? Cat got his tongue? He didn't know which, and if she asked, he couldn't hear her. He was focused on her hands rubbing together and then her arms lifting to reach his head.

"Get shorter." She tapped the inside of his bare feet wider apart, leaving enough room between them to breathe without touching.

"So, what *is* your favorite star?" he asked, closing his eyes and enjoying her fingers lightly massaging his scalp as she liberally put gel on every strand. He couldn't look.

"Wolf 359. Isn't that an awesome name for a star?" She took the tube a second time. "Just a bit more. Your hair's really thick and wavy."

He was dang lucky he'd put his pants on quickly. If he hadn't…

"See?"

All he could see was the roundness of each breast under the thin layer of hospital garb.

"All you have to do is squeeze some on your hands and rub it around like this. Then it should stay looking deliberately messed up all day." She wiped her hands on his towel and admired her handiwork. "That will look much better later when it's dry."

She twisted one last piece of hair and placed her hands on his shoulders. It seemed like the most natural gesture in his memory for his fingers to move and span either side of her waist. Drawing her closer to him was just as easy.

They were forehead to forehead. Her slow, warm exhale smelled sweet like the cola she'd insisted on before the officer had arrived. She'd called it her wake-up drink of choice. He, on the other hand, loved coffee and lots of it.

Concentrate on the job. What job? All he had to do was hang around here, keep her in sight till she was someone else's problem. Maybe even escort her home.

"I'm not a rule breaker, Andrea."

"Then why are your hands still around me?"

Kissing her was destined as soon as she'd told him they'd never get along. "What's about to happen probably shouldn't. But you won't find me apologizing for it later."

"You better not, Pete. Bad first kissers don't get a second chance."

He liked her. A lot. Too much. Too fast.

He leaned his lips to touch hers for the first time. Soft and wet, they parted just enough to encourage him. His hands spread up her back, noticing the firm muscles.

There wasn't anything between them now except a thin layer of cotton. He stopped himself from getting the shirt out of his way. This was their first kiss but sure didn't feel like it.

Their lips slid together, teasing, seeming to know their way without conscious effort. A perfect fit? Practiced. Confident.

He wanted his hands to wander but forced them to stay put. Andrea's arms encircled his neck, shifting her body next to his. Her tennis shoes snuggled next to his size-thirteen feet. That one layer kept him both sane and drove him crazy at the same time.

He wanted it off. Wanted her bare skin under his flesh. Wanted to forget exactly where they were and remember everything much too late.

The attraction turned to mutual pure hunger and he liked her even more.

Chapter Six

Maybe it was defying her father, the Commander. Maybe it was a bit of the rebellious daughter in her that forced the need to push him at every turn. Or maybe she saw something in this man that she recognized as rare. A part of him that was wise beyond his years.

Attraction or defiance. It didn't matter for Andrea. Not at this moment. She was totally enthralled by Pete's kissing abilities. Something she hadn't experienced in a long time, if ever.

"Did I pass?" he asked when they came up for air, continuing small kisses and nips down her neck.

"I think you've earned a second audition." She tilted her head back to give him better access.

A few light touches of those incredible lips across her shoulder where the large scrubs top fell to the side and then he stood straight. She was close enough to notice the tiny gold flecks in his dark brown eyes. Hard chest, hard shoulders, hard biceps. This man was all man, yet playful. And those dimples were just killer.

She liked him. He was perfect for her plan to ignore her father.

"And just when is this second audition to take place?" he asked, his voice rich with the desire displayed in his eyes.

"How long does it take to get back to the observatory?" She had to entice him into taking her home.

"I thought you were ordered to stay put?" His hands slid under her loose top, warming her bare back and exposing her belly as the top inched higher.

"Technically, but I'd be safe with you. We came to an understanding." She did a little of her own exploring, dragging her nails across his well-sculpted muscles.

"I think you may have gotten the wrong impression about me." He gently circled her wrists with his fingers and returned their hands to their sides.

"Why do you say that?" Andrea painted the words with innocence.

He took a couple of steps backward and opened the door. "Honey?"

"Yes, Pete?"

"Did the Commander leave any parting words?"

"You mean when he said, 'I expect my daughter to be here when I return'? That's pretty much everything."

When Pete smiled a really healthy smile that made it all the way to his eyes, he had dimpled cheeks to match the one in his chin. She truly was a sucker for dimples. He let the door close, crossed his arms and leaned that bare back against the gray paint. "So he's your father. How did you understand those specific instructions to include a drive up the mountain?"

"Are you going to let him order you around? You aren't in the Navy. Technically, he doesn't have any jurisdiction. He's only here because I'm involved." Her dad was assigned to the Customs and Border Protection Office, reporting directly to the DHS. He had every right to ask the local sheriff for cooperation in a case. But he hadn't. And forcing her to stay at the county jail wasn't about any case. It was about controlling her life.

"To use a word you seem to love—*technically* he's with Homeland Security. I haven't been filled in yet, but he does have some authority around here. Your dad wants you to stay put and be safe. My dad wants me to stay put and see that you are." He pushed off the door, twisted the combination on a lock and lifted the latch of a locker. He pulled out a crisply starched uniform shirt and shoved his hands through the sleeves.

"Your jerky movements may be revealing your true feelings. Or they could be showing me your true nature."

"Maybe I just failed the second audition." After turning his back, he pushed the tail of his shirt inside his pants.

"I know my rights. You can't keep me here against my will. You certainly can't use the excuse *her daddy made me do it*. It will all be on you when I sue the county."

"At the moment, I'm too tired to care. I've gone without sleep for a couple of nights and haven't had the privilege of napping like you. So let me spell this out real plain like. You have two choices. Spend your time here in protective custody locked in a cell or walk down the street and have breakfast with me. Simple. You choose."

"You won't change your mind about that audition?" She added a wink, teasing him.

"I'm too hungry to change my mind." He stretched his neck, swiveling his head from side to side.

She made a grand gesture to follow him. "Lead on."

"Be right there. I walk better in my boots."

If she could get through the door before he buckled his gun around his hips, she might have enough of a head start to ditch the impromptu bodyguard her father had assigned. Then what? Downtown wasn't filled with public transportation and there certainly wasn't a taxi waiting on the corner.

The heavy door to the restricted area slammed behind her. She'd at least wait in the comfy chair in his office. Getting far away from his dimples seemed a good idea. The more he smiled at her, the more she was willing to change the venue of his *audition*.

Who was she trying to fool? Pete had already passed any audition with flying colors. She had one more Saturday night in West Texas and hoped this was the last time she thought about being bored.

Before she could sit, the restricted door slammed again. Pete scooted through, one boot on and one boot in his hand. With the office door open, she could watch his head turn, searching and landing on the receptionist.

He looked straight at her, let out a deep breath, showing his relief, and pulled on his second boot. "Good. I'm too tired to run."

"Don't get comfortable. There's been a disturbance near Doug Fossen's place. A burning vehicle on the side of the road near the state park."

"That's Davis County jurisdiction. Give Mike Barber a call."

"They know that but think you need to see it."

"Send Griggs, then."

"He hasn't reported in this morning and they're asking for the sheriff. That's you."

"What the…" He took a piece of paper from the woman. She looked a lot like the receptionist who had been at the front desk when they arrived. "Honey, please call Peach and see if she forgot to give me a message about Griggs."

"Pete, you know she didn't forget. I can get Joe to write Griggs up if you don't want to do it. But right now we have a problem at the Fossens'."

"I have babysitting duty."

Andrea stuck her head out the office door. "Don't mind this baby. I can sleep in that nice jail cell you suggested. I'm sure the Commander would prefer me safe and sound, guarded by a senior citizen." She nodded toward the receptionist. "No offense."

"None taken," Honey said, bringing the ringing handset up to her ear. "Presidio County Sheriff's Department." Honey wrote more notes. "We'll get someone out there shortly, Mrs. Fossen." She waved the slips in the air.

"I'm not heading anywhere, Honey. I smell a mess brewing and there's no way I'm taking anyone with me on a call." Pete reached for his hat on a nearby desk. He almost shoved his hair off his forehead. He stopped, tapped the styling gel now hardened in place and then scratched the bridge of his nose.

"Sounds like you need to get a move on." She raised her wrists to him. "Do your duty, Sheriff Pete. Lock me away."

His moment of indecision played on his handsome face. Then it was chased away with confidence. "Honey, get my dad or somebody from the accident last night on the radio."

"Yes, sir," the receptionist said.

"I'm not doing it. Send Dominguez and Hardy." He muttered something under his breath. "Come on, Andrea."

"Mind if I take the jacket from your office?"

"It's not my office, but I'm sure the sheriff won't mind."

With Honey answering the ringing phone and Pete rubbing the bridge of his nose, she walked to the coatrack in the corner. All the framed pictures on the wall were of Pete growing up. There was no mistaking the cleft in his chin or the tall, lanky frame. They were snapshots from his life of sports, school and graduation. One caught him shoving his hand through his hair and setting his hat on his head.

"That one's my favorite. He looks so uncomplicated, don't you think?" Honey stood in the doorway, arms crossed over her Davis Mountains souvenir T-shirt.

"I imagine he's rarely uncomplicated."

"You're a smart woman for picking up on that so quickly. He went for breakfast or he's using you as the excuse to fill his belly. We didn't get to officially meet earlier. I'm Honey, part-time dispatcher and unofficial receptionist around here. You met my sister, Peach, when you arrived earlier."

"You look alike."

"Don't tell her that." Honey laughed. "Do you have everything you need?"

"Yes, thanks. Sorry if the Commander offended you earlier. I wish I could say he was stressed and this wasn't his usual behavior, but today is just business as usual. I love him, but sometimes he's rather rude."

"I totally understand, sweetie. I hope you like breakfast burritos. That's just about all Pete ever has time to grab from that café." Honey crossed her arms over her heaving bosom and planted herself in the middle of the doorway.

"Anything's fine. Some of these pictures are really good. Have you known them long?" She quickly received the message that Pete had gone to the café alone and she was staying put. She might as well glean useful information about her adversary.

"Pete's worked with his dad since he was— Actually, I can't remember a time Pete wasn't here in this office. The sheriff prior to Joe paid him to empty the trash and sweep up as soon as he could hold a broom."

"Was his mom behind the camera in all these?" Andrea pointed at the wall, noticing that there weren't any with women.

"No. One of Pete's parents was a second cousin or something to Joe. They died and Pete came to live in Marfa. Poor man never considered marrying, but adopted a three-year-old without missing a beat. Peach and I moved here close to the same time."

"I'm glad Pete found someone and things worked out for him. And thanks. I would have really stepped in it asking about his mom if you hadn't shared."

"The whole community's been contributing to that wall. He's like one of our own, you know."

"I sure didn't want to spend all morning locked in that cell. Maybe we should go back to your desk." She got close enough to hug Honey—even though that was the furthest thing from her mind. She gestured to move out of the room, and then it hit her. "I get it. You're supposed to watch me until Pete gets back. Aren't you?"

Honey smiled, crossing her arms and planting her large frame in the doorway. "He reminded me that it's part of my job responsibilities designated under 'other.' I offered to get his breakfast, but he said he needed a break. Sorry, but you aren't going anywhere until Pete comes for you. He's smarter than he is cute."

"Ha, he is pretty darn cute. This doesn't have anything to do with him. Not really. I'll lose two years of work if I'm here when the Commander comes back. He'll haul me to Austin or worse, DC. I'll be unable to finish my thesis and…" Trying to talk her way out of the office wasn't working. "You don't care one rogue meteor what this is going to do to my life."

This couldn't be happening. She only needed six more days.

"Take a seat, Miss Allen." Honey crossed her arms and stood as straight as her aged body would allow. "I do know that *caring* about prisoners is not in my job description."

For a split second she considered making a run for it out the restricted door through the back exit. But there was nowhere for her to go. Staying with Pete wasn't a bad idea. He was the only one who could solve her current problem. She had to avoid her father and stay in West Texas for at least six more days.

Chapter Seven

"I can't be here when my father comes for me."

"You won't be. Let's go." Pete waited for Andrea to follow, cell phone still to his ear.

"Some days are busier than others. Enjoy your ride." Honey answered her ringing phone.

He escorted Andrea to the Tahoe without any instruction. She hopped in and quickly dropped her head against the headrest, closing her eyes and looking completely relaxed.

Pete knew different. He recognized the compliance she thought was necessary until she could talk herself into a different position.

Pete tapped his smartphone and left another message for his dad. "We didn't finish our conversation. Be prepared. I'm dropping Miss Allen off with her father and returning with you. I will lock you up to make you rest. Honey's plumping the pillows in the holding for you. No scene or I swear you won't like being cuffed and thrown into the backseat of your old service vehicle."

He disconnected, debating the logic of moving his witness. She was safer here, in a building filled with law enforcement officers. Yet Commander Allen had been adamant when they spoke. His daughter would be brought to him at the Viewing Area immediately. A chopper was on its way to airlift them home. The directive had included instructions not to inform Andrea where they were heading or why.

Prisoners were kept better informed than this guy treated his daughter.

"When did he call?" Andrea asked as soon as he sat behind the wheel. Questioning arched brows, innocent open eyes and an impish suggestive grin—she looked totally in control.

"Who?" That wouldn't fly. She knew that *he* knew who she was talking about.

"The Commander. I've seen the look of having to swallow his orders many times."

"What you witnessed was me leaving a message for my dad."

"Oh." She looked at him and then her chin went up a notch with her aha moment. "You aren't denying that the Commander called."

"No, I'm not. Why do you call him Commander?"

"I've always addressed him by his rank. Well, at least since I was a teenager. It was easier. He answered to it faster when we were in a crowd and he's never seemed to mind. Since you aren't sharing our destination, I suppose he told you not to tell me. Afraid I'd pitch a fit or something?"

"He didn't mention fits of any sort. In fact, he didn't explain his reasoning with me at all. He seems very concerned about your safety. Why is that exactly?" It had to be finding that man from the desert. Whoever he escaped from—that didn't take a genius to determine—knew he'd made contact with Andrea and they thought she knew something. Including her father.

"I don't know what you mean. I spent all of five minutes in his presence. How does that make him appear concerned?"

"We can skip all the tippytoeing around." He took another look behind them and yet another along the horizon, searching for he didn't know what. "Your father asked me to bring you to the accident site. I disagreed. If men are after you, then you're much more vulnerable alone with me in this vehicle. Doesn't matter that it's only nine miles to their location."

"Did he mention why he wants me there?"

"To leave."

Either Andrea had seen or heard something from her passenger or these men were so well connected they knew she was the daughter of the man investigating them. That would account for a DHS impostor trying to remove her from the hospital.

Her fingers curled into her palms. "I've said this before, but I'm an adult and he has no right—"

"Pete?" Honey's shaky voice broke through on the radio. "Pete, are you there?"

He could tell she was upset. "What's wrong?"

"Jeff Davis County just called. They found our missing deputy's car abandoned near the state park. You want me to send one of the new guys to check it out?"

"Negative. Ask Hardy to head over." He released the button on the microphone.

"You need to go and I'm in the way," Andrea said. "You can drop me off with Honey. I promise to be good."

He pulled the car to the side of the road. "The Viewing Area is still three or four miles. I could drop you off, then hightail it back north."

"Or?"

Something hadn't been sitting right about the facts in this case. Too many coincidences. Too many orders issued. Too many gut feelings that he needed to be doing something active instead of reactive.

"Did I lose you, Pete?" Honey asked.

He spun the vehicle around and brought the microphone

up to his mouth. "I'm here. Tell Jeff Davis County I'm on my way and ask if they can wait to move anything."

"That's what they wanted to hear, Pete. They're searching for our deputy as we speak." The radio clicked off and back on. "You still babysitting?"

Andrea rolled her eyes and shook her head. A laugh escaped as he answered, "That's an affirmative."

Honey laughed into the microphone. "Think they'll find our deputy passed out on a park bench?"

"I'll write the reprimand myself. On my way."

Pete's rash decision about bringing a witness to a crime scene would come back and bite him. He was certain about that. He was also certain she'd done her best to manipulate him with the make-out session and talk about second auditions. Andrea Allen sat next to him because *she* wanted to be there. She might have just hypnotized him or something with those large, dark blue eyes. Yep, this decision would definitely bite him in the end.

"I never stood a chance," he mumbled aloud.

"Did you say something?"

"Yeah, stay in the car when we arrive until I give you permission to get out. Or I'll put you in cuffs for your own protection."

"Sure thing. That was a good breakfast burrito."

Was she agreeing just a little too quickly? Changing the subject even quicker? If she wanted it changed, he could roll with that.

"Always is from the café. I'm thinking you should tell me what's going on between you and your dad. Why are you afraid he's going to take you home? You're a little old for a runaway."

"That's funny, but not far from the truth. I've been running from my parents since I was twenty and wanted to change my major the first time."

"You've changed more than once?"

"Not really. I let them talk me into completing three."

"So you're an overachiever. Will this be a fourth?"

"Not an overachiever as much as... Well, I feel more like a compliant child. I'm working on my doctorate in space studies and need to be here to finish up."

"Sounds like a complicated relationship."

"You know how parents and college are," she said casually.

"Not really." He repeated her words, wanting to avoid his life history as much as possible.

"You didn't have to go to become a police officer?" She looked genuinely confused. "You're looking at me like I'm a cat with two heads."

"My dad has been sheriff in this county since I graduated from high school. He was a deputy before that. I've been around that office my entire life. I didn't need any references or education except what he could teach me."

"Is this all you ever want to do? Be sheriff?"

"You say that like it's a bad thing."

"No, I'm sorry. I always have an uncanny ability to say exactly what makes people uncomfortable or just end up insulting them."

"Well, now that you mention it..."

"Seriously, I apologize. I just meant...is being sheriff your dream or your father's?"

"Both, I guess. I haven't ever given it much thought. Everyone just assumed I would be."

He hadn't given it much thought until his dad's heart attack and he'd been asked to step in. It was always one day in a future he assumed was way down the road. Now? His father's bombshell had exploded and was a constant distraction.

He couldn't dwell on that problem. Andrea was enough distraction for any man to handle.

"Not too many people have wanted the job. It's a lot of territory and a lot of nothing. It's just so excitin' and all."

"Now you're just teasing. You've had alien visitors, a missing body, an attempted homicide and Homeland Security taking over an investigation all in less than twelve hours. I am very confident that everyone wants to be in your shoes." Andrea smiled, teasing him at every turn.

"Yeah, I see what you mean." He did have a decision to make about the election. Soon. But not before he needed to find a missing deputy and determine what was really going on in his county. And if he let this woman go before he had some basic questions answered, they might go unanswered for quite a long while.

He drove. Quickly, efficiently. He knew every shortcut not only in his county, but also to the north and east.

"I've always been told I'd achieve certain things. There are only problems when I assume I can go about them in my own fashion..." Her voice drifted off and she looked out the window.

"Sheriff, this is Honey. Where are you?"

He picked up the car radio. "About three miles south of Fort Davis."

"They found Logan."

He heard the shakiness to her voice. She wasn't irritated—a tone he'd heard plenty of times from her being interrupted. She'd been crying. "What aren't you saying?"

"It's not good, Pete."

"Are you talking about Logan Griggs?" Andrea asked, gripping his arm.

He nodded. "Why? Do you know him?"

"That's Sharon's boyfriend. She's the woman I was covering for last night. They had a date. Do you— Do you think...?"

He knew what she didn't want to ask. If they'd been

returning from Alpine and were stopped by the same men who had tried to kill her...

"Both of your fathers are headed there now. Should I tell them you're on your way?"

"Negative. They'll find out soon enough. Inform the searchers there may be a woman missing."

"Come again?"

"A UT student may have been with Griggs. Tell them and keep me posted."

What a mess.

"Before you try to convince me to take you someplace other than to meet your father, we need to stop the secretiveness."

"Absolutely. Do you really think Sharon was with him?"

"There's more to your accident than you're telling me. Homeland doesn't send teams to investigate car accidents for six hours. Not even when daughters are involved. Now, what's going on?"

"I...I swear I don't know. Sharon asked me to cover for her at the last minute. That's all. She had a date, didn't want to watch for the lights, asked me to take pictures if anything happened and even let me borrow her car." She raised fingers as she went through her mental list.

"Did you take pictures?" That had to be what they were after. "Where is the camera? I didn't find one in the car."

"I...I dropped it in the front seat when I dragged the man into the back. It had to be in the car. Do you think it got thrown out during the crash?"

"I made a cursory search in the dark, then followed your tracks and took you to the hospital."

"Then those men followed you to the hospital."

Pete turned the Tahoe into the state park entrance, eager to confirm that this accident was connected to the other. Dreading the sight of one of his deputies—and friend—being the victim of a homicide. Dreading more that he knew it wasn't an accident and that he needed to warn the woman next to him.

"Andrea, as more information comes to light, I have a gnawing feeling that none of this has been coincidence. I don't think anyone followed me to the hospital. I think they were prepared for the possibility you might get away. That they expected you to be at the Viewing Area last night."

She stared at her hands, shaking her head in disbelief. "No way."

"Do you think they could be setting a trap to get rid of your father? Has anything like this ever happened before?"

"He's only been DHS for a year or so, but no. Never."

"You're staying with me. I'm responsible for you. You will listen to me, understand? I tell you to stay in the car, you stay in the car. I tell you to do anything, you do it. Got it?"

A man had tried to abduct her, had knocked her across the room just hours ago and she hadn't looked as worried as right now, staring at him.

"You can't be right about this, Pete. But even if you aren't, you're beginning to scare me a little."

"Well, damn. I meant to scare you a lot."

Chapter Eight

Andrea waited in the car as instructed. Not because Pete had sworn her to obedience or issued orders. If waiting in the car hadn't been the safest place physically, it was the safest place mentally. Logan's body had been found not far from the car on the other side of the hill.

The car fire had brought the park rangers to the main road. They'd extinguished the dry brush before it had gotten out of control about the time she and Pete arrived. She'd put her face in her hands and refused to watch after Pete parked. She didn't want the image of a wrecked car, possibly with charred bodies, forever in her memory. The fake ones in movies were bad enough to fuel her imagination.

The sunlight began chasing shadows away at the bottom of the nearby hills where officers searched for evidence. And for Sharon, who hadn't returned to the observatory housing last night.

Plain, simple, old-fashioned apprehension had her short, practical nails digging into her palms. It built in her chest, clogging her throat until she wanted to jump from the SUV. She pushed the door open and was greeted by the horrible acrid smell of burning plastic. Dark smoke continued to billow into the sparse trees.

The guilt and uncertainty of what she should do played

with her mind. Pete had scared her with his declaration before jumping out of the truck to identify Logan's body.

Was she in danger if she stayed to finish her study? She swiped the tears trickling down her face. Sharon had been so full of life…

Had her young coworker died because those monsters thought it had been Pete returning her to the observatory? Was this her fault? What was she supposed to do now? Or had Sharon set her up to be kidnapped so they could manipulate the Commander?

After what they'd been through at the hospital, she trusted Pete to defend her and do it well. She respected his honesty along with his ability. She also appreciated that he wasn't bossing her around because he could. He had every right, and he could have left her in a jail cell waiting on the Commander. She knew what her father would do. A decree would be made and if she didn't follow his instructions to the letter, an agent or officer she didn't know would enforce his orders.

Parents shouldn't have that type of authority over their twenty-six-year-old children. Especially since she'd been paying her own way since her first degree. And most didn't. She was the only person who gave her parents the authority. This was her life, but she had the feeling it was about to spin completely out of her control.

Six days was all she needed to finish her dissertation and get the dream job halfway around the world. Far away from Commander Tony Allen, former astronaut now working for the Department of Homeland Security. And farther away from Dr. Beatrice Allen, wife, perfect mother and foremost authority on the Brontë sisters in the United States.

Even with three degrees behind her, Andrea felt compelled to argue for a thesis on a once-in-a-lifetime star. She'd fought for her allotted time tracking it over the next week. Even though the observatory had been perfectly willing to record what the telescope found and send it to her, she'd insisted on being here. Personally overseeing the collection of data, trying to impress experts halfway around the world.

If she failed…what then? Another degree? In another subject? Another direction? Give in and teach with her mother? Hear all the reasons she'd failed because she'd chosen a terrible topic or that she must not have applied herself enough?

Her parents' voices saying "I told you so" rang through her head. They'd been right too many times to ignore.

This was her last shot. One star was certain to rise over the next six days. The question was if she'd watch it from behind an international telescope or if she'd see it on TV designated by her father as secure.

Pete tapped on the driver's window, and she unlocked the doors. "No, she's with me and staying with me. Especially now." He carefully set his hat in the backseat, kept the phone to his ear and made a motion for the keys.

While he was gone, she'd kept them in her hand. She placed the key in the ignition and started the car. Pete looked at her strangely and agreed with whomever he was talking to. Cell still to his ear, he put the car in gear and took off quickly, a cloud of dust billowing behind them.

"Two males. About a hundred yards from the vehicle. No, that's not in question." He paused, listening. "No, she's not staying. I agree, not over the phone. I assume someone's listening and I won't risk it."

"What's not a problem?" she asked, but he hadn't hung up and just waved her question aside.

"Yes, sir. I understand, sir." Pete stuck the phone in his shirt pocket.

"I can tell that was my father. What are our orders now?"

"Your transport is meeting us at the observatory."

"And I have no say in it." She wanted to fight for her right to stay and yet…two men were dead.

"No, Andrea, you don't. It's obvious to everyone now that *you* were the target. The man beside Griggs in that ditch is the same one from the car."

"And Sharon?" She'd barely known the young woman, but her heart sank under the guilt. Sharon was probably dead because Pete had taken her to Marfa instead of to the observatory. If it hadn't been for Pete finding her when he did, she'd be dead, too.

Pete's phone rang, squealing a hard-rock tune she loved before he tapped it and raised it to his ear. "Come on, Dad. Take it easy on the man and work with him. Right. You, too. See you at the ranch."

Question after question rammed their way into her mind and needed to be asked as soon as Pete set the phone down.

"They thought they were us. That could have been you. Oh, my God, I can't believe— I mean, I know what that suit tried to do last night, but it all sort of seemed surreal. You were there to stop him. What do we do now? I mean, I heard what you said, but are you taking me to the Commander? He's going to ship me home on the first plane headed in that direction. Or any direction, for that matter."

"Honestly, Andrea, you throw out so many questions that I don't know where to start. They haven't found your friend. Were you close?"

"Not really. I just can't believe she's dead."

"The body from last night is an undercover agent working for your father." His grip tightened on the wheel. He was obviously upset, too. "I'll wait with you until your father's helicopter arrives. He's ordered—"

"I'm not leaving."

"Someone's trying to kill you. Two people are dead, maybe three. What do you mean you aren't going?"

"I've waited two years for this one week. This one specific week. I'm scheduled to use the telescope for the next six nights. If I don't, all of my research is useless."

"And that's more important than your life?"

"I have one shot at this star."

"In the right wind, one shot's all any sniper needs."

"You really believe that my life is in danger?"

"Yes. Or worse," he mumbled, but she heard him loud and clear.

"Then I'll go." She really had no choice. The longer she stayed here, the more people she put in danger. Her father had loosely warned about threats a year ago when he was transferred. Until that very moment, she'd never believed anyone would actually threaten her.

Now she was indirectly responsible for at least one man dying. She couldn't handle another—specifically Pete—losing his life, too.

"You're not just saying the words that I want to hear. You're going to leave when the time comes?" He reached out and tipped her chin upward. Her eyes raised from her hands and focused on the dimples apparent in his cheeks.

His smile relieved the apprehension, lessened the guilt, made her want to spar with him again. "Do you need me to pinkie-swear or something, Sheriff?"

"Acting sheriff, and no." He rested the crook of his arm on the back of the seat between them. "So…um…I guess this will be it. I don't suppose you'll be back for another look at the stars anytime soon. I was sort of looking forward to that second audition."

"Yeah, me, too."

Chapter Nine

"If you know where this woman will be, why not just let the men shoot to kill?" Patrice Orlando strummed her extra-long nails against each other in a ghastly rhythm. "Homeland Security will surely bring in extra patrols we'll need to avoid."

"I'd like to find out what she knows before we disrupt months of planning." He disliked repeating himself, especially to the same person.

He moved around his library, passing the multiple chess-boards along one wall. If Patrice would satisfy her thirst—either for his wine or her delusion that she had any part in the decision making of this operation—he could achieve checkmate in three moves with board four. He contemplated his next play on chessboard one.

"But Homeland is involved now," she whined.

He hated whiners, but she was necessary for a major component of his plan.

"Yes, it does present a challenge that needs a complex solution. And yet I've dealt with complicated problems before, if you recall."

"Not like this."

"My dear, why do you continually doubt my ability? Didn't you say that the last time we faced an adversary?"

"Getting rid of two Texas Rangers is not the same as the

Department of Homeland Security. Why would they send a man undercover into our operation, anyway?"

Explaining oneself was the tedious part of working with expendable assets. Yet sometimes it was necessary to ease their minds and clue them in to the big picture, as someone once reminded him. He might be able to see several moves ahead, but he did have a propensity to forget others could not.

"I'll begin with your question. One small reminder, Patrice, that Homeland is in charge of our borders. We have outwitted them on several occasions regarding our gun trade. And we are a major drug supplier in the south. Soon to be number one, I might add. Therefore, it makes perfect sense for DHS to weasel an operative into our business."

"Can't you stop talking down to me, Mr. Rook? I get all that. I'm not a dummy." Patrice guzzled the remainder of the California pinot noir.

She might not be a "dummy" about certain components of their business dealings, but when it came to wine, she needed a great deal of schooling. After four years of her visits, he didn't bother any longer. "I meant no offense, dear."

"Just spell it out. We've been lucky. I just want to keep that trend trending."

Luck? Dozens of plans had been considered and one had been carefully chosen, then manipulated into action. There had been no *luck* involved.

"The Texas Rangers were out of the picture for almost four years because of one of my simple plans, as you referred to it." He sat at board number two, wanting the intricately carved pieces to fill his vision instead of Patrice's continual pacing around the room. "Once they reappeared, they were distracted with their wild-goose chase. Patrice, come sit down."

"We're wasting our time and resources. I don't want anything to go wrong. What's the point of capturing this woman who happened to see the crew last night? Don't we already know she switched at the last minute?"

"Patrice, Patrice, Patrice." He rose and placed his hands on her shoulders, patting them like a pet dog.

He'd never had a dog. He couldn't abide the shedding, drooling or constant neediness. He'd tried a cat once, but soon disposed of it. He supposed the people who worked for him were pets enough, but he preferred to think of them all as pawns.

"Why can't you appreciate the fine chessboard that I've set into motion? This is the part I enjoy."

"Chess has never been my thing." She smiled uncomfortably. He saw her reaction in one of the many mirrors he had strategically placed around the room for just this occasion.

"And still you've accomplished so many aspects of a refined chessman," he complimented her, forcing the words he barely could say, squeezing her shoulders a bit. Patrice was far from a disciplined chess player. "You are very good at guile, manipulation and distraction. Dispatch four of your best, dear. I want this accomplished this morning."

"Four of my best?"

"If you want to achieve your goal, then you must be willing to sacrifice your players." He moved his queen's bishop, knowing the piece would be captured. He'd left his opponent no choice. The sacrifice would be seen as a potential deadly mistake, but in the long run it would help him achieve his goal of checkmate.

"That...that...hurts—"

"They are easily replaced. More can be trained."

He applied even more pressure, certain her skin would be bruised the next time he saw it.

To her triumph, she didn't pout or ask him to stop. "Where should she be taken?"

"I will make the arrangements. Notify me when the

deed is done." He released the pressure and petted the bruised flesh.

"Yes, sir." She carefully wiped a tear from the corner of her eye.

Pain could remind pawns faster than any words.

"We shall give the authorities another bone to dig their teeth into for a while. It appeases the American taxpayers and we go on our merry way for some time before they drag their hungry behinds back to the border for more."

"And what is this bone?"

"Andrea Allen."

Chapter Ten

Andrea's bags were packed and would be shipped later. Her laptop and change of clothes were in her shoulder bag. She looked around the observatory with a feeling of desolation. Everyone around her was determined she'd leave on that helicopter with her dad and…

That was the problem. There was no "and." If she left the McDonald Observatory and her research, there wasn't an option left for her. Nothing except a second-rate teaching job at a university already overstaffed with more than enough astronomers twiddling their thumbs. Well, it might not be that horrible.

But it wasn't her dream job. Nor did it sound exciting at all. Definitely not as exciting as working in Germany, Australia or South Africa.

"You don't look too happy."

"You think?" she smarted off to her rescuer turned guard. "I'm sorry, Pete. It's just that my dad is so over-protective. Because of his position and authority, everyone just falls into line with any decision, complying with his every wish."

"Got it."

Sheriff Morrison opened his stance and placed himself back to the wall, facing the entrance, staring straight ahead. Straight over her head. He probably didn't realize his hands rested on his belt, his right very near the hilt of his pistol. He was ready for whatever might come their way.

It was just plain selfish of her not to acknowledge the risk he was taking or the friend he'd just lost.

"I'm sorry, I realize you'd rather be investigating your friend's death."

"My job's right here." He continued his guard duty, never meeting her eyes, looking anywhere—everywhere—but at her.

"Forget it. I'm not running away. I know I have to leave. I can't let anyone else get hurt because of me." *Or murdered.* She saw the words on his face with the minuscule clenching of his jaw. "I appreciate you staying with me until the Commander arrives."

"I gave my word," he said matter-of-factly, without much inflection or a shrug. He looked like every soldier who had ever stood guard over her growing up.

"Of course you did. I'm appreciative nonetheless." Not only did he look the same as those soldiers, he acted the same, too. "They should be here any minute. I think I'll wait outside."

"I don't think the patio's a good idea."

"I don't really care what you think. I can't stand it in here another minute." On her way through the door, she punched the release bar a little too hard, causing her injured wrist to sting. It was just enough to make her eyes water. Or make her realize they were watering. And once they started there'd be no stopping the tears.

"Hold on," Pete said, coming after her. "If someone followed us, they could be waiting for you to show yourself."

"You're right again, Sheriff." She let her hands slap her thighs, frustrated she couldn't do anything right. More frustrated that he was about to witness a meltdown. She rubbed the protective bandage, determined he'd interpret that as the reason for the tears.

"Come on, Andrea. This isn't my fault."

She knew that and was about to blab it to him. The words weren't going to stop and she wouldn't be able to pick and choose which she said out loud.

"Dang it, I'm not blaming you for anything. I've lost the only job I've ever wanted because I was…I was bored on a Friday night. It's all my fault. I know that." She swiped at the silent tears. Tears for Sharon and a deputy she'd never met. For an injured man who walked out of the desert and died anyway when she wrecked the car. And selfish tears for her lost career. Crying for herself seemed petty, but she couldn't stop.

Before she knew it, Pete had his arms around her, turning her face into his shoulder. His name tag poked her cheek, but she didn't care. She could smell the starch used on his shirt. Feel the rock-hard muscles again under her palms. It was so easy to be safe wrapped in his arms. It defied logic, but there was nothing logical in anything that had happened since yesterday evening.

Nothing logical at all.

"You can't blame yourself, either, Andrea. If you hadn't volunteered to take Sharon's place, they would have found another way to get to you. It could have been here, surrounded by tourists with lots of kids running everywhere."

Since the fire he'd been professional to the extreme. She preferred him closer with his words a warm whisper against her ear. His hands a steadying force cupping her shoulders. Standing in the circle of his arms seemed both natural and enchanting in spite of the circumstances.

"I wish I'd met you two weeks ago," she said softly into his uniform.

"You might not have found this place so boring." He gently moved her away from hiding her face in his shoulder.

Her chin momentarily rested in the crook of his index finger before he quickly extended his others to circle the back of her neck. Angling her lips closer to his, sweeping down to make a claim.

His lips captured hers, or hers captured his. She didn't care. They meshed together while their bodies screamed to get closer. He was right yet again. If she'd met him when she first arrived in West Texas, she definitely wouldn't have been bored.

"I don't know how many rules we're breaking. At the moment, I'm not really sure I want to know." There was nothing soft about Pete's kiss.

No auditioning necessary.

He was an easy person to like, to admire. Maybe it was a good thing she wasn't sticking around, because she could fall for him. Easy.

The sounds of a helicopter bounced through the mountains. Her father would be here any minute. The Commander hadn't revealed what location she'd be whisked off to. If she was the only person this situation affected, she'd be kicking everyone controlling her life to the curb.

Including the handsome young sheriff holding her in his arms.

"I don't want to go, Pete. I'm not saying that because of the Commander or my dissertation. I haven't wanted to stay with anyone in a long time." She searched his eyes and melted a little more when his dimples appeared. "Have you?"

"I thought that was a pretty good second audition, if I do say so myself." He caught her lips to his again but quickly released them, too. "Just makes me want you on that chopper that much more. You aren't safe here."

"At least give me your number. Do you have a card or something?"

He laughed and shook his head. "You know how to reach me, Andrea."

"True, but Honey doesn't like me. She might not give

you the message." She had to joke. They were talking about a call that would never happen. She'd never be allowed to come back to Fort Davis or see the Marfa lights. No matter what position her father held, he'd put her under house arrest before she got close to the border alone.

"Your ride's here." He casually dipped that chiseled chin toward the chest she'd just cried her heart out against. His Adam's apple dipped as he swallowed hard. The brim of his hat cast a shadow over his tanned cheek.

Before he could release her, she leaned in for one last kiss. Pete didn't disappoint. Their lips connected and there wasn't a thought of what they should or shouldn't be doing. Just feeling.

The sad goodbye got her hotter than the desert sun. Then the chopper approached and she recognized the sound. She'd heard it the night before. She'd been racking her brains trying to match the distinct *whomp, whomp, whomp* that had been chasing her. Mixed as it was with the engine noise of Sharon's car, she hadn't been able to distinguish its distinctiveness.

But she knew helicopters and planes. She might not have had much in common with her father...but she had that. It had been their game. They knew their engines.

"That's not my father." Andrea pointed in the direction the chopper was approaching. "You have to trust me, Pete. That's a Hiller, a training helicopter. My dad wouldn't be traveling in anything that small. It only holds three people."

"You know what kind of helicopter just by the sound?"

"What do these idiots want? I can't believe they're coming here in broad daylight with my father ten minutes behind them. It's insane. Do they think they're going to swoop in and—"

Cut off by a shotgun blast, Pete pushed her between him and the building. People eating snacks at the table ran, ducking for cover behind the low brick wall separating them from the field.

"Pete! They don't care who they hurt!"

The doors were a couple of steps away. Another shot burst the brick just above their heads. She ducked to the side, but Pete kept his head down and drew his weapon, retreating to the people pinned down outside.

The gunfire shifted to the other side of the building. Pete searched the direction of the field, stood and helped a family inside the building.

"Everyone back from the windows! Go!" He waved people away from the doors made of glass toward an open classroom. "Get those kids into the classrooms. Everybody stay low. You'll be safe."

"What's going on?" an older man yelled from behind the information desk. "Who's attacking?"

"I'm Sheriff Morrison, Presidio County. Get on the speaker and tell everyone to get to an inside room. Stay away from the windows. No one goes outside. Anyone outside needs to stay in their vehicles."

Pete had her backed up against a wall, literally. He directed people, having holstered his weapon when the threat didn't follow him indoors. He pressed her against the paneling well away from the outer doors.

"I can help. I'm a pretty good shot," she offered.

"You don't leave my sight. That's what they want. Chaos and for me to lose focus. You're the prize, Andrea. They want you for leverage and are obviously willing to risk an open attack."

"I can call the Commander."

"They're listening to the police frequency, maybe even my phone. It's the only way they could have known you were here or that your father was sending a chopper for you."

His body completely blocked her view. She shifted to her right and so did he. Hand on his weapon, ready to go.

"How did they even know who my father is? Oh, God, my ID. They have my name and found out who I am." It really was all her fault. A stupid series of mistakes or events that were ending with innocent people's deaths. "If they are listening, the sooner my father says he's coming, the faster they'll leave. Please, Pete. I can't let anyone else get hurt."

"Here." He shoved his cell between their bodies. "Make it quick. The men after you are aggressive bas—" He cut himself off while two women herded kids into the classroom, shutting the door behind them.

She punched in her father's cell number. "No luck. There's no reception here." She tried to wriggle free from behind Pete's back. "I need the observatory phone."

"Stay where you are, Andrea. Wait, you should get into the classroom with everyone else. You'll be safer and can make the call from there. It sounds like they're landing." Pete moved along the perimeter of the room, closer to the glass patio exit.

She felt exposed, even though she was safe from any gunfire.

"Where are you going?"

"I can't let them enter the building."

She ran across the room to the information desk. "Where are the keys to the doors?"

"Right here," the volunteer answered, slapping the keys on a pile of Star Party pamphlets. "But I ain't getting paid to risk my life."

"Of course not," she said, soothing his hand and looking at his name tag. "But, Ben, can you dial 911? Tell them to find Commander Tony Allen to let him know what's happening. I swear he'll help us."

"Don't even think about locking those front doors, Andrea. That's what they want," Pete instructed, handgun finally drawn and in a ready position. She recognized the stance as the same one her father had taught her. Her gun was inside her travel bag and the bag was on the patio.

"Hurry," she whispered to Ben, who had the landline in his hand but hesitated to reach for the base to dial. "Please."

"It's too dangerous."

"I can do this, Pete. Are they on the ground yet?" She'd feel better if she could get to her gun on the patio.

"What the hell do you think you're doing?" Pete said beside her, taking the keys from her hands. He stood and pulled her back behind the information desk.

"Trying to slow them down."

"Locking the doors won't do that, hon. We don't know what's out there. And I won't let you—or anyone—risk being exposed." He jerked his head at the volunteer still holding the phone. "Get into the classroom and bar the door with anything you can find."

"Yes, sir." Ben crawled extremely fast for an older gentleman.

"Hello?" a voice coming from the receiver yelled. Pete clicked a speaker button. "Morrison here. Did you get through to Commander Allen?"

"They're still trying to locate him. Sheriff and deputies are about twenty minutes out."

"That's what I figured." Pete raised himself far enough to see over the counter. "He's probably with my dad. Try his cell. Tell them we're pinned inside the Observatory Visitor Center. I'm leaving the line open."

Andrea tried to peek over the counter with him, and he shoved her shoulder down before she could get a look. There was nothing to see anyway. Chairs had been knocked over, but the center was empty. This was the first time she actually wished her dad was closer.

PETE SEARCHED THE WALL. Maintenance. Office. Auditorium. Café. He needed someplace safe to hide Andrea before an unknown force burst through the unlocked doors and over-powered them. He wasn't wearing his vest. His dad would tan his hide…if he had one left to hang out to dry.

The extra protectiveness and responsibility weighed on him. It had nothing to do with giving anyone his word. Had nothing to do with his job responsibility. He flat out liked this woman. Everything about her shouted that she was special.

He'd never forgive himself if she was shot or—worse—abducted.

"We've got to get you out of here."

"I am not helpless, Pete. I've been in self-defense courses my entire life. And I know how to shoot. My gun's in the bag we left outside."

Good to know, but he wasn't letting her near that bag. He dropped the key ring on the floor near her hands. "Find one that looks like it's to a regular inside door. Like a broom closet. I'm going to lock you inside."

"Are you sure they're still out there?"

"The chopper's on the ground. The blades are still rotating. No telling how many were already here ready to ambush us." He watched two shadows cross the patio. "Let's move. Next to the snack bar, there's a maintenance door. Run. I'll lay down cover if we need it."

They ran. He could see the shadows but no one followed. Hopefully they didn't have eyes on him or Andrea. He heard the keys and a couple of curses behind him, then a door swung open enough for his charge to squeeze through.

He saw the glint of sun off a mirror outside. They were watching.

"Can you lock the door? Will it lock without the key?"

"I think so."

"Keep the keys with you. I don't need them. Less risky." Bullets could work as a key to unlock, but they might not risk injuring Andrea. He was counting on that.

"But, Pete—"

"Let me do my job, Andrea. Once you're inside, see if you can get into the crawl space. They just saw you open the door. Hide till the cavalry arrives."

"You mean the Navy. He won't let us down," she said from the other side of the door. "This is his thing, after all."

Pete had done all he could do to hide her. Now he needed to protect her. He turned the café tables on their sides. If he had to run, it would give him some cover. The thickest defense was the café counter itself. He plunged over the bar—taking the condiments with him—just as the first shots pierced the windows.

He heard the shouts—in Spanish—and the entrance doors open. More shots, from a machine pistol. The cartel's weapon of choice. Another burst of fire hit the café's menu.

"We know the *chica* is in here. You give her to us and nobody gets hurt."

Pete answered in not so flattering Spanish and blindly fired two rounds toward the front. He was answered with another burst from a machine pistol and plenty of curses.

Static over his radio. Maybe the cavalry would arrive sooner than he'd anticipated. He couldn't make out any words, but he turned the volume down so none of his adversaries would hear them when he could. He spoke into the microphone with a low voice. "This is Morrison. Pinned in the café. Numerous civilians in the classroom area. No eyes on multiple hostiles with machine pistols."

"We know it's you and you be all alone, Sheriff. We got no problem with you, man. We just want the girl."

"Didn't hear me the first time?" He popped off two rounds over the counter again, preserving his ammo. Cursing exploded from his opponents, followed by scrambling. "Why her?"

"No help's getting up the mountain."

So did they know about Commander Allen's helicopter

or not? He knew how many rounds he had left. There wasn't much he could do until they made a move on the door.

Rapid fire pinned him to the floor, ricocheting off metal objects in the kitchen. His biggest worry yesterday had been if he'd have a job after the election. Today the only future he was worried about was surviving the next couple of hours.

And making certain Andrea did, too.

Chapter Eleven

Andrea could hear them through the door. Balancing on the mop bucket wasn't easy, but it did get her close enough to the ceiling to push the tile to the side. Her wrist ached before the men trying to kill her had landed. She was extremely aware of every tendon as she did a chin-up into the ceiling.

Her muscles shook with the strain. She bit her lip to silence the grunt of pain. She spread her weight over the steel supports, breathing hard, wanting nothing more than to roll over to her back and rest. But that wasn't an option.

Silently, she moved the tile back into place. Shouting. More gunfire sounding like a machine gun. *Come on, Commander! Where are you?*

The ceiling wasn't the safest place. One wrong move and she could fall through. One wrong sound would alert the men with the automatic weapons that could penetrate the tiles hiding her.

So she needed a way out.

They both did. That rapid fire would cut through Pete in a matter of seconds. She heard him, heard his weapon. He was still alive, but for how long? She could do this. She wasn't your average astronomy PhD student. She'd never been average, with a dad who trained her well. She could shoot and hold her own in a fight. If those men were on the inside of the center, then she needed to get to the outside and her gun.

"PETE, PETE, ARE you there? We're in the parking lot. You doing okay, son?" His dad's voice was a welcome reprieve from the bullets flying over his head.

"Just great."

"Let's assume they're tuned in to our frequency, son. Let's change it up. Remember the colt's birthday last month?"

"Do it."

Pete changed frequencies on the hand radio. They wouldn't have long before the men sitting on top of him would circle through the numbers and overhear.

"Pete? You know what these guys want?"

"Yeah, Andrea. Is Commander Allen with you?"

"Separate entry point. How many?"

"Four that arrived by chopper. I don't know about outside."

"We've cleared the parking lot and are ready to evacuate the classroom through the emergency exit. Change frequency to Peach's birthday."

"Got it." Pete twisted the dial again. It was another date easily remembered. They had just celebrated it last week.

"Sit tight, Pete. Just sit tight. We'll have you out of there in two shakes."

He checked his rounds. Three remained.

He'd left his extra clips in the truck and hadn't been prepared for a shoot-out.

Sit tight. As if he had a choice. He heard low grumbling in Spanish, words he couldn't distinguish other than complaints about a madwoman. Shuffling.

"Who's out there?" one of the men asked in English.

Pete slid to the edge of the counter and peered around,

expecting one of the Jeff Davis deputies to be in a position to take these guys down. Shocker of shocks. Andrea drew her hand out of her bag and raised a weapon.

Three shots. That was all he had to get to her. He couldn't stay put. She fired, and he ran straight through the shattered door under her cover. She stood at the ready, waiting for him.

A fifth man came around the brick wall, a large gun barrel pointed at them. "Down!" Pete shouted. He reached Andrea, they spun, the man fired, Andrea fired.

The bullet seared Pete's flesh and knocked him sideways. Their assailant fell to the patio concrete. Pete managed to stay on his feet and kept them moving forward. "Run!"

They both took cover at the wall of the ramp leading to the closest telescopes. A five-foot-wide path bordered on either side with a three-foot-high brick wall that was one foot thick. It would stop a spray of machine-pistol bullets.

Too much space. Wide-open fields. No cover.

But if he jumped the brick wall he could draw fire and possibly disable their helicopter. Andrea could make it to the front of the building and his father.

"Follow the sidewalk to the front. Deputies are on sight evacuating the civilians."

One of the men jumped through the glass, and Pete tugged Andrea to the ground behind the brick. He covered her with his body. They heard several rounds and saw red shards splinter into the air. The strength in his left arm where he'd been shot was waning.

"Where are you going?" Andrea didn't seem fazed. She spoke from under the protection of his body, taking everything that happened with a deep breath and calm logic.

"We need a distraction so you can get around front," he answered, breathing hard from the exertion. "I'm heading to their ride and you're heading to my dad."

"The helicopter? Can you fly that old relic? I can."

He shook his head. "But I can disable it. We go on three."

"But I said I could fly—"

When a new blast broke more of the brick into splinters, he ducked his head again, reaching around Andrea, tugging her closer, covering as much of her body as he could. If she wouldn't cooperate, he'd take her to the front himself. The men might be able to escape, but that wasn't his highest priority. Getting Andrea to safety was.

The burst ended and he moved past her, clasping her hand with his right to get her started in a low crouch below the wall and up the path. His left arm was getting harder to move, but he still had clear vision and a clear head. "I don't need your help. We need to move."

She tugged him to a stop. "You're getting my help, so don't argue. I don't want those men to get away. So, do you want to jump the wall or go around the far end by the telescopes? I'm thinking jumping is faster. I'll lay down a cover while you run."

"Hand me your gun." He stuck his weapon in its holster and covered her weapon with his hand. "I'll disable the chopper. You're going around front."

She placed the handle of her Glock in his. "We're wasting time. It's not a one-way ticket if I fly that hunk of junk out of here. Cover me."

Spunk or confidence or just plain stubbornness. He didn't know which. She stuck her head up, evidently didn't see anyone and took off, crossing the path and rolling over the brick wall separating it from the field. He didn't have the chance to stop her and didn't think he could have. He hadn't radioed his dad to say they'd left the building.

He stood a little slower than normal—probably the blood loss—he could see it soaking through the sleeve of his shirt. He backed to the opposite wall, keeping his eyes on the doorway to the Visitor Center. He heard gunfire, but from the opposite side of the building.

Those men would want to make their escape...fast. They'd be heading toward their escape, and Andrea was almost at the chopper. Dammit, all they had to do was sit tight as his dad had instructed.

A man came through the door again. Pete fired two shots, breaking the glass next to him. His aim was off, missing the man's body mass, but he'd forced him back inside. Maybe he was closer to passing out than he'd thought. The chopper was warming up. Pete ran, firing his last rounds that kept the machine pistol inside the building silent.

Now, if he could just keep his feet moving.

FORTUNATELY, THE HILLER wasn't that far and there wasn't anyone inside it to deal with. The man who had come up behind her had probably been left to stand guard. Andrea concentrated on getting ready to get in the air and let Pete deal with the men wanting to kill her.

Pete opened the opposite door and slowly climbed inside. "You sure you can fly this thing?"

He leaned on the door, so tired his head thudded against the plastic.

"Definitely. Buckle up." She didn't wait on him, moving the stick and lifting into the air.

They were away from the observatory in seconds. She could hear machine gun fire but didn't hover to see how many men or find out what they looked like. The former sheriff could round up the bad guys.

She was a bit rusty, but it felt good to be behind a stick again. She'd loved flying with her dad while she was growing up. He'd take her into the air with him as often as he could get private fly time. He'd been Dad then, back before he'd permanently become the Commander.

"Hey, I meant it when I said buckle up, Pete." She swatted his arm to get his attention. Her hand came back bloody. "You were shot? Stay with me, Sheriff! Don't you dare pass out."

He didn't answer. She took a quick glance at her passenger, who was seriously slumped toward his door. Shoot, she wasn't even certain he'd closed the thing correctly. He was out cold.

There were a couple of wild bumps as she jerked him closer to the middle. It was a nervous couple of minutes as she looped his arm through the seat's shoulder strap.

One thing missing on the Hiller was the radio. She couldn't call anyone. She couldn't reach Pete's cell phone and couldn't see his department radio.

"I guess I should put this thing down somewhere and try to keep you alive."

The controls weren't responding as fast as she would have liked. They were as sluggish as peddling through pudding. They had probably been hit by the last gunfire as they were taking off. She wouldn't let them crash. But wherever she set this thing down, they were going to be trapped there.

Stuck without medical supplies, food or water. Each minute they were in the air, the controls got worse.

"Hold on, Pete. We're going to land."

Chapter Twelve

Soft lips. Pete wasn't too familiar with being awakened by a kiss, but he recognized the sweetness. He reached out with his arms to catch Andrea's body and hissed between his teeth instead. The pain in his left arm was manageable, but he'd rather not push it.

"I was shot."

"Yes, you were. I've been patiently waiting for you to wake up. But let me tell you, it was getting pretty boring around here again without your company."

"Can't have that." He sat up with a little help from Andrea. "We know what happens when you get bored."

"Ha. Ha. Ha," she said, plopping down next to him and crossing her legs.

He carefully lifted his arm without the same pain he'd experienced a few minutes earlier. The chopper was thirty or forty yards away, seemingly intact. Drag marks from his boots left a trail to where they currently sat. He'd be lucky if there weren't holes in his jeans.

"I'm sort of glad I wasn't awake for that." He nodded toward the chopper.

"We've been here awhile. I couldn't leave you baking in the sun. You lost your hat."

"It's late afternoon already." They had an hour, maybe

an hour and a half of light left before the sun was obscured by the mountains.

"That's right, tough guy." She swayed into his good arm before bringing her knees up and resting on them. "You finally got that nap you needed."

"No cell reception?"

"No nothing reception." She pointed to the department radio, then jumped up to retrieve it. "I thought for sure the Commander would be swooping in for the ultimate I-told-you-so. But I haven't heard anything except a cow mooing."

"Thanks for fixing my arm."

"I can't believe you were shot. Okay, never mind, I can believe it. I mean, there were a lot of bullets flying around. You should have told me when it happened. You might have at least tried to tell me before I ran to the Hiller. Though, honestly, I don't think I gave you time to tell me—"

"Andrea," he said, covering her hand with his good one. She was talking fast without taking a breath. Nervous or scared or maybe a little of both.

"Yeah?"

"You didn't shoot me. We got out of there and I doubt those men escaped. There was nowhere for them to run when you took the helicopter.

"Can I assume something's wrong with that thing?" He pointed toward the chopper.

"One of those men shot the engine before we got safely away. Well, almost safely away. We were very lucky, considering he could have sliced that trainer in half with his machine gun."

"Machine pistol. We've known they were smuggling those for some time, but it was the first time I'd faced one."

"How's your arm? You know, you were lucky. The bullet tore a hunk of your flesh away. You'll just have a wicked scar." She picked up a pebble and tossed it across the path. "But I got the bleeding stopped and didn't have to dig around with a penknife for a bullet. And believe me, I could have, too. My dad saw fit that I have lots of practical survival training."

"I see that. You're pretty good with a gun, too." He held her hand, resting it on his thigh. "Come on, just catch your breath and give me a minute to figure this out."

"Oh, sorry. I'm babbling again, aren't I? I do better when I'm moving. Less stressed." She tried to release his fingers with the intent of getting to her feet. "I'm not certain why you passed out. It bled a lot, but did you hit your head or something?"

"I'm fine. Don't worry about it." Pete kept a firm grip on her hand, wanting her next to him for multiple reasons, but touching her skin was the first one that came to mind. "Give me a second. Then we'll take a look around. See if I recognize where we are." He knew they hadn't flown far and were still pretty much close to nowhere.

"Oh, I know exactly where we're at," she said with confidence.

He knew the peaks, the general vicinity. "Maybe twenty-five miles northeast from the observatory."

"Very good, Sheriff."

"I've traveled these mountains enough to recognize the terrain. That puts us darn close to the Scout ranch. We'll need to get started up one of those trails if we want to sleep in a bed tonight."

"Is that an invitation?" She winked. "If so, I think you could at least buy a girl dinner first."

"I've already bought you breakfast," he teased in return. "But I'm sure your father will have strong words objecting to your spending another night in Marfa."

He groaned as he stood up. Feeling like he hadn't slept

in a week and that he was as old as sin. Andrea helped him until he was steady on his feet.

"You know, I am an adult. I make decisions all on my own."

"Maybe we should start with dinner after we determine exactly why those men would make such a stupid move today."

"I can go with that."

"No radio in the helicopter?" he asked as they passed it. She answered with a look and a long sigh. "Right. First thing you would have tried."

They headed up the trail. He was a lot weaker than he could let on, but they needed higher ground for cell reception.

"You okay?"

"I'll manage." He would.

"Mind if I stay close to make sure you do?" She shouldered up next to his right side.

"Going to hold my hand?"

"Maybe." She smiled.

"Why hasn't your father found you yet?"

"I've been asking myself the same question."

"I'll take your Glock back." He extended his palm.

She slapped her hand on his, wrapping her fingers tight and keeping hold. "No offense, Pete, but I think I'll keep it. You aren't quite yourself at the moment."

Perhaps she was right. She was definitely right about him not being one hundred percent. He'd seen her shoot. They'd both hit their target on the café patio and she hadn't fallen to pieces when the body hit the ground. He didn't know yet how he actually felt about shooting someone. It wasn't like they'd had much time to think about their actions. Their assailant had been attempting to kill them. They didn't need to think about it at the moment, either. There'd be plenty of time later.

"So, I've been thinking, since I haven't had much else to do all afternoon waiting on you to wake up."

Unless he wanted to walk home, they had another good fifteen-minute hike before they got a phone signal. They'd never manage a call at the bottom of one of these gullies, even if it was the easiest route home.

"What conclusion did you come to?" He was gaining confidence with each step. Up it was and then down the other side to the Scout camp he'd gone to in his youth.

She took a step away from him, angling toward a path cows and horses had beaten over time. "You can't be serious?"

He pointed toward the butte. "E.T. should phone home."

She faced him with both hands on her hips. "You are never going to let me live down that *aliens* were chasing me, are you?"

He laughed. Really laughed. There was something about the way she stood there along with the way she held her mouth and tilted her head. "No, I don't think I am."

She didn't ask if he was up to the climb, just took a step and looped her bandaged wrist through his right arm. One wobbly step at a time, he stayed on his feet.

"As I was saying, I've had a lot of time to think. When the *aliens* showed up at the observatory—" she used her original description of the men trying to kill her without skipping a beat "—it didn't make a lot of sense."

"How did they know you were leaving? And why are they trying to grab you?" They kept a steady pace on the inclined path. "After we make the call, we need to take cover. We can't be certain they aren't listening to my phone, but it's more likely they were monitoring the police bands."

"Right. So we're thinking along the same lines."

"You're a valuable asset just because of your father. But why risk losing men and a helicopter?"

"Exactly. They might think I know something, yet kill-

ing me would be the fastest, most reliable way to elimi-
nate that threat."

He'd never met anyone like her. She wasn't upset or falling apart. "Does this happen to you all the time?"

"Hardly. I grew up preparing for it, though. I wanted
to please my parents and did everything possible to make
them proud."

"Like learning to fly helicopters?"

"That's actually fun. All of it has been to some degree,
I guess." She squeezed his biceps. "You'll have to tell me
about your treks into the mountains sometime. Right now,
concentrate on breathing. We'll have time to get to know
each other later."

He was surprised how much he wanted that to be true.
"The aliens either think you know something or they
wanted to hold you hostage in order to exchange you for
something."

"That is the same conclusion I came to earlier. Unfortunately, neither of those reasons explains why they attacked
in broad daylight using a helicopter. I mean, wouldn't it
have made more sense to enter through the door, take us
by surprise and then signal for the chopper once they were
successful?"

He stopped and checked his pockets for the phone.

"Looking for this?" She handed him his cell after pulling
it from her back pocket. "I turned it off to save the battery."

He turned it on, then continued their climb. He wanted
this point to be high enough for a connection but it wasn't.
They climbed in silence for a while, thinking. "You're right.
Their attack doesn't make sense. They would have assured
themselves of your location, been ready to get in and out,
not hang back. They could have overrun me easily."

"Unless it's all a diversion."

"You're brilliant." She was gorgeous and brilliant. The

phone was ready. He pulled up his dad's cell number and
tapped the speaker.

"Pete?"

"Hey, Dad."

"Thank God. Is Andrea with you?"

"We're both great. I think my cell might be compromised."

"We assumed communications weren't safe. Do you
know your location?"

"Yeah, I could go for a Buffalo swim if it were open."

"Ah, gotcha. Nicely done, son. We'll be there ASAP."
Andrea looked around, obviously wondering about his
coded message.

"Sort of wondered why you haven't found us already,"
he asked his dad.

"We lost the helicopter soon after takeoff. Took us until
about half an hour ago to discover that neither of you was
with the last man who escaped to the south."

"Five men. Three in the chopper and two in a vehicle?"

"Correct and all accounted for. Commander Allen wants
to talk to his daughter."

"Are you all right, Andrea?" her father asked.

"Yes, sir. Not a scratch."

"That's my girl. Mechanical difficulties?"

"Yes, sir."

"The search team got a late start. We'll steer them to
you soon. You're certain you're fine?"

"She's brilliant, sir," Pete answered when he noticed
the tears in Andrea's eyes. "We better save the battery, sir.
Just in case."

"Certainly." He disconnected.

"HE'S NOT MUCH for goodbyes." Andrea used a knuckle to
wipe the moisture from her eyes. Pete might get the wrong

impression...or the right one. Either way, she could break down later. Think about everything...later.

With the exception that Pete thought she was brilliant.

"This is a pretty good place to wait. If you hear the wrong helicopter again, we can dart down this side of the hill." He nodded behind her. "Closer to the road."

She squinted, noticing the buildings at the bottom of the canyon. There was a well-marked trail zigzagging down. "You mean I was one hill away from civilization?"

"Yeah, but to its credit, it was a large hill." He was still breathing hard from their hike, but smiling.

"We're resting. Sit." They chose one of the smoother rocks and kept their backs to the sun. It was quiet. A gentle wind was the only sound. If whoever was chasing her did understand Pete's description of their location, she'd be able to hear them straightaway.

"So, a diversion? That makes sense."

"Whatever happened this afternoon had to be a profitable enough deal to sacrifice five men and a helicopter. It wasn't rigged for the light show they used to imitate the phenomenon near Marfa. It sounded like this type of Hiller, but this one is bare bones."

"So they have another chopper."

"It's logical to assume so."

"Whoever's behind this discovered who you were and used the opportunity presented to them to their advantage." Pete wiped his brow. "Are you certain you don't have experience being a detective?"

"I had an hour and a half to myself, and deductive reasoning just happens to be my strength."

"So your switching places with Sharon last night was purely coincidental. If I were them, I might assume you work at the observatory. I don't think I'd assume you're the daughter of a director with Homeland Security."

"Sharon. Sharon knew. I talked about it last week. About

how difficult it was for me to convince the university to let me come, since my dad was opposed." She had to move, so she jumped to her feet. "Shoot. I forgot the first rule my dad taught me. He's been paranoid about my mother and me since he joined the DHS. Afraid someone would attempt exactly what they did today."

"Then we can't assume Sharon's switching with you was a coincidence. This might have been the plan all along."

"They couldn't have known I'd say yes. And what about the man in the desert?" She walked a few feet and tugged a long leaf off a bush, nervously tearing the ends off.

"He's an undercover agent who discovers the plan to abduct his commander's daughter. I can think of a lot of reasons he'd risk warning someone. So last night the aliens aren't smuggling drugs across the border, they're searching for an escaped hostage—your dad's undercover man. He's got details they can't let be exposed, but he finds his way to you. They run you off the road and would have abducted you."

"But you came along. They don't know that the agent didn't tell me anything, but they want to make certain."

"Somehow they know he's Homeland Security and send someone in posing as..."

"The phony agent," they said together.

"How would they have known he was DHS? Your dad's man from the desert was pretty beat up. They could have gotten the info from him." Pete stood, shaded his eyes and checked out the terrain behind him. "Then again, it makes more sense that they discovered him if he was trying to warn your dad about the danger you were in."

"If all of this is just coincidence, though... Why is Sharon still missing?"

Not answering said more than trying to soothe her guilty conscience. He thought Sharon was dead. Once they got the necessary information from her, they wouldn't need her any longer. "Do you think they killed Sharon or that she was working with them?"

"I don't believe these men think twice about eliminating anyone who stands in their way."

"I'm sorry one of those people was your deputy. Logan seemed nice."

"I had to cover for him a lot. Now I know why. He was a good kid. I didn't have much else to do. If I hadn't worked all night, I'd be up taking care of ranch chores. I'd rather ride on patrol."

He lifted an eyebrow, smiled and she knew the subject was changing. "Hey, you going to share how you got outside from the maintenance closet?"

She waved her injured wrist. "Let me tell you, it wasn't easy. Good thing I can pull my own weight, injured or not. Once I got into the crawl space and found a way to the roof, I climbed down the steel beams that formed the partial shade over the door. They were at a slant and got me close enough to the ground that I could drop."

"Is that the Commander's chopper?" he asked, facing the south to catch a glimpse. She nodded, and he dusted off his jeans with his good hand. "You're a very competent, capable woman."

"Tell that to my father." She followed him back the way they'd come. There was plenty of room for another chopper to land. "He's going to command me to leave. I doubt he'll hang around long enough to drop you by the hospital."

"I don't blame him."

"I'm not certain I'm leaving." There was too much unfinished business here. "I don't want to run away."

"Of course you should." He stopped, grabbing her upper arms, wincing at the sudden movement of his own injury. "Seven men are dead. You can't just shrug that off. It's dangerous for you here."

"Whatever reason they had to abduct me, it's gone now."

"You don't know that." His grip tightened, but it didn't hurt. It seemed he was fighting to keep her at arm's length. She would have preferred to be pulled next to his chest.

"But you agreed with me."

The chopper was getting closer.

"A good guess doesn't mean we're correct." His good hand cupped her shoulder.

"I know you're right." Then why was the first thought in her head how to ditch her new escort that hadn't even been assigned to her yet? Then find a way back to Pete's place. She didn't even know where Pete's place was. "What if I don't go back with my father?"

"But you agreed—" Pete searched her eyes and she wasn't certain what he saw, but he dropped his hands to his sides. "Come on, Andrea. What would be gained from staying? You have nothing to prove."

She didn't want to stay just for Pete. She barely knew him. But her heart dropped when he started back down the path, leaving her to follow again. "How are you going to catch the men responsible for Logan's death? What about Sharon? You said I was good at this detective stuff."

"Do you really think your father's going to allow you to stay? He was packing you off before the attack. There's no way he's saying yes."

That was true. She'd rarely stood up to her parents. Their advice was usually firm and logical. So there had never been a reason to question them. The exception was when her father had declared she couldn't come to West Texas in person. Perhaps if he'd explained his reasons instead of dictating, seven men wouldn't be dead and a young woman wouldn't still be missing.

"There's one thing that everyone around me keeps forgetting. You can't force me to leave the observatory."

Chapter Thirteen

There had been many times throughout Pete's teenage years that he'd argued with his dad. During the past six weeks, he'd been holding back because of his dad's heart attack, but he was building up to a doozy of a fight. If he confronted him, he'd been thinking that all hell would break loose.

"They still at it?" Honey asked from her desk.

"I didn't know people could yell that long without a drink or shot of tequila," his dad joked.

Andrea and her father might not have the exact family problems, but they definitely had a lot of words to *share*. If he'd known, he would have taken them to the middle of the desert for this confrontation instead of his dad's old office.

The door flew open and the Commander marched out, eyes front without any acknowledgment as he passed them. Pete had no illusions. That was not the expression of a man who had achieved his goal—which was to get Andrea on the next transport home.

Commander Allen executed a one-eighty to be face-to-face with him. "You should get that wound seen to." His voice was void of inflection yet full of buried emotion.

Or maybe it was just Pete's own anxiety pushing its way onto others. He didn't need the responsibility of an attractive woman in his life or workplace. It was time for decisions.

"She's determined to stay," Allen continued. "And mad as hell at me because she's not."

"Yes, sir. I understand your frustration." She wasn't going to be his responsibility. That was good. Very good. His personal desire didn't amount to anything in this decision.

"I need coffee before round two."

"Does it matter if it's good?" his dad asked.

"I'm used to the worst."

"Around the corner and you'll smell the sludge," his dad directed but walked beside the Commander, who threw back his head laughing at something else his father had said.

Pete could only scratch his head.

"Everyone show up for their shift?" he asked Honey. "When will the Griggs family arrive?" Could he pull off business as usual? Swing by the café for a break without the rest of the town asking what the hell was going on? He needed a minute to take care of his responsibilities. Another minute to think. But where? His best bet for a reprieve was his house.

"Yes, and in about forty-five minutes," Honey answered.

No time to make it to the house and back. He needed a real meal, not just a package of pretzels from the vending machine, before he could face Logan's parents. He glanced up to see Andrea standing in the office doorway and then their dads rounded the corner with smiles on both their faces.

"Pete, would you join me a minute?" Andrea's father asked, gesturing to the office.

Did anyone lower on the totem pole ever tell this man no?

"We've been tracking a high number of gun purchases by a few individuals. We believe something big's in the works, that the cartel is tired of receiving their guns one or two at a time. Homeland likes your distraction theory, Pete," Commander Allen stated once the door was closed.

Pete kept his hands tucked in his armpits and his mouth shut. Andrea had let her father believe he had thought up the distraction angle. He was sure they both sort of followed that trail together.

"We checked out some satellite pictures and discovered a large number of trucks crossing the border at Presidio into Manuel Ojinaga. You were right. They wanted us focused on the attempted abduction instead of the payment delivery for a major drug deal. I think it's time I brought you onto the team, Sheriff."

There wasn't any doubt which sheriff their visitor from Homeland Security was directing his comment to. Pete caught himself swallowing hard, nervous. He knew his job and his county and didn't have anything to feel nervous about. Nothing except losing everything if DHS checked into his background.

Pete understood the sideways glance from his father. A look that said keep your mouth shut and let me do the talking.

Easy for his dad, who had kept his mouth shut for over twenty-six years. He'd kept a secret that could potentially destroy them both. Andrea sat in his father's chair, head down, not making eye contact.

"I'm setting up a task force and I need you to be a part of it."

Pete snapped his attention back to the Commander. "You need me. Why?"

"You're familiar with the area and think on your feet. We need some of that and someone to coordinate with the other county sheriffs or local police."

"Thank you, sir, but I have to pass. My plate's about as full as it can get right now." He ignored his dad's attempt to get his attention. "I have work to do. I'm actually in charge of a few things around here and need to get ready for Logan's family. Excuse me."

The two older men parted, and he passed between them.

"Maybe I should explain?" Andrea asked behind him.

"No, this one's my responsibility," his dad said. "Wait here a minute, will ya?" He followed him out the door. "Son, this is a great op—"

Pete bit down hard—teeth on teeth. He knew where the conversation was headed and didn't want to have it publicly, so he pushed through to the locker room. His dad caught the employee only door before it slammed in his face. Pete verified no one was there so they could talk freely. "You're really for me joining a Homeland task force?"

"Of course I am. It's a big step for you."

"It's a family power struggle. She wants to stay, he wants her to go. The last thing I need is to be around any of that mess." He lowered his voice. "Especially involved with the daughter of one of the top dogs in Homeland Security."

"She's leaving with her father. Besides, no one's going to uncover who you really are. You don't need to think of that right now."

"Hell, Dad, it's all I ever think about since you dropped this bomb on me."

"Keeping your identity a secret is for your own safety."

He dropped his hands onto his dad's shoulders. The muscle under his fingertips was less solid than two months ago. A lot less solid than two years ago. He shook his head. He wasn't a crying man—neither one of them was. But the only man he'd ever called family stared at him with his brown eyes about to overflow.

"I love you, you old coot. But I already know who I am and who my biological father was. I've just been waiting for you to tell me why it all happened."

"How did you find out?"

"I'm the sheriff. At least that's what you all are telling

me. It didn't take much investigating to discover where I came from twenty-six years ago or the identity of the man I assume was my biological father."

"We'll talk about that at a more appropriate time. Right now Commander Allen needs your help." Pride or excitement or envy weaved its way into his father's words. Maybe because of the times their department had been overlooked for opportunities like this one.

Would his dad be let down to know that it was Andrea's idea and had nothing to do with the Commander's need for help?

"What happens if he decides to run a background check on me? What then? How much trouble are you going to be in? You're right. This isn't the place to talk about forging our relationship with the Department of Homeland Security or why that's impossible. The best thing is to bow out and assist where needed."

His dad's face grew older under the fluorescent lights. "I know you have a lot of questions, but you're right. This is a talk more appropriate for home. I do wish you'd reconsider working on the task force."

"Not a chance. It's just a disaster waiting to happen."

"It can't be all bad, son." His dad winked. "I've seen the way his daughter looks at you."

"You haven't seen anything. And it'll never happen. It might have been fun while she was here, but I have no future. A woman like that needs a future." He couldn't risk the complications of becoming involved with the daughter of such a powerful man.

"What are you talking about? You have job security here. You're running unopposed."

"Let's drop it." Now wasn't the time to tell his dad he hadn't submitted the election paperwork to run for sheriff. He hadn't decided—yet—if he would. But he could set him straight on one thing. "I'm not getting involved with anyone, especially Andrea Allen. My babysitting days are long behind me."

OUCH. ANDREA WAS careful not to allow the door to slam, hearing a gentle clicking noise as it closed. She'd completely misread their friendship. Following him to apologize, ready to abide by her father's wishes and leave Marfa, she hadn't meant to eavesdrop, especially on a father-and-son chat that seemed very private. But now she was glad she'd overheard Pete say he wasn't getting involved with anyone...especially her.

Now she was having second or third or fourth thoughts. She'd lost track of how many times she'd changed her mind about staying here. It was as if her decision-making ability had evaporated with one look at Pete's dimples.

Pete's earlier look of disappointment had deflated her desire to be around him. She'd thought staying in the area worked to everyone's advantage. Before the shooting at the observatory, she thought she'd keep her promise to her father and get her dissertation finished and maybe allow a few distractions with the sheriff.

Not anymore. Not now that she knew those men were willing to kill anyone. And not now that she knew how Pete really felt.

It could be all business for her and not matter who stood guard outside the telescope. No. She was acting like a scorned lover. Staying meant putting more people at risk and she couldn't do that. She'd have to find another way to obtain telescope time.

It wouldn't be the end of everything if she finished up the thesis in Austin. But she could be disappointed for not being able to finish here. She couldn't stay. It would be horribly selfish. She hit the employees only door as she pushed it open again, catching Pete with a hand on the other side and a surprised look on his face.

"You aren't going to talk me into joining his task force," Pete said to his father, then turning to Andrea, "and neither are you."

"I came to apologize before leaving Marfa. But now…"

"Nothing to apologize for. Excuse me."

"Man, you really are something." She blocked the door. Pete could have moved her easily but seemed reluctant to.

"Can you leave us alone a minute, Dad?"

The retiring sheriff squeezed past. Pete clasped hands with her, gently pulling her to where the door could shut with a loud bang. She shook his hand free as quickly as she could.

"You don't need to be talked into anything." She knew what calls her father would make as soon as they all left the office. "The people who sign your paychecks are already being contacted. You no longer have a choice."

"Why is this so important to you?"

"Not me. I don't force myself on anyone. My dad's limiting the number of people who know about the incident. You're already a part of his small circle. It's logical—therefore, it'll happen."

"As much as I hate that logic, I understand it."

"Oh, and don't worry about having to be around me. You know you can assign anyone you want as my *babysitter*. It doesn't matter to me." Telling him she'd changed her mind and wouldn't be heading back was on the tip of her tongue. "I really don't understand why you're so reluctant to help the Commander. This is an amazing opportunity that could take you places. After this is over you could name your assignment."

"I'll make sure Commander Allen gets the help he needs. And who says I want to leave Marfa? That's a lot of presuming you're doing after knowing me for such a short time. I actually like it here."

He smiled, and her heart melted a little. He was delightful when he wanted to be, but right now was obviously not one of those times.

"You should use that wicked charm of yours more often, especially with strangers. I bet your father and the rest of the community who raised you gave in every time you smiled. Is that why you're so spoiled?"

"Me? You think *I'm* spoiled?" His deep voice rose a couple of octaves with that accusation. "Where do you get off calling anyone spoiled? Have you taken a look at the way you have your father wrapped around your pinkie finger? Never mind, I don't care to know the answer. It's not worth it."

"Man, do you have that wrong. I don't call him the Commander because of his rank."

Andrea didn't really think Pete was spoiled. She was hurt from his private remarks to his father and she was striking out. She wanted to apologize, take it back, tell him she didn't mean it. But she couldn't. She'd thought he'd liked her and the wound was too fresh.

Later. She'd apologize later. She'd calm down while looking into deep space or on the plane back to Austin. She was still uncertain which route was in her future.

"If you'll excuse me, I need to get in touch with the observatory. I've already confirmed that my telescope will be ready at seven-thirty and need to make arrangements." Arrangements for the information and her things to be sent to her, but she wouldn't admit that to him. She reached for the door. His arm stopped her. She spun to face him, landing against his chest, looking straight at that dimpled chin.

"You aren't going anywhere on your own. You can wait in the office while I make the arrangements."

"Fine."

"Okay."

Earlier today, being this close would have ended in some serious kissing. The disappointment she was experiencing that it was no longer a possibility froze her in place. She focused her stare at his chin, unable to meet his eyes.

His hands were snug around her waist and she was ready to forgive him and explain her harsh words. Ready for those kisses to take over and there not be a need for any explanations from either of them. Then he gently moved her to the side.

If she had looked at him, she might have known that he was trying to open the door. By the time she figured it out, she added embarrassment to the long list of emotions she was scrolling through.

"You stick with me or your dad until I find a deputy to escort you. Or you can wait in a locked office."

Without uttering a word, she veered left, choosing to stand near Reception instead of sitting in the chair waiting on her father to finish his calls. Pete went about his business, giving instructions, signing some papers…man-in-charge stuff. When he was done, the mayor or someone equivalent called to speak to him. He looked at the glass front doors and told Peach—the sisters had switched positions—to take a message.

A couple entered the front. The man's face looked confused and the woman cried into an old-fashioned handkerchief. Peach pointed to Pete without a word. He tapped on the open office door and brought a third chair inside.

"Sorry, Commander Allen, but I need this room for a bit."

Her father glanced at the couple and left, walking to a corner, placing another phone call on his cell while she watched Pete hug each of them before they sat.

"Logan's parents. They wanted to talk to Pete about what happened," Peach said softly next to her.

"I wish I'd known him better."

"He was a nice young man. They're still searching for the student he was on a date with," Peach stated, then answered the phone.

Andrea's guilt was growing. She'd been so caught up in her own world she hadn't thought about Sharon or that her body hadn't been found. Had she been abducted or murdered and her body dumped in a remote spot? They might never know, but she had to find out.

Chapter Fourteen

"Is there another office my father could use, Peach?"

"Sure." She pulled open a drawer and handed Andrea a key. "Through the back hallway next to Pete's office, then second door on the right."

Andrea tugged gently on her father's sleeve, and he followed, arguing with someone else for a change. She sat in a straight-back chair and let him take a seat behind the desk, waiting for him to finish the call.

"I'm staying. I was going to return with you, until I saw Logan's parents. I meant what I said. I think you should come up with a plan and let me help find Sharon or whoever abducted or murdered her. Will you let me do this and include me?"

The office was empty except for the desk and chairs. No pictures of Pete on the wall to distract her.

"Why do you think you're qualified to help?"

"I don't, but those men were after me for some reason today. They might be again."

"Therein lies the problem. You aren't safe here," the Commander stated firmly. His men never argued with that tone, but it always brought out the rebellious teenager in her.

"I don't want you to be disappointed with me again."

"Why do you think I would be?"

"I thought... Well, you and Mom argued so vehemently

against my coming out here." She looked at the secrets he hid beneath the stoic naval-commander expression. "Oh my gosh. You couldn't tell me the real reason you didn't want me to come."

"No, I couldn't. I'm not supposed to speak about it now. I had a man undercover and I knew how explosive this region is. I didn't want you in danger."

"I have to do this, Dad."

He reluctantly nodded. "My boss is twisting my arm to get you to cooperate. They want to use you for bait."

"It's not very appealing or noble when you put it like that."

He stood and pulled her to her feet. "Andrea, this is serious. You aren't trained to be an operative, and any number of things can go wrong. Probably will go wrong. We've already lost a very experienced agent."

"I know, Dad. I just don't think I could live with myself if I walked away. Could you?"

He shook his head. She liked it when Commander Allen left the room and he was her father again. "Whoever's arranging for this gun shipment to Mexico has to be high up in the cartel."

"I wish you'd reconsider." Her father's voice dropped so soft she could barely hear.

"You let me think you were the overprotective commander to try to keep me from coming. You've got to remember that I'm your daughter. I need to do this. The entire time I was growing up I heard you say how important it was to finish what you started, to be a part of a team and not leave anyone behind. How can you ask me to walk away from all three of the most important things to you?" She wanted to hug him, but they really didn't hug a lot in her family.

"The most important thing to me is keeping the two women I love the most safe from harm. What kind of father would deliberately let his daughter be abducted by drug dealers?"

"One who understands how much this means to me. I can make a difference. Please let me help."

He gave a reluctant nod. "For you. Not for the men twisting my arm. I do understand about not leaving a man behind. Responsibility can sometimes weigh you down. I should have a team with you every moment—that's what your mother would want—but we're shorthanded as it is. Would you consider a professional bodyguard…would you allow—I see by your expression that's not a possibility, either."

"You know a military detail or bodyguard won't allow these men to feel comfortable enough to act. I'll finish the study at the observatory. I promise I won't leave until you're ready for me to draw out these murderers again. I'll call as often as you need me to. I don't want to be a burden…"

"But that's not the most important reason you want to stay." He finally had his dad face on, the one she could relate to, the person she loved so much because he understood her. "You sure?"

"It's more than the study or potentially helping catch the murderers. Sharon's still missing. What if she was abducted because they thought she was me? That's on my head. Oh, don't you give me that look that it's your fault. No. You've warned me for years to be aware and on my toes, one step ahead of anything like this. I let my guard down, Dad. I feel so selfish—"

"It's okay, Andrea. This isn't anyone's fault except the men with no thought to human life. I completely understand why you need to stay here. I'll explain everything to your mother. But we do this my way. When my team is ready. Make everyone believe you're here only to finish your thesis. No one knows the truth except my liaison."

She remembered Pete's arm around Mrs. Griggs, wondering who the liaison would be. If not Pete, then she'd be forced to act like a selfish, spoiled woman with no thought for anyone else other than herself, lying to Pete.

"My men said the Hiller was a piece of trash. That was some nice flying this afternoon. Reminds me of our Sunday afternoon flights. That was a lot of years ago."

"Yes, sir. I miss them."

"We'll have to do it again sometime soon." He squeezed her hand. The closest thing to a hug she'd ever get in public.

"It's a date."

"For the record, I'm damn proud of you, Andrea. Very proud. And regarding the attempted abduction, you touched on several points that had already been considered by my team. They believe they're going to try again as another distraction. I'll be couriering a pair of earrings to you. Wear them at all times and I'll be able to find you."

They walked from the spare office and witnessed Logan's parents leaving.

"You don't have to do this." Her father spoke quietly, hope apparent in his voice. "You don't owe anyone anything."

"Yes, I do. For them, for Sharon and especially for me."

"Only one person will know the real reason you're staying. He'll be fully briefed and ready to move without my permission. You and I both will have to trust him with your life. I'll assign him to be in charge of your protection detail, but you can't tell him why you're really staying here. You can't tell anyone."

"I want Pete to be in charge."

"He's already declined my offer."

"I know that won't stop you. It would look more realistic for the sheriff to be in charge."

"I should lock you up and throw away the key."

She nodded and her father left her standing at the edge of the office. More like on the edge of reality. She couldn't believe she'd insisted on putting her life on the line. Something these men and women did daily.

Homeland Security. Texas Rangers. Drug Enforcement Administration. Presidio County Sheriff's Department. Pete would be another valued member of their new task force. But her role? She was the bait. She felt every bit exposed as if she were dangling midair on a small hook, holding on for dear life but her fingers were slipping.

Andrea was determined to stay, determined to help find Sharon, determined to put the creep behind all this confusion in jail. And like it or not, she was determined to find out why Sheriff Pete Morrison had no future.

It was a shame that to accomplish her goal she had to let him think her a selfish human being.

"I NEED TO speak with you, Sheriff Morrison," Commander Allen commanded, but remained outside the office.

No choice. He'd already received a phone call from the mayor ordering him to help in any capacity. He was sunk, but at least Andrea would be returning with her father and remain safe.

"Did they find your hat?" she asked out of the blue.

He was certain she had a look of mischief, just a slight tilt to those luscious lips and a twinkle in her eyes.

"I didn't check, but someone brought back the Tahoe. I imagine it'll turn up."

"This picture is great." She pointed to one his dad had caught of him shoving his hat on his head. "It'd be a shame to lose that hat."

"Andrea—"

"Were you on duty?"

"What? Oh, in the picture? No. I'd just been pitched from a bucking bronc at a local rodeo. Can you wait with Peach till I can get a protection detail together to take you back to the observatory?"

"I don't mind at all. The Commander actually threatened to arrest me to get me home. Fortunately, we came up with another arrangement. I want to help find Sharon. To do that, I had to concede to his terms. And if you're in here, that means he's given in to mine."

"What terms?"

"I hope you can forgive me, Pete. It really is the only way, but I'm not picking up my things and running home."

He was afraid to ask, and for some idiotic reason he felt like he'd been waylaid. He crossed his arms over his chest and backed to the door, wishing he had his hat brim to hide behind. "What terms?"

"I'm trusting you with my daughter's life," the Commander said through the doorway.

Why would her father state that she was leaving only to give in to Andrea's demands moments later? A quick glance at the enthusiasm on his dad's face, then a sharp stare at the woman who couldn't meet his eyes. A sliver of secretiveness was still there no matter how much she tried to hide it. And no matter how good an opportunity this sounded, Pete didn't think he would like working for her father.

She still hadn't answered his question. "One more time, Andrea. What terms?"

Victory was displayed in her smile as she finally met his eyes. "I'm staying as long as you're my personal escort and that you agree I'll stay at your ranch when not at the observatory."

"You mean, glorified babysitter." He turned to Commander Allen. "You said she was leaving."

"She was—now she's not. She agreed to stay put at the observatory and in your home."

Not only was he responsible for her every move miles away in another county, but she was supposed to bunk at their ranch? Live with him?

"You're willing to bring me onto your team so you can

order me to play bodyguard for your daughter? Seems like
you could have just asked me to assign her a protection
detail."

"I'm a bit surprised by Andrea's change of heart, but
I assure you there's much more involved than protecting
my daughter." Another couple entered the sheriff's office. "Looks like my state liaison is here. Please escort
my daughter to the conference room, Sheriff. You're both
needed for the briefing."

Pete recognized the Texas Ranger entering his building
and directed to the office. The woman next to him looked
completely out of place. With an expensive suit and heels
that belonged on a television show—completely ridiculous
and useless for West Texas.

"Commander Allen? Cord McCrea, Texas Rangers. Nice
to meet you in person. Good to see you, Pete." He turned to
the woman next to him. "This is Special Agent Beth Conrad, Drug Enforcement Administration."

"We've got the upstairs briefing room cleared out and
ready to go."

Everyone turned toward the stairs, with the exception
of the woman in high-end heels. "Where's the elevator,
please?"

"I'll show you the way," his father said, draping her
arm over his.

When everyone except Andrea had left, he asked,
"Why?"

She shrugged and averted her eyes. "I need to finish
my thesis. If you're too busy for this opportunity I'm dropping in your lap, you can always ask your father to take
on the job."

"That's not the reason I said no. You aren't safe here."

His new charge was hiding something and he had a really bad feeling he knew what it was.

Chapter Fifteen

Andrea followed the others upstairs to a vacant briefing room since Joe's old office was no longer big enough. Each person grabbed a chair and made introductions. Pete crossed his arms and leaned against the wall instead of taking the empty seat next to her.

The Commander was back in full force and sitting at the head of the table, definitely in charge. "I'm keeping this task force small for a reason. I would prefer we stay under the radar and not let our enemy know we're searching for him."

They all glanced in her direction, except Pete. "I'm not going to blab about it."

"We know. At approximately 2200 hours Friday evening, a severely beaten man came from the desert and—"

"If I may, Commander." Pete pulled his notebook from his back pocket. "McCrea and I are pretty familiar with this area. It might help to hear a detailed account of events."

"Then we're all up to speed. Sounds good," McCrea said.

The woman from the DEA compressed her lips and took out an electronic notepad.

"Andrea Allen was at the Viewing Area on Highway 90. People stop and watch for the lights to appear this direction—" he pointed to a spot on the map hanging behind him "—southwest toward the Chinati Mountains. A trucker reported seeing the lights at 2204. Andrea returned to her vehicle searching for a camera."

The camera. What had happened to it? She needed to ask her father, or maybe Joe would know. Pete recited the details of their adventure. She rubbed her wrist, which was still sore from all the climbing she'd done to escape that supply closet. She couldn't remember how she'd kept her wits to find her way out of the building. His mention of how she'd escaped got her a nod from both the Ranger and the DEA agent.

"Which brings us back to Commander Allen," Pete concluded. He remained standing and didn't look at her.

"The man who had been beaten was Lyle Moreland. He was one of mine. Trained to fly just about anything. Mc-Crea had given us a tip that a new gang could be using helicopters to move drugs. We know that this has been done before, but whoever's in charge of this new group is smart and, unfortunately, patient."

"Did you know about this, Dad?" Pete asked.

"Not until I went to the car accident and met the Homeland crew."

"While you were there, did anyone find the observatory's video camera?" she asked quietly.

"Did you manage to record part of the altercation or anything Moreland might have said?" the DEA agent asked from across the table.

"I remember turning it on. Then he was there and unconscious."

"I didn't see it," Pete answered. Their fathers shook their heads.

"Perhaps that's why they believe Miss Allen knows something of importance," Agent Conrad surmised.

Andrea had just come to that same conclusion while waiting for a break to ask about the camera. The statement carried more weight with a real agent stating it as a possibility. Andrea knew how these things worked. It was like dealing with four "commanders." Only four because Joe watched them all chat, too.

Pete wanted answers as to why his department hadn't been included. The Ranger said, "Need-to-know basis." Pete seemed to keep his cool but didn't let the conversation end.

She quietly scooted her chair from the table. If she could get out of the room, she wouldn't have to lie about her real reason for staying in the area. She made it to the hallway without anyone asking her to take her seat again.

"Need a cup of coffee?"

"Oh, Joe. You scared me. Yes, I'd love a cup."

"I'm thinking you haven't had anything to eat. Want a bite, too?"

"No, thank you. I better hang around for my dad and I need to find a ride to the observatory."

"Pete's taking care of that."

"But—"

"No need to argue. He's already made up his mind. Tahoe's gassed and sitting out front." He waved his hand and started walking away but turned around, waving her closer to him and farther from the door. "There's a solid reason he believes he can't get involved with anyone. You should ask him. He might even tell ya."

Joe dropped this statement into her lap and headed down the stairs.

How did the man know that she'd overheard any portion of their conversation? It didn't really matter. Any connection with Pete would be based on the lies she promised to tell. After all this was over, he'd find out the truth and really have no reason to become involved with her. No matter how determined she'd been an hour ago, his reasons were none of her business. Period.

PETE NOTICED THE moment Andrea had crept out of the conference room. He wanted to stop the discussion, to follow her, but his dad had given him a thumbs-up and taken that job on himself.

Half an hour later she was still on a bench in the hallway. She might even be asleep.

"So we're agreed on a plan?" Commander Allen flattened his palms on the table, ready to push up out of the chair.

"Yes," everyone confirmed. Pete nodded his agreement.

He would funnel information to the Commander and the DEA through McCrea—who also had an informant in Presidio on the border. And as he'd been warned earlier, he'd been assigned the duty of keeping the witness safe. Although he'd never promised that he'd be with Andrea 24/7, he had agreed to provide her with a protection detail.

Beginning with him.

It was going to be a long night.

"Wondering if you should wake her?" her father asked from just behind him. He placed a hand on Pete's shoulder. "The answer would be yes. Back to that dang observatory and searching the stars for who knows what. Her mother can't understand her passion but I do. I was in the program at NASA for several years while she was growing up."

"You wanted to be an astronaut?"

"Damn right. Didn't you?"

"Afraid I wasn't at the top of my class." Close enough, but studying had never been his thing. "Are you staying the night, sir?"

"I did everything right, still didn't make it to space." Regret passed quickly over his face. "I'm confident that you've got this under control."

"You mean McCrea."

"I know who I meant." He patted his shoulder in a

fatherly fashion and passed through to the hallway. "Andrea, time to get a move on."

"You leaving?" she said midyawn.

Pete went downstairs, collected messages and checked out an extra shotgun. He secured everything in the Tahoe, including the fast food Peach had ordered during the meeting. A government vehicle pulled up next to him. The driver was on his phone and stayed behind the wheel.

"Thanks for the eats."

"I told Brandie to double your usual and put it on your tab. You know, one of these days you're going to have to learn how to cook."

"Peach, you know dang well I haven't been home since Thursday. When would I have had time to cook?"

"I'll let my book club know you're ready for some casseroles. Looks like you're going to need them with company at your house."

"Lord save me from a death by casseroles." *And a frustrating woman living in the guest room.* He put his hands together in prayer just in time for Andrea and her father to enter the hallway.

The Commander shook Pete's hand, then took his daughter's between his own before saying good-night and leaving.

Andrea turned to Pete. "Well, what now, Sheriff? Where's the escort?"

"You sure about this? I could catch your father before he pulls away. You were ready to leave with him this morning. I'm not certain I understand what's changed."

"Do you have a ride for me or not?"

"Right this way."

Five minutes down the road, he thought she'd given up the battle to stay awake again. Catching a nap before she worked all night seemed to be a good idea. He reached in his bag and pulled out a hamburger.

"That smells absolutely delicious."

"There's one for you."

He heard the bag rustle.

"Oh, my goodness. That's awesome. Thanks for thinking about me."

"Peach took care of it."

"Okay. Be sure and thank her for me," she said with her mouth full.

"I'll need to know your routine when we get there. And I need your word you won't vary from it."

"I promise. No playing, no hikes, no exception. Just straight to and from the telescope."

"I'm in charge of scheduling your escorts and protection. No one has authorization to make changes and I won't send a message via anyone else to do so. Not even my father. Is that clear? If you don't hear it from me, you can assume the message is bogus."

"That works."

Her tone was short and abrupt. She acted mad at him, but for what? She'd actually called *him* spoiled when she was the one using her father's position, demanding to stay to finish her research. But what did he know? They'd kissed a few times. He didn't know anything about her.

There hadn't been time for much else. And there wouldn't be. He hadn't just been spouting words that she deserved a man with a future to his dad to shut him up. Without his job, he'd work their ranch with the few cattle they currently had. They couldn't keep the place up just on his dad's retirement. Hiring out as a ranch hand was his best option to help make ends meet.

But right now he had a job to do. Get Andrea to the observatory and ensure her safety until she left next week. He could do that and do it well. She didn't have to like him.

"What's so important about watching a star?" he asked. His curiosity had gotten the better of him. "What made you change your mind about leaving?"

"I'm working with a University of Texas astronomer who verified the most distant galaxy in the universe using several telescopes. For me this study is more about securing time with the actual telescope than studying the stars. If I finish my thesis and publish, I'll have a good chance of obtaining a position with one of the best telescopes in the world."

"This is about a job you may or may not get?"

"The Chilean Giant Magellan Telescope will begin construction soon and will have nearly five times the light-gathering power of the best infrared in the world. We'll see more distant galaxies and watch stars being formed. Someday I'd love to get on a team studying reionization."

Under different circumstances he'd appreciate the enthusiasm in her voice, the excitement displayed through her hands as she spoke of something she truly loved. Another time he'd ask her what all that meant. At the moment, he was confused.

"You're willing to risk your life, not to mention the men on your protection detail, for a potential job? And you called me selfish." *You're an idiot, Morrison!* He could keep his distance without insulting her.

"You asked about my work. I…um…understand that Logan is dead and Sharon is still missing. I can't change any of that."

"*You* could be missing. Do you understand that?"

"Yes, I do," she admitted quietly.

Then it hit him. "Son of a gun, your father stated three separate times that you were a witness and not an active member of the task force. You're both lying. Aren't you?"

"I'm staying at the observatory to finish my study."

"And hoping that those maniacs will try to get to you again. Dammit." He hit the steering wheel hard enough to make his palm sting. "This is a stupid plan. I can't stand guard twenty-four hours a day."

"You aren't supposed to. They won't make a move if you're too close."

There it was, the admission. He was right and she was staying behind to draw the murderers out.

He jerked the car to the side of the road as soon as there was room to safely do so. "We're going back. Or I'm taking you to Alpine to catch the first flight to Austin. You can't go through with this. You have no idea what you're doing."

"You'd be surprised, but it doesn't matter. You don't have a say in the decision."

"Andrea," he beseeched, hoping her name and his tone could say more than the words that wouldn't form into sentences.

The closeness between them was strained. She'd pulled away after spending time with her dad. He knew why he had distanced himself, but why had she changed?

The soft gleam from the dashboard lights gave her a glow like one from a full moon. Perfect for someone who worked with the stars. He wanted to take her in his arms. Their attraction had them both leaning toward each other, until bright headlights interrupted and they both pulled back.

"I appreciate your concern, but I have to do this." She retreated as far as possible, wrapping her arms around herself like she was freezing to death. "This was my idea, Pete. But the Commander's superiors agree. Please believe me. Even my father's respecting my decision."

The nonstop nervous chatter he'd grown accustomed to had disappeared. This woman seemed completely in control. He faced forward, ready to continue to the observatory, wanting to know why it was so important to her yet holding back.

"You're right. It's not my call." Easing the vehicle back onto the empty road, he wanted to ask but couldn't allow himself to get closer to her. "Aw, hell, mind sharing why your dad insisted you weren't involved? Or why he wants the very task force he formed out of the loop?"

"It's better this way. Less chance of word getting out that it's a trap."

"I see. He said a couple of times that he didn't think you'd be part of the equation again. So no one's supposed to know except Cord. He knows, right?"

"Yes. Please don't think badly about my dad. He understands why I need to stay. Sharon's still missing, and if there's the slimmest chance..."

"I need to assign you a larger protection detail."

"No. Please, Pete." She leaned toward him. Close enough for him to see the strain on her face. "I have to do this."

"Not at the expense of losing your life."

"Again, it's not your call. If you refuse to help, then you're not part of the loop. You can step away, and we'll get the Jeff Davis County sheriff to help."

"Over my dead body you will."

"Nothing that extreme, please. Like I told my dad, I promise I won't make any detours. Straight to work. Straight back to your ranch. I won't ditch my guard or anything like that. But if there's a chance that Sharon's alive and they still think I have some information, I need to be here to help."

"I admire your determination and courage, even if I think you're insane for volunteering to do this."

"Thanks, I think."

He'd already planned to handpick her protection detail from both counties. He'd already spoken with his father about driving her and made arrangements for the house to be cleaned. It would be a pain driving her back and forth, but he didn't care.

Nothing would happen to Andrea on his watch. They might not have a future together, but she definitely had places to go and stars to discover.

Chapter Sixteen

The operation had lost one helicopter and five men. Patrice would be upset. More accurately, her employer would be angry. Indeed, she was due here any moment. He uncorked her favorite California wine to let it breathe.

Homeland Security's spy had stolen from him and had the power to bring down more than what Patrice had lost. He was certain Andrea Allen had been given information at her car in the desert—whether she knew it or not.

Tomas had been too inquisitive. His intelligence should have given him away immediately as an undercover agent. But to his credit, he'd kept himself in the background operations for months. Unfortunately, their methods hadn't been able to obtain how he was making contact with DHS to pass any information back to his superiors.

If they hadn't learned of Miss Allen's importance, they might never have ferreted out the spy. He still wanted the young woman. Having her in his control was key to the next phase of operations.

It had been highly improbable Patrice's men would succeed in the abduction but well worth the try. The benefits far outweighed the losses. He heard the front door open.

"Miss Orlando, please come in."

"I told you it wouldn't work, Mr. Rook." She dropped her purse on the floor and stripped off her jacket, tossing it haphazardly across a brocade chair. She saw the wine, tilted some into a glass and gulped the fine red elixir too fast.

"Yes, you did." He bit his tongue to remain pleasant. "But I also informed you that it didn't matter to me what the cost was to you. The trucks made it into Manuel Ojinaga and we're on schedule."

"I'll need compensation for the men I've lost. Replacing them will cost me a bundle. I don't want to dip into my reserve, drawing attention to myself."

"Naturally. These men will be worth the higher price. Unless you'd like to reconsider?"

His fingers caught her exposed throat as she tossed back the last of the wine in the glass. She choked—partly on the wine, partly from the pressure of his grasp. The fragile handblown wineglass shattered on the floor. He should have waited until she'd set it on the table. Her fingers curled around his own, attempting to pry them away from her skin.

As her oxygen waned, her eyes grew enormous as she realized he controlled whether she lived or died. He saw the acknowledgment in her face, in the desperation of her clawing hands and kicking feet. Her dress rose to show the tops of her stockings.

Had she worn them for him today? Sex with her might be a satisfying distraction while he waited. He released his grip, immediately turning his back to give her a moment to recover.

As he was concentrating on board three, his next move presented itself. "Aw, thank you, Patrice. Nc6 is a very nice move."

She coughed and sputtered behind him, then began tugging on her dress. Yes, it was time to remind her who was in control. He gathered her things and offered his hand to help her stand.

"I'm in the mood to postpone the doldrums of business for a while. How about you?"

The fright in her eyes spurred his movements. He controlled himself, restraining from pulling her along. He glanced at the six boards, committing the pieces to memory. Ready to be inspired while Patrice was at his fingertips.

He opened the door, waving off his assistant. "Delay dinner an hour. Oh, wait, Mr. Oscuro."

Patrice's stylish dress had a visible zipper down the back. He'd noticed straightaway that she was also braless underneath. It had been a long while since he'd reminded her where her place was. He jerked her to a halt in the hallway, tugged the zipper and waited to see if she'd let the dress fall.

A small gasp of surprise was her only protest, and he'd let her have it. She dropped her arms to her sides and the dress amassed around her ankles with a gentle tug over her hips. He offered his hand again to help her step over the sleek red pile. She took it. The bruises on her shoulder and neck visible against her flawless skin.

"Marvelous. Simply marvelous. That's all, Oscuro."

He nodded to the near-naked woman. She brought a smile to his lips like no other could. But she needed to know he'd sacrifice her faster than a knight's pawn if she defied him or took his courtesy for granted.

Chapter Seventeen

There's a solid reason he believes he can't get involved with anyone. You should ask him.

Andrea tried to work on entering new information into her database. She'd managed to eke out a couple of sentences on her dissertation during the past two hours. Useless. Her mind kept coming back to Joe's statement and wondering why he couldn't just tell her what the reason was himself.

"This is hopeless." She shut the laptop lid and rubbed her aching eyes. All her things had been moved to the Morrison ranch house, but she still had her assigned room at the dormitory where she could work. She'd come early today, hoping to get caught up without any distractions.

Distractions like Pete sleeping in the next room or working horses in the late afternoon. Yesterday from her window she'd seen him thrown from a horse. She'd wanted to run to him to make sure he was okay. Willpower hadn't stopped her. She'd been frozen to the windowsill watching him take off his shirt to shake out the dirt.

So she'd come to the observatory early in order to avoid those type of incidents today.

Studying, applying herself or stringing words together for a paper had never been a problem…until now. She'd never had trouble sleeping at odd hours before. You got used to that when you studied the stars. Who was she kidding? Sleep deprivation had nothing to do with it. Every thought centered on Pete and the cryptic advice his father had given her.

Just concentrate.

Three nights watching the farthest regions of the galaxy and she couldn't type up her notes. Learning the nuances of the 9.2 meter mirror on the telescope hadn't relieved her or excited her the way it usually did. And if she did manage to keep on track for a few minutes, the next person entering the room would ask her about the shooting or share how she and Pete had escaped. Or they'd tell her what they were doing during the shooting. She'd either commend them or apologize to them.

During the day, construction crews were down the hill at the Visitor Center repairing windows and bullet holes. The shattered glass had been swept up and thrown away. Pete's dad had tried to capture her would-be abductors alive, but they'd all chosen to fight to the death. One had escaped into the woods and been tracked for several hours until he also stepped in front of a bullet.

The manhunt was the reason authorities had delayed searching for them after she'd landed the Hiller chopper in the middle of nowhere. It was ridiculously hard not to think about the incident. Much harder not to think about Pete.

Her hands smoothed the laptop. Was she ready to open it and get serious? *No.* She wanted to stop thinking of Pete. Andrea stepped out of the main room of the dormitory.

"Hi, Bill. Need anything?" She spoke to the guards throughout each day, making a point to learn the names of the men who accepted the risk of protecting her.

Pete had warned the deputies not to take the assignment for granted. Joe reminded them each morning when dropping her off at the ranch about potential attacks. He stressed the danger without disclosing specifics about the task force or possible trap they could be setting.

"No, thanks, Andrea," Bill answered, tipping his hat and resuming his watch.

The crime scene and repairs had closed the main building and classroom. Neither was necessary for the star parties. From out here she could see the visitors lining up on the sidewalk, claiming their telescopes. It would be a beautiful night for stargazing.

The observatory was short on staff and volunteers. She'd received an email asking for all volunteers to help with the class tonight. Her telescope was sct and she wasn't needed until much later. Why not help?

There was no reason other than writing or compiling data. If she wasn't going to do either of those, then she could give back a little. After all, she was the reason all the windows were broken.

Technically, she'd promised not to do anything other than study at the observatory and sleep at Pete's ranch. The Commander had forced a promise and then Pete had asked for one. But it had been two full days and three nights without another person making an untoward move against her.

The closed spaces were beginning to make her twitch. She needed to move, feel a little free.

Wasn't volunteering to help kids considered part of her job? She'd helped a couple of times her first week and loved it. The star parties were so much fun and, man, oh, man, she needed some fun. It wasn't like getting in her car and driving into town. She would still be at the observatory and keeping her promise.

She pulled on tennis shoes and practically ran down the hill from her dormitory room. Bill stayed close after jumping into his squad car and repeating ten times that she needed to wait. She slowed and took a deep breath of the

crisp clean air as she got closer to the café patio and where
Pete had been shot.

Last Friday afternoon, she'd taken the same walk to get
to Sharon's car. On that journey she hadn't nearly been
killed in a car accident, shot at on the observatory patio,
stranded in the mountains or kissed by a sheriff. The very
same sheriff who seemed to avoid her as often as possible.

His days were full of work—doubly so since he'd joined
the task force. Her days were full of sleep. Her nights were
busy with calculations and stars. His were surrounded by
dreams. At least she hoped they were.

Stubborn man.

Right now, this very minute, was about sharing her love
for the stars. Helping someone—child or adult—find a con-
stellation or a crater on the nearly full moon.

*There's a solid reason he believes he can't get involved
with anyone. You should ask him.* Joe's words orbited
around in her mind like a moon around its planet. They
were constantly there with no choice but to continue.

The next time she saw the sheriff of Presidio County…
she was going to ask.

"The source is reliable. They're going to use the cover of
the UFO Border Zone to move something major." Cord Mc-
Crea had been trying to stop drug trafficking since trans-
ferring to West Texas almost ten years before. He knew the
area and could get information from a dried cactus.

The men who had followed Andrea to the observatory
had inside information—from either the police radio or
bugged cell phones. So he met Cord in an open area dead
cell coverage zone between their properties. Making certain their conversations weren't monitored or overheard.
Pete wasn't taking a chance with Andrea's life. Not a second time.

"How would they use the UFO convention? It's not like

there are crowds and crowds of people wandering every-where. The thing draws a couple of thousand at best. And that's during the concerts. They've only been having the conference for a couple of years now." Pete caught himself shoving his hair back and resituating his hat. A habit Andrea had drawn to his attention when she'd arranged his hair with gel. His fingers had gotten stuck a couple of times in the stiff edges. After every shower now, he stopped himself when he reached for the styling tube.

"I don't know, Pete. All I can confirm is what my informant tells me. And that's all he's got."

"What's the deal with your task force? Do I need to be doing anything differently?"

Cord stretched his back. He'd been shot several years before by drug traffickers. All those men were behind bars or hadn't survived a second confrontation. "Naw. Just keep being the sheriff and keep Allen's daughter safe. You could let me know who you'll be sending to the aliens conference."

"You got it." Exactly what he'd thought. He'd been put on the task force only because of Andrea. "Cord, I know Andrea's being used as bait."

"I didn't think it would stay a secret from you long."

"Is that right? Why?"

Cord raised a curious eyebrow. "Come on, man. I saw the way you two looked at each other. The tension the other night could be cut with a knife. She insisted on staying at your place, having you as her protection detail. Allen wanted you in charge of the border detail."

So those were her terms.

Cord clapped him on the back. "I can see that brain of yours working, pal. That's right. Miss Allen wouldn't trust anyone else with her life. Just you. Go ahead, stick that chest out a little farther. Does that make you feel more important?"

They both laughed, but he did feel more competent.

"Just so you know, I'll be filling her in on our suspicions that something's happening. I want her to be prepared."

"Makes sense."

"Kate and the new baby okay? We haven't seen much of her around town."

"They stay close to the house, but they're great. Danver's a regular roly-poly. Kate's brother David is coming in at the end of the month, which is a code word for barbecue with the McCreas. Bring your dad."

"Sure. As long as this thing's over by then."

"You realize that we're never going to be done with drug traffickers trying to make a buck. We stop this group, another one is standing right behind it ready to take up the reins and harness a new set of horses. It'll never be over," Cord said sadly.

"Job security. What more can a man ask for?" He shrugged. At least Cord had job security. The position of sheriff—no matter how competent Pete felt—might be out of the question for him.

"There's more to life, man. I hope you'll find out what soon." He tipped his hat. "See you around. I'll give you a holler if my guy comes through with more info about the shipment."

"I'll have additional deputies in or near Presidio. They were already on the schedule to be at the UFO conference. Hard to understand that's the date they're choosing…when we have *more* men posted there."

"My source is more reliable than they normally come. It ain't gospel, but it's close. Take care now." Cord closed the door of his truck and drove out on the broken trail.

Pete stayed put, leaning on his Tahoe, watching the first evening star shine in the darkening sky. Andrea would have been dropped off about an hour ago. His dad was driving her from the ranch to the observatory and a deputy would pick her up in the morning and drive her to the ranch.

He would have to talk to her sooner or later. They couldn't keep successfully avoiding each other. He finished his soda and crushed the can, tossing it into the back. A couple of minutes on the road and he could make a call.

"Dispatch, reassign the driver for Miss Allen in the morning. I'll be picking her up myself."

"You don't say," Peach answered. "I told Honey you'd come around."

"Thanks for the confidence."

"Well, we did raise you as a hero, not a coward."

"I'll be signing off now, Dispatch."

"'Night, Sheriff."

Not a coward. For the past three days, he sure as hell had been one where Andrea Allen was concerned. Dammit.

PETE WAVED AT Randy Grady still on his feet at the door where Andrea was working. "Didn't they have a chair for your shift?"

"I didn't want to get too comfortable and nod off. You said to stay on our toes. I thought your dad was picking up Miss Allen?" They shook hands.

"He had an errand this morning, so I'm filling in."

"How's the arm?"

Pete stretched it across his chest. "Surprisingly good."

"Heard you passed out." Randy snickered under his breath.

"More from a lack of sleep than this thing."

"Right." Randy sang a song as he said the one word, doubting. He trotted down the sidewalk and stopped. "She's a nice woman. Any chance this protective detail will be over before she blows town?"

"Don't think so. Not with her father."

"Totally understand. I'd keep her for myself, too. I'll head out, then."

"It's not like that." But at the back of his mind, he knew it was. Randy disappeared down the path, and Pete stopped himself from shouting a denial.

He watched the sky lighten in the east through the tree-tops. Andrea would be out any minute. Why had he decided to pick her up? The dare from Peach? He had nothing to prove. Andrea would be gone at the end of the week without a glance back in his direction.

She didn't need any of the complications that getting involved with him would bring. The door opened.

"Oh, hi," Andrea said, then waved behind her. "My ride's here, guys. See you tomorrow."

Pete scanned the perimeter, including the skyline for a possible chopper, avoiding eye contact with his assignment. There had been three days without a hint of an incident. None of the deputies had reported any unusual activity. No one had reported any unusual cars or visitors hanging around either Fort Davis or Marfa.

"I'm surprised to see you."

"Why?"

"Well, Randy was here earlier."

"He just left. I thought I'd give you a ride back to the ranch. Do you need anything else?"

"Nope, I've got everything." She patted her laptop bag. "Gorgeous morning."

"That it is." She was a step ahead of him. He could take a long, good look at her. Gone was the bandage around her wrist, and the bruise was fading. Tight-fitting jeans covered her slender figure. A McDonald Observatory souvenir T-shirt hugged a tiny waist, giving him a terrific view.

They both got inside the Tahoe, and he drove away from the observatory, watching for stalled cars or men on the road. He noticed Andrea's constant movement and glances behind them. "You seem kind of antsy. Something on your mind?" he asked after a few minutes.

"I was just waiting for you to drop the real reason you're personally picking me up. I know you've been avoiding me. Did something happen? Did they send a new threat?"

"Nothing like that. I thought I'd give you a chance to pick up anything you might need. Our schedules haven't been conducive for much socializing, that's all." *And let you know about the possible threat for the next three days.* But those words stuck in his throat.

"And whose fault is that?"

"I wouldn't place blame on anyone. It's just the way it happened to turn out." Peach's words argued with his conscience. If he did say something, what good would it do?

"So, did something happen? Do you have a message from my father?"

"Wouldn't Commander Allen be calling you directly?"

"I really don't know. This isn't exactly our normal situation. We normally don't talk that often."

"That's a downright shame."

Andrea laughed. "You've heard all about the educational differences I've had with my family. Now it's your turn to share."

"My dad and I get along just fine."

"You can't get off that easy. I've been living in your house. Joe's walking on eggshells and you guys barely say three words to each other."

"He had a heart attack, and I've sort of been busy."

"Oh, I know all about that. It's nothing to take lightly, but he's exercising and has lost seventeen pounds by changing his diet."

"How did you know that?"

"He brags about using a new belt hole all the time. You'd know if you were around him for more than five minutes.

Is it the upcoming election? Are you afraid he's going to be upset that you're taking his job?"

The desire to spill everything to Andrea was tempting. In spite of the nonstop chatter and her irresistible kissing ability, she was easy to talk with. He'd kept his dad's secret without saying a word for six weeks.

"I take your silence for a yes."

"Joe Morrison has been ready to retire. I know he'll miss the people, but he's been frustrated with the day-to-day stuff for a while now."

"He said you're running unopposed, so what's the problem? Why are you nervous?" she asked.

"You seem pretty cozy with my dad, but I'm not sure this is any of your business."

"What can I say? I like to talk."

"I've noticed."

"Are you mad at him because of me? I mean, Joe agreed to help the Commander. I know all this is an added strain. Especially having to drive me back and forth to the observatory."

"I have an idea. Why don't we listen to the radio and you take a break from thinking too hard on my problems."

"Okay, but I don't do country. Are there any classic rock stations around here?" Andrea turned away.

Pete immediately wanted to spill his guts. He'd been rude in order to stop himself from telling her everything. By the time they turned south into Fort Davis, he was ready to beg her to chatter again. He liked her voice and hadn't realized how much he'd missed it.

"You're right," he said, unable to take the silence.

At least she looked at him, eyebrows arched, waiting for him to continue.

"It's not…" Could he appease her curiosity without sharing all the details of his problem? No. In a very short time, this woman had gotten into his psyche. He wanted to be honest with her. But he just didn't know if he could be.

Telling anyone would be risking everything his dad had worked to achieve for thirty years.

"If things were different—" He clammed up...again.

"I get it. This is personal and I'm a stranger."

"Why is it so important to you?"

"You and your dad have been a big help this week. I owe you a lot. I hate to see your relationship strained because of me."

"It has nothing to do with you."

"Okay, I'd believe that. Except, after my dad formed this task force, you didn't want to have anything to do with me. And Joe said I should just ask you why. I would have sooner, but you made it pretty clear—"

"Wait a minute. Slow down. Dad told you to ask me why?"

"Yes, when he left the meeting Saturday, he said you had a good reason for acting like a jerk."

"He's called me worse."

Andrea turned a nice shade of embarrassed pink. "Sorry, that's actually my description. But you didn't even give me a chance to say thanks for saving my life before you completely brushed me off."

"I think we sort of saved each other. We made a good team."

"And that has to end?"

He took the vehicle through Marfa and made the last couple of turns to the ranch without responding.

"Look, Andrea, I don't see the point. You'll be on a military chopper out of here in four days. I have no doubts your father will keep you as far away as he can from Marfa, Texas, and this drug cartel. After that, you're trying to get a job on the other side of the world."

"Oh, so that's it. You're afraid of short-term relationships. Have you been burned before?"

He pulled past the front of the house, waving to his dad on the front porch. The grin and waggling eyebrows on his dad's face were enough of a sign that everything appeared normal. He parked, cut the engine and got a strange feeling his dad expected something to happen with Andrea and him.

She unbuckled, turning his direction. A playful grin replaced the serious expression from earlier. "I got the impression from the nurses the other night that you were a popular guy."

"Popular? I've had a few dates, nothing serious—"

"Hold that thought. Do you hear something?" She opened her door and hopped out before he could react. "Is that a helicopter? Was it following us?"

He drew his weapon as he jumped from the Tahoe, searching, seeing nothing. Andrea continued to the far side of the barn, her face turned to the sky.

"Wait! Don't run out in the open! Dammit, exactly like what you're doing."

Chapter Eighteen

Andrea ran until she got a good look at the helicopter heading away from the ranch. A sense of relief that their day wouldn't be interrupted swept over her as fast as the pleasant northern breeze. She stopped, and a second later, Pete skidded to a halt behind her. He stretched out his arms to steady her but quickly dropped them to his sides.

"Still alive." She shrugged. Hopefully indicating that running had been the wrong thing to do. "We don't have to make a big deal out of this, Pete. I know I shouldn't run off like that. It won't happen again."

"When am I supposed to make a big deal out of it? After they succeed in abducting you?"

Andrea was tired of seeing Pete's face worried instead of smiling. In the past few days, when that deep furrow appeared across his brow it was because of her. She was also tired of avoiding her attraction. Deep down, she knew that part of the reason she'd stayed in the area was her attraction to this man.

There was just something about him. Something sweet about his silence, though he was strong to his core. She wanted to discover what centered him and made him so easily confident without conceit. Simply put...she wanted to know him better.

So it made perfect sense to kiss him again.

"Did I finally ask something you don't have an answer for?"

Shrugging a little, she couldn't help smiling at the confusion in Pete's eyes. His hat was already in his hand or she might have pushed it off his head to the ground. He took a step back. She followed with two steps, catching his shoulders. With one small twist, she had him next to the barn wall.

He knew what was coming. She knew because his head tilted sideways and his face dropped even with hers.

"This is a bad idea, Andrea."

"You've got to have a better reason."

There was a hairbreadth between their lips. They stayed there, taking in each other's air. The minty clean made her wish she'd taken him up on the lifesaver he'd offered in his car. His chest began to rise and fall quicker, matching hers. His hands tightened around her waist, and she draped hers around his shoulders.

"Bad, bad idea," he said before crushing his lips to hers.

Sheriff Pete Morrison might think kissing her was a bad idea, but the man hauling her hips to his... Well, he left nothing but good sensations behind.

"The suggestion that any part of this is bad...absolutely ridiculous," she whispered close to his ear. "You are such a good kisser."

"You make me crazy," he said. He smashed his mouth to hers again, not allowing her to respond.

The returning kiss she gave him should have been answer enough. She was desperate not to let him go this time. Her body needed him, and his needed her.

She pulled back, dipping her mouth, tasting the salt on his skin, nipping the curve where his shoulder muscle met his neck. She tilted her head back, encouraging him to taste the V of her throat, sending additional shivers of anticipation down her spine.

His lips traveled down her breastbone, lightly scraping his teeth across her sensitive skin. His tongue darted under the lacy edge of her bra. His hands stretched along her sides, then tugged at her T-shirt, making her wish she'd worn the button-up hanging in her bedroom.

Oh, gosh, a bedroom would be nice. They could take their desire to the next level. But they couldn't... They weren't alone. But that didn't stop the exploring.

Pete's cool hands slid under her shirt, up her back and to her sides. He skimmed her breasts, just the thin lace separated the tips of his fingers and her flesh.

More shivers. At this rate there would be endless shivers and no relief in sight. She wanted his shirt off, but it was firmly tucked into his pants. She settled for skimming the tops of his ears, dragging her nails gently across his scalp and filling her hands with his thick hair.

Pete caught her mouth to his again, plunging his tongue inside. He captured her whimper as their hips gnashed together again. Wanting more than either could deliver in broad daylight on the side of the Morrison barn.

"Ahem." Joe cleared his throat from the corner of the barn.

Breathing too hard to speak, Andrea looked in his direction and could only see the toe of one boot and a long, tall shadow.

Breathing a little hard himself, Pete dropped his forehead just above her ear. Then he whispered, "Very bad idea."

"Not at all," she whispered back, noticing his hands settled on her hips, his thumbs comfortably hooked inside her jeans.

"Um, son. Since you're going to be here with our guest, I thought I'd take Rowdy into town. We need feed and supplies. I have a few errands. We'll probably be gone a good three or four hours, so I thought we'd grab lunch at the café."

"You don't have—"

She placed a finger over Pete's lips, fearing he'd convince his father not to leave. She lowered her voice again. "I promise to be good…and not run away."

Pete dropped his head against the barn, then his eyes seared her with their heat. "Fine, Dad. I got this covered."

Yes, he did.

PETE NEEDED TO drop his hands and lock the county's guest in her bedroom. That would be the right thing to do. The responsible thing. The sheriff thing. He could try. But the way his body was throbbing it would take every ounce of control he no longer had.

Holding Andrea in his arms, he'd lost control. If his dad hadn't interrupted them, there was no telling what he would have done. His heart rate was still thrumming at top speed. If he didn't have a grip on her hips, his hands would be shaking.

The horn from the truck sounded a couple of blasts. A minute later he heard it leaving. He stayed put, reluctant to let Andrea go because he knew what needed to be done.

"We should get inside." He reluctantly dropped his hands, pressing them against the barn.

Andrea stepped to the side and picked up his hat. She handed it to him, then put her fists on her slim hips. "What's wrong? You embarrassed?"

He shoved his hat on his head and circled her wrist, tugging a little to get her started. "Inside and no. Or yes, a little."

Once they were around the corner and headed to the house, she twisted her wrist free. "I've been walking on my own for a while now."

"Come on, Andrea. You're under my protection. We

can't— I shouldn't let my guard down or take advantage of our situation." He opened the screen door, ready to let her go through and plant himself on the porch until his father returned.

Looking him up one side and down the other, she seemed to read his mind and paused. To add to his misery, she took a seat on the porch swing and gestured for him to join her.

The chain suspending the swing creaked above their heads in a gentle rhythm as they sat shoulder to shoulder, silent. The horses clopped around in the corral. The breeze was picking up and blowing the top branches in the tree. Then just like high school, Pete found his hand inching toward Andrea's, then lacing their fingers together.

"This is nice. My mom would love this porch. She'd decorate it with all sorts of plants and small statues. She loves statues." She didn't seem mad.

In fact, she seemed to be in a great mood. Just like before their make-out session. Man, she was completely different from any woman he'd ever met. Shouldn't she be furious with him instead of holding his hand, sending lightning bolts up his arm or making small talk?

"Plants don't do so well out here in the winter." He could make small talk and ignore the energy surging through his body at her touch. Could he ignore that they had the house to themselves for the next three hours?

"Your dad is convinced that your reason for halting a potential relationship between the two of us is *solid*, as he put it. I, on the other hand, am not convinced."

So much for small talk.

"I have a lot of good reasons." It was easier to remember they couldn't be together when he wasn't touching her. He just couldn't force himself not to enjoy the smoothness of her skin. In fact, the memory of her incredible breasts made it hard to keep his seat.

"Why can't you tell me, Pete?"

"It's complicated."

"Then why is your dad so eager for you to share these reasons?"

"I don't know."

"One more question and then I'll go to my room." She looked down, dragged her toes and stopped the swing.

"Go for it."

"I think I will." She arched those beautiful brows again and winked. "Does it really matter for the next three hours?"

Chapter Nineteen

Pete watched Andrea's eyes slowly look into his and with his free hand, he tilted her chin until he could brush her lips again. Close enough to share her breath, her softness and her taste, and still far enough apart to quit. All he had to do was release her hand and let her go.

"What about all your reasons?" she asked.

His mind raced to find one legitimate objection not to finish what they'd started.

They'd only known each other a few days. That wasn't cause enough to stop. He felt drawn to Andrea like he'd known her all his life. And he wanted to know her better. Completely.

He wanted to taste the rest of her, working his way down from her slightly salty neck to her cute little toes. He wanted to find out if she was ticklish behind her knees or at the curve above her hip. He wanted to keep her to himself for a week of Sundays and forget the rest of the world and his list of reasons.

He didn't have a future. Hell, she only wanted three hours. The way his body was humming, he could guarantee that short time would be a long unforgettable adventure.

He was in charge of her protection. Her father working with Border Protection and Homeland Security still wasn't enough to make him stop. He'd take his chances.

But could the biggest reason on his list be ignored? *He was a phony.* He didn't want to lie to her, but it wasn't his secret. No matter how much she liked him, he couldn't take a chance telling anyone. Ever.

Pete stood quickly and jerked her into his arms. Her blue eyes were a perfect match with the sky. A perfect backdrop to kiss her again. He wanted to consume her, but he managed to keep his hands on her upper arms. He pressed his mouth to hers, coaxing her lips apart enough to enjoy the luxurious softness.

He wanted her with a fierce need that made nothing else matter. It had started in the hospital with each cheeky answer she'd given to his questions. And he honestly didn't see an end happening soon. It would, just not today. He'd already wasted enough of her remaining time in town. He tapered off their kiss in order to coax her to the door.

Andrea curved her hips into his, leaning back as she'd done on the far side of the barn. Her smile was sultry, sexy. "Does this mean you've changed your mind about the next three hours?"

With her looking like that at him, they weren't going to make it to the bedroom.

PETE KISSED HER hard and wrapped his arms around her waist as she wrapped hers around his neck. He moved toward the door, almost dragging her feet across the porch as he lifted her body next to his. Andrea didn't care. She was in just as big a hurry. Give the man too much time to think and he might change his mind.

Their limbs tangled as they helped each other take off their shirts. Hers pulled straight over her head, while she could only get his unbuttoned. Still kissing and touching, they dashed down the hall to the bedrooms.

"Mine," she said, bouncing against the closed door and struggling to turn the knob.

Pete didn't object. He skimmed her black bra—thank goodness she'd worn the sexy one—then traced her collarbone, moving higher until he cupped her neck with one hand and opened the door with the other. They backed into her bedroom, lips frantically finding each other again.

The belt holding his holster was unlatched. Andrea shoved his uniform over his shoulders and tugged his undershirt loose. Her hands skimmed his chest, hot flesh against her palms.

She returned his hard, deepening kisses, breaking long enough to stretch the white cotton over his head and let it fall to the floor. His hands slid down her back and seconds later her bra fell. Pete took a step back, his eyes smoldering as they saw her for the first time. She paused, letting him, not feeling vulnerable or self-conscious.

Andrea couldn't pretend to be a shy girl. She wasn't. Neither could she act coy and tiptoe around what she wanted. She'd wanted Pete Morrison since noticing his dimples back in the hospital. And what girl wouldn't want to make out with the man responsible for saving her life, not just once but twice?

"This has to be the *best* bad decision I've ever made."

"Oh, yeah?" She reached for the button on his fly and couldn't miss his physical reaction to her body as she unzipped his pants. "Then why are we slowing down?"

"Some things are worth savoring."

The smolder in his eyes turned to pure flame, spreading the heat to his entire body. He held her, letting her arch her back over his arm as he kissed and nipped a hot trail to her breast. By the time he reached the second, he laid her on the bed, taking his time to explore.

Pete stood between her legs, which were still encased in the heavy denim. His strong hands glided slowly down her thighs. If she hadn't been going crazy with anticipation, she might have screamed for him to hurry. But the anticipation was exquisite as he undressed her, giving a final tug to the tight jeans.

"You are more than beautiful. I could stare at you like this all day."

"You better not. What's good for the gander is good for the goose, you know." She winked suggestively and scooted farther onto the bed, pointed at his pants and propped her head up for a more comfortable look. "Strip, mister."

"Yes, ma'am."

Without much effort, Pete divested himself of all clothing and stood at the side of the bed a second before he looked uncomfortable. But that was only for a second. He got onto the bed, leaning on his side, and worked magic with his hands again.

Feather-soft strokes up and down her breastbone sent tingles all over her body. He drew concentric circles until her nipples drew tight, making her shiver multiple times. The strokes became longer, including her hips and thighs. Then tiny circles at the back of her knees.

"You've got a gentle touch," she gasped a little before he created a trail up her body with his lips. Then silenced her again with decadent kissing.

Andrea eagerly explored Pete's body, too. His sinewy muscles, long powerful thighs, lean hips and sheer strength left her breathless. When he reached between their bodies, she grabbed his shoulders, unable to keep her nails from lightly scraping into his skin. Moments later, her body hummed in fleeting perfection as she cried out.

Pete rolled to his side next to her, kissing her along her shoulder up to her neck, following the line of her jaw back to her lips. There wasn't an inch of relaxed parts on the man as she reached out and explored more.

It took a slight nudge to reverse their positions. Seconds later, Pete was on his back. She rose to her knees, massaging his chest, admiring the muscles extending to his hips.

She mimicked his technique of touch. She loved the fine dusting of manly hair on his legs, drew circles behind his knees, where he jerked away and laughed.

As much as she loved those dimples, another touch made him suck in his breath and tighten his abs. She shimmied up his body, her breasts sensitive as they flattened against his chest.

"I need my...my pants," he said, gulping air.

"Oh, no, you don't, mister. You aren't getting away now."

"Not...leaving." He smiled, pushing gently at her shoulders, then cupping her breasts, making her join him on a long sigh. Then he whispered, "Condom."

He groaned when she sat up, connecting them and then again when she left to retrieve his slacks. She tossed his wallet to him, repositioning herself across his thighs, hand extended for the foil packet. Once the condom was on, she was no longer in control. His smile was replaced with a look of longing. His gentle, slow touch was replaced with a frenzy she could barely control. He flipped her to her back and filled her.

Their joining was more than she'd thought it could be. They settled into a rhythm that belonged only to them. It couldn't be duplicated with anyone else.

"Meant to be" kept repeating in her head. No words were needed and none were said as their lips opened for each other just like their bodies. The perfection she'd experienced at his touch shortly before returned in extended stellar abundance. Pete joined her, tossing back his head as his body went supernova.

Chapter Twenty

"Think you could tell me about your list of reasons now?" Andrea asked, her head nestled in the crook of his shoulder. Her body was only half covered with the sheet, so he could still admire her flawless skin and curves.

"I'd rather make love to you again before I go remembering why I shouldn't."

"Don't get all hot and bothered because you're my protection detail."

"That's easy for you to say. What am I supposed to write in the report?"

"You can say I spent a pleasant morning in my room. You don't really write everything down for my father, do you?"

He'd pass answering that question honestly because the answer had been yes until an hour ago. "So now you know the real reason why I've tried to talk us out of this."

She climbed on top of him, close enough to kiss, her breasts gently grazing his chest. "I really want to know, Pete. I meant what I said about staying in touch when I leave." She paused, her head cocking to the side with realization. "I thought you were kidding earlier about long-distance relationships. But you really don't want that."

He gently held her in place when she tried to roll away. "Just hold your horses. Before you start rapid-firing questions off only an assumption. I never said I didn't want a relationship, close or long-distance."

"Then what is it? I can tell that something's bothering you. Is it my dad?" She turned her head again. "I knew it. The Commander is such a turnoff to potential boyfriends. But good grief, Pete. You're the sheriff. You can't possibly think he'll find out something about you…"

He couldn't look into her eyes. She was reading his mind—or doing a dang good job interpreting his expressions. She scooted to his side, pulling the sheet higher and tucking it around her like a toga. He threw his legs over the side of the bed.

And once again, Andrea surprised him with a comforting hand soothing his back muscles. She didn't seem indignant or curious. She just ran her fingertips lightly up and down, giving him a chance to think of what he should say.

"I should have just made love to you again."

She laughed and pressed her body to his, her arms lightly circling his neck. Her tongue flicked out enticingly against his earlobe.

"You don't have to tell me anything else," she whispered. "I'm very happy to take you up on your offer."

He twisted in her arms and dropped them both nose to nose on their sides.

"This isn't about you or your father, Andrea."

"All right. Since you don't know me very well, perhaps I should inform you that I'm pretty good keeping a secret. I once kept a secret for my best friend for almost two years. That actually might be because I forgot about it, but it should still—"

"Shh," he said just before covering her lips.

The long kisses kept them both silent. He wanted to tell her. She deserved to know that it had nothing to do with her. The frenzy slowed but not the intensity. Soon he was kissing his way down her body and loving every part of her.

"THAT WAS INSANE," Andrea said, collapsing next to Pete. "I can barely breathe. How much of our three hours is left?"

She'd fallen for Pete faster than a shooting star fleeted through the sky. And she was glad. He was a complex man, very intriguing and just plain adorable. Plus, he was a heck of a lover. A seriously wonderful lover. She had to be careful she didn't meet the same fate as a shooting star and burn up when it hit the atmosphere.

"Enough for a shower and breakfast." He was propped on the pillows, the corner of the sheet modestly covering his vulnerable parts.

"You mean lunch," she teased.

"Or dinner if you look at the fact that we both worked all night and neither of us has slept in a while."

"Wow, Sheriff. You did all that on no sleep? I can't wait until you're functioning at full capacity." She laughed, but she was also impressed at how this man could be wide awake for just over thirty hours.

"Shower, food and sleep. In that order."

"Sounds like a plan. If I can move, that is. Maybe I'll just stay here for a couple of days and recover."

He pushed off the bed and she admired his backside as he gathered his clothes. "Race you."

"You're on. First one finished has to cook."

"I might have a better idea. We wash each other's backs, finish together and both cook." He caught her wrist and pulled her to him. His sexy definition of "cook" was pressed between them.

"I really am hungry," she said only because she'd noticed their time was running short. Otherwise she would have been all over the possibility of another romp. "Didn't Joe say they'd be back around one?"

"You're right. We'll save the shower for next time."

"I love a good plan of action." She winked at him as he patted her behind, then swaggered down the hallway.

He beat her out of the shower only because she made certain her legs were shaved again. Who knew? They might actually get time alone together before heading to work. She slid the understated tracking devices back into her ears and yawned. They needed something upbeat to keep them alert, at least long enough to eat.

Music. Shoot, hers had been stolen. Well, at least the device had been kept by the men in the desert. Fortunately, all her music was stored electronically and could be accessed via Wi-Fi. She grabbed the university-issued tablet from her bag and followed the aroma of sizzling bacon.

"Oh, my gosh, that smells delicious." She got close to Pete, stealing a kiss when he faced her. She didn't want him to retreat to their relationship status prior to the front porch. So she stood right next to him, hoping the popping grease wouldn't reach her bare arms.

"Nothing fancy. I'm too tired for anything other than breakfast." He pulled her close, then let her back away from the frying pan.

"I don't mind. I'm starving." She suddenly wanted to know more about him. What could he cook? What did he like to eat? There were so many unanswered, frivolous details. The only conversations they'd had were about parents or Sharon or madmen who might still be trying to abduct her. She powered the tablet on and set it on the table. "Hey, what kind of music do you like? Are you a good ol' country boy? A hard rocker? Oh, please don't be a closet classical music guy. That might just be a deal breaker."

He threw his head back, laughing. She loved getting that reaction from him and watching those dimples. Spatula in hand, he drew her into the circle of his arms and just looked at her. She dropped her head onto his chest, hugging him.

"You are so lucky you're the sheriff."

"What do you mean?"

"Well, my dad's probably running an extensive background check on you, verifying that you're good enough to date his only child."

"Are you serious?" He broke their embrace faster than she could wonder what was happening. "He can't. You've got to ask him to stop."

"What's wrong?" She knew something major had changed. The smile had disappeared and was instantly replaced with a look so serious it frightened her.

"I like you, Andrea. Give your dad a call, will ya?"

"I like you, too. I know my dad can be a bit overwhelming. This is no big deal. Really. He was probably already running one for the task force."

"I should have thought of that. Explain there's nothing between us, so he'll call off the background. I just hope it's not too late." He scooped the eggs out of the pan and set their plates on the table, treating his command like any other friendly suggestion.

He was clearly worried something awful would be revealed. But what? He couldn't be the county sheriff if he'd broken the law. That couldn't be a possibility. So what or who was he trying to protect?

"First off, do you really think I have that kind of control over the Commander? And second, I thought there was something between us. Am I wrong?"

"Go ahead and eat."

They both sat, coffee and breakfast growing cold while they sort of just stared at all of it. She didn't know what to do, almost afraid to say anything that might change his mind about telling her—whatever was horrible enough that he thought it would keep them apart. At least she assumed it would keep them apart. His seriousness seemed to indicate that, but it was hard to hypothesize correctly without any facts.

Silence was not her thing. She asked questions, got people to spill the beans all the time. Pete seemed to have mastered how to keep his mouth shut. How typical that she'd fallen hard and fast for someone who fit the strong-and-silent stereotype.

"Other than the professional reasons we shouldn't be involved, there's something very basic you should know," he finally said.

"Okay." That hurt. She really hadn't anticipated he'd say they shouldn't be involved. She better understood what biting your tongue meant. She literally bit the end of her tongue to keep her silence.

Neither of them lifted a fork. She was glued to the endless expressions crossing Pete's face. She might pass out from holding her breath waiting for him to talk.

"I can't leave Marfa."

"Is that all? I didn't expect you to. At least not now. If I do get the post outside the country, maybe you can visit. If you want to, that is. I mean, I'm not assuming anything because of what happened this morning." The words spilled out.

"I would if I could, but it's just not possible."

"Do you need a passport or are you afraid of flying?" He was so earnest and didn't seem as if he was going to explain the background comment. A million reasons popped into her head. Reasons she wanted to be true instead of the one thing that kept reverberating in the back of her mind.

"No and no." He shook his head and pushed his damp hair away from his face, clearly struggling with the decision to tell her.

She covered his hand, now on the table. "Whatever it is, you can trust me."

"Pete Morrison is not my real name."

"Honey told me about your adoption last week." She couldn't wait for his explanation and rushed forward, following the illogic of what he'd revealed. "So what is it? What secret are you protecting? I mean, you live here, everyone knows you. Those pictures back at the sheriff's office prove you grew up here. Your life looks like an open book."

"I'm not explaining this correctly."

He shoved back from the table and stared out the window. "God, I don't know why I'm trying to explain this to you at all. I shouldn't. I wouldn't have brought it up if you hadn't warned me about the background check. I need you to call your father before it's too late, but I can't tell you why."

"Oh, no, you don't. You can't just drop that kind of...of request and not allow a question and answer." She stayed remarkably calm. She didn't know how, she just did. Much the same way she'd encouraged him this morning to face his attraction for her. She wanted him to trust her. Becoming all shrewish wouldn't accomplish that. "I didn't mean to rush you. I'm overly curious, if you couldn't tell that from knowing me a few days."

Waiting, she forced a bite of the bacon down without choking. Then a sip of cooling coffee.

"It's complicated," he said, dropping his chin to his chest.

"All the better to talk it through with a person who has an objective mind and can be unbiased." *Be patient.*

"I can't. I want to. It would be easier, but I can't." He walked around the kitchen, agitated.

Andrea placed her hands in her lap and watched without anxiously following him around the room. Part of the question on her mind was why Pete wanted her to know something he was clearly conflicted about revealing. Then again, why was she so excited that he'd begun to share with her?

"Whatever your real name, it won't change anything about our...friendship." If not a relationship, they could at least be friends.

"Not even if I'm the son of a murderer and never legally adopted by Joe?"

She swallowed hard after realizing her jaw had dropped open, totally unable to believe his statement. He was the son of a murderer and never adopted? It was more than a little hard to believe. "Those exact possibilities never crossed my mind."

"Believe me, I thought Joe was delusional from the heart attack when he told me what he'd done." The hurt he experienced was easy to see. His entire body slumped as he sat in the chair.

Andrea wanted to pull him into her arms and hold on as tight as he'd let her. She couldn't immediately call her dad. He'd want to know why, and if he hadn't begun the background check already, he would as soon as they hung up. "I hate to ask, Pete, but I'll need details to convince my father. Have you talked about this with Joe?"

"We've managed to avoid the conversation for six weeks."

"I don't think I could have waited. I'm too impatient and would want answers."

"Yeah, well. I didn't wait. My job does have some advantages. With a little research, I could put the facts together. I just don't know why my dad doesn't think it's a big deal. It could ruin everything he's worked for his entire life."

"You're talking about the illegal adoption? Maybe there were extenuating circumstances. I'm sure he'd be forgiven."

Elbows on the table, Pete blocked showing his emotions to her by resting his head on his hands. There were very few times when she felt completely lost. This was one of them. Did he need comforting or someone to vent to?

He looked up, and his eyes sparkled with near tears. And she knew…no matter what he needed, she wanted to comfort him. She also knew exactly why it all mattered… she was falling in love with the whole man. Not just his dimples.

Chapter Twenty-One

Stupid. He'd blurted out his dad's well-kept secret. Just spilled his guts to a woman he hadn't known a week. The daughter of a man who could dig into his past and destroy everything he knew. And everything his father had sacrificed for his entire life.

"Are you okay, Pete?" Andrea asked.

Yeah, he was okay. He wanted to be angry at his dad. He was angry. Then he felt guilty. That had been the cycle for the past six weeks. How could he blame the man who'd raised him with no obligation to do so? It hurt...the betrayal. Pete hadn't realized how much.

"I'm not sure I can forgive him. He's lied to me for over twenty-five years. Upholding the law has been his entire life. He made it my entire life. And yet everything's been a lie."

"Not the way he feels about you." Her hand rubbed his shoulder, trying to comfort him. "Anyone who meets the two of you can tell how much he cares."

"I don't want to be the reason he loses everything. Can you call Commander Allen?"

"I don't think it's a good idea to bring the situation to his attention. Maybe he's not digging into your past at all. He hasn't removed you from the task force, which would happen if he'd discovered your identity doesn't exist. Where did Joe get your birth certificate? Things like that?"

"I don't have one. That's what started this whole mess. County Administration entered my interim-sheriff status into the system and notified me they didn't have a copy of my Social Security card or birth certificate. Dad admitted that he twisted some arms to get me hired back before the updated system was installed. He also said my Social Security number is a fake. He bought it before I started school, so I had no idea."

Andrea's jaw dropped again. Sort of the way his had done when he'd found out.

She quickly recovered. "That seems…"

"Very illegal, as in he's bound to do jail time." Thus his dilemma. Having a government agency dig into his past would expose his father no matter what good intentions he had long ago.

"No wonder you're worried for him. He must have had a good reason to go to such lengths."

"I wouldn't know. I haven't asked."

"You have to be the least curious man I've ever met." She left the table to microwave her breakfast. "Obviously, you're going to ask him, right? I mean, you need to hear the entire story. Want me to heat up your plate?"

No longer hungry, he shook his head. If he didn't know how smart Andrea Allen was, he'd wonder about her stream-of-consciousness conversation. All in all, he liked it. More often than he'd admit out loud, he silently chuckled at how her mind worked and made him stay on his toes.

Every time he turned around he was amazed by how casual and accepting she was of their situation. Telling her he was the son of a murderer stopped her as long as it took to hiccup. Then she was asking to warm his breakfast.

Damn, the woman made him want more. More of her. More of life. Just…more. Until he'd met her, it had never crossed his mind. Now that it was out of his reach, he ached for a chance.

She was back at the table, silently eating and occasionally looking at him. He could tell she was dying to ask more questions. He didn't know if he was ready to answer.

"Do I smell bacon?" his dad asked as soon as the front door opened.

"In here, Dad."

He barreled around the corner. "Good, you're still awake." He looked at the table, grabbed a slice of bacon from Pete's plate and nodded toward Andrea. "I can see by the look on his face that you asked him. About dang time. You tell her?" he asked his son.

Pete nodded, and Andrea sipped the last of her coffee. He wondered how long her silence would last before she'd shoot a list of questions for his father.

"Good," his dad continued, twirling the chair around to sit. "We need to get this out in the open, and you need to stop trying to protect me."

"Outside." Pete liked Andrea, but this was private. He needed the reason before he shared it with anyone—if he ever shared it.

"You don't want her to know why?"

"I was just telling Pete that I'm really tired. You guys talk. I'm plugging in my earphones, turning on some music." She lifted the tablet and forced a yawn. "I'll be out before you can say right ascension." The blank look on his dad's face must have encouraged her to explain. "It's an astronomer's term that... Sorry, never mind me. I'm heading to bed."

Andrea backed out of the room. Her bedroom door clicked shut softly, and he was alone with his dad. Biological or adopted, legal or not—Joe Morrison would always be his dad. He'd already forgiven him.

"I shouldn't be surprised at not being able to follow her

talk too much. Andrea tried to tell me what she was looking at through the telescope the first time I picked her up.
Couldn't make hide nor hair of it. She let me take a peek,
though. It was almost as pretty as her." His dad poured
himself a cup of coffee from the pot that rarely turned off.

"She's definitely a smart woman." Pete realized what
he'd said and tried to ignore his dad's inquisitive raised
eyebrow. "Yeah, you meant the picture in the telescope. I
got it. But she is smart and gives good advice."

"Like…"

"Like how I should have asked you about my *adoption*
as soon as you were out of the hospital. I can't believe that
the man who preached at me about doing what was right
my entire life had been breaking the law the entire time."

Joe leaned on the counter, just as Pete had earlier, talking
to Andrea. He held his coffee cup the same way as his dad.

"The first four months you were here, I never had to ask
for a babysitter when I went to work. The church organized
it. You know, people say we look alike. It was easy for everyone to believe you were my grand-nephew. It was also
easy for them to look the other way about certain things."

"Seriously, Dad, you risked everything. Why did you
do it?"

"The why part is an easy answer. You. I did it for you."

"I need a little more than that, Dad."

"It was the right thing to do, son. And I'd do it again."

Joe sat at the table, taking Andrea's place. The tanned
skin around his eyes crinkled with his smile. "When you
said you knew who your father was, I'm assuming you figured it out after I said I arrested him."

"I figured it had to be someone outside Presidio County
about the time I came to live with you. You only arrested
three people. Two were transferred to San Antonio and one
ended up in Huntsville State Prison. Philip Stanley sat on
death row for eleven years. Just after my fourteenth birth-

day you took a trip to see him, didn't you? Did you go for the execution?"

"That's right." He sipped from the cup. "Sad day. He'd robbed a liquor store in El Paso. Shot and killed the attendant."

"The report said you talked him into releasing hostages at a house south of here."

"A family of four. They moved not too long after that. I think their five-year-old son made more of an impact on Phil than I did trying to get him to let them go. Something the kid did made him want you to grow up in a home and be happy. He loved you in his own way. He let the people go when I gave my word I'd find your maternal grandparents. His were already gone. I tried. Believe me. I verified straight off that your mother was deceased. It took nine months to discover that her parents had passed on before you were born."

"And I lived with you for that time? Why didn't you turn me over to foster care?"

"Gave my word I wouldn't. He was scared you'd turn out like him and made me promise no foster homes." He cleared his throat and leaned back in the chair. "I'd already told everyone you were my nephew. Hell, Sheriff Grimshaw is the one who encouraged me to give my word at the house. He's the one who helped me find information on your family."

"So Uncle Russ knew and even helped you."

"Yeah. He vouched for me and thought of you as part of his family, too. We convinced ourselves we were doing the right thing. Two old bachelors taking on a kid who we were determined would not end up like his old man. We thought about the foster program, but after you'd been here that long, they wouldn't have given you to me."

"How'd you enroll me in school? Didn't I need records?"

"We actually used his wife's Social Security number for

school. It's not so hard to enroll as long as you had shot records. Everyone around here knew your story by then. No
one pressed us. Russ got the county to hire you. I winked
a couple of times to make people forget your paperwork
was incomplete."

"You know you can go to jail."

"Son, no one cares. You're a good man. This won't make
any difference in you being sheriff."

"Dad, Andrea's father made me a part of his task force.
He's probably got people vetting me right now. That means
a background check. They'll find the falsified information.
Believe me, the government cares."

"I don't see why it should matter now. We can get everything straightened out, maybe legally change your name.
You haven't done anything wrong."

"Dammit, Dad. Don't sit there and act like this isn't a
game changer." He would have been yelling. If there wasn't
a guest in the house, he probably would have been ranting
a little at how nonchalantly his dad was accepting their
secret was out.

Yes, it was their secret now. People would assume Pete
had known about his adoption circumstances. As close as
he was to Joe, no one would believe otherwise.

His dad seemed remarkably calm when he turned to him
with no smile, just a gleam in his eyes. He looked free of a
huge burden. "Son, I know the gravity of the situation. I'm
accepting full responsibility. If the world finds out, then
the world finds out."

"They don't have to find out. I can resign, stop Commander Allen from moving forward with the vetting process."

"No way. Absolutely not."

"Dad, what's impossible is to ignore this ticking time
bomb. No ifs, ands or buts. It's going off. Only a question
of when."

"I disagree. There's—"

"Excuse me." Andrea dashed into the room. One ear pod dangling, one still in position, tablet in hand, looking as bright as sunshine. "I know you two need to talk, but this… It just can't wait. I'm so sorry for interrupting. But can I? Interrupt, I mean?"

"Sure," his father said. "Have a seat."

Pete would have rather finished their conversation, devising a game plan. Whatever she'd found, Andrea seemed about to burst with excitement. She probably couldn't wait.

"Oh, I can't sit, thanks. This is… Well, you have to read it for yourself, but I think Sharon was working with those men. Or at least it seems that way to me. Do you want to call the rest of the task force? Maybe get their take on it?"

"You might want to show us what you're talking about first." Pete tried to slow her down.

"Oh, I was doing it again. My apologies." Standing between him and his father, she set the tablet on the table and swiped the screen. "An email popped up addressed to Sharon from an unknown sender."

She touched the screen a second time, bringing up the email program.

We'll pay $500 if you get her on her own. Let us know when and where. Don't cross us, Sharon. You know what kind of trouble you'll be in if things go wrong.

"So what do you think?" she asked.

"This could mean anything," he answered. "Are there more emails?"

"A couple. She sent the information about me taking her place on Friday night at the Viewing Area, right down to the license tag on her car."

"Then you were set up."

"How did you find the emails?" his dad asked.

Andrea leaned on his shoulder. The movement was so casual he wasn't certain she knew she was there. Nice, yet very telling when his dad raised an eyebrow and the corner of his mouth in a half smile.

"This is a university-issued tablet. I've been utilizing it, inputting my data and notes. Those creeps stole my music last week, so I thought I'd listen from my cloud. I haven't been on the internet, since Dad asked me not to. But when I went to sign in, the device automatically logged in as Sharon. She must have been the last user and forgotten to log out." She shook his shoulders with her excitement.

Pete scrolled through some of the other messages. "Why wasn't this turned over to Commander Allen's team? They're better equipped to trace where the message came from. They collected her laptop and cell from the car fire— or at least what was left of it."

"I guess no one thought about the tablet. The University of Texas owns it and all the students use it."

"I'll drive the tablet over to Cord's place."

"Not so fast, please," Andrea said, trying unsuccessfully to snatch it from his grasp. They both held it inches above the tabletop.

The look on her face sort of shouted that she wanted to use the clue herself. "No way, Andrea. We've got to get this to Cord's team. I'm not putting you in danger again."

"We should check with the DEA agent at the task force meeting. Maybe she knows how to trace the sender or who to contact about it."

Pete stood, grabbing her shoulders securely enough to get her attention. "We are not tracking down whoever sent this email."

"But they might have Sharon."

"I agree. But it's not my job." He'd guessed why she'd stayed at the observatory just after her father left. He'd come right out and accused them of using her to draw

Logan's murderers into the open. But no one else had confirmed it. If they didn't give him a direct order, he could play along and focus on his assignment.

"You're kidding. Why are you on the task force, then?"

"To babysit."

His decision not to search for her friend wasn't the only contribution to her look of dissatisfaction. She was disappointed in him. And he could live with that. As long as it kept her safe.

Chapter Twenty-Two

Studying the chessboards along the edge of his study was comforting. It took his mind off other problems and somehow helped him eventually resolve those problems. Then his eyes landed on Patrice.

Once again, she sat on the edge of her chair, sipping her wine, ready for his instructions. She'd behaved well during their last encounter, following his instructions to the letter. As a result, she was conducting herself with cautious obedience.

The delivery was scheduled to take place in two days' time. The details were complete, with the exception of Andrea Allen in his possession. The risks were much higher without her as a pawn. He kept reworking the board, wanting a different outcome.

The only way to guarantee victory was his original plan. Throw another distraction into the laps of the Border Protection officers and they'd weaken. If they were searching for their commander's daughter, there would be fewer officers searching for his shipment.

Yes, his tactics might need to change, but the fundamental overall strategy was sound and needed to stay in play. Therefore, it was essential to capture his opponent's queen.

"Do you still have the college girl?"

Patrice looked up quickly, setting her wine on his glass

table. "Yes, of course. You said to ship her south with the guns and let the men split the money when they sold her. Blondes bring a good price."

"Good. Good." He studied his third game board, anticipating a Steinitz strategy.

"There's one more thing, Mr. Rook. Our mutual friends would like you to oversee the transfer yourself."

"Certainly. Patrice, have I ever told you about Wilhelm Steinitz? He developed several rules of chess. The first states that the right to attack belongs to the person with the positional advantage. Since I am in the superior position of knowing what lies ahead, I believe I have an obligation to attack or lead. If I fail to attack, I deserve for the advantage to evaporate."

"I think I know what you're saying." Her look of utter confusion confirmed she did not.

"Steinitz thought the attack should always be made on your opponent's weakest square. Do you know what that is for the men trying to find us?"

She shook her head.

"Andrea Allen."

"She has around-the-clock protection. Do you have a plan to abduct her?"

"I do. And I'll need the university student. How soon can we have her available?"

"I can get her back by tomorrow. I'll need a drop-off point."

"Certainly." Ah, yes. If he moved his king's rook...

"Hand me my phone."

She complied, and he texted the new position of his rook. If his opponent's moves were as predictable as he projected, in two moves he would run the board.

"Based on Miss Allen's personality and the inexperience of the new sheriff, I think our problem will be resolved soon. Let's drop her roommate near the abandoned southwest camp."

"And what then?"

"I'll provide you instructions. Do you need more wine?" She shook her head, and he locked the door. "After a very long week, I'm in the mood for a bit of fun."

There was a moment—just a slight raise of her delicate eyebrow—where Patrice had a look of calculated control. He didn't care to think about it twice. She unzipped her leather skirt and let it fall over her slim hips. She could make the arrangements for the girl's transportation soon.

The thought of Andrea Allen sitting in Patrice's place excited him to his core. Extracting his pleasure shouldn't take long at all.

Chapter Twenty-Three

Father and son had both picked her up from the observatory this morning. They held a conversation in the front seat while Andrea stared out the window at the same rocks as yesterday and the day before and the day before that. Boring terrain? She wouldn't admit to anyone that she secretly loved it. Watching the sun rise here was different from anyplace she'd ever lived, and the stars... The stars were amazing. She could look at them every night for a lifetime.

"Not a word since I told her no yesterday," Pete answered Joe.

Joe had offered the front passenger seat to her, but she'd moved past him and climbed into the back. Alone, free from distractions. Without staring at Pete, she could search the sunrise for answers to all the confusing questions she'd been left with yesterday.

Search, but not find. She was still as confused as ever. Needing to be involved in finding Sharon. Scared that she might be allowed to participate. Frightened that she wouldn't. Ultimate confusion.

She forced herself to count the different varieties of trees instead of sneaking a peek at Pete. The conversation with his dad was obviously meant to pique her curiosity. Both men were blatantly attempting to get her to jump in and talk to them. She'd easily ignored them both yesterday afternoon, closed off in her bedroom sanctuary. Today would definitely be harder.

Especially when she wanted to ask if the task force had discovered anything from the tablet Sharon had used. Nope, she wasn't going to talk to him. She might ask Joe later, but he was helping Pete annoy her at the moment.

"I'm just doing my job. You'd think she'd understand how a protection detail works," Joe said. "Someone protects the gal needing protecting. The rest of the task force runs down the information about secretive emails implicating a missing student."

"Secret?" she began, then stopped herself. No talking. Pete had insulted her and hadn't bothered to apologize. Point in fact, when she'd taken her dinner to her room he'd shouted after she was around the corner that he wouldn't apologize for thinking of her safety first.

It was killing her not to ask a gazillion questions. Where was Sharon? Why hadn't Joe just legally adopted Pete? What made him lie all these years? But more important, how did Pete feel about his father's explanation?

It appeared that whatever the explanation, Pete had accepted it and moved on. His relationship with his dad seemed as strong as ever. Another reason she wanted to talk was that she had her own news to share. Each morning, she'd enjoyed filling Joe in on her project, even if he rarely understood what she said. It felt good to talk about the progress and the setbacks. Darn it. And last night had been one setback after another.

Pete made the final turn onto the last road to their house when the county radio squeaked. "Pete, you there?"

"Yeah, Honey. What do you need?"

"We've got a call here for Miss Allen. She still with you? Want us to patch it through?"

"Who's calling?"

"A woman just keeps saying it's an emergency and asks

for a number to reach her. I'd assume it's no one from her work, since she was there all night. Her parents have your number, right?"

"Patch it through and run a trace." Pete passed the microphone to her. "This doesn't seem right, Andrea. You will not give them a number to call you directly. Not until we establish who it really is. Got it?"

"Yes."

He pulled next to the barn when the radio crackled again. "Andrea?"

"Sharon? Thank God, you're alive. Where are you? What happened?"

Pete covered her hand and lifted her thumb from the microphone. "Let her talk, Andrea. We need some details."

"They won't let me go unless you bring…" Sharon whimpered. "I'm sorry, I don't understand."

Andrea was frozen with fear. She couldn't press the button to ask if Sharon was still connected. She could hardly breathe, wondering what demands these vultures were going to make. And she was scared to death she wouldn't be able to help.

All the questions from earlier dissipated into the ozone. They seemed petty in comparison to someone's life.

"Sharon? Are you there?" Andrea jumped when she heard a short scream, then crying. "Sharon!"

"Three thousand dollars. They want money…you and only you…" Sharon continued to cry. "Bring it at sunset tonight. The…coordinates… Oh, God, are you ready to write this down?"

Joe wrote the numbers on Pete's notepad he'd removed from the glove box.

"Do you know where you are?" Andrea asked, her eyes locking with Pete's.

"No." More crying. "Andrea, please come. I'll pay you

back, I swear." Sharon's sobbing was followed by another short scream as if she'd been struck.

"Whoever you are, the money's not a problem. Don't hurt her!"

"I'm scared." The static from the call stopped.

"We'll find you." She'd moved closer to the front seat and didn't realize that she was clinging to Pete's hand. "Do you think she heard me?"

"Yes," Joe said, patting her shoulder.

She kept her eyes on Pete. His lips flattened, and he nodded ever so slightly. He didn't like it. "Those coordinates sound like the box canyon on Nick Burke's place where they had the shoot-out with the McCreas."

"I was thinking the same thing," Joe said. "That means we need horses, and they don't actually expect her to be alone. I'll get in touch with Burke. I assume you're heading to talk to Cord. You taking Andrea?"

"Of course he is," she said to both men, who continued to ignore her.

"She's got to go somewhere. She won't be safe here alone."

"You know it's an ambush." Joe nodded, reaffirming his statement.

"I think they've had a reason for everything they've done." Pete kept hold of her hand. "This fits in with Cord's informant hearing something would be going down during the UFO Border Zone conference." He looked at her. "I meant to tell you about the potential threat yesterday, but we sort of changed the subject."

She liked the feel of his strong fingers wrapped around hers. She could get used to that feeling, the sense of having someone there for you. Even if he was carefully controlling his emotions and hiding behind circumstances.

"Son of a—" Joe mumbled. "That's a couple of thousand extra faces to sort through. Half of 'em will be in alien costumes."

"Does anyone care what I think?" Andrea asked. Father and son stared at each other instead of laughing outright. They were the ones with experience. She knew that.

Fortunately, their silent laughter was interrupted by another squawk of the radio. "We couldn't get a trace, Pete. You want me to bring the deputies in to help? What kind of support do you need?"

"Keep them in Presidio with the want-to-be aliens until McCrea orders otherwise." He set the microphone down and rubbed his chin.

"Why ransom the girl back today?" Joe asked.

Pete snapped his fingers. "Another distraction. The UFO Border Zone starts this afternoon. It's the perfect time to smuggle guns with all those aliens running around all night."

"Night of aliens?" The phrase popped into her mind and she knew exactly where she'd first heard it. "The undercover man in the desert said 'night of aliens' before he passed out. The camera was in the back with him."

"Maybe he tried to warn you or give you the group's location. Maybe he knew more and left the info on the camera after the accident. There was no way to know when he actually died, especially when they stole his body."

"If he did say something else, I don't remember. The recording would be on that missing camera. Didn't anyone look for it after the meeting?" She sat on the edge of the seat, then fell backward as realization dawned. "Oh, my gosh, whoever has Sharon must not have the camera or they'd know what was recorded, right? That's why they need me. To see if I know the plans. Do you think the agent could have hidden the camera and it's still in the car?"

"It's possible," Joe said. "We weren't looking for a camera at the crime scene."

"I'll have Hardy go over and take another look. Maybe he'll get lucky and we can get you out of this mess."

"You know it doesn't matter if he finds it." Andrea knew this was the reason she'd agreed to stay. "We don't have any choice. We still have to go or they'll know we've figured out their plans. Sharon will be at those coordinates and we need to save her. That's all that matters. Three men have died already. Sharon has her whole life in front of her."

"So do you," Pete stated simply. "You aren't going."

"I know, I know. Your job is to babysit me." She dropped the warmth of his hand, scooted across the seat and opened her door before looking his direction. "Look for the camera. I hope the information we need is on it. But I'm still going. You can't stop me."

"Is that a challenge?"

She wouldn't argue now. She knew how to defend a position and had even taken classes on the subject. Her dad's instructions were clear. She just needed to prepare her plan of attack.

"Just wanted to say again how much I appreciate you coming here to the ranch, Cord." Pete was relieved he hadn't needed to demand the task force come to them. "I don't want to move Andrea yet."

"It made sense. Half of us were already here," Agent Conrad said, then shrugged.

Andrea smiled at him, suggesting her position on the task force had been confirmed.

"Miss Allen is not a member of this team," he corrected, and no one challenged him. "Did you discover anything about the emails?"

He moved behind Andrea, keeping his hands on the back of her chair instead of reaching out to touch the back of her neck. If he looked at her, someone might overanalyze how long he stared or why he felt such a strong urge to shout that she needed to be flown out of the area immediately.

"Mind you, I'm only working with this one account, but I don't think she meant Andrea any harm. At least it doesn't seem so. If I took a guess, I think the person making the suggestions to her is a female."

"How can you get that?" Cord asked.

"The sentence structure and choice of words. I've had a little profiling. In an earlier email, the sender states they're friends with you, Andrea."

Everyone looked first at Andrea and then toward him, standing directly behind her. Everyone, with the exception of his dad, who just shook his head and sighed.

"That's ridiculous. I don't know anyone around here and even if I did, does it really make sense to want to meet me in the middle of nowhere? I would never have agreed to that." Andrea tried to stand up.

Pete placed his hand on her shoulder, keeping her in the chair. They hadn't really spoken since the day before, but it didn't seem to matter. She immediately responded with a deep breath and seemed a little less tense. By Cord's compressed lips, he hadn't missed the gesture.

Agent Conrad sat on her hands. Her gaze dropped to her lap. She was busting buttons to keep herself from responding.

"I think Beth is implying that someone told Sharon they were trying to surprise you and not to ask you about it. And no one here thinks she did," his dad said to Andrea with complete calm.

Absolutely the calmest man he knew, Joe stretched back in his favorite chair, hands behind his neck, ankles crossed under the coffee table. He didn't seem worried that a woman's life was in danger. The others in the room might misinterpret his calmness for not caring, but Pete knew different.

In that moment, the clarity of how his father had been

over twenty-five years ago smacked into Pete. Calm and rational. Two things his father had always been. He would have been no different confronting a murderer and promising that man his son wouldn't face the same fate.

He would have meant every word. And then kept his word. And he had. The price just might be the expense of his entire career.

There was nothing Pete could do at the moment to help his dad. He caught his hands slipping toward Andrea's shoulders and pulled them away, tucking them into his pockets before taking a step back. He glanced around the room. Only Cord had a disapproving frown on his face.

Andrea popped up and went to the window. "I just need to get to a bank to withdraw the three thousand dollars."

"Why that amount?" Agent Conrad asked. "Does it strike anyone else as an odd amount for a ransom? I mean, it's not an overly large sum. Many would have that in their bank account."

"It's not a problem for me to pay."

"Why do you think it's a low amount?" Cord rose and guided Andrea away from the windows.

Her long sigh assured everyone in the room just how tired she was of being kept safe. Pete knew she was ready for the forced protective custody to be over. "Shouldn't we get started? It takes forever to get from place to place around here."

Cord swiped a hand over the bottom half of his face. "Nick's bringing extra horses and will help with the tracking—if necessary. We're leaving from here, Andrea."

"When? I need to change and then get to the bank."

"Cord brought the ransom. You're not going," Pete stated, again waiting for someone to tell him different. He knew the bomb would be dropped. Just not by whom.

"What do you mean?" Andrea marched toward him, sticking her hands on her hips, ready to do battle. "Of course I'm going. I have to go. They won't release Sharon if I don't."

"No. Agent Conrad's going in your place." He could try. They all knew why she'd stayed in Marfa even if no one said it out loud. She was the bait. But he could try to keep her out of the frying pan.

"Um, Pete," Cord interrupted.

At the same time, Beth Conrad shook her head. "I'm not sure that's wise."

Pete had made a decision. He no longer cared about being politically correct or following orders or whose orders needed to be considered. "My job is to make sure this woman stays safe. That's not going to happen taking her into a trap. We all know it's a trap. The responsible thing is to have her stay with my dad."

He wanted to be the one to stay with her, protect her, make love to her again. But safe with his dad and a couple of trusted ranch hands would have to do.

"The responsibility isn't yours," Andrea stated firmly. "You know what my father already decided."

"I don't know how to ride a horse," Beth Conrad mumbled behind him.

"She'll be safer with us," Cord said, clapping a hand on his shoulder. "We can't do this without her."

He shrugged out from under the hand of the official leader of the task force. "This is a joke. Plain and simple. What you really mean to say is that Andrea's father has already decided she should go. Does he have a death wish for his daughter?"

A red haze seemed to tint the entire front room. Pete's blood pumped loudly through his veins while he concentrated on relaxing the tightness in his chest. Nick's truck and trailer turned onto the driveway. They'd be leaving soon. All of them.

Overruled again. At least he'd made his objections well-known.

"Nothing good's gonna come from this. Nothing." He slammed out the screen door, taking a deep breath, surprised at how betrayed he felt. "Acting sheriff or actual sheriff. Makes no difference when no one listens to a word you say."

Chapter Twenty-Four

They were on their way to rescue Sharon and had officially crossed over onto the Burke family ranch. Andrea had won and was with the rescue party. It was obvious to her that every person around her disagreed with the decision. No argument needed. Her father had left instructions that if the opportunity presented itself, she'd take an active role and try to lead them to the murderers.

So here she sat, sure to be saddle sore tomorrow even though the riding wasn't that difficult. Pete, Cord and the DEA agent—maybe even Joe—all considered her the weakest link. She knew that. The new guy who'd brought the extra horses, Nick, had raised a ruckus about bringing either woman.

None of them would allow her to carry a weapon. Ironically, her father had probably had a gun in her hands earlier than any of them. Well, maybe with the exception of Pete since Joe didn't have a wife telling him not to teach his son anything and everything.

The DEA agent tugged at the reins again, upsetting the beautiful sorrel she rode. Beth would be lucky if the mare didn't buck her off just to escape the woman's obvious inexperience. Then where would Sharon's rescue be?

"Loosen your grip and she'll follow the trail just fine," Nick Burke said to Agent Conrad.

"You're kidding me, right?" the agent replied, jerking the reins to the side. They continued arguing, exchanging little digs back and forth. Some under their breath, but mostly not.

"This will never work." Andrea was furious but kept her voice low enough for just Pete to hear her. "Agent Conrad might be the same height, but stuffing her hair into a hat won't fool anyone that she's me. She doesn't even know how to sit a horse. It's obvious to everyone she's petrified of the animal. It's old, as slow as Christmas, and she's still having trouble controlling it."

"We'll get there in time." Pete stayed calm and relaxed in the saddle.

In the week she'd known him, anxiety rarely showed through his controlled exterior. Stressful situations seemed to make him even more laid-back. He watched, waited.

And she was just the opposite. The more frustrated or excited she became, the more questions she asked. And at the moment she was very anxious for Sharon's benefit.

"What if they're watching us right now? I mean, anyone can tell she's not me."

He took a long look at Andrea's outfit. She knew exactly what he was thinking. They'd gone to great lengths to make her look like a guy, even setting her on a smaller, shorter horse so she'd look larger. The oversize Western hat on her head stayed in place with a leather tie.

"They don't know you're the one who can ride a horse. We're not certain they know about Agent Conrad being here at all. Keep your eyes open."

Beth Conrad's horse whinnied loudly and began dancing in circles. They'd never make it to the rendezvous point at this rate. Pete brought his horse closer. It was the first time since their task force meeting that the frown on his face had relaxed.

"Andrea, we won't be able to stop them from taking

you. Do you know that?" The concern on his face broke her heart.

It should have frightened her.

"Cord informed Dad's team. They're tracking me. It'll be okay." As hard as it was to say the words, it was harder to believe them while she looked at the worry on Pete's face. He hadn't smiled all day and probably shouldn't, but she missed it. Missed the man who had teased her to nervous, unending babble.

Pete leaned in close, tugging her even closer. If anyone had fallen for her outfit before, her cover was totally blown when his lips devoured hers. Excitement returned even with the cautioning clearing of Cord's throat.

"I know you think you have to go through with this, but you don't." Pete let his horse put a couple of feet between them.

"He's right," Cord added. "Say the word and we're heading back at a full gallop. There's no guarantee that Sharon will be released."

"But there's a chance."

Nick tried to help Beth by jumping off his horse and soothing the older mare.

"Very slim," Pete said.

"I have to do this. And we all know the real objective is to find their camp and the men responsible. We'll put a stop to the murders and find Sharon."

Pete exchanged a glance with Cord, making her feel naive. Well, maybe she was, but she had to try catching the person responsible for Logan's death.

"Remember what we said. Try to keep an idea of where you are. Landmarks, if you cross water, sounds like a train or lots of people." Pete rubbed her back. "If I can't stop you, just remember that I'm not far behind. I *will* find you. Got that?"

"Yes."

"Don't be a hero, Andrea. Just do what they say. Please," Pete whispered.

"If things don't go according to plan, just listen to us and do what we say. Okay?" Cord added. "You ready, Nick?"

Before Nick could respond, Beth exploded with confidence behind them. "I can do this!" But a loud crack sounding like a single gunshot echoed through the mountains, giving their horses a different opinion. While the rest of them regained control, Beth's old mare bolted into the open area toward the wider end of the ravine.

"Dammit, she's lost control of the reins," Cord said, rising straighter in his saddle as if he could see more than a runaway horse carrying away their bait.

"I'll get her," Nick exclaimed, taking off before anyone could object. "Don't wait for us."

"You want to wait here?" Pete asked. "Or do we turn around and forget this farce?"

"We can't." Andrea could only think of her mission. The shadows were growing long behind them as the sun sank lower on the other side of the mountains. "We have to keep going for Sharon."

She shoved the hat off her head, letting the leather string dig a little into her throat as the wind caught it like a sail behind her. She tussled her short hair around, fluffing it a bit to let anyone watching know it was her. Pete was still close so she leaned and kissed him with all the passion she could. He kissed her back and looked stunned when she sat in her saddle again.

"We have to find Sharon." She kicked her horse and took the lead, trotting up the trail they'd been following.

"Andrea! Wait!" Pete shouted. "What are you doing?"

Both men called for her to stop. She would, just as soon as she got over the next rise and it was too late to follow the DEA agent whose horse was still galloping in the opposite direction. She clicked to her own mare, kicking her sides just a little to get her to break the trotting motion. The path was smooth and level enough for a short, steady lope.

She topped the rise, slowing and coming face-to-face with six armed men. Horses and ATVs and gun barrels. No Sharon in sight. Her escort was several seconds behind her.

It was the trap Pete had anticipated. She'd been so determined—or stubborn—to save the young college student that she'd disregarded all the men's warnings. Midway in turning her horse around to get back to safety, a man leaped out and grabbed her waist. They fell to the ground and rolled, lucky four hooves didn't trample them. She kicked out, threw an elbow in the soft spot under his rib cage, but he held tight.

Nothing deterred him. They ended up with him on the ground, her on top of him. He slapped a dirty hand over her mouth tightly so she couldn't shout out and warn the men. She kept throwing punches until another man put his boot on her stomach and pointed his gun at her head.

"That's far enough," the man holding the gun said. "Throw your weapons to the ground. We don't want any death today."

At first, Andrea thought he was talking to her. Then she realized that Pete and Cord had topped the hill.

"Let her go," Pete shouted.

"We have your money. Where's the girl?" Cord's weapon was still holstered.

Pete moved, his eyes searching hers. They both knew that these men weren't there for a hostage exchange. They were there to abduct the daughter of the man in charge of border patrol.

The man holding Andrea released her to two others, who quickly yanked her to her feet and zip-tied her wrists behind her. Pete began to swing his leg over the back of his horse to dismount, but the man with the gun shoved it in her back, tsking.

Pete cursed and kept his seat.

"I'll be okay." She answered his unasked question. Her father would certainly be tracking her, but she could see the determination in Pete's eyes that he'd find her no matter what the cost. She knew he'd keep his promise.

Countless times she told herself to expect this scenario, yet it was still frightening. They wanted her alive, otherwise they would have shot them all earlier. Why was the million-dollar question that her father and the DHS needed answered.

The men half lifted, half dragged her to an empty ATV.

"Wait. Isn't there some deal we can make?" Pete asked.

"Don't you want your money?" Cord shouted.

"You keep your pittance. The women are worth a lot more to me. We'll get more for not taking your money." The one pointing the gun laughed at their attempt. He straddled the ATV in front of her. "You can get off your horses now."

Two other men on horseback pointed their guns at Cord and Pete, waiting for them to follow instructions. The weapons they'd dropped earlier had already been picked up. They bent low against their own horses, grabbing the lawmen's fallen reins and leading them away.

As the horses passed Pete, he lunged, catching one of the men off guard and pulling him to the ground. The big man giving the orders held up his hand to stop his men. All stayed where they were while the one closest to Cord put a gun to his head. He froze while the fight continued.

The man Pete fought was young and seemed inexperienced. Pete got two or three punches in for every one he took. A final uppercut to the younger man's jaw had him out cold against the rocky trail.

Pete took a deep breath and wiped a little blood away from a split lip. A pistol was quickly pointed at the back of his neck, keeping him from moving.

"That was quite a show. The fight was good experience

for my man and seemed only fair since he helped kill one of yours." He gestured for one of the ATV riders to drag the unconscious man to his vehicle. "Useless to make a move. There are many of us. Too many to fight, I think."

"No harm in trying." Pete spit blood toward the man who had murdered Logan.

"I think Jimmy would disagree with you."

"I will find you," Pete growled with confidence but kicked rocks with his feet. The leader laughed.

It could have been encouragement for her or a threat to the man calling the shots. She didn't know. His words gave her hope and she'd hang on to them as long as possible.

Both ATVs were started.

"If it were up to me, *amigos*, you'd never walk out of here. Not up to me today. Maybe next time. *Si*?" He saluted Cord and Pete and put the ATV in gear with a jerk. "Take their phones."

Pete and Cord had brought hand radios, which the armed men tossed to the ground and smashed. She looked at Pete as long as she could. She knew he was yelling, but she couldn't hear his words over the ATV engines. Hoping above all else that this would end quickly and positively, she tried to get her bearings.

Then they were bouncing over rough terrain and all she could think about was hanging on for dear life. She barely had a grip on the edge of the seat with her hands tied. One good bump and she could be dead against the rocks.

They were on the north side of a state highway. So she doubted they'd be riding horses and ATVs all the way to the border. So where would they take her? They hadn't scanned her for tracking devices and she could only pray they wouldn't before they arrived at their destination.

And if they did?

Would she vanish like Sharon?

Chapter Twenty-Five

"They lost one of the signals twenty minutes in. Just lost the second." Cord hung up the cell.

"Where? Where's the last place they had her?" The look on the Ranger's face told him he'd been instructed not to disclose that information. "Dammit, Cord. Tell me. You knew this was going to happen. We all did and we let her go through with it anyway. Stupid. I should have stopped her."

"Take a minute. You tried to talk her out of it."

"I didn't try hard enough."

"We're to wait here. Burke and Beth Conrad are still missing." Cord calmly pocketed the cell they'd picked up from his truck.

"Do you think they're dead? We didn't hear any shots. And if they'd wanted more hostages, why didn't they take us?"

"Too much trouble, I imagine. Same as killing us would have brought too many law enforcement agencies in here to muck up their plans. We sit tight and wait."

"No. Whatever's happening is going down in Presidio. That's what your informant said. You going to sit in the corner and accept your punishment or are you coming with me?"

"Now, hold on just one damn minute. We aren't being punished. We're part of a team." Cord defended the task force.

At the moment, the only loyalty Pete felt was to Andrea. He'd promised her. He wouldn't sit around and let that promise be broken by following orders. He'd already broken a couple.

"Well, this player's tired of sitting on the bench." He threw out the challenge, wanting the backup but willing to go alone. "You coming?"

Cord hesitated long enough to blink. "Yeah, I need my shotgun."

"Dispatch," Pete said into the microphone while he was waiting.

"Whatcha need, Pete?"

"Anyone heard from Hardy? I sent him on an errand and thought to hear back by now."

"I'll ask him. Be right back."

And what if they were monitoring the police bands? "Peach, have him call my dad at the house."

"You got it, Sheriff."

Pete pulled out the tracking device he'd borrowed from the county. He'd been using it with Andrea since dropping her off the first day at the observatory. "Good, it's still working."

"You can't be tracking Andrea."

"Nope. Do you think I risked getting shot in a fight I knew I couldn't win? I planted a tracker on that guy, Jimmy."

"You could have told us."

"What's the fun in that?" He switched the box on and watched for a light. Nothing. "If I had told anyone, Andrea would probably have found out. I didn't want her to give it away. I also wasn't certain you guys would approve. We need to get closer for it to pick up the signal."

"Or they found it and got rid of it just like Andrea's. The fight was risky." Cord shook his head in disbelief.

"But worth it since my tracker still has a chance. Let's get going."

It would be the fastest he'd ever driven the sixty miles from Marfa to Presidio. Also one of the blackest nights until the full moon came up. He passed one other car, his flashing lights lit the fields on either side. They were taking a risk. Mainly him. Not with just the speed of the Tahoe...

"What if they took her somewhere else? I should have stayed in the mountains and tried to track them."

"Don't second-guess your decisions, Pete. You took a big risk dropping the pocketknife during the fight, then kicking rocks on top of it. If you hadn't, we might still be waiting on Nick and Agent Conrad to untie us."

"I was lucky they didn't just shoot me."

"If they'd planned to shoot us, they would have as soon as we got within range." Cord glanced at his cell again. "Still no word from Nick."

"He knows those mountains as good as either of us. The DEA agent's horse looked pretty spooked. Probably took him a while to catch up." Pete couldn't put much thought into Nick's problems. Every thought came back to getting to Presidio fast. A plan wouldn't hurt, either. But he had nothing. "Do you think we should have stuck with tracking Andrea's abductors?"

"Forget it. You couldn't see a trail in the dark. They had horses and ATVs. Three each, three pairs or six different possibilities. Presidio is our best shot. We both know that."

It was worse than trying to find a needle in a haystack. At least you had the haystack right in front of you. This time they had a town and all the surrounding area. Miles of border and no way of knowing which way the illegal goods were crossing. Guns into Mexico or drugs into the States. There'd be mass confusion with too many law enforcement agencies trying to call the shots.

"What are we looking for when we get there?" He

knew it was a long shot. "Other than Jimmy's jacket that I'm tracking?"

"Your guess is as good as mine," Cord finally admitted.

"I was afraid you'd say that."

ANDREA WAS STILL WET. The men who'd abducted her had been prepared for any electronics that she carried. By dumping her in a barrel of water the tracking earrings her father had sent would be useless. They'd held her under until she'd almost passed out.

Afterward, the six men had split up. Their leader drove them both to an awaiting helicopter. They didn't bother to blindfold her for the first part of the trip, so she could see all the terrain. They hadn't crossed the Rio Grande, so they were still on the U.S. side of the border. That, at least, was something in her favor. The nearest town to the east would have been Marfa, but they flew south.

The only city or town that direction was Presidio. Once they landed they'd covered her eyes with a sleeping mask. She could see nothing but her feet. And there hadn't been one clue about Sharon. Nothing had been mentioned.

Cord's informant had been right. The undercover agent had been right. And Pete had definitely been right. She, on the other hand, had been terribly wrong. There was little hope that Pete or her father would find her. But hope was all she had...and her wits.

What could these men gain from her being here? Especially tonight?

Alone in a small metal room, no bigger than a storage crate, she could hear the low bass of a speaker. It wasn't coming from the other side of the door as she'd first thought. It was behind her, through the wall. Vibrating. She must be close to the concert in Presidio.

Low lighting from a battery-operated lamp. Two chairs and a card table. It didn't feel like a normal room. The low ceiling was made of the same material. She was in a storage container. Driving from Austin to West Texas, she must have seen hundreds of these containers transported by train.

If she could only get word to Pete. She didn't know how much time had passed while sitting there. She'd counted every rusty plank of the container and knew how many rivets held it together. Her wrists were numb, still tucked behind her back in the folding chair. It made it impossible to rest her head.

The door opened and in marched an unusual man. Unusual because he was tall, well-dressed in a very expensive suit and had white-blond hair. His hair among all the darker Hispanics in the city would stand out. He smoothed it flat before clapping his hands.

"Come now, don't tell me that no one cut your hands free." A guy appeared with a knife.

Who claps their hands for the hired help? But that's how he acted…as if everyone around him was beneath him. So far beneath him he didn't give any direction to the men who'd abducted her, just facial expressions that shouted to everyone.

"Who are you?"

"You may call me Mr. Rook."

A comfy armchair was brought in for him to use. Then a glass of wine. Andrea would have settled for a sip of water. Her mouth was so dry she'd seriously thought about sucking some of the water out of her shirt. Then she remembered the dirty barrel they'd tossed her inside.

Mr. Rook sat and sipped his wine while one of the hired help cut her restraints. A sigh escaped from her as she massaged life back into her arms.

"There's no reason to think about trying to leave. My men surround this little box. No one will hear your screams because of the concert. And no one will trace you to our little town on the border since we got rid of anything on your person."

"I..." Her hoarse voice sounded ancient. "I wouldn't be so sure of that."

"Yes, you think your incompetent sheriff will find you like he promised? We've taken every precaution to make certain he doesn't. And this time tomorrow, you'll be secured in my home away from home so I can make a longer-lasting deal with your father."

"And where's that?"

"You'll find out when the time comes." He sipped his wine again and didn't look the least bit rushed.

The crate door opened and a beautiful blonde in a tight-fitting leather skirt and jacket joined them. She slid a phone across the table without a word. Mr. Rook held it to his ear and locked eyes with Andrea. Her spine and body shivered. The polite captor had disappeared. Hate and disgust oozed from him.

"I have your daughter. Speak, Andrea." He didn't switch the speaker on. She could barely hear her father's voice asking if she was okay.

"Can you hear me, Dad? I'm fine after my short trip. You were right—"

The woman cut her off by pressing three fingers against the base of her throat, choking her. Andrea jerked away, finally knocking the woman's grasp loose. She missed Rook's instructions for her father while coughing and trying to get her breath back.

He placed the phone on the table. "Time to get started."

The woman left.

"Start what?" She searched the small opening, but the door quickly closed. She couldn't see a thing except the woman walking down the stairs immediately at the door. "What are you really doing?"

The man stood, slapping her left cheek. "Tie her up and store her in one of the containers."

Andrea averted her face and watched through the hair hiding her eyes. The blond man spoke well, wore the suit well. She remembered what Pete said how most criminals forgot the shoes. This man's shoes were old but expensive and well-kept. His nails were well manicured like a businessman's.

There would be no answers from Rook. Just like the man who had brought her here had no answers.

Two men in green alien heads blindfolded her, grabbed her arms and then hauled her out the door. They kept her tight between them, dragging her about fifty yards before throwing her into another dark container. Was it strange that they hadn't hurt her? At least not yet?

Once the door was bolted shut, it was blacker than the blindfold she'd removed. She was stuck unless Pete found her. Her father's hands were tied because of national security.

She had to have faith in Pete. She did.

The confidence that Pete would find her was the strangest thing she'd ever experienced. It was more than just attraction. She admired his kindness, his humbleness. She especially admired—maybe even envied—his relationship with his father and how he was determined not to ruin him.

The darkness didn't seem as dark. She was surrounded by wooden crates probably filled with guns heading to Mexico. Her father and his men would be watching for a truckload of drugs headed north. Not a cargo container filled with guns going south.

She climbed to the top of the stack to wait.

Pete would be there. She just hoped it was soon.

Chapter Twenty-Six

Pete and Cord followed the tracking blip to the outskirts of Presidio. If they could find the man he'd fought with in the mountains, they might find Andrea. They were close. He'd been stopped about half a block from them for a while.

"Our chances are slim to none this is going to work." Cord adjusted the shoulder strap holding his weapons and slipped into his jacket.

"Better than just aimlessly searching through a thousand people dressed as aliens."

Cord's phone rang. "It's Commander Allen." He answered, "McCrea...Yes, sir." He punched the speaker button.

"He's using her to guarantee safe passage for a shipment of drugs," the Commander said. "Wants to drive straight up Highway 67 through the Port of Entry. He knows most of your men are here and wants me to personally wave the truck through. He's a brazen son of a bitch, that's for sure. When he called, I could hear loud concert music. He may be holding her at the festival like you thought. Can you find my girl before his truck gets away from us?"

Music? The band was scheduled to begin in fifteen minutes. Did they just want them to *think* she was at the concert?

"We might have a chance, sir. Pete dropped a tracker in

one of the men's pockets. It was risky but seems to be paying off. We're on his trail now."

"Good thinking, son. I'm less than seven minutes away via helicopter from the Port of Entry. Call when you find her. I want this crazy SOB alive to uncover the extent of his operation. He has to know that I can't let drugs through even to save my daughter. Out."

Cord stuck the phone back inside his jacket. Pete couldn't see his face, hidden in shadow from the brim of his hat. But that meant the Ranger couldn't see Pete's, either. If he could, it would be filled with worry and doubt.

It was up to him to save Andrea. The Commander had as much as said there was nothing he could do. He dropped his chin to his chest again to watch the green dot on his screen inch forward.

"He's on the move," Pete told his partner. They'd left the vehicle about half a block back. "He's heading for the festival. If he gets there, it'll be easier for him to disappear."

They turned and ran, this time with Cord driving while Pete watched the blip.

"Not if we have anything to do with it." Cord shoved his foot on the gas.

They both buckled up as they sped through the backstreets. They stopped midblock just ahead of whatever vehicle Jimmy—or his jacket—was in. An old pickup barreled down the street, skidding to a halt when its occupants spied the flashing lights.

Fortunately, it was late at night and Cord was a good driver. He spun the Tahoe, pushed the gas and missed the old vehicles on the side of the street. Within minutes they had Jimmy and his *compadre* in cuffs. Pointing the shotgun out the window at the driver helped.

"Hands flat on the dashboard, you murdering son of a bitch," Pete yelled from the window as he covered Cord heading toward the truck.

Both men complied. Jimmy was in the driver's seat. When he recognized Pete, his head dropped backward in defeat. Then he began chattering in Spanish to his passenger, who Pete recognized as one of the other horsemen at Andrea's abduction.

It didn't take long to get Jimmy's story. Hired help for a few days. The guy who had hired him for the trip to the mountains said to meet him at the festival. Everyone helping tonight was to wear an alien mask that covered their entire head. Those were the only instructions. Just show up.

Pete looked inside Jimmy's truck, picking up an alien mask. *Why the mask? Who does he need to hide from?* "Distractions."

"What?" Cord looked up from settling the second prisoner into the backseat. The Tahoe had been equipped with handles to handcuff passengers into place.

"Everything this head honcho has done so far has been about distractions. So why tell the head of Border Security that you're bringing a shipment into the States? Why abduct his daughter and threaten him when you could continue to sneak under the radar?" Pete looked at the crate in the pickup bed.

"If it's a distraction, then what's he really up to?" Cord asked, not dismissing Pete's theory. "Probable cause applies if we open a sealed crate."

Pete retrieved the tire iron from the Tahoe and jumped into the back of the truck. "We up the security coming into the country and don't concentrate on what's going out." He pried the top off the crate, then lifted a .38 Special to show Cord. "Second possibility is that he's ferrying guns south just like usual. There's a variety of handguns here. Not packed well. Probably straw purchases."

Cord slapped the hood of the Tahoe. "It's so simple it has to be right. That's why his men are meeting on this side of the border. Allen should be able to get some air support, but I don't know how quick. I'm guessing that you're going to search for Andrea."

"It's my job, my primary assignment."

"And the right thing to do." Cord clapped his shoulder as he walked around the front of the service vehicle. "I'll call Allen with the update. We shouldn't split up, but I don't see that we have a choice."

"I'll pose as Jimmy, find out what's going down and where if I can. But I will find Andrea." Pete dropped his hat onto the front seat for safekeeping. It wouldn't fit on top of the alien mask he intended to wear when he found Andrea. "Keep your head down, man."

"You, too, and good luck," Cord called out as he got in the Tahoe. He'd take Jimmy and his partner with him to the border crossing. He'd meet up with Commander Allen to see if either man had more information about their un-named opponent or his plans.

Saving Andrea was Pete's duty, but much more than that. He'd promised to find her and he meant to keep his promise. The first step was to infiltrate wherever they were gathering.

He drove Jimmy's truck to the outskirts of the festival. The concert was in full swing. If there were any people attending not in costume, he couldn't see them. But since both the men they'd arrested were supposed to wear identical masks, he'd look for more of the same. Jimmy was slightly larger around than Pete, but the extra fabric of his denim jacket covered the pistol at the small of Pete's back. He was ready to pull the mask over his head when his cell rang.

"Pete, I found it," Hardy yelled excitedly. "The camera was hooked under the seat and stuck clear up at the top of the metal springs. I guess it got wrapped there during the crash. There's a recording with a picture before the car rolls. Shoot, that dude was messed up bad. Then there's only sound… Man oh man, the guy you found had a lot to say about a drug operation and a Mr. Rook who runs the whole dang thing. He lives in Mexico, but he's supposed to be there in Presidio tonight. You want me to bring it to you?"

"Hardy, slow down. Lock the camera in evidence. Did he say where they're meeting?"

"Something about masked men and a stage. Oh, and the password is…I have it here in my notes. I wrote it down. There, king's rook checkmate."

"Thanks, Hardy. You've done a great job. Secure the camera and you can get back to patrol now."

"Yes, sir."

Pete stowed his phone in the truck along with his identification and county-issued shirt. His white tee fit in with the crowd better and he couldn't risk being spotted as the sheriff. He pulled the mask over his head and drove the perimeter of the parking lot, searching for more green aliens.

The plastic mask was hot, hard to breathe through and limited his line of sight. But it did its job protecting his identity. He passed right by two of his deputies without a second glance. The variety of costumes—some elaborate and some just face paint—were impressive. The people impersonating aliens posed for pictures with those who weren't. Some took it seriously, beeping a make-believe language in the background.

On the edge of the crowd, an identical alien spun full circle. Trying to find something or someone? Pete hung back, waiting for the fellow to lead the way.

A couple of minutes later he was following four or five little green men and a woman. These were most likely ordinary people purchasing guns with cartel money. The smaller crates they carried weren't disguised. No bogus labeling. Different sizes and styles. Most weren't crates at all, just plastic tubs. He stayed at the back of the group. No one asked him for a password. No one acted like he was there at all.

At the back of the stage were half a dozen men all in the same masks, loading wooden crates, boxes or tubs like what was in the back of Jimmy's truck into a twenty-foot steel shipping container. Mask or no mask, he recognized the big guy from the ATV earlier. He was wearing the same clothes and carrying the same shotgun.

Where was Andrea?

The boxes brought in were stored in wooden crates that were then loaded inside the steel containers on the big rigs. But where were the trucks going? No one would be stupid enough to drive across the border so openly. Of course, he wouldn't think that the cartel would so openly gather the guns they were going to smuggle at a concert where county deputies and Presidio cops were stationed.

"Hey, you," the big guy said in his direction. "Where's your shipment? Get it loaded in the second rig."

Pete acknowledged him with a nod and ran back to Jimmy's truck. He had to send a message to McCrea. He dialed, and another alien tapped on the window, and a guy pulled off his mask to talk.

"Hey, man. You need help carrying— You ain't Jimmy."

Pete dropped the cell on the seat and shoved the door open, knocking the alien back a step. "Sorry, man. Jimmy said I could charge my phone."

"You're lying. No way Jimmy lets you in his truck." The guy's alien mask dropped to the ground.

"No, really. I don't want trouble."

The man punched him hard in the stomach, stealing Pete's breath for a second. He straightened, fighting the pain. "You got this all wrong."

Pete didn't want any attention. If law enforcement broke up the fight, his deputies would recognize him. Then the smugglers would know. He'd never find Andrea.

Pete allowed Jimmy's friend to grab his collar and drag him back to the light of the truck cab. He reached for his gun when the man saw the badge on his shirt. Before the guy could open his mouth, Pete had the barrel shoved under his chin.

"Not a damn word. Where do they have the girl?"

His prisoner shook his head and shrugged. Which was probably the truth. The likelihood that she was here was slim to none. What was he going to do with him? He cuffed the guy's hands behind his back and shoved him to the pickup seat. "Now what?"

"Now you're a dead man. That's what."

"Pete? Did you find something?" McCrea had answered and was still on the phone.

Pete clicked the speaker button and shoved the tail of his shirt into his prisoner's mouth. "Yeah, they're smuggling guns across the border on big rigs. Don't know the route yet. Send men behind the concert stage and locate Jimmy's truck in the lot. Out." He tied the sleeves behind the man's head, effectively gagging him before he shoved the door shut and dropped the cell in the jacket pocket, then grabbed the guns.

This area would be swarming with law enforcement, alerting the smugglers to the bust. He had to find Andrea's location in the next few minutes or it would be hopeless. Disguised and carrying the tub of handguns, he fell into a short line and set it inside the shipping container. It was easy to get a good look inside in spite of the late hour because of the concert lights. But there was nothing but boxes of guns or ammo. Four steel containers and very few people in masks left around. He sneaked around to the opposite side.

"Andrea?" He knocked on each container, wanting to shout at the top of his lungs, but keeping his voice normal. "Come on, you've got to be in one of these."

The first rig pulled away, and Pete ran behind the second. If Andrea wasn't inside, he had to stay with the con-

tainers in order to find her. He pulled himself on top of
the second rig and used the tie-down straps to hold on. He
didn't wait long before the second truck slowly bounced
across the field, west a few minutes and then south onto
Rio Grande Road. The trucks turned toward the border at
the railroad.

Above the roar of the wind and road noise, he heard the
loud rotation of giant helicopter blades as the trucks came
to a halt before the ground dropped away.

He dialed McCrea. "They're at the burned-out rail
bridge. There's a heavy-lifting chopper hovering over the
water. How fast can you get here?"

"Back off, Pete. We're spread thin on four fronts. We can
notify the Mexican authorities to pick them up."

"I'm not leaving. She has to be here." He shoved the
phone in his pocket and pulled his weapon. He crawled
forward using the cover of the engines to beat on each of
the containers, shouting her name, "Andrea!"

"Pete? Pete! It's about time you guys showed up. Let
me out of here!"

"It's just me. Pipe down and hold on while I figure out
a way to get us out of here."

Men climbed atop the first container, hooking cables
so the helicopter could airlift it over the river. Pete ducked
his head, desperately trying to come up with a plan. Before he could free Andrea, he needed keys to the padlock
on the door.

Ten guys would come crashing down on him if he fought
the big guy shouting orders. He couldn't get close without
being recognized as the sheriff. He climbed down the tail
end of the truck. Mimicking the smugglers, he tugged at
the tie-downs, keeping his face hidden.

Across the river, he saw a train arrive. The chopper
stayed low until the last hooks were in place, then took off
transporting the first container to the train. At this rate,

the exchange wouldn't take long and the smugglers would be out of reach before authorities could track them down.

Pete didn't have much time.

Taking on the leader would only get his head blown off. The solution was dangerous. His timing would have to be perfect and he'd most likely get shot. But he was willing to risk it for Andrea. He couldn't live with himself if he did nothing.

He coiled a tie-down and casually dropped it by the last container. By the time Andrea's was being hooked to the chopper, everything was in place—including himself. The leader gave a thumbs-up to the pilot just as he had for the previous three containers.

Gun in hand, Pete tackled the leader to the ground while everyone was looking up. He threw a punch, connecting the grip of his 9mm with the man's jawbone. Pulling the key ring, he ran to the back of the container. It was a stretch, but he caught the loop he'd tied for a handhold.

Curses. Gunfire. Pings from the ricochets off the steel. He dropped the gun down his T-shirt so he wouldn't lose it while crashing against the side, then pulling himself to the top.

They were flying through the air. Andrea yelled below him, asking what was going on, but there was no time to explain. He slipped his arms through the loop and dropped slowly down in front of the lock. The Rio Grande was below him as he banged around. He finally reached the door, kicking it with his boots to get Andrea's attention.

"Grab hold of something, I'm going to open this thing!"

"Ready."

The lock fell, clanging against the train below. He pushed out from the container. Gravity helped open the door as the chopper got closer to the empty flat car of the train. The darkness helped hide him against the black container. Shots from below. Andrea's smiling face in front of him. Apprehension that he might fail stabbed at his gut.

"Do I pull you inside? Or do you have an escape ladder?" she shouted.

The container was almost in place. A bullet ricocheted too close for comfort. "Steel between us and them might be a good thing." His hand caught the opening, and she caught his waistband.

Once inside, she pulled him close, kissing him before he could get the loop from his body. "So, what's the plan?"

"This is as far as I got."

"Can anyone come to our rescue on this side of the border?" she asked, lifting a handgun, arming it and aiming behind him.

"Not officially. All we have to do is get to the Port of Entry." He pulled the tie-down loop off his body and caught men taking cover behind several vehicles.

"Well, there's plenty of guns and ammo in here." She turned over a tub similar to the one he'd carried to the smugglers. Then she sorted through the smaller boxes in search of the right ammo. "All we need is a getaway car."

"Are you hurt?" He tugged her back into his arms and searched her eyes while she shook her head. "It'll be risky. No brave stunts. You run and you keep running. No matter what happens."

"I promise." She softly touched his split lip, then brought hers to his, clinging for the briefest of moments. Then she darted to the other side of the opening, drawing a couple of shots. "Grab what you need before they shut the door and lock us both in here."

He found ammo, pulled his shirt from his pants and retrieved his weapon. He took another, quickly loading and dropping it in his boot. She was right. If the smugglers were smart, all they had to do was close the door. One thing to their advantage was that the chopper was still attached, so the container was still wobbling around a bit.

"I'll lay down cover while you get to the other side of the train."

"Then I'll do the same for you."

"Look, Andrea. This isn't the same as shooting targets."

"Come on, Pete, we don't have time for lectures. I got this." She placed one gun at the small of her back and had the second ready to fire. "I'll see you in a minute."

He fired. She jumped, rolling out of sight below him. He didn't wait, just reloaded, fired in the direction of movement and followed her.

Backs to a train wheel, Andrea pointed to floodlights from a helicopter hovering on the other side of the river. "Do you think that's my dad? Can we swim across?"

"We can probably walk." He dialed the cell. McCrea answered on the first ring. Pete stated their plans and disconnected. "They agree that it looks like our best way out without your father flying over the river and causing an international incident. Stay low, drop to your belly if you hear anything and don't say a word."

"Got it. But before I stop rambling, thanks for coming to rescue me."

"No problem. It was my—"

"Let's shut up now before you say it was just your job. Go."

She ran. It wasn't far, but it was dangerous. He kept a close eye on the activity behind them. The men at the railroad were no longer worried about the prisoner's escape. They were more worried about their own. Pete followed, knowing that as soon as they crossed that river, he'd lose Andrea for sure.

Chapter Twenty-Seven

Andrea ran. And when her lungs were screaming, she ran some more.

There was very little ground cover, but apparently losing her as a hostage was less important than getting their train out of there quickly. No one followed her and Pete, and in no time at all they were back on U.S. soil. Her father was waiting, hugging her as soon as she sloshed out of the river. Publicly.

"You're not hurt? Thanks to heaven for that. Now your mother won't divorce me," he joked.

Andrea was handed a bottle of water and gulped it down. "What about Sharon?" she finally got out when her dry throat was soothed.

"She was with the men in the truck with the shipment of drugs—if you could really call it a shipment. We stopped it six miles up the road. She looks okay, but drugged so she would cooperate." Her dad squeezed her shoulder, pulling her closer to his side. "We rounded up more than a dozen men at the concert. All in all, I think we can call this a successful operation."

Sharon was okay. She'd helped find her. All the risk had been worth it.

The man who had abducted her on the ATV was lying on his stomach with the rest of the smugglers, hands behind their backs. She felt safe next to her father, but she wanted Pete. She watched him about twenty feet away accepting slaps on the back from his deputies. Their eyes finally met. She gestured for him to come closer. He stayed where he was, his face full of sadness.

"And what about the guy who orchestrated it all?" she asked her dad. "What happened to Mr. Rook?"

"Ranger McCrea radioed that they found him speeding to Alpine and an awaiting private airplane."

"So everything's okay and I can go back to the observatory."

"Absolutely not. We don't know the extent of this operation. You're heading back to Austin with me. In about three minutes. No arguments."

"Yes, sir." She knew Pete heard. His chin dropped to his chest, but he didn't move.

There was so much she wanted to say.

"Pete?" She ran to him, leaving her pride behind. "Come with us," she said, hugging him, not wanting to let him go, wanting to beg him, knowing she wouldn't.

"I can't." He lowered his voice, his breath close across her ear. "You know why, Andrea." He pulled back, his mouth only a whisper away. "I'm resigning. I can't let my dad's reputation be destroyed."

"But you love being sheriff. I could stay, I don't have to go…"

Pete looked around her to the waiting helicopter and her father. "Yes, you do, darlin', and I have to stay in Marfa. As much as I'd like things to be different, they aren't."

"But I lo—" He covered her lips with a soft touch of his fingers, stopping the words but not the thought. She loved him. Yes, it had only been a week, but she was certain of it. Her heart felt heavenly with the realization, then plummeted with the miserable look on his face.

· "Don't say it," he whispered hoarsely. "I couldn't let you go if you said it."

"We can work this out. It doesn't have to be your father or me."

"Dammit. I'm not choosing my dad over you. It's just rotten luck that our fathers are who they are."

"You make us sound like Romeo and Juliet. This can all be worked out. Our families aren't at war. They actually like each other."

"That's just it. You can't lie to your dad. It wouldn't be fair to you. And I can't tell the truth. Not after everything my father did for me. I just can't turn my back on him. If they found him guilty of perjury or forgery, what then? Think of every criminal he's ever put away. They'd appeal their cases. They'd be out of jail faster than a jackrabbit back in its hole."

"I understand, but there has to be a better solution than never seeing each other again."

"Andrea, it's time," her father called behind her.

She wrapped her arm around Pete's neck and gave a little tug. He came closer—a willing partner, knowing her intention. He meant their kiss to be a goodbye. She couldn't stand that it was. Hot, hurried, desperate. Their bodies molded together. She didn't want to let him go.

She couldn't let him go.

"Please don't cry, Andrea," he said against her lips, wiping a tear that had fallen to her cheek. "You've got to go. He's waiting." He reached up, holding her hands as they slid across his chest.

She already ached to touch his warm skin and play with the hair falling across his forehead. She turned and ran, afraid to look back at him. She'd scream how wrong he had to be. Or she'd shout over the whirling blades that she loved him. Then everyone would know she'd been rejected, that he was letting her go, practically chasing her away.

The door of the chopper closed, and they lifted off.

"I was thinking about offering Pete Morrison a job," her father said without the benefit of the headset and microphone. No one else could hear their conversation. "Funny thing. Pete Morrison doesn't exist on paper. At least not the man you just desperately kissed goodbye."

"And you didn't arrest him?"

"I'm assuming there's a logical explanation. I don't know the particulars yet. Do you?" He smiled. Totally her father. The Commander was nowhere in sight. He could tell Pete was a good man.

"Dad, I have a huge favor to ask you as soon as we get back."

Chapter Twenty-Eight

It was a night just like all the rest before Pete had met Andrea. He was in his service vehicle driving Highway 90. Everything was quiet. Too quiet. The quieter it was, the more he thought about the mistake he'd made letting Andrea go.

Would he be destined to live on the ranch alone like his dad? Keeping secrets, scraping together enough to keep a few head of cattle.

His father was angry with him and as a result so were Peach and Honey. His family. And they were all disappointed that he'd let Andrea leave and hadn't called her in the week since.

There wasn't another way round it. He couldn't ask her to live a lie with him. It was his burden to bear.

"That sounds so stupid. Just get a grip on yourself. It wasn't a mistake. You were protecting her." He hit the steering wheel, leaving the palm of his hand stinging.

"Sheriff?" Honey's voice came through the radio.

"Yes, ma'am."

"We have a report of unusual activity at the Viewing Area. Do you think the smugglers are back?"

"I'm heading there now. Out."

He was only a couple of miles away. Heading east, he couldn't see if the Marfa lights were visible behind him.

There wasn't anything to the south—at least not in his line of sight. He slowed his approach.

There was one car in the lot, one person standing on the platform. Tight jeans hugging a figure he remembered all too well.

Andrea?

That was wishful thinking. Her father would never let her set foot in this town again. He got out of the car, not mentioning to Honey that he'd arrived. His feet wanted to run and spin the woman around to verify what his heart told him. It was her. It had to be.

And in that moment he knew beyond a doubt that he couldn't stay away from her. He loved Andrea Allen. Sure, they needed to learn more about each other, but this was different than anything he'd experienced. And he wanted more.

"Did you call for assistance, miss?"

"No. Honey thought it would get you here faster." Andrea turned, leaning on the railing with a large envelope in her hand.

"What are you doing— Should you— Why are you here?" he stammered.

"I need to ask you a question."

"Right here? Couldn't you just ask on the phone?"

"No. I needed to see your face. But out here in only starlight might not have been such a good idea." She slid her fingers around the edge of the envelope, nervously touching every side as it rotated in her hands.

"What's your question?"

"To answer your second question, I didn't want an audience when I asked. Or when I gave you this."

"What's in the envelope?"

"First, my question. Do you like me?"

"Of course. Is there more?"

"Do you like me enough to give whatever's between us

a shot? I mean, if you're not forcing me to lie to my father. That was the only reason you gave, but it could have just been an easy way out for you."

"There was nothing easy about letting you get on that helicopter." Protective emotions slammed him. She shouldn't be anywhere close to Marfa and yet he couldn't let her go. Not again.

She sighed and turned to face the mountains. He didn't analyze his actions. He simply walked to her and dropped his arms around her waist, pulling her into the curve of his body. He wanted to spin her around and kiss her into oblivion, but that's where he stopped. She'd come a long way to say whatever she was trying to say.

"I could get used to this." She linked her fingers with his and rested her head on his shoulder.

He could, too.

"I thought the only thing I wanted was to make my own discovery. A distant star that no one had ever seen before. Then I came here. With all the stars up there to see every night, I ran out of reasons to find another." She twisted in his arms, staying close, then skimmed her fingers through his hair, ending at the back of his neck. The envelope stayed in her left hand, dangling behind his back.

"I missed you. Missed the conversations that I didn't totally understand. Missed smelling your shampoo and soap when the steam from your bathroom found its way into the hall. Everything you feel about stars…I feel about you. I—" He was choking up, but had to tell her. It might be his only chance, and she deserved the truth. "If things were different, I wouldn't let you go. I've never felt this way about anyone, Andrea."

He leaned in to kiss her, but his lips found her neck instead.

She tilted her head enough to meet his eyes. "I feel the

same and I'm so happy. I think you should know that I accepted a job."

Gut kicked. Stomped by a bronc. The pain shooting through him was worse. His lonely life passed before his eyes. He'd looked up just how far away those jobs were. They might as well be on one of those stars she studied, since he couldn't follow her.

"I'm not sure I understand. Why'd you risk coming here to tell me you'll be living halfway round the world?"

"It's actually not that far." Her voice had the twinkle in it that made his mouth curl in a smile.

But not today. He didn't have the patience for teasing. He gently set her away from him and saw the laughter in her eyes. "Just where is this job?"

"At the observatory. I never thought I'd enjoy teaching, but I love it. Love the kids and all their questions. The stargazing parties turned me on to a new way of seeing the sky."

"But that means—"

"That we can work on this chemistry we seem to have?" She tapped the envelope against her thigh.

"What's inside?"

"Well, turns out my father knew about your false identity."

His mind exploded, running every scenario through his brain at once. What would happen to his dad?

"Before you go off the deep end. After a conversation with Joe, my dad used some connections and fixed everything." She handed him the envelope. "Meet Pete Morrison. Passport, birth certificate, adoption papers. Don't be mad at your dad for keeping it a secret. I asked to be the one to tell you."

"I don't know what to say. I never thought…"

"I know. When I asked him, I didn't think he could manage all this. I thought he might smooth things over, keep it out of the courts. But he does know some influential people who obviously believed in you both. You're completely legit, Sheriff." She pressed the envelope to his chest.

"Come here." Capturing her lips under his reemphasized just what a fool he'd been. No other woman would ever take Andrea's place. She was his, but more important, he belonged with her.

"There is one little catch my dad insisted on," she whispered.

"Whatever he wants," he whispered back, "we'll manage. I'm not letting you go again."

"Good, because he's insisting I stay at your place and act as if I'm under house arrest until your task force is finished."

"That's not a favor, it's a reward." He kissed her again to seal the deal. "Are you sure you'll be satisfied looking at the stars from West Texas?"

"As long as I look at them occasionally with the man I love…I'll be more than happy."

* * * * *

Don't miss the next book in Angi Morgan's miniseries,
WEST TEXAS WATCHMEN, *when*
THE CATTLEMAN goes on sale next month.

MILLS & BOON®

Why shop at millsandboon.co.uk?

Each year, thousands of romance readers find their perfect read at millsandboon.co.uk. That's because we're passionate about bringing you the very best romantic fiction. Here are some of the advantages of shopping at www.millsandboon.co.uk:

* **Get new books first**—you'll be able to buy your favourite books one month before they hit the shops

* **Get exclusive discounts**—you'll also be able to buy our specially created monthly collections, with up to 50% off the RRP

* **Find your favourite authors**—latest news, interviews and new releases for all your favourite authors and series on our website, plus ideas for what to try next

* **Join in**—once you've bought your favourite books, don't forget to register with us to rate, review and join in the discussions

Visit **www.millsandboon.co.uk**
for all this and more today!